TOURNER

THE IRONSIDE SERIES
BOOK TWO

JANE WASHINGTON

Washington, Jane
Tourner

www.janewashington.com

ISBN: 9798856020662

CONTENTS

Also by Jane Washington

Ironside Academy
Book 1: Plier
Book 2: Tourner
Book 3: Sauter

A Tempest of Shadows
Book 1: A Tempest of Shadows
Book 2: A City of Whispers
Book 3: Dream of Embers
Book 4: A Castle of Ash
Book 5: A World of Lost Words

Bastan Hollow
Standalone: Charming
Standalone: Disobedience

Standalone Books
I Am Grey

Curse of the Gods
Book 1: Trickery
Book 2: Persuasion
Book 3: Seduction
Book 4: Strength
Novella: Neutral
Book 5: Pain

Oh, the irony of this prestigious stage,
Where stars are sold, wrapped in a cage,
Topped with a bow and a sweet serenade,
Iron on all sides, the insides in suede.

TRIGGER WARNINGS

panic attacks/flashbacks
bullying/torture (not within main group)
neglect and abuse (not within main group)
references to sexual assault
mild sexual harassment
traumatic and violent crime resulting in death
(mostly off-page, not within main group)

If you or anyone you know needs support, please visit
lifeline.org.au.

Ironside Academy Map

To view the map of Ironside, please scan the QR code below.

IRONSIDE ACADEMY PLAYLIST

To listen to the playlist for the Ironside series, please scan the QR code below.

IRONSIDE ACADEMY CHEAT SHEET

To view the character cheat sheet for the Ironside series, please scan the QR code below.

Acknowledgments

I just wanted take a really quick moment to say a massive massive thank you to everyone who has supported the Ironside series since Plier's release. I'm so humbled and grateful for everyone's support, but especially the following people.

Thank you Andrea Velasquez and Kass Bruinier, my Beta readers for the first version of Plier!

Thank you Michelle, for too many things to even start listing. You're the best.

Thank you Taylor, as always. I'm sorry Michelle keeps kicking you out of my groups. She's just way too good at her job and you're a bit of a creeper. An adorable one who I love with all my heart, but still.

Thank you to the Release Chaps. There are too many of you to list but I really mean this for every single one of you: you guys fuel me and without you, I would probably just be writing very sad (and awful) poems and publishing them under @notjanewashington. And I hate poetry. I can't thank any of you enough.

A super special thank you to all the bookish people who shared their thoughts on Plier. Your stunning photos, hilarious videos and thesis-level reviews have absolutely blown me away, and it makes me want to work so much harder to give you everything I have for the rest of the series.

Thank you!!
Jane xx

I

THE SECRET

Isobel sat cross-legged on Kilian's bed, watching him. He seemed too tired to push back the pale golden hair that had fallen in the way of his light, yellow-green stare. His usually proud and graceful posture was slumped, his eyes shadowed, the smooth skin beneath bruised and marred by puffiness. He had spent three days looking after her while she had been unconscious, but that seemed to be at the expense of himself. Her hair was smooth and shiny, waving in soft little ripples of strawberry blonde over her shoulders. His was messy, the pale strands drifting fretfully around his strained expression.

Almost dying and then waking up with pupils a completely different colour and the word "mate" being thrown around should have limited her capacity to care about anyone else, but her concern for Kilian spiked anyway. Especially when he started to pace, his jaw clenched like he was struggling to speak.

There's something else you need to know, he had said, before he started with the pacing and the furtive glances at the door.

She remained where she was, occasionally dropping her gaze to stare at her knees. She didn't bother trying to dress herself properly. She had already known that Kilian didn't like her in that way, but when he kissed her seemingly to reassure himself that she *definitely* wasn't his mate, it really made that fact painfully apparent.

It was confusing for her mind and body to be kissed by someone who looked like Kilian, who smelled like Kilian, who was as kind and caring and *touchy* as Kilian ... only to have him declare that it meant nothing. It was confusing because she had already known it would mean nothing to him. So why had she enjoyed it?

It can't be me, you understand?

He had insisted.

"It's about Theo." The words he had been troubling over finally spilled out of him as he spun to face her again. He looked a little wild. His hands shook as he rubbed his arms, his posture fidgety, like he didn't know what to do with his limbs.

"What about Theo?" Her entire body locked up, frozen, bracing for bad news. "You said he was okay." She tried not to sound accusatory, but her tone carried a hint of sharpness.

"He's fine," Kilian assured her, coming to sit on the bed beside her. He placed a pale hand against her leg, his thumb brushing along her knee, his other fingers lightly grazing her thigh. "Look, nobody else is going to tell you this and I probably shouldn't either, but he likes you. Maybe he doesn't even realise it himself, but we've all noticed."

"You can't say you know him better than he knows himself." She pulled her shoulders back a little, dropping her attention to her folded legs, and to the hand against her thigh. To the thumb brushing back and forth over her knee. "It's just ... if you're about to tell me to stop hanging out with Theo—"

"I'm not," he interrupted, biting down on his pillowy lower lip. He released it on a deep breath. "I'm trying to warn you. You need to be better prepared when he loses it next time. He's going to be even more volatile than usual because ... he likes you and your eyes have changed. You need to keep that in mind and keep yourself safe. And under no circumstances can you use your ability on him again. The next time you die, it *will* be permanent."

"Kilian?" She raised her head, fixing him with a look. "Are you trying to be my friend?"

"I thought I already was?" His brows drew together, but his eyes were too guarded for her to figure out how he felt about her question.

"Then stop trying to be my dad. I already have one of those and he's more than enough." She slid off the bed again, searching the room until she caught sight of the clothes she had been wearing before she passed out several days ago. They were folded neatly on a side table by the door. "Thanks for washing my clothes and brushing my hair and feeding me soup and taking care of me, though." She had to rush those words out without a pause, her face flaming as she quickly scooped up the clothes and escaped into his bathroom, his light chuckle chasing her.

She got dressed as fast as she could, needing to pause a few times as her head spun and her body grew so weak she thought she might pitch sideways into the tiled floor.

"I'll get you some food," Kilian called through the door. "You don't need to come out until you're ready."

She heard the door to his room open and close before she could even thank him, and she leaned over the sink, sucking in a long, shaky breath before she raised her head.

Those eyes were not hers.

And yet ... that little piece of her was still there. Gold flecks. Little starbursts in the strange galaxy of colour her eyes had become. Most of the tones were dark, a splotchy background bleeding into her onyx Sigma ring—but some of them were lighter. Twinkling blips and specks that shifted when she turned her head, like her eyes hadn't even settled yet. Like they were still shifting. Evolving. *Searching?*

Did that mean she hadn't met her mate yet?

Or that they didn't exist?

Would it be a boy, or a girl? Kilian's fear had become infectious, and she stood there weakly, wondering how awful he must have felt, waiting for her to wake up and wondering if it could possibly be him. Maybe a girl would have been better for her. She didn't *want* a mate. Her mate could be her best friend like her mother used to be. Or maybe it didn't work like that.

The Alphas on the rooftop must not have been able to see her eyes clearly. They had probably all been waiting, wondering if it was one of them, even though Kilian had said their eyes didn't match hers. But they would find out, now. Kilian would reassure them.

She didn't really need to be there.

She didn't *really* need to face everyone after the mess she had caused. She didn't need to explain to Ashford why she was hearing strange voices in her head. She didn't need to talk to Theodore after his eyes had bled black and chaos had descended. She didn't need to check if he was okay, and she didn't need to reassure him that she was okay.

What she needed was to get better at lying to herself.

"Ugh." She pushed away from the mirror and tiptoed through Kilian's room, opening the large panes over his window seat. She caught sight of her phone charging on his bedside table and quickly stuffed it into her pocket before sticking a leg out of the window and feeling for the ground.

She closed the window behind her, straightening out her shirt before hurrying around the lake toward the steps leading down Alpha Hill. The pain in her chest was growing worse, and she paused halfway down, her hands on her knees, her breath wheezing as darkness swam over her vision.

"Going somewhere?" a rough voice asked a few feet behind her.

She snapped up straight, glancing over her shoulder. Oscar Sato was the last person she wanted to run into while running away from the other Alphas. Or had she run into him? It looked like he had followed her. He was wearing an oversized shirt and long pants, his comfortable style somehow managing to look fashionable. His arms were folded, the dusky skin rippling as his muscles shifted. She couldn't see his hands, but he was probably forming fists. His deep-set eyes were shadowed, his black lashes almost kissing his cheeks as he stared down his nose at her.

Sato wasn't handsome like Theodore and Ashford, and he sure as hell wasn't beautiful like Kilian, but the Ironside forums didn't gossip about how "ugly" he was, either. Not like they did with Mikel Easton.

Sato was like a magnet, sometimes drawing people in and sometimes repelling them away. Most people couldn't decide if they were obsessed with being scared of him or just plain scared of him. There was a terrifying pull in the way he made eye contact, his deep stare unblinking. He drew attention and didn't let it stray ... and he currently had all the little hairs along Isobel's arm rising in alarm.

"Do you have a problem with that?" she asked carefully. *Just apologise, idiot.*

With everyone else, her Sigma nature always rose to the surface, but with Sato, it seemed to be stuck behind a rock that wouldn't budge. The words she needed to say lodged in her throat, threatening to choke her before they allowed her to voice them.

"Just what were you going to do, exactly?" He cocked his head to the side. An eagle observing a worm. "Stroll into a dorm full of people who would do anything to sabotage you ... with rainbow eyes?" He started walking toward her, stepping down until he was right in front of her, towering over her, and then he bent, sticking his face a few inches from hers. He looked between her eyes, pulled in a short breath, and shook his head, easing back a little. "Seriously, rabbit?"

"D-Don't call me that." She shakily felt behind her with her foot, moving down a step without breaking eye contact. "I just needed a minute. I would have come back to apologise."

"We don't want your apologies."

"You don't?" She scrunched up her face, trying to read his impassive expression.

"Of course we fucking do," he growled. "You almost died in our dorm. You think the officials love Alphas so much that there wouldn't be any consequences to a *body* turning up on our rooftop?"

"It wasn't deliberate." She reclaimed the step, quickly crossing her arms to control her trembling. "I was only trying to help Theo. I ... I didn't mean to ...

with Moses." She tossed her hands up, feeling hot temper suddenly flare in her eyes. "It was an accident. I don't need to explain my ability to you. You think either of them explained their fera—"

He was on her in an instant, one hand wrapping over her mouth, the other catching the back of her head, his grip tightening hard enough that she felt a flash of panic, her hands immediately gripping his wrists, her nails digging in.

"I told you not to say that word," he said lowly, breathing the warning right against the back of his hand.

Ferality.

The illegal ability.

The forbidden word.

The reason everything had happened in the first place.

She dug her nails in further, pulling at his wrists. He breathed in deeply, almost like he was savouring the pain before he released her. But he didn't move away. He fixed her hair, twisting a flyaway, strawberry-gold strand around his finger before tucking it behind her ear.

"I won't go out of my way to hurt you," he muttered, gold-ringed black eyes drifting over her face.

"Why would you say that?" she rasped.

He blinked, focussing on her eyes again. "I was talking to myself."

Yikes. "Are you actually stopping me from leaving?"

"Yes." His hand drifted over hers, the tips of his fingers grazing against the softness of her skin. The touch was surprisingly gentle, but purposeful, reminding her of the careful way he had tucked her hair behind her ear. It was a lie. A manipulation. Just like his scent. A cloying, poisonous nectar meant to draw her in until she was fully under his control and he could do what he wanted with her. And with Sato ... that could be anything.

"Are you seriously asking me to apologise for an ability I can't control?" she bit out, unable to pull her hand away for some reason.

His touch grew more insistent, his fingers twisting between hers. They were much bigger than hers, and the stretch actually hurt a little, but he didn't leave their hands hanging together loosely to ease the discomfort, he pulled her palm against his tightly, locking his hold on her.

"Yes," he muttered.

"Even though it was two of *your* Alphas who started all of this?" she asked. "With abilities *they* can't control?"

Sato's lips lifted, his canines catching against his bottom lip as he tried to bite back what looked like dark amusement. Possibly at her expense. "Don't you mean one of *your* Alphas started all this?"

She tried to tear her hand away, but he only gripped her harder. A strange sensation shot up her arm, like pins and needles.

"Carter. You're awake."

The voice sounded behind her, where Sato's inky stare had lifted, fixing to the speaker.

Great.

She closed her eyes, steadying herself, and then she turned—as much as Sato's unbreakable grip on her hand allowed.

"Professor Easton." She didn't know what else to say.

"Were you going somewhere?" He frowned at her, moving closer until he was on her eye level, still several steps away.

His attention switched between her eyes the same way Kilian's and Sato's had, but it was a brief, cursory glance, simply categorising the odd colour of her irises.

"I ... was," she finished lamely.

"Would you come back for a brief moment?" He sounded so polite, so friendly, so reasonable ... but

11

there was an undercurrent of authority there, subtly letting her know that she didn't really have a choice. "We should discuss what happened on the rooftop."

He sounded so *opposite* to the emotion emanating off him, battering against her chest. There were too many negative feelings vying for dominance; it was hard to tell exactly what they were, but it was pretty clear he was very unhappy to see her. His face lied, but his emotions didn't.

His sharp, scarred features were arranged perfectly, allowing no emotion to shine through. His dark blue, slightly mismatched eyes with the differently shaped black splotches in them were hard to focus on, so she directed her attention to his polished shoes.

"Sure," she said, a little too quietly. "I'll be right there."

"Oscar will accompany you," Easton added, forcing her head to jerk immediately back up.

He wasn't looking at Sato, his expression sharpening for just a moment as he stared at her, a shrewdness peeking through before he fixed the crack in his mask, smoothing it out again. "You must still be feeling very weak. We wouldn't want anything to happen to you."

Sato made no move to follow Easton, who passed

by them both with the barest brush of a sleeve. Once the professor was out of earshot, Sato softened his grip on her hand and then released her, flexing his fingers before stuffing them into his pocket. "Come on," he muttered, already looking back toward the dorm. "Let's get this over with."

She followed silently, grateful he didn't seem to be in a rush, because, after a few steps, she was already out of breath and fighting off dizziness again. He walked slowly and calmly, somehow knowing how much she was struggling without once turning around.

As soon as they figured out Isobel had slipped out of Kilian's window, Theodore's throat had tightened with panic. He had been trying to run after her when Mikel intercepted, walking toward the dorm from the hill where he must have passed Isobel at some point.

He pushed Theodore back through the door. "She's coming," he said, pointing to the common room. "Go and wait for her in there."

Theodore nodded stiffly, shoving down his restless, panicky energy as he strode back to the common room and planted himself in front of the window. Waking up after going feral was always hard.

Aside from the wounds and the guilt, there was usually a maelstrom of fear in his gut, swirling around with indecision, wondering at the damage he had caused. He could never remember much. Sometimes he was left to wonder about the people he might have hurt and the impossible position he might have put his friends in.

This time had been different. Two days ago, he woke up with a single thought blaring like a siren in the forefront of his brain.

It's like she's already dead.

Isobel is dead.

Except she wasn't dead. She was ... his. His Tether. Drifting somewhere on the other end of a half-formed mate-bond. It was easy to believe, though he kept that to himself. It was easy to believe she was his, that he really was responsible for her, that it really was his job to protect her, that she was made to fit tucked beneath his arm, hugged into his side as he tempted one of those unwilling smiles to her lush lips. He had felt responsible for her from the moment he met her and had chalked it up to feeling indebted to her. She had saved him in his most vulnerable moment and hadn't asked for a single thing in return. Except to be friends. Not that she knew Kilian had taken a photo of the note she never gave him.

He had never dreamed he would have a mate—he definitely didn't deserve one—but as soon as Isobel whispered to him in the pool that she hated Alphas, he could suddenly picture it. The little Sigma was exactly what his mate would look like. Anything less would be a disappointment. It would have to be a *she*, and she would have to have sunlit silk for hair, the waves dwarfing her small face. She would have to have skin so pale it was ethereal, like the petals of a white rose with a slight translucency that let him see a hint of her veins. She would have to have eyes lit by a constant wariness sparking behind the honeyed colour of her iris, a jumpiness that didn't match the blessed life of a spoiled rich girl.

But he might have been able to trade all of that in just as long as she had lips like a perfect bow, a subtle plumpness and a velvety-looking texture that made them look like they were crafted to be kissed. Because he really fucking liked staring at her mouth. He liked the shock of the words she uttered, sometimes sharp, sometimes soft, always perfect.

He should have known it from the first time she parted those lips and spoke to him.

Are you okay?

Because *that's* what you say to a monster.

"Fucking hell." *Stop it*. He shook his head, trying to

dislodge the thoughts as she appeared at the top of the stairs on the other side of the lake, trailing slowly behind Oscar.

Theodore was completely fucking *delusional*.

The mate-bond made sense to him, but that was still a far cry from *accepting* it. There was no way in hell he was sharing his mate. He'd rather go without one. Even if it was her. And then there was the other problem.

There was the game.

"Stop glaring at them." Kilian nudged his arm. "You'll freak her out."

"You're also the person she's close to in here," Elijah added, walking into the room with a notebook tucked under his arm—it had been attached to his side since Theodore had woken up, and Elijah was constantly researching everything he could find about mate-bonds and adding notes to it. Gabriel was close behind, looking disgruntled. Mikel was obviously summoning everybody.

"We need her to not feel threatened or scared," Elijah continued. "Or she might run off and start blabbing things she shouldn't to people who don't need to know."

"Or ... maybe we don't want to be bringing a Sigma into a room full of tense Alphas just to scare the shit out of her," Kilian added, giving Elijah an exasperated look.

"Or that." Elijah shrugged. "Whatever you need to tell yourself. Where's Moses?" He directed that to Theodore, who frowned.

"He won't be joining," Theodore predicted. "He said he didn't want anything to do with this."

"So did Oscar," Gabriel noted calmly, nodding toward the glass wall. "But look who ran after her."

"Just count your lucky stars he didn't push her down the stairs," Cian noted, striding in from the hallway as Kalen entered from the office closest to the front door.

"Mikki probably interrupted his plans," Gabriel pointed out.

"Niko not joining?" Kalen asked as Mikel returned, his scarred lips twisted into a heavy frown.

"No," Mikel answered, the word full of exasperation and anger. "Moses and Niko have decided it would be best if they removed themselves from the situation."

"Because you can just *remove* a mat—" Theodore snapped his lips shut as the door to the dorm opened, and they all turned to watch as Oscar led Isobel into the common room.

She stood there at the edge of the hallway, staring

at her shoes, tucking trembling arms against her sides. His throat burned again, and he could feel eyes on him. They were monitoring him just as much as they were monitoring her, and that pissed him off.

Plastering an easy smile on his face, he strode forward, watching some of the tension ease from her stiff shoulders as she lifted her head to watch his approach.

"Welcome back to the world of the living, sleeping beauty." He tucked her under his arm, feeling her little hand flutter against his stomach as he hugged her sideways, like she didn't know whether to embrace him in return or not. "How are you feeling?"

He ruffled her hair, mostly to tease out Kilian's scent. The dickhead liked to saturate her just to fuck with him, but Kilian wouldn't do that today, not with everyone's emotions stretched so thin. Which meant he had been all over her for a different reason. Theodore tried not to think about it as he rubbed his hand along her arm, trying to coax a smile out of her, almost biting his tongue when it appeared, shaky and hesitant.

"I feel fine," she whispered, her fascinating eyes searching his face. They were still soft, still gentle, still wide and doe-like, but now they were filled with confusing colour. He focussed on the familiar gold specks.

"Were you really going to run away without checking on me?" he teased, slowly walking her over to the couch.

She only looked at him, nobody else, as she allowed him to lead her. He dropped onto her left side and tucked her beneath his arm once she was seated. It wasn't a mate-bond thing. The need to wipe away the scents of his friends on her skin. He did it even before the bond happened. He tried to hold himself back from scenting her in front of everyone else, forcing himself to relax back into the couch, but his fingers slipped up along her shoulder to play with her hair again.

Fuck, he couldn't stop.

She was *his* friend first. He saw her first. She should smell like him, not them.

He should think about something else.

"Obviously, something happened on the rooftop," he said. "Your eyes changed."

"But none of yours did," she quickly added, like she needed that acknowledged. Out loud. Something they couldn't do.

"None of our eyes match yours, as you can see." Kalen avoided answering her in her own words. His mouth kept pinching down at the sides like he hated talking about mate-bonds at all, in any context, with a student.

"And there was nobody else here?" she pressed, lifting her chin to meet Kalen's uncomfortable stare.

Behind him, Oscar hesitated, seemingly torn between the hallway and the common room. He accidentally met Theodore's eyes, and Theodore cocked a brow in challenge.

Are you going to stay or leave?

Oscar scowled. Twitched. Stayed.

He was staying.

Theodore's other brow jumped up, his eyes widening momentarily, but then all of a sudden, Oscar let out a small growl and turned, striding off.

"Not that we know of," Kalen answered. "I'm just going to come out and say it. I think you should keep what happened to yourself, Carter."

ISOBEL TAPPED HER FINGERS TOGETHER IN HER LAP distractedly. She didn't understand why almost all of them had to be there for the discussion they were having, but she was too tired to question it. They were probably just protecting each other.

"Obviously it would be better if nobody had to

know what happened." She sighed out the words, exhaustion dropping her shoulders even though she had only just woken up. "But how am I supposed to lie about this?" She pointed at her eyes.

"You could wear contacts," Reed suggested. He was sitting on one of the couches set a few feet back from the window, the afternoon sun straining to reach him, barely managing to touch the sweep of silvery blond hair that brushed his forehead, or the delicate, aristocratic features that somehow made him handsome instead of feminine. It was probably the frosty, hard look in his eyes and the tense squareness of his jaw.

"All the time?" Isobel frowned at him. "While I'm sleeping? While I'm showering? While I'm dancing and swimming? I live in Dorm O. There are cameras and people everywhere. It isn't like h-here ..." Her words trailed off on a stutter as she sought out the cameras carefully disguised around the common room.

"The cameras have been malfunctioning since the storm." It was Kalen West who answered her again. The large, intimidating professor didn't even try to put on a friendly face like the other scarred Alpha professor—even if Easton's smiles were fake. "That's why this discussion needed to happen today. Before the cameras are fixed."

"Oh." She went back to playing with her fingers, pulling in a deep breath. It wasn't until her lungs were filled to the brim with a rich, earthy, resinous aroma that she realised she was trying to pull Theodore's amber scent into her body.

Theodore was staying quiet, holding her loosely against his side, his body relaxing languidly into the couch. It was like he didn't have a care in the world— he *definitely* wasn't acting crazy or jealous like Kilian had hinted he might. They were so wrong about him. Still, she was grateful for the support. There was something infinitely comforting about Theodore, even if he did make her nervous sometimes. He was so charismatic that it felt like he could turn the tide of a crowd with a single look or a single word. Watching the nuances of his tight facial muscles working felt like watching someone solve an incredibly satisfying, incredibly complex puzzle. He was just ... Theodore. Powerful and dangerous, with a smile that had the whole world fooled. All of those qualities that made her fear ever disappointing him or being on his bad side were the same qualities that had her stomach twisting whenever he positioned himself as her ally, her friend. Like he was doing now, tucking her into his side so she wouldn't feel ambushed by the other Alphas.

"What do you think?" West prompted. His voice was deep and a little raspy. It was like he was trying to make himself sound soft and approachable, but it didn't really land. It wasn't natural for him.

Shit. She had been silent for too long.

She peeked up at the huge man. "How bad was the storm? Kilian said it was too dangerous to get me to the hospital. How long have the cameras been out?"

"The cameras didn't see anything." Theodore spoke up before West could answer. "And the storm was bad enough to completely destroy the rooftop. They're starting renovations tomorrow. It also tore up the mountain behind the dorm."

"There's a fire trail up the mountain. I saw it in the *Creating Ironside* documentary." Isobel chewed the inside of her cheek as her sluggish thoughts tried to formulate a plan. "I could say I was hiking up there when the storm hit, and I just woke up today. That nobody was around me. There aren't any cameras out the front of the dorm, so even if the last footage they have of me is walking to the front of the dorm, there would be no footage of me leaving again and walking straight to the track."

"That was the seventh scenario I brainstormed,"

Reed said, crossing his arms and looking impressed.

What the heck were the others?

"Could work," West agreed, after a moment. "It would take the attention off us and keep you safe. If they don't know who your mate is, they have less of a reason to pull you from Ironside. They might just keep you on-screen, waiting for the drama to play out, even if your eyes haven't changed in a normal way."

She had briefly wondered what it meant that both her eyes had changed instead of one of them, but clearly West had considered it much further. He had thought about the real-world consequences. The dangers of being an "unknown" to the officials. Suddenly, the contacts seemed like a good idea.

"Or you could wear one contact," Spade spoke up, his russet gaze narrowing on her face, like he had sensed the sudden change in her thoughts. "Then the officials won't be alarmed at all. Only curious—and probably overjoyed, since you've become a trending topic on the show."

"It'll give you those popularity points you need to get a room in this dorm," Theodore added casually.

She froze, barely daring to look around at the other faces in the room, but none of them appeared shocked at the knowledge that she was trying to get a room in Dorm A. Ashford was frowning, staring off toward the hallway, while Reed and Spade seemed distracted and fidgety, ready for the meeting to be over so that they could go about their days. Of course, this didn't really have anything to do with them. She understood why Kilian and Theodore were there—they were her friends. Maybe the others were just being nosy. Reed and Spade definitely seemed the kind to prefer to be in control of most situations.

Kilian was looking up at her through pale eyelashes, but he dropped his eyes as soon as she turned to him. West was frowning like it was his standard expression, and Easton was actually scrolling through his phone like he wasn't even paying attention to their discussion in the first place.

"Okay—" she began, but Spade stood suddenly, shocking her. He strolled over, picking up a paper bag that had been sitting beside the couch.

He held out the bag to her. "I already got you some," he said plainly. "You probably already know, since you lived in the human world, but they're obsessed with our eyes. There's an app where you can design your own contacts with your choice of rank ring around the pupil. They offer next business day shipping."

"Oh. Wow. That's prepared." She took the bag, peeking inside as though the right words to say in that situation might be conveniently sitting on top of the box of contacts.

Spade knew the exact shade and pattern of her eyes? Somehow, that didn't surprise her as much as it would have with anyone else. It was just so ... Spade. He seemed very intelligent, precise and exacting. And that was just the surface of his personality.

Thankfully, he wasn't the type of person to linger. He gave her a nod and left the room, Reed following without looking at her. Ashford stopped frowning down at the ground, but he seemed to hesitate before leaving, meeting her gaze before he stood. Something unspoken passed between them. It wasn't quite an acknowledgment that they needed to talk, but more of a demand. Issued from him. To her.

She quickly dipped her head, staring into the bag.

"Carter." West's deep voice had her head snapping up again. "We're here for you." He was doing that thing where he tried to make himself sound unthreatening again. And failing, of course. If he had been speaking a different language, she would have easily believed subtitles revealing that he was there to arrest her, and she should probably contact a lawyer. "If anyone gives you a hard time or you run into any trouble, I want you to come straight to me. Can you do that?"

"Yes," she lied, glancing over to Kilian for a moment.

His lips twitched.

"You can come to any of us," Easton amended, catching the look on her face.

"Th-Thank you." She tried to look at him but couldn't hold his mismatched eyes for very long.

There was something about Mikel Easton. Something she couldn't put her finger on. But it wasn't ... right. *He* wasn't right ... and she had absolutely no evidence to back up that theory.

"Good." He slid his phone back into his pocket, shared a loaded look with West, and left the common room.

"You should head to the hiking path," West advised, checking his watch. "They'll be sending technicians to fix the cameras soon."

Isobel nodded numbly, waiting until everyone except Theodore had left the room before the breath she had been holding finally stuttered out of her chest.

"It didn't seem this complicated when I woke up," she whispered to her knees.

"You haven't been awake long, Illy." Theodore's arm fell from her shoulders, his body twisting to face her. "You were probably in shock, and you still haven't had much of a chance to absorb everything."

"Am I doing the right thing?" She lifted her eyes to his. "I've never lied to the officials before. My father would kill me."

Possibly literally, but he didn't need to know that part.

He stiffened slightly, his attention drifting over her face, landing on her mouth for a moment. "You grew up in the human world." He paused, choosing his words carefully. "It's different in here, in the settlements. You had choices out there. Now you don't. Now, you play by their rules. And the first rule of their game is that there are heroes, there are villains, and there are supporting characters who can only ever become a hero or a villain. Villains can be vanquished, and everyone will still cheer for Ironside. *Never* give them a reason to cast you as the villain."

"And this ... anomaly"—she gestured to her eyes—"it makes me a villain?"

"It gives them an opening to twist the story however they like." His big hand landed on her knee, his grip squeezing slightly. Some of the calm, relaxed energy he had been putting off slipped away. "You don't want them filling in the blanks when you present them with a mystery. Decide the story before they do, and make sure it's the only version they see."

2

BLOOD

She climbed up the fire trail slowly, listening out for other people. She had one contact covering the strange colour of her left iris, but her clothes were freshly washed and her shoes were clean. In her current state, nobody would believe that she had been stuck out there for days.

"One hell of a storm," she muttered, picking over torn-up shrubbery as twigs crunched beneath her soles. She eventually stopped and plopped herself onto a rock, pausing a moment to sit there and stare out over the chaos of the torn-apart hillside around her. A drone whirred above, and she quickly shifted from the rock to the ground, sighing out an annoyed sound before shoving her hands into the dirt by her sneakers and beginning to streak it over her skin and clothes. She worked fast, aware of the drone drawing nearer, and messed up her hair before starting back down the hill toward Dorm A.

She didn't need to fake her unsteady walk, or the way she needed to pause every few steps to brace herself against a tree to catch her breath. She *was* sick. She *had* almost died.

The drone locked onto her at some point and followed her the rest of the way down. She expected it to lose interest in her as she passed Dorm A, but it stuck with her all the way to the medical centre. If it was possible that she might have made it without anyone paying her any attention, the drone put a stop to that. The students immediately picked up their heads at the sound, trying to figure out who it was following.

They stared at her, but none of them offered to help.

Not even for the views.

She pushed into the lobby of the medical centre, rubbing at the pain in her chest as she stopped before the triage desk. The woman behind the Perspex barrier glanced up from her computer and locked eyes on Isobel before freezing, her fingers falling off the keyboard. She switched her attention between one eye and the other.

"Are you here to report an incident?" she asked, clearly struck by shock.

"Yeah, hi." Isobel scratched her arm awkwardly, where it looked like a hive was forming. Maybe she was allergic to something she had rubbed on herself. "I was ... um ... hiking—"

"Haven't had one of these for a while." The woman wasn't even listening to her. She surged to her feet and grabbed the desk phone, coming around the other side of the barrier to get a closer look at Isobel's face as she spoke rapidly into the mouthpiece.

"Send down a crew and a bond specialist. Where's your mate?" She barely paused between words, so it took Isobel a moment to realise the last question had been aimed at her.

"I don't know."

"What?" The woman pulled the phone away from her ear, frowning. "Did you have an accident? Did you enter the Death Phase?"

"Well, yes. I think so."

"You think so?"

This wasn't going well. She was tired, and her head was pounding. Her skin was itchy, and she just wanted to sink into the corner of a shower and cry, because everything was moving too fast. Everything had changed. Her future was now set in stone.

She had a mate.

Just like her mother.

"It's the Sigma." The woman was talking into the phone again, walking away from Isobel. "She seems very confused. She's probably the Tether—she doesn't seem to remember anything, and she looks like she's been in an accident. Are you wounded, Sigma?" She looked back at Isobel.

Isobel shook her head, rubbing her chest.

"Inform her parents," the woman said, before hanging up the phone and sliding it back onto the bench. "Why do you keep rubbing your chest?" She frowned at Isobel's hand. "Are you sure you aren't injured?"

"Yes." Isobel dropped her hand. "I get sick sometimes. I had to go to hospital a lot when I was a kid. My heart stopped. It's happened before."

"Who was with you? I'm Mrs Gomez, by the way. This is very exciting. If it's true."

"If it's true?" Isobel was led through the office and into a small sickbay room with a single bed in it and some basic medical equipment.

She had seen the "hospital" portion of the Ironside

Medical Centre on the show, and this wasn't it. This was more of an interrogation chamber.

"Yes." Gomez patted the bed, waiting for her to sit gingerly on the edge of it. "It happens. More often than you might think. Those damn contacts the humans are so obsessed with."

Isobel's hands began to sweat, and she quickly tucked them beneath her thighs.

"Just a few months ago we had a Beta come in with a purple eye. Not nearly as creative as yours." Gomez prattled on as she untangled a blood pressure cuff and attached it to Isobel's arm. She picked up a small, handheld mirror from the workstation tucked into the corner of the room, shoving it beneath Isobel's nose. "Take a look. That colour is really something."

Isobel only nodded as Gomez tossed the mirror aside, allowing the woman to poke and prod her, noting things down on a chart until there was a knock at the door. The camera crew came in first, trying to find the best position in the cramped room as another woman entered after them. She had soft brown eyes that bled into a black Sigma ring. The first Sigma Isobel had seen since ...

Don't think about her.

Not now.

Not when her mother's deepest fear was coming true.

"Hi, Miss Carter?" The Sigma woman ignored the cameras, shifting around Gomez to stand in front of Isobel. She had a nice smile, a soft face, and straight brown hair tucked behind her ears. "My name is Annalise Teak. I'm a bond specialist. Do you mind if I have a quick look at your eye?"

Eye. Singular.

Still, Isobel turned her head to the side a little, trying to hide her normal-looking iris. "Okay."

"It won't hurt," Teak assured, pulling a small black torch from her pocket. "It's just a special light designed exactly for this purpose." She flashed it quickly, dropped the beam down, and then flashed it again, her own eyes widening. When she dropped it the second time, her whole demeanour changed. She tucked the torch away and rocked back on her heels, crossing her arms as her brow dipped down. "Where is your mate, Miss Carter? They should be here."

Isobel could see Gomez's mouth dropping from her position by the door, and the cameraman's face popped out from behind the camera as he pushed his cap up, staring at her.

"I don't know who they are." Isobel frowned, shifting her fingers out from beneath her thighs to play with them in her lap. "I went hiking up the mountain behind Dorm A, and then ... I think a storm hit?"

"But you're not hurt?" Teak flicked a look between Isobel and Gomez, asking them both the question.

Isobel chewed on her lip. The "my heart sometimes stops" reason worked on Gomez just fine because she was a human, but Teak was a *Sigma*. She would know. Isobel would have had to use her ability for her heart to stop, and she had to use her ability on a *person*, which implied that a person had been near her.

"I don't remember anything," she said instead. "But when I woke up, my mate wasn't there."

"It could be a supernatural attack? Something that doesn't cause any exterior wounds?" Gomez suggested in a whisper, causing Teak's mouth to immediately dip into a frown.

Gomez was outright accusing someone at Ironside of being an anti-loyalist with an illegal ability. Isobel winced, rubbing at her chest again. She needed to fix this. *But how?*

"I get sick a lot." She dared to look at Teak but couldn't quite lift her eyes higher than Teak's arrow-shaped chin. "Sometimes I have fits, and when I was younger, my heart would stop."

Teak stayed silent, but her frown deepened, tightening the skin around her chin. "We need to transfer you to the hospital. The Death Phase is exactly what it sounds like—it's not something to be messed with. We have to check your heart and monitor your vitals while the officials try to find the student who matches your new eye colour. Is that okay with you?"

"I don't know anyone with this eye colour," Isobel dared to reply, slipping off the edge of the bed to follow Teak. "Maybe they don't exist. Maybe that's why they weren't there. Maybe that's why my eye looks so weird."

"It's possible," Teak admitted. "But that's all the more reason to monitor you for a few days. We need to make sure you aren't going to suffer any adverse effects emerging from the Death Phase without a mate."

"WELL, AT LEAST YOU'RE PROPER FAMOUS NOW," EVE JOKED several days later, perching on the end of Isobel's hospital bed and opening up her bag to reveal a random stash of chocolate bars. "It's barely been a week, and it's already out. I haven't seen it yet, but everyone's talking about it." She handed one of the chocolate bars to Isobel, tearing open the wrapping of another and stretching out along the end of the bed.

Isobel wasn't surprised. Ironside didn't air an episode on Saturday, only an announcement that they would be doing a special double episode on Sunday, so she had been dreading this all day. Even though she really didn't know who her mate was, she could still feel the pressure of lying to everyone, of pretending the Alphas had nothing to do with it, that they weren't all there when the accident happened.

Still, it was necessary. Ferality wasn't just an illegal ability; it was a death sentence. If anyone found out what had really happened, it would be the end of Theodore and Moses—and the others would also likely be labelled anti-loyalists for protecting them for so long.

"Any news on the mate?" Eve drew her from her thoughts.

"No." She nibbled on the chocolate, her stomach churning uneasily. It was like this sometimes. The stomach aches, the headaches, the low-grade fevers. Teak had said it was her body rebelling because she wasn't near her mate, but there was no mate for her to be near.

"Has the bond specialist come back yet?" Eve clued

in to Isobel's mood immediately, straightening up and casting her eyes over Isobel's drawn face.

"Not yet." Isobel sighed, setting the chocolate aside. "She was supposed to come today but she didn't make it. They won't let me out of here until she gives me a health plan for living without a mate. She said the officials need to approve it first."

Eve sighed, pulling her laptop out of her bag and setting it up at the end of the bed. She crawled up to the top of the bed to sit beside Isobel, and they both quietened to watch the latest episode of the *Ironside Show*.

It began with her stumbling down the hiking trail, with Ed Jones and Jack Ransom keeping relatively quiet for once. They let a crescendo of suspenseful music build in the background instead of their usual commentary. The cameras followed her to the medical centre and showed some rare, behind-the-scenes footage of crew reporting the possibility of a mate-bond to an Ironside official standing in a room full of screens, like a vast control centre for a newsroom.

"*Where are they?*" the official asked, stepping away from the screens and hitting a button on his headset.

"*There's just one, sir. The Sigma. No sign of a mate. She's with a triage nurse.*"

"*The Sigma?*" He leaned over someone's desk,

tapping out a few things against their keyboard as they shifted out of the way and off camera. "*We haven't seen her in days. We've been trying to track her down.*"

He pulled an image up on the screen closest to him, and the camera zoomed right in on it, showing Isobel and Ashford sitting on the ledge at the top of the library building.

"*Is it Cian Ashford?*" the official asked. "*That's who she was last seen with.*"

"*No, sir,*" the staff member replied. "*Her eye doesn't match up with any of the Alphas. It was the first thing we checked.*"

"*You're absolutely certain?*" the official asked.

"*It's vastly different.*" The staff member cleared her throat, lowering her voice slightly. "*If it's real.*"

"*Get a bond specialist in there fast,*" the official ordered.

The scene changed immediately, switching between a shaky vision of the hallways the camera crews were running down and the view of them from above using the fixed cameras. It showed the plaque on the door of an office in the admin building.

Annalise Teak - Gifted - Bond Specialist

"I didn't know they had Gifted on staff," Eve noted quietly, her usually excited tone subdued.

"Maybe she's bonded?" Isobel suggested.

"Would make sense." Eve lifted one of her shoulders. "It's something the humans will never fully understand. Do you think she's stuck here like the professors, or do you think she's free—"

"*It's possible her mate is dead,*" Teak was saying on-screen, drawing their attention back to the episode. She was shrugging into a short blazer, a disturbed expression on her face. "*I've heard of it happening before, the Anchor dying in the same accident that started the Death Phase. It will be interesting to see if the Tether will surviv—*"

"*Carter,*" one of the crew interrupted. "*The Tether is the Sigma: Carter.*"

Teak paused, and the camera zoomed right into her own Sigma ring, catching the way Teak quickly arranged her expression into a polite mask. She brushed over the front of her jacket, gave the camera a smile, and turned for the door. "*If it is true.*" She pulled open the door, and the cameras followed her into the hallway. "*It will be interesting to see if Carter survives. But she may not be the Tether. She may not be the one who entered the Death Phase. She may be the Anchor. She might have lost her Tether to their Death Phase, in which case, she will likely recover and go on living unchanged, except for her eye.*"

Eve sucked in a breath, and Isobel could feel her

glancing sideways, but Isobel only folded her arms, staring at the laptop screen. Not that she was really seeing it anymore. She could barely focus as she watched herself on-screen: body language hunched, hands tucked beneath her thighs, her limbs trembling. She barely registered when Ed and Jack's silence suddenly burst in the moment Teak confirmed her eye change was real. She wanted to sink back into the pillows, close her eyes, and erase what she had heard.

Kilian was right: the next time she died, she would stay dead.

She didn't doubt that she was the Tether, that she really had almost died, but if she had lost her Anchor … didn't that mean she was in free-fall? Her soul attached to nothing, nothing anchoring her to this world, to life?

The door opened before the episode had even finished and both girls looked up, scrambling to turn off the show and clean up the messy surface of the bed as Teak walked in.

"Miss Carter," she greeted warmly, her friendly smile transforming her face. It was a soft-featured face, with the exception of her arrowed chin. Her skin was dark mahogany with a rosy tinge, and there were several gold hoops in her ears, as well as a small gold stud in her nose—all details that Isobel had been too distracted to notice last time.

Teak shrugged off her jacket, pulling a chair up to the bedside. "Don't mind me." She waved off Eve's efforts to scuttle out of the room. "I still need to check out her chart before we can chat."

"Oh." Eve calmed a little, shooting Isobel a wide-eyed look. "I'll just … I'll come and see you tomorrow before breakfast?"

"You can wait in the hallway," Teak assured her. "Miss Carter will be free to leave after our conversation."

An excited smile split over Eve's face, and Isobel felt her whole body deflate, the horrible doubt trickling out of her.

"Really?" she asked, as Eve finished gathering her stuff and left the room.

"Really." Teak finished with her chart and set it aside, propping her folded arms over a black folder that she rested on her thighs. "Your condition hasn't deteriorated in the least. You've gotten stronger. We believe your mate is still alive, but for some reason, they weren't there when you died."

"Maybe they ran away—"

"They aren't even at Ironside," Teak announced, puffing out a laugh that sounded impressed. "The officials have a database for exactly this reason. Your new eye colour doesn't match any student or professor here."

"P-Professor?" Isobel spluttered, drawing her legs up to her chest.

"As I said ..." Teak's voice turned soothing. "You aren't a match to anyone. You may be the first Gifted to bond to a person over distance, which would make you quite the anomaly. The officials will be conducting searches through the settlements, but for now, your focus should be on Ironside." She straightened away from the folder, turning it and placing it onto the bed beside Isobel. "This is your healthcare plan. It explains all the possible side-effects that we know of when it comes to prolonging bonds and half-formed bonds, which is what you have. You will need to prolong your bond until we find your mate."

"What if I don't want to find them?" Isobel hugged her legs tighter, wedging her chin in between her knees as she stared at the innocuous black folder.

Teak leaned back, crossing her arms loosely. She looked young, all of a sudden, a flash of sympathy racing across her expression. She didn't answer with words but let her silence hang heavy between them.

She didn't want to say it, but Isobel knew.

She didn't have a choice.

"You're in a unique position." Teak finally spoke again, her tone careful. "You can't be sent back to the settlements because of your father—you're still considered a member of his household until you're twenty-one—but you can be removed from the academy and enrolled in a research program. I guarantee you won't like it. There won't be any cameras."

It seemed like a strange thing to add. *There won't be any cameras.* But then Isobel understood, and her heart dropped into her stomach. They would be able to do whatever they wanted with her. The humans always did whatever they wanted.

"Right." She forced her body to unwind and scooped up the folder, pulling it into her lap. "Can I go now?"

"Just one last thing." Teak watched her carefully, pulling out her phone. "We're going to need to have regular appointments. I'm the only one here qualified to assess the health of your bond, and how it might be affecting you physically and mentally."

"What makes you qualified?" Isobel asked the question before she could stop herself and immediately regretted it.

She didn't have to be from the settlements to know it was extremely rude to enquire about a person's bonded status, and that was essentially what she was doing. But Teak didn't seem to mind. She rolled up one of the silk sleeves of her business shirt, turning her taupe-and-rose dusted wrist to reveal a small, black tattoo, right in the centre of her forearm.

C.T.

"My wife's initials," she explained. "We decided this was the most fitting way to complete our bond with a permanent marking instead of waiting around for an accident to happen."

Isobel nodded, chewing on her lip. "How long have you been bonded?"

"Five years now. She was a student here. It happened after she graduated and came back to my settlement. She will also be attending some of our sessions—it was something I fought the officials quite hard for. I thought you might appreciate the added perspective of someone who has gone through what you're going through here at Ironside, though I have to admit, she was nowhere near as popular as you're becoming." Teak's lips lifted into a grin. "She was a bit of a disaster, to be honest."

Her fondness for her mate was obvious, and it didn't settle Isobel's mind at all.

"How's Thursday?" Teak asked, tapping on her phone screen. "I can see you next week, and then the

Thursday after that is the last day of term before spring break."

"Sounds good." Isobel edged toward the door. It had been days since she had been alone in her own space, and she was suddenly desperate to be back in her shitty little room in Dorm O, curled up on the floor beneath a blanket.

Her head wasn't right. She was depressed, and she couldn't figure out why. For almost two years she had endured Ironside, refusing to let them see her break, but now she felt broken, and she couldn't identify the moment it had happened.

Teak said something about sending her an email reminder of their appointment, and Isobel thanked her dutifully before walking back to the dorm with Eve, neither of them knowing what to say.

"It's all going to be fine, you know." Eve attempted cheering her up. "The scariest part of bonding is the Death Phase, and you're through that."

Isobel grimaced, refusing to let her brain jump back, to let it roll through memories like a rolodex, showing image after image of her parents. Of their "bond." The Death Phase wasn't the scariest part of bonding, in her opinion. It was the happily never after. It was being tied to a person who would use her, suck her dry, and rule over her until she disappeared without even an aftershock to prove she was ever alive or a funeral to prove she had ever died.

Ironside, as terrible as it had been, was an escape from that life. An escape from her father. The idea of going home to someone like him after she finished her five years at the academy—after she was no longer owned by her father—was unbearable.

"Hey!" Eve gripped her shoulders, shaking her a little. "Cheer up, girl. Whoever they are, they're an obscurity right now. Let's not waste our time worrying about obscurities. Be an opportunist. *Use* this." She lowered her voice to a whisper. "Don't become their puppet. Don't just sit around waiting for them to decide what to do with you. Seriously. Build up your popularity. This is your opportunity to really make it happen."

Isobel sucked in a breath, stepping into the dorm as Eve held the door open for her, patting her on the back as she moved past.

"You're right." She released the breath on a short laugh. "You usually are."

"I know." Eve grinned, shifting Isobel a sideways look. "Strategy meeting over breakfast?"

"Okay." Isobel chuckled, feeling a little lighter as she climbed the stairs.

Eve pulled her into a hug before they separated.

"You know most of the students here would *kill* to be in your position right now?" she whispered into Isobel's hair.

"I know." Isobel felt a pang of gratefulness for the other girl, squeezing her tighter than usual before breaking off to go to her own room.

It was that gratefulness that stopped her running right back out again.

She carefully shut the door, cutting off the light from the hallway before switching on the overhead light, illuminating the dozens of heavy balloons hanging from the ceiling. Water balloons, it looked like, filled with some kind of dark liquid.

She took a single step forward, and that was when it happened. Her ankle pressed into a wire tied across the room, triggering something to explode. One of her remaining windowpanes shattered, and a few items were knocked off her shelf, the balloons exploding at once. Dark red liquid rained down over her room, and her. She just stood there, shuddering, her attention fixed to the wall beside her head, where several tiny nails were embedded in the paint.

And then she started hyperventilating.

Her legs buckled, and she caught herself against the slippery floor, her chest squeezing and constricting. The door behind her opened, a soft curse sounding.

"Jesus fucking Christ." Kilian appeared before her, his hands gripping her shoulders as he pulled her up. "Is that blood? Is any of this your blood?"

She couldn't find the words to answer.

He snatched something off her bookshelf and started wiping her with it, his movements lacking the usual care and softness he usually showed her. "Isobel?"

She felt like she was choking.

"Fucking hell." He gave up trying to wipe her down, picking her up like she weighed nothing at all. He held her against his chest as he stepped back to the door, kicking his shoes off before moving into the hallway.

"N-No." She found her voice and started to struggle, pushing against his chest. "Cameras."

"We're invisible," he informed her, his tone cold.

She stopped struggling, listening to her own ragged breathing.

"Are you hurt?" he asked, moving toward the bathroom. There weren't any students in the hallway, but he whispered for the cameras.

She tried to take stock of her body, but she just felt

numb everywhere. "I don't think so. You can put me down."

He ignored her, waiting by the wall until an Omega girl walked out of the bathroom, and then he caught the door with his foot, slipping inside. He carried her right into a shower room and locked the door before grabbing a towel and throwing it over the stool of a wing-backed armchair that stood apart from the shower and bath. He placed her on the towel and set a finger against her lips, asking her to keep quiet before he ducked into the tiled shower alcove, turning the water on full and filling the room with a comfortable hum of white noise. He came back to her, lowering close to her face.

"Don't move," he whispered, before slipping out of the room.

Isobel stared at the door, hoping the noise of the shower would be enough to stop anyone else from entering. When he returned, he had her toiletries bag, and he set it down before holding out a hand to her.

She blinked at his hand, her mind flashing back to their kiss before she quickly shoved the memory from her mind. He was there to help. Maybe her feelings were a little confused—it was impossible *not* to be confused by someone who looked like Kilian—but that didn't mean *his* feelings were confused. He was safe.

She put her hand in his, letting him draw her silently up and into the shower, where steam curled around them. He didn't say anything as he angled her under the spray, his hands cupping her face, rubbing over her cheekbones as she scrunched her eyes closed and let him tilt her face to the water. When she came out of the spray for breath, he was examining her with so much care and intensity it had her heart stuttering.

He stepped out of the shower to rummage through her toiletries bag, and she found herself confronted with a very wet, very serious Alpha as he returned. His face had tightened into hard lines, his jaw clenched, little lines furrowing around his pale eyes. He had only been wearing a stretched-out, faded terracotta tank and plain black pants—the thin polyester type with the drawstring. Basically, he wasn't wearing enough to hide any of the beautiful, streamlined muscles of his body. The wet material now clung to him like a second skin.

"Why are you so fit?" she mumbled. It was too quiet, apparently, because he lifted an inquisitive brow, shampoo in one hand and conditioner in the other.

"Hmm?" he asked lowly.

"What do you do for exercise?" she whispered.

He tipped her head back again and traced his fingers across her scalp, the focussed look back on his face. He was looking for nails. She shuddered, and his eyes immediately snapped down to hers. His chest was so close to hers that she could feel it expand as he took a deep breath.

"Dance," he admitted.

"What?" She blinked up at him. "But—"

"Privately." He finished checking her scalp and bent to squeeze shampoo into his palm.

"No shit?" Her lips tugged into a small frown, and his eyes dipped to follow the movement, fixing there as his chest expanded against hers again.

He massaged the shampoo into her hair, moving slowly and treating her scalp like it was made of glass. "Not showing them everything is a tactic," he told her quietly, his tone carrying a warning in such a subtle way that she wasn't even sure he was doing it deliberately. "You might not be on the Icon track, but that doesn't mean the rest of us aren't playing the game."

She ducked her head down, but then started shaking again at the sight of the red-tinged water washing away from her feet. Her body locked up, and

Kilian caught her chin, gently lifting her gaze back to his.

"Just focus on me." His tone was hushed, his expression gentle. "It doesn't look like you have any cuts, but I'll double-check."

She stared at him as he washed her hair and kept staring as he unbuttoned her shirt, drawing it off her shoulders and leaving her in a plain black bra and shorts. He washed it clean before wringing it out and hanging it up on one of the towel racks. When he came back, his jaw was even tighter, his hands drifting carefully over her neck, shoulders, and arms. He only flicked his eyes back to hers once, right before his hands settled on her stomach. His fingers drifted first, fluttering over her skin like butterflies, searching for any wounds before he began to rub the blood away.

It was awful, having him touch her. Awful because his hands on the outside seemed to be connected to something on the inside of her. Every brush and scrape from the pads of his fingers had her stomach clenching, weird tingly feelings shooting through her from somewhere low in her belly. She was worried he could feel it, but his expression never changed. She hadn't experienced a lot of gentleness in her life, unless it was from her mother. Receiving it from Kilian was like a drug, and it completely intoxicated her.

"Is it a little weird that you're doing this?" she asked, just as he began those butterfly touches over her chest, tracing the skin above her bra and making the frantic organ inside her chest do somersaults. She was fascinated with the way her flesh dipped lightly beneath the drag of his touch.

He paused, but only for a fraction of a second. "Is Theo the only one allowed to be friends with you?"

"Theo doesn't shower me."

"His loss." Kilian's lips twitched, the first softening of his expression that she had seen since he appeared in her room.

"Wait." She squinted at him, completely sidetracked. "Why were you in my room? How did you know I was getting released from the medical centre?"

He chewed on his lip, his hands dropping to grip her hips and spin her around. He took a few moments to answer while his fingers drifted over the backs of her shoulders. When he started to rub the blood off her skin, his fingers dug in a little harder, almost like a massage. She released a quiet groan and sagged back against him. His head dropped near hers, his voice changing until his whisper was a husky one.

"Feel good, baby?"

"Yeah." She closed her eyes, focussing on the way his fingers worked her muscles. "I used to get massages every week back home. My father said I couldn't afford any injuries because I wasn't allowed to skip practice."

"Your dad was intense." His fingers slipped down from her shoulders. "But it paid off. You dance like you were born for it. I'm going to touch your ass."

"Thanks for the warning." She almost laughed. He sounded so serious.

But then he was pushing down her shorts, his hands gripping her waist as he lifted her up, kicked them away, and set her back down again. She didn't really feel like laughing anymore, especially when he skipped the butterfly touches, his palms dragging down the swell of her ass cheeks. The water must have already washed away enough of the blood for him to see that she wasn't injured, and she looked down at herself for the first time since he had told her to focus on him. The shower water was no longer running red, though her legs were still stained in some places.

Her stomach clenched as he knelt behind her, firmly rubbing down her thighs, and then her calves. He washed away all the blood and then stood, spinning her back around again, his eyes cataloguing her skin for any specks he might have missed.

She quickly wound her arms around his neck

before she could second guess herself, muttering into the skin of his collarbone.

"Thank you."

He caught her hips, holding her a few inches away, but when he realised she wasn't trying to plaster herself along the front of his body, he relaxed, his arms cocooning her and cuddling her chest close to his.

He wasn't speaking, and that was a little weird for Kilian.

"You still haven't answered," she accused, realising he had successfully distracted her from her question. She drew back to meet his guarded yellow-green eyes. "Why did you come to my room?"

"We have connections inside the surveillance room. They told Kalen you were being released."

"And he told you?"

Kilian rolled his lips together. "Not exactly." He reached around her, turned off the taps, and ducked his head close to her ear to whisper, "I was spying."

He plucked one of the fluffy robes from the dressing area and then came back to wrap it around her. "You can't stay in that room tonight."

"I know." She managed to conjure a smile. "I'll go and sleep in Eve's room."

He looked down at her, that serious expression still holding his features hostage, a strange thump of emotion emanating off him and hitting against her own chest. She frowned, but just as she tried to focus on it, to figure out what it was, the darkness lifted from his expression, a familiar gentleness stepping into place even as his lips lifted at the corners, the curve of his mouth familiar and wily.

"I'd tell you to keep this a secret." He kept his voice low. "But it might do Theo some good to know he isn't your only Alpha crush."

"I don't have a crush on you, you idiot," she scoffed, tightening the fluffy robe.

"But you do have a crush on Theo?" His teasing tone remained the same, but his eyes were sharp enough to cut through steel, and she wasn't used to that from Kilian.

Was he jealous? Did he *like Theodore?*

"We're friends." She hunted down a pair of the plush slippers that were always provided in the dressing area.

"You're broken records, that's what you are." Kilian caught the neck of her robe, pulling her up and forcing her to look at him. "Are you okay? I don't feel right leaving you."

"Remember that discussion we had where we agreed you aren't my dad?"

"Was this after I folded your underwear, brushed your hair, or bathed you?"

Isobel bit down hard on her lip so that she wouldn't burst into laughter, but a loud sound escaped her anyway, and they both paused, heads cocked, as they tried to listen through the door of her shower room.

"I need to follow you out," he whispered, returning his attention to her. "Just promise you'll text me or Theo if anything else happens."

"Okay." It was a lie, and they both knew it.

3

TAKE ME BACK

Isobel returned to her room after Kilian left. She retrieved her black folder and bag—both now covered in blood—and searched for clothes on her shelf that had managed to evade the deluge from the ceiling. After quickly changing and switching the items from her bag into the only clean tote she could find, she left the dorm.

It was almost midnight, and the pathways were quiet, only a few lights on near the fitness centre. She walked to the library, swiped her access card, and climbed to the top floor, her posture stiff with tension. Her neck had prickled the entire way there, the hair on her arms standing on end, but no matter how many times she turned around, nobody was ever following her. The uneasy feeling didn't leave her until she slipped into the chair behind her desk.

She cleaned the folder as best she could before flipping it open and scanning through the first page. It was a schedule for her final week of the term, saying that she had been excused from classes until Friday, when spring break started, though her dance sessions in the practise rooms remained.

Not only that, but private lessons had been added. There was one on Wednesday with Kalen West.

Private Piano Tutoring.

She sat back, staring at the little block of time, her brows shooting up, her mouth parting in shock. An *Alpha* professor had agreed to privately tutor a *Sigma*? She wasn't even in her third year, yet. Teak must have pulled some serious strings ... and Isobel wished she hadn't. Not only was West terrifying, but she also had no interest in the Icon track. She wasn't in this game to win it. She needed popularity points before the summer break and private lessons were rarely filmed —at least until the officials decided to send out crews on foot. Private lessons were for people on the Icon track to work with their mentors on special projects that they would only debut to the public when they were ready.

She had absolutely no use for private lessons with West.

The other new addition was a small group session that had replaced her second period time slot, but it didn't list the professor or the subject. Only the location.

On the next page was a note from Teak, explaining the timetable changes.

Miss Carter,

I've managed to clear your schedule for the last week of term to give you some time to acclimate to your newly half-bonded status. There are a few exceptions, namely the private lessons with Professor West and the small group session.

After being informed of your deal with the Officials to move to Dorm A with a provisional amount of popularity points (of which I am sure you will accumulate), I tracked down the Alpha professors and asked them to consider adding you to their private tutoring schedule. It was more of a formality to make sure you were on their radar, since I believe you will be living there next year.

To my surprise, Professor West agreed.

This is a rare opportunity, as I am sure you understand, and a very big vote of confidence from the Alphas. If they welcome you into their fold, it goes without saying that you will benefit immensely. I fear the other ranks may begin to target you soon for the attention you are receiving as a Sigma at Ironside.

Isobel snorted, rubbing her eyes as she dropped the folder. Teak had no idea.

She shrugged off the deflated feeling before it could settle over her shoulders, pushing her chair back and turning off the lights on the upper level. She returned to her desk in the dark and crawled beneath it.

It was dusty. It was cramped.

It was safe.

WHEN SHE WOKE UP, IT WAS WITH A GASP IN HER THROAT and the memory of blood flooding down over her face, but it wasn't her red-soaked room that she saw. It was a tall boy sitting up against the wall behind her chair, his head tipped back, his eyes closed. She blinked the bleariness from her eyes, but barely dared to move as she stared at Theodore.

There was a takeaway cup of coffee by his thigh, and she dragged her eyes over the black pants that somehow managed to show how muscled and firm his thighs were to the second cup in his hands, tilting dangerously. His long, dark lashes dusted his sharp cheeks, the harsh lines and angles of his face somehow still tight, full of tension even while he slept. She carefully pulled herself up, but as soon as she shifted near him, reaching out to save the tipping coffee cup, his eyes flicked open, immediately focussed, his pupils expanding and contracting.

"Illy." His voice was husky. He set his cup down and stretched his limbs, something cracking as he winced. And then he handed her the other cup.

"How did you find me here?" she asked, sipping the still-warm liquid. As soon as the bitterness hit the back of her tongue, she started to drink it faster, greedy to consume it all before it lost its heat. "Christ, I needed this," she groaned. "Thanks."

He watched her, the elegant, arched shape of his brows pitching down. "You aren't that hard to find. Why were you under the desk?"

"I had a little incident in Dorm O." She took another few gulps of coffee and then tried to change the subject. "You don't look very happy to see me."

His face softened instantly, one of his arms held out, like he wanted a hug. "I am. Sorry I didn't come to see you in the hospital."

"It's okay." She knee-walked over to him and then awkwardly bent into the hug. He had been texting her every day, but he never actually explained why he wasn't coming to see her. She just assumed it was the same reason he got himself a fake girlfriend. To deflect attention.

He patted her back as she leaned over him, and she could feel him inhaling at the same time as her, both of them holding their breath, but then he suddenly stood, drawing her up with him. She yelped, holding her cup with one hand and grabbing a handful of his shirt with the other. He chuckled, setting her down before he swiped up her tote.

"As much as I like you clinging to me, we're late for our group session," he said, looking her over. His expression slipped for just a moment, showing a brief flash of darkness in his stormy eyes. "What happened?"

"What group session?" She tried to ignore his question, stepping back to her desk to snatch up the black folder with her new schedule inside.

"Private small group session," he replied, eyeing her folder. "We all have one for second period. You've just been invited to the club."

"We?" she asked as he pulled her toward the stairs. "What club?"

"The other Alph—"

She dug her heels in, pulling them both up short.

He looked her over again, his brows drawing low. "It's okay. They won't do anything to you."

"They don't *want* me in their club!" she insisted, her words almost hissing out between clenched teeth.

"Who doesn't want you?" His lips were twisting into a grin, but he managed to fight it back. "Me? Kilian?"

"Moses," she added tonelessly, folding her arms. "Ashford? Niko? Spade? Reed? *Sato? All the rest of them?*"

Theodore blew out a sharp breath, waving his hand. "Never heard of them. Gabriel got you those contacts, didn't he?" Theodore managed to get her walking toward the stairs again. "And Elijah set up the sensor on your door."

"Wait, what? Reed put a sensor on my door? What does that even mean?" She halted once more, whipping around to face Theodore, who quickly turned his attention to his watch.

"We're going to be really late." His cheeks were tinged with the slightest hint of colour.

"What sensor?" She folded her arms.

"He thought the camera might not be enough." Theodore shrugged lightly, but there was caution in the way he returned her stare. "He set up a sensor to bring the camera feed up on his phone whenever someone uses your door. That's why Kilian was on his way to your room. He was going to take down the blood trap before you got there. None of us were expecting you to be released last night."

"Kilian didn't tell me that."

"We weren't supposed to tell you that."

"Did they see who set the trap?"

"No." The word was almost growled out. "Someone flooded the room with darkness, and then they covered the camera while they set it up. Elijah waited until he had visibility again to tell us what had happened since you were already safe in the hospital."

She was reeling, but Theodore had given up trying to gently coax her into movement. His bigger hand wrapped around hers, and he practically dragged her down the steps and out of the library, muttering something about her thanking him later when she didn't get punished for being late. She was silent as they walked to class, his hand releasing hers as soon as they were outside, though his arm landed over her shoulders instead, maintaining his fast pace as he steered her.

Halfway there, he seemed to remember that he had brought her a protein bar, and he switched it out for her empty coffee cup, which he dropped into a bin outside the fitness centre before pulling her toward the entrance.

"Eat quickly," he encouraged. "Mikki won't go easy on you."

"*Professor Easton*?" she spluttered, choking on the first mouthful she had hastily bitten off.

"That's right." Theodore gave her a droll look. "Our group session is your new second period. You want to live with the Alphas? You're going to need to learn to keep up with us."

"I'm never going to be able to keep up," she grumbled beneath her breath, tearing into the protein bar to ease her nerves. It tasted terrible. It was one of the health bars, not the "full of sugar and pretending to be healthy" bars that she preferred. It made sense that Theodore would choose the nutritious option though, with muscles like his. "Why is the group session in here?" She glanced down the hall.

"Mikki does things a little differently," he answered, leading her through the centre toward the gym rooms.

She stared at the back of his tousled dark head, wondering if those heavy words had been a promise or a warning. The protein bar inside her mouth turned to ash, and she quickly tossed the rest of it out right before Theodore paused before a door, knocking three times.

It opened to Easton's annoyed face as he checked

his watch. "Two minutes late," he growled, all traces of the forced politeness in his scarred features vanishing. He stepped back, waving Theodore through, and then settled his splotchy black eyes on her, quirking a brow with a scar cutting through it. "Rough night, Carter?"

Did they all know? She squared her shoulders, edging past him into the room. "No, Professor. Good morning."

"Here." He dangled a bag before her face. "I didn't think you'd be prepared, and I don't like to waste time. There's a bathroom behind the treadmills. Get changed quickly."

Her hands were shaking when she took the bag from him, careful not to accidentally touch his fingers when she slipped hers through the handle. He stepped back, pointing to a door at the back of the room. It was a full gym with a large stretching area, at least five treadmills, and two walls of mirrors ... and it looked like every single one of the Alphas were already there, except Professor West.

They were stretching, Theodore chatting with Kilian while he kept his eyes on her. She felt the others looking at her too. Assessing, wary, watchful. They weren't sure about inviting her into their group, but they were opening the door a crack. Which meant they thought she was going to succeed in getting a room in their dorm. It didn't mean they were accepting her, but they were taking the possibility seriously. She didn't know whether to be flattered at their confidence in her growing popularity, or terrified by their careful planning.

She ducked her head and hurried to the bathroom, trying not to trip over any of the equipment in her nervous haste. The Omegas didn't scare her half as much as the Alphas, but the Alphas were the only ones —other than Eve—who were making any small effort to somewhat include her. They weren't rigging her room with nail bombs and water balloons filled with blood.

But they were asking her to … to what? Be better? To not embarrass them?

She shook out the contents in the bag Easton had given her, blinking at the brand-new gym shorts, sports bra, and loose shirt. There were also socks and sneakers, and she changed as quickly as she could, frowning over at herself in the mirror as she quickly slung her hair into a ponytail. Everything fit perfectly, right down to her shoe and bra size. It was unsettling. Had he asked Theodore? Had he looked up her official records? Was her bra size in her official records? Almost definitely. Had he done this because he knew her clothes had been soaked in blood? No matter how she looked at it, it was disturbing.

As soon as she entered the gym, she was hit with a wall of sound. Niko, Theodore, Kilian, Spade, and Reed were running on the treadmills. No ... *sprinting*. Niko, who was closest to her, darted a quick look at her as she walked past, his striking eyes blank, the meld of hazel and green cold, wiped of emotion. He had his wavy, bleached hair pulled into a bun, but most of it had escaped to bounce against his forehead, covering his eyes when he turned away from her. A light sheen of sweat already covered his caramel skin, his breath loud. *Everything* was loud.

Ashford, Sato, and Moses were lined up in a row before one of the mirrored walls, rhythmically punching tear-drop boxing bags hanging from the ceiling.

"I'm grateful to be invited, but what kind of lesson is this?" she asked, meeting Easton in the middle of the room.

He was looking at her outfit, his dark frown refusing to loosen until he seemed to find the hem of her shorts, barely peeking beneath her shirt. His forehead smoothed out slightly and he crossed his arms, rocking back on his heels. Maybe the shirt was too big. It did kind of look like she wasn't wearing any pants. She tucked part of the shirt into her shorts, to make it more obvious.

"For you? It's a singing lesson," he told her.

She wasn't sure if she was supposed to laugh or not.

"Niko!" he barked. "Move to a bag."

Niko jumped off the treadmill, giving her another blank look as he crossed to the boxing bags, picking up a set of gloves and falling into the other workout without batting an eyelid.

"Jump on," Easton offered, waving at the freed-up treadmill.

She swallowed, stepping toward the machine. Spade didn't break stride beside her as she stepped up and Easton immediately started pressing buttons.

"This is a warm-up," he told her. "The aim isn't to kill yourself. Tell me when to stop."

Suddenly, her legs were kicked into a jog and then a run. "S-Stop," she begged as she felt the strain of maintaining the speed he had set. He switched it down a level before walking away.

She tried not to stare at the others in the mirror as they ran in silence, Kilian occasionally muttering to Theodore, Spade ignoring everyone as he blasted music through his headphones. When her machine hit the ten-minute mark, Easton called for them all to stop and stretch, and she followed the others to the mat-strewn section of the room, drawn to the sunshine grin Theodore shot at her. Something in her gut was pulled by the gesture, guiding her to his side as she copied the stretches he was doing. Every time he shifted and she mirrored him, his smile grew a little more amused.

"Right." Easton stood over them, looking through his phone. "Feeling loose? Feeling warm?"

"Loose as I get," Sato grunted, jumping up and down on the spot like he was preparing to pounce on somebody.

"Also warm as he gets," Reed added, making a few of them chuckle.

"Can you sing, Isobel?"

Easton's sudden question—and all the attention that swung her way—had her frozen to the spot. She really thought he was being sarcastic about the singing lesson.

"N-No. Yes. Sort of. Not well."

"If you could only pick one?" He was still staring at his phone, the inflection in his voice a bit impatient.

"Not well, Professor."

He slipped his phone away, his arms crossed. "You're at the most expensive arts academy in the world, *and* on the most famous reality *or* talent show in the world. Not to mention you're Braun Carter's daughter. So ... I find that hard to believe. Even as the daughter of an Icon, they wouldn't have let you take a fucking picture of this place unless they were impressed with what you could do. Show me. Sing something."

Her mind immediately flashed back to her first year, to the professor who had forced her to sit at the piano and play for the class, and how her fingers had refused to move. The students had dismissed her as a lost cause almost immediately, and she couldn't afford to repeat that mistake with the Alphas. Dorm A was her only escape. If they thought she would embarrass them, they might find a way to refuse her entry. She registered the impatient look on Easton's face and quickly grappled for the first song she could think of, opening her mouth to begin it, but his head was already shaking.

"No, no. Stand up."

Blushing, she pushed to her feet and moved between Theodore and Moses to stand before Easton, right at the point on the floor he had indicated. When he seemed satisfied, she began. Her voice cracked immediately, but she closed her eyes and blocked them all out, determined to finish before she froze up.

It was an old settlement song her mother used to

sing, and she started to think about her mother's soft voice as the words passed naturally across her lips. She relaxed, seeing her mother leaning over the bathtub, testing the water. Boiling the kettle. Mixing something on the stove. Watering the ferns around the apartment. Standing on the balcony at night, her silken robe flapping as she stared down, down, down.

Take me back to where it all began,
Seas of sand and sun-kissed land,
Take me home before I'm buried here.
Show me the spot where the sun falls,
Somewhere far beyond these walls.
Take my hand, be my guide,
To the light on the other side.
Through this maze, we'll find our way,
Before these walls claim my last day.

She snapped her eyes open mid-chorus, her fists clenched by her sides, her chest rising and falling quickly, a hint of panic at the edge of her mind. Maybe she needed to talk to someone about her mother.

Maybe that someone was her father.

She sucked in a shuddering breath, turning her eyes up to Easton's. "I forgot the rest," she lied. "Sorry."

He didn't look annoyed anymore. He looked almost surprised, but his brow was also furrowed.

"Never mind." He stared at her for a few more seconds, cataloguing her features. It was the first time he had *really* looked at her. "You're clearly very comfortable in your mezzo range. Your voice is lyrical and airy ... you didn't push your range at all. You must have started singing young."

"As young as possible." She was shocked with the compliments.

"You need to work on your stability, though." Easton pulled out his phone again and started up a song over the speakers before handing the phone over to her. "Pick a song from this playlist, and we'll use that as our base today. Something with a lower register. I want to experiment with your range."

He turned away from her and began firing off orders to the others. The song playing over the speakers had been recorded by Theodore, his clear, hypnotising voice ringing about the room—but it seemed to be a demo track, and each of them knew their parts. They were all practising this song. Even Sato and Moses, who were the last people she had expected to see *singing*. She couldn't distinguish their voices very well in the loudness of the room and quickly stopped trying when Easton shot her a sharp look.

She returned her attention to his phone screen just as a message appeared across the top of it.

Tilda: It's no surprise, but you forgot to call this morning. Can you do anything right?

Isobel winced, trying to ignore the message as she scanned the list of songs, settling on the first familiar name she saw. She quickly turned off his screen, but his phone vibrated again, making something flip sickeningly in her chest. When he returned, she quickly handed the phone back, the vibrations threatening to burn her palm.

"Billie Eilish. 'Ilomilo,'" she quickly said, hoping to stop him from looking at his phone. "I'll search the lyrics." She already had her phone in her hand, her fingers flying across the screen.

"Good choice." He watched her search for the song and then brought a stand over for her to rest her phone on.

He had her sing it through once, somehow able to block out all the other noise in the room as he focussed solely on her. The other Alphas had divided up into pairs, a line of them standing up against the wall and singing different parts of their demo song on repeat over the loudspeaker. The others put on boxing gloves and faced off against one of the boys against the wall.

And then they started punching, sending light but

fast jabs into their partner's abdomen. Isobel started, stepping away from the podium, but Easton dragged her back, tapping on the podium for her to focus.

"Don't worry, that won't be part of your vocal training." He had a small, tight smile on his face.

"Why are they doing that?" she asked, wide-eyed as Theodore took a particularly nasty punch from Sato.

"Alphas are ..." Easton trailed off, cutting a glance over to them. "Different," he finished. "We have a side that only comes out when triggered by adrenaline. That's the side I need them to tap into when they're performing. You have other talents."

"You want me to make everyone calm when I perform?" she asked.

For just a moment, he almost looked amused. But it also might have been exasperation. "Your voice has an ethereal quality. That's what I want you to tap into. It's the opposite of what they're doing."

Another compliment? Last week, she would never have believed this scene. Her, training with the Alphas, being complimented on her talent by Mikel Easton.

This was not the Ironside she was used to.

"Sing it through again," Easton ordered. "But this time, try to breathe more through your diaphragm." His hand tapped against her chest. "I can see you breathing from here. It should be here." His hand dropped to her stomach, flattening there. "Your tutors should have taught you that."

She swallowed, blinking at her phone screen. With him so close, she could discern his scent, like cedar leaves crushed beneath a storm, like lightning striking too close and rain falling too heavy. He still hadn't moved his hand.

Why did they all have such distinct scents? Easton's was probably the oddest one she had encountered.

"Sing," he prompted. "When you breathe, I need to feel you pushing against my hand. Direct your breath here."

She remembered these lessons. He was right; her tutors had taught her this. It should have been second nature to her, but she hadn't had lessons in some time, and it was easy to forget all the technicalities.

Her voice was a little wobbly when she restarted the song, too much of her focus on the man beside her. It was strange to be touched in such a clinical manner, but nothing was as strange as when she lifted her eyes from the lyrics and found that Sato had turned around and was staring at them, pulling his gloves off with his teeth, his glittering dark eyes narrowing. Theodore lifted away from the wall, also glancing over, reaching beneath his shirt to rub at his abused muscles before his focus narrowed in on the hand against her stomach. He caught the gloves Sato tossed at him and didn't look away until the last minute, sending a vicious punch straight into Sato's gut. The other Alpha grunted and then laughed, pulling up his shirt to reveal clean, defined ridges of sinew and muscle.

He sneered something at Theodore, something that looked like *do better*, but Theodore backed off, shaking his head and then shaking out his arms, returning with a more measured jab.

"Carter," Easton snapped.

Her eyes snapped up to his, touching on his hard, downturned lips. She trailed off, falling silent.

"Try again." He lightly tapped her stomach. "You aren't making me feel it."

She started again, and he pulled out his phone with his free hand. The screen was already lit up, so it must have been vibrating in his pocket for a while. His frown darkened as he glanced at it, and the fingers against her stomach flexed, the movement seeming unconscious. He had a big hand, and one of his fingers was digging into the dip of her waist, almost pinching painfully as he stared at his phone, but she kept singing, kept trying to breathe through her diaphragm, kept pretending she didn't notice all the tension. Eventually, he seemed to realise, and he dropped his phone back into his pocket, easing his hand away from her. She tried not to stare at it hanging by his side, clenching and unclenching.

"Relax your face," he growled, his voice rough and grating. There was a strong emotion pressing into her chest, emanating pain of some kind. He felt wrong, suddenly. Like something had shifted inside him, flicking a switch somewhere in his body and mind. His eyes were detached, his body tense.

"There's too much tension here." He tapped her jaw. Very light and gentle compared to the violence that seemed to suddenly curl beneath his skin.

"I can't help it," she broke off, sighing out a frustrated sound. "I'm a Sigma."

I'm feeling what you're feeling.

It took him a second to understand, and then he looked down at the ground, hiding his unnerving eyes behind a fan of dark lashes. His broad shoulders rolled back, and when he looked up again, the pressure against her chest had eased. His expression had smoothed out. His fingers were lax by his side.

"Again," he said calmly.

4

YES, FATHER

Isobel stood at the entrance to her room, a sigh depleting some of the rigidity from her posture. She had planned to still attend her other classes until the end of the term despite Teak's permission to skip them, but then she had overslept in the library that morning, missing first period, and now she was faced with a blood-soaked room that would likely take her the rest of the day to clean.

She was grateful the dorm was empty, at least. The Alphas might have had the run of the academy—people like Sato, Reed, and Spade were able to drift in and out of classes at will—but there was no way the Omegas would be able to get away with that.

After setting her bag aside from the mess, she left the room to hunt down one of the dorm supervisors.

Finding Professor Yarrow at her usual desk, she explained that she needed cleaning supplies and new bedding. Yarrow looked like she might question why, but then she just shook her head and reached for a phone to call one of the cleaners.

A few hours later, Isobel had hauled all her stained belongings to the laundry on the lower level and sorted through everything else, throwing away what was unsalvageable and writing out a list of what she needed to replace. She only had one term to go before she would be a third year, and then she would be able to access the shops on Market Street. Putting up with a limited wardrobe until then seemed like a preferable option to contacting her father and asking him to bring her new clothes.

Hell, having no clothes at all would have been preferable.

It was almost dinnertime when she finally emerged from her room, dragging buckets and trash bags behind her. Yarrow appeared at the other end of the hallway, looking far more frazzled than she had when Isobel had inferred that her room had been trashed again. She dodged the other students, her eyes locked onto Isobel.

"Carter." She was wringing her hands. "The

officials have summoned you to the family centre. You
need to go there immediately."

Isobel's hands turned numb, the mop falling out
from where it had been cinched between her arm and
her side.

"Leave all of this here." Yarrow started trying to
wrestle one of the buckets off her.

Isobel released it, setting everything else down. "I
need to shower," she said dumbly. She looked terrible.
She had stains all over her knees and elbows from
scrubbing the congealed red mess from the floors.

"No time for that. Hurry now." Yarrow gave her a
little push toward the staircase, but Isobel ducked
back into her room and grabbed her phone before
stepping out.

It was getting dark outside, but there were still a
lot of students around. The dinner rush was starting
and she had to weave around so many groups of
Omegas that she didn't notice the large, lumbering
form that was following a few steps behind her until a
second form emerged, like a shadow snapping into
place beside her.

"Fuck off." The snarled order was delivered in a
gravelly Alpha voice, forcing the huge Beta in her
peripheral to stop in his tracks, and Isobel to turn in

shock, watching wide-eyed as Crowe lumbered away, glaring at her over his shoulder.

Sato remained, looming over her. "What could have you so distracted that you don't even notice Frankenstein's Monster stalking you halfway across campus?"

"You've been following me that long?" She turned and strode away before he could retaliate, because she was a coward.

"Longer." He fell into step beside her again. "Elijah is forwarding his fucking door-sensor alerts to me, and you've been in and out all day. At some point I lost my mind and decided to come and demand an explanation."

"Why?" She didn't even break stride, and she was quite proud of that. But then again, she was a little distracted.

Had they found her mate?

Was it happening?

She had been gifted with more time to prepare than anyone else usually got, but it still wasn't enough. It would never be enough.

"Why demand an explanation, or why is Elijah forwarding the alerts to me? You look great, by the way. Very murdery. The bloodstains are a nice touch."

Sato was remarkably talkative for once. It didn't seem like a good sign.

"Both."

Students were now actively scattering out of her way, making her progress that much faster. They took one look at Sato and scurried away like mice into crevices, pretending like they were never there in the first place. Hoping he didn't remember their faces.

"Elijah is a sadistic bastard. I respect that about him." He didn't seem inclined to explain further, his dark eyes fixed to the path ahead, his cold expression trapping unsuspecting students as they accidentally made eye contact before all the colour drained from their skin. More than one of them turned around and headed in the opposite direction, acting like they suddenly realised that they left something important back in their dorm.

Sato didn't have the best reputation, but there was no solid evidence as to why. It was like he broadcast exactly what violence he was capable of without ever acting it out or spelling it out.

People just *knew*.

She swallowed, shooting him a sideways look. "What do you want—"

"You still owe me a favour," he smoothly inserted,

his gravelly voice low. "Ashford's birthday party was rescheduled for this Sunday. Wallis will be there."

She slowed a little, looking at him a little more carefully. He had asked her to steal Theodore's fake girlfriend's phone, but Isobel still didn't know why. Then again, it didn't really matter why.

"Okay." She breathed out a sigh. "Is that all?"

He looked like he was amused, though she wasn't sure how she could tell. The cold expression on his face barely shifted, only the slightest twitch of his mouth giving anything away.

"That's all, Carter."

She glanced at him a few more times as he walked with her, his strides easy and measured beside her more hurried movements. He wasn't breaking away or going about his business, but it didn't occur to her that he was actually deliberately escorting her until they reached the front of the family centre and he stopped at the base of the stairs, watching her approach the door.

She turned in the doorway, frowning down at him. "Is this about Crowe?"

"This?" He plastered on an expression of confusion that didn't even look like he was *trying* to mimic the confusion of a normal, non-sociopathic person. His hands disappeared into his pockets as he rocked back on his heels, the wind teasing mahogany-and-oak curls against dark bronze skin.

With the sun threatening to set in the background behind him, he almost looked handsome instead of terrifying. If she squinted. His scars disappeared into shadow, his emotionless eyes warmed with the golden hue of dusk, and his hard slash of a mouth softened with her imagination.

"Is that why you're following me? Why you came to the dorm?" Her hand tightened around the door handle as she tilted her head at him.

"Maybe." He shrugged, his expression uncaring. "Maybe I should have killed him when I had the chance. Maybe I'm waiting for another chance. Maybe I thought he would give me a chance just now."

Her hand shook against the warm metal, her brows jumping up. "You shouldn't joke about that."

"You're right." He smiled. It was terrifying. No matter how much she squinted. "That's why I never joke."

"O-Okay." She twisted the handle, unsure what else to say. "Just don't ... do anything. I can handle Crowe."

He narrowed his eyes at her, the darkness of his expression tunnelling into her throat and forming a stiff ball of tension that was hard to swallow around.

He didn't say anything, but that look seemed to scream louder than anything.

"See you round, rabbit." He turned on his heel, leaving her in the doorway, unease settling so deeply into her limbs that for a good few minutes, she completely forgot all about why she was there.

After watching Sato disappear back the way he had come, she finally pushed open the door and stepped inside, scanning the empty waiting room until her gaze landed on a bulky body sitting at one of the small meeting tables up against a window. The setting sun slanted across his broad shoulders, illuminating the way he stiffened slightly, his head turning a few inches to the left, giving her a glimpse of his side profile.

"Father." She was rooted to the spot, the door falling slowly closed behind her.

"Isobel." He still hadn't turned fully. "Take a seat."

She couldn't move. Her feet wouldn't work. Or at least that was what she thought, until his chair began to scrape against the ground, and then suddenly she was jerked forwards by adrenaline alone, her heart leaping up into her throat as she hurried to obey. She took a seat across from him, her hands folded in her lap, her eyes downcast.

"You haven't been responding to my emails." He

settled back into his chair, tapping the cell phone sitting on the table before him.

"I was in the hospital."

"And you didn't think I should know about that?" He snatched up his phone, tucking it away before reaching over the table and pinching her chin. "Hmm?"

She no longer had his eyes.

Why that thought occurred to her in that moment, she had no idea, but it ... settled her. His attention flicked between her irises, a strong brow quirking.

"I thought you had been notified," she eased out between stiff lips. He was pinching her chin too hard for her to comfortably talk.

He squeezed harder, his anger battering her. "Why do you have to ruin everything?" he seethed, his sharp words accompanied by a bolt of pain that travelled through the lower half of her face. Any harder and he would crack her jaw. "This is the only thing that could have possibly made you half as interesting as the Alphas. We could have capitalised on this. We should have involved my publicist, and my agent, at the minimum. Instead, we're playing fucking catch-up."

Pack it away. Her mother's voice floated across her consciousness, and then, suddenly, it wasn't just her voice.

Her mother was sitting right there, across the table from her, beside her father. She was wearing a silk robe, her hair loose about her shoulders, her expression despairing.

"Pack it away." Her mother reached out like she would take Isobel's hand. "Remember what I taught you? When he's in a mood like that? Take all the things you want to say and put them in a box, until only obedience remains. Just say what he wants to hear."

Isobel flicked her eyes between her father and mother, but her father was still glaring at her, pinching her chin to the point of bruising. He couldn't hear the woman beside him. He didn't know she was there.

"Yes, Father." She forced the words out, her hand inching across the table to where her mother's hands were. If she could just touch her. Just once.

Her father released her chin with a disgusted sound, sending her jolting back into her chair with the force of it. Her fingers barely managed to brush those of her mother on the table, but there was no substance to them. Her touch passed right through, like her mother was made of air. She curled over in her chair, hugging her midsection, the tips of her fingers pricking with a strange kind of awareness.

"I should have known better than to give you the freedom to manage yourself at Ironside," he announced, folding thick arms and regarding her with eyes weighed down by disappointment. "They've allowed me to move into one of the units upstairs thanks to your *unique* situation. I expect you to report to me every afternoon for one hour. During that time, you will keep me appraised of *all* new developments, and we will strategise with your new PR team. Is that clear?"

She chewed on her tongue, staring at the seat beside him. Her mother was just sitting there, looking back. There was a small, sad smile tugging at her lips, and a heaviness in her eyes.

"Is this really happening?" Isobel asked quietly, directing the question to her mother, and hoping it would pass as a response to her father's lecture.

"Yes," her mother whispered, just as her father barked out his response.

"You'd better stop wasting the opportunity I've given you here at Ironside. You're here to *represent* me, not to fuck around and embarrass me. Do you understand?"

"Yes, Father."

Her mother dissipated like evaporating steam, like a dream Isobel had tried to hold onto despite it slipping further and further from her consciousness. She turned her attention back to her father.

"Good. We'll start with our promotional activities in the settlements. We'll have a photoshoot in my apartment tomorrow afternoon for the settlement posters and take it from there."

"What settlement posters?" she asked warily.

"Your 'Mate Finder' campaign," he answered dismissively, already standing from his seat. "We'll be doing a tour of the settlements over the break. We want *crowds* when we arrive. Men and women begging to be your mate. Begging for a second of your time. A reverse-Cinderella, except you're the shoe and they're all hoping to fit you. I've already suggested to the officials that they should send a crew with us to get it all on camera, and they're seriously considering it. Be here at 5:00 p.m. tomorrow. I've already changed your schedule to accommodate our meetings."

He strode away without looking back, hitting the button for the elevator that would take him to the upper levels of the family centre. She watched as he got inside and the doors closed on his impassive face. He moved with the confidence of a man sure of his position at the top of the ladder. He wasn't just a revered Alpha, he was also a recognised citizen, with all the rights of a regular human. He had the best of both worlds, and he had her right where he wanted her. Right back under his complete control.

Resisting the urge to break something, she stalked out of the family centre, skipping dinner to go straight to the training rooms. She searched for a free room before kicking off her shoes and hooking up her phone, scrolling through for a song that made her blood pound and her ears hurt. She shrugged off the oversized shirt Easton had bought her, pacing before the mirrored wall in her exercise shorts and sports bra.

When she finally faced herself, she tried to see herself as her father had. She wasn't the same girl he had dropped off down the bottom of the mountain a couple of years ago, and she wasn't the girl who'd had a breakdown in the chapel only months ago.

She was a whole new creature entirely. There were bloodstains on her knees and stars in her eyes. Little spots and specks that weren't hers. Just another part of herself syphoned off to belong to someone else. Her entire existence, she hadn't been allowed to live for *her*. She existed as her mother did: to support Braun Carter.

And soon she would exist for someone else ... but not before her father paraded her around the settlements like a prized horse up for auction.

She stepped back from the mirror with a

disgusted growl and fell into the rhythm of the song, dancing faster and harder and faster and harder until her ankle gave way. She crawled into the corner of the room and curled into a ball, hugging the shadows around herself as she viciously fought back tears.

She should have been surprised when Theodore appeared in the doorway to the practise room, but the only thought that occurred to her was that they had switched places. She was the one huddled in the shadows, and he was the one cautiously approaching her. Her eyes had changed, and while they weren't bleeding black with ferality, she almost wished they were.

Then nobody would mess with her.

For the short time they allowed her to live, anyway.

Theodore sat beside her without a word, his arm wrapping around her shoulders, pulling her into his chest. She rested her head there, lulled by the way his fingers dragged slowly through her hair.

"What's with you guys popping up out of nowhere and following me around?" she grumbled against his delicious-smelling shirt, her hands twitching to rest there, to feel the beating of his heart through the material, the tempered rise and fall of his chest, to soak up some of his calm and strong energy through her palms.

He ducked his head, hiding it from the cameras as his lips brushed against the shell of her ear. "We're monitoring you."

She reared back, a full-body shudder taking hold of her before she could suppress it. "What?"

He only looked at her, his head tilted slightly. Waiting. Waiting for her to figure it out so he wouldn't have to say it.

"In case I talk," she surmised, her lips pursed.

He nodded.

"And you agreed to this?" she asked, her brow furrowing deeper. It was important to her, whether Theodore trusted her or not, though she tried to tell herself it wasn't. Nobody ever trusted Sigmas. Even the ones who believed Sigmas had no power.

"Oh, I agreed," Theodore said easily, his usual smile teasing at the edges of his mouth. "But only because it means I get to follow you around and avoid my *fake* girlfriend." The word *fake* wasn't spoken out loud, only mouthed, his head still ducked, hiding from the cameras.

The laugh that trickled out of her tense body surprised her, and she felt some of that tension escaping with it.

"Come on." Theodore jumped up, offering her his hand. "Let's get you settled in."

"Settled in?" She let him pull her up and they walked over to her belongings. He had taken her bag hostage before she even finished pulling her shirt over her head.

"You're crashing with me," he announced, walking to the door and leaving her standing there with her mouth hanging open.

And then she did the thing you were never supposed to do at Ironside. She swung her gaze to the nearest camera and looked at it dead-on, her eyes wide with shock.

"W-What?" She quickly looked away, her face turning bright red as she scrambled after him.

"Someone doused your room in fake blood, Isobel—"

"Isobel?" She laughed nervously. "Am I in trouble now?"

"No." He gave her a flat look. "But you will be if you go back there tonight. Or ever."

"I have to go back there." She rolled her eyes, having to take two steps for every one of his. "It's my room. And why are you saying this in front of the cameras?" She tried to hurriedly whisper the last part.

"To avoid rumours," he whispered back, before

raising his voice again. "Besides, students have sleepovers all the time." He shrugged. "I guess you just have to be on a permanent sleepover until summer break."

"That's two and a half months away, Theo."

"That's better than a mile away."

"What?"

"A mile." He flashed her a tight smile. "That's how far Dorm A is from Dorm O. And what's with that big-ass Beta following you around all the time?"

"Who? Crowe? Why are you changing the subject?"

"Why are *you* changing the subject? Who the fuck is Crowe and why is he stalking you?"

"I can't sleep in your room. You only have one bed."

"I'll sleep on the couch. Avoid my question again, I dare you."

She rolled her eyes, reaching for the bag hanging over his shoulder. He didn't release it.

"Illy," he warned lowly.

"Theo." She tried to mimic his growly tone.

"That's it." He suddenly switched direction, moving toward the path that would lead around the opposite side of the lake to Dorm A. She followed him because he had her bag and because he couldn't possibly be forcing her back to his dorm if they weren't even walking toward it.

"Where are you going?" She skipped ahead, trying to keep pace with him.

"Dorm B." He cast her a quick, hard look. "I can't use my Alpha voice on you, but I sure as fuck can use it on Crowe."

"What?" She forced her legs to pump harder. She was almost jogging. "You can't use your Alpha voice on me? Why?"

He slowed a little, the corners of his mouth downturned. "I don't know." His forehead crinkled, his jaw working as he clenched his teeth together before he released all that tension with a sunny smile. "Doesn't seem right." Then he was striding forward again, even faster than before. "You can come with me to Dorm B, or you can wait for me in Dorm A. Choose anything else and you'll be punished."

"Punished how?" She slowed, her ankle twinging from practice, her voice raised to reach him.

"You don't want to know! Oh, and Illy?" He turned, his phone pulled up, facing her. "I dare you not to tell them why you're there."

She groaned, coming to a proper stop to catch her breath. Theodore laughed as he turned back to the path, putting his phone away. The asshole still had all her stuff, but she had slipped her phone into the waistband of her exercise shorts before they left the training room, and was reminded of it when it vibrated against her skin. She slipped it out, tapping on the new message.

Theodore: Make sure you film it.

After everything that had happened on the rooftop, she had almost forgotten about their plan to start an ongoing dare war online to cover up the real reason she had ended up in the middle of the lake one morning. Totally naked. This was his second dare for her, and she still hadn't thought of anything for him. They weren't allowed to post videos for seven days after taking them, just in case they spoiled anything for the show, but Theodore's first dare had already gone live, and people were probably waiting for her to retaliate.

She tucked her head down, marvelling over how she managed to turn invisible again as soon as there were no Alphas at her side. She dragged her feet a little as she made her way to Dorm A, pausing at the bottom of Alpha Hill when the nerves decided to rush through her body, making her hands shake. She curled her fingers into fists and marched up the stairs, pushing it all down and trying to assemble a cool, impassive expression.

It didn't work in the slightest. She could feel the nervous arrangement of her features. The tremble in her lower lip. The forward hunch of her shoulders. She almost dropped her phone when she fumbled to turn on the camera, but managed to catch it at the last second, cursing quietly under her breath. She pushed into the dorm without knocking, because it wasn't going to be very entertaining if she stood outside and refused to tell anyone why she was there.

She couldn't hear any sounds in the hallway as she crept toward the common room and was immensely relieved to find the lounge empty. She quickly sat on an armchair in the corner, propping her phone against the lamp table beside her so that it had a good view of her side profile and the hallway leading into the common room.

She briefly wondered if Theodore would arrive back before anyone else discovered she was there, but the thought was dashed as Spade entered the room. His damp, dark-blond hair was combed back from his angular face, not a single strand daring to flop over his forehead. He was wearing a soft cotton shirt and dark grey sweatpants with pristine white socks, and there wasn't a single droplet of water anywhere to be seen. He didn't look like a guy who had just finished showering. He looked like he had been prepped by a pedantic make-up artist to look like a model pretending to have just showered. His russet eyes landed on her instantly, and he stopped walking, his head tilting to the side. He seemed more surprised that he was surprised than surprised by the fact that she was there.

"Not often people sneak up on me," he noted, accepting her presence just like that. He glanced down at the notebook in his hand before setting it on the coffee table and seating himself in the long sectional against the window, just out of frame of her phone.

She waited, but after a moment of staring at the notebook he had placed down, he seemed to decide that he wasn't willing to put aside whatever he had come out there to do. He swiped it up, opening it on his lap, and began to write on the page in a calm and measured way.

She wanted to laugh.

All the nervous energy about inviting herself into the Alpha dorm and *this* was the reaction she got? She thought for sure they would have ordered her straight back out, or at least ask why she was there.

A short sigh from Spade distracted her for a moment, and she glanced up to find him suddenly staring at her.

"Could you stop?" He chewed on his pink lower lip,

the movement drawing her eye for a moment. His nose was scrunched, the look in his eyes hard. He was bothered by something.

"H-Huh?" she managed.

"Stop smelling so scared. I'm not the one you have to worry about, and I much prefer the sweet cherry smell."

She swallowed. *What?* "Uh. Okay. I'll change how I ... smell."

He opened his mouth again, but whatever he had been about to say was interrupted when Moses entered the room, a dark look on his face like he already knew she was there, somehow.

"What are you doing here?" he snapped immediately, dark grey eyes drilling right through her.

"I don't know," she said.

Whatever he had been expecting, it wasn't that. His eyes widened, a flutter of panic brushing against her chest, reaching out to her from where he stood across the room.

"Ah." Spade slapped his book shut, like he had just figured something out, but that was all he said.

Moses glanced from Spade to her, his frown deepening. He picked up a game controller and fell into the seat furthest away from her, turning on the TV.

"This is a bit of a letdown," she mumbled to herself.

"What?" Moses' dark glare slammed immediately back into her, making her shrink back in the armchair.

"It's another one of Theo's dares," Spade explained calmly. "You didn't notice the phone?"

Moses' expression turned sour, roaming around her until he found where she had set up her phone. She expected him to explode or something, but he only let out a sharp sigh, some of the tension seeping out of his body. "I thought ..." He shook his head.

"Moses is having an off day," Spade offered, still in that same calm tone. "You'll have better luck with the next one."

"The next—" Isobel cut herself off as Sato strode into the room. His hair was also wet, the curls weighed down to trickle around his face, his shirt scattered with droplets of water. He froze a step into the room, his eyes fixing to her immediately.

He catalogued her like he was searching for some kind of discrepancy. A spot the difference between who he saw now and the girl he had left at the family centre a couple of hours ago. His nose twitched, much like Spade's had, and his gaze rested on her jaw for a moment too long.

Had her father bruised her?

His examination swept over to Spade, who was sitting there stiffly, watching them all. Spade didn't so much as twitch an eyelid, and then Sato turned his attention to Moses, who just quirked an eyebrow in response. It was clear neither of them had invited her inside.

"Just let yourself in, did you?" Sato growled.

Did Theodore want her to die?

"I did." She couldn't hold his eyes, dropping her attention down to her fingers instead. She wrapped them together in her lap, waiting for Moses to tell him it was a dare. But Moses didn't speak up.

"So, you're one of us now?" Sato drawled, his voice dripping in malice. The way he switched up his personality so quickly was terrifying. "If that's true ... then maybe you should prove it."

THE SIGMA WAS CLOSE TO PETRIFIED. OSCAR COULD SMELL it. He could almost *feel* it. He could definitely see the flush against her chest. It made his own heartbeat pick up, like her fear was breathing life into him. He knew that was fucked up, but he didn't really care.

"I don't know what you mean." Her voice was small. She was lying. Her eyes darted up for a second, just long enough to lock with his. Just long enough for a silent conversation to pass between them.

He knew she was trying to get a room in their dorm.

They all knew.

But it wasn't just the officials she needed approval from. That was only the first hurdle. They wouldn't just accept anyone. Fuck. Normally, they quite literally wouldn't accept *anyone*. Under any circumstances.

"It's time you proved yourself," he said quietly, drawing her eyes back to his. He preferred it when she looked at him, even if that multicoloured eye was a direct punch to his gut. "If you really want to be one of us."

Her slender shoulder lifted slightly, shrugging just a little. "Okay."

Something curled through his body. Something like ... hunger. Or pride. Or adrenaline. She was accepting his challenge, but his challenge was for her to run. She had no idea what she was saying yes to.

"What do you want me to do?" she asked, leaning back and crossing her arms, tucking her fingers against her sides to hide the tremble in them. "I'll do anything."

Her scent gave her away. She smelled like spilled sap and crushed cherries. Like someone had stomped through her fruit to hack at her branches. She was wounded and scared, and he wanted to retrace her steps to find out exactly what caused the change. What weighed on her shoulders and who the fuck put it there. He was also curious about the discolouration along her jaw that wasn't there before. It almost looked like fingerprints.

She was *his* toy to play with. *He* was the only one who should be able to tease that sweet, crushed scent from her veins. He claimed her the minute he breathed air back into her chest.

Not that he wanted her.

He just didn't want anyone else to play with her.

"We're all equal here." He spread his arms, his lips twitching slightly as Moses rolled his eyes at the lie. "So we all deserve a chance to test you. You'll face a trial from each of us. Who would you like to go first? It can't be Kilian." He smiled slightly.

Her chin inched up, and that was when he realised it.

He was providing her a distraction from her *real* issue.

Whatever that was.

And she was diving right into it.

5

DARE

"Niko." Isobel mumbled the name, unsure. None of them were a *great* choice, except Kilian.

Even Theodore wasn't a good choice. He liked to challenge her, and he had a little current of sadism that ran just beneath his surface, despite how much of a good person he was most of the time. He would probably like to make her squirm.

"Niko?" Sato quirked a dark brow, doing that thing with his face where he managed to look amused without really changing his expression at all. He pulled out his phone, tapping the screen quickly. "I've sent him your number. You'll get your first task soon."

"Fine." She moved to the edge of her seat, debating how much longer she could keep this up before Theodore got back.

"You definitely chose wrong, by the way." That comment had come from Spade, who had picked up a controller to join Moses' game. He didn't seem to be trying to bait her. He wasn't even waiting for a response. He was just stating a fact.

"This is boring." Sato frowned at the screen.

Moses sighed, throwing the controller aside. "I know."

"Let's drink instead." Sato disappeared and Moses got up to follow him.

Spade picked up their discarded controllers, arranging them in one of the drawers below the TV set into the wall. Even from where she sat, it was obvious that he was arranging them in a very exact way. He made a sound of disgust, pulling a cord from the drawer and rolling it up. He opened another drawer of neatly arranged cords, returning it to its place before rubbing his fingers together like he suddenly needed to wash his hands.

He glanced at his notebook, then at his fingers, his frown growing.

"Are you coming?" he asked distractedly, his movements a little jerkier when he turned for the hallway, dismissing the notebook.

She quickly turned off her phone, sliding it into her pocket. "Ah ... do you want me to bring your book?"

He stopped, narrowing his russet eyes on her.

"Yes," he said plainly.

She picked it up and followed him, expecting him to go up to the rooftop, but he opened the door to his room and stepped inside, leaving the door hanging half open.

"Put it on the desk with the others, please." He disappeared into his bathroom, and she entered his room, casting her eyes around.

She had expected it to be clean. Exact. But this was ... something else.

He had a single pillow on his king-sized bed, exactly in the centre, and pristine white sheets so fitted they looked like they had been pressed into place. No blankets.

There were small, white square sticky notes everywhere. *Everywhere.* They were arranged in perfect, ordered lines and groups. She swallowed, moving toward his desk, which was set up beside the window seat. It was far bigger than Theodore's desk, with two large monitors and three neat piles of notebooks, ordered by colour and size. His desk had some sort of clear cover over it, and beneath it, the surface was a checkerboard of black and white sticky notes.

She placed the notebook on the desk, turning her

head to read the nearest note.

Your hands are not dirty.

And the next one.

You do not need to wash your hands.

She whipped her head up when she heard the sound of water running in his bathroom, and then decided to add the notebook to the pile with others of its size and colour. She tried not to read any of the other notes but stopped short at the sight of the back of his door. Down the very middle of a cloud of notes was a message, written one letter at a time on individual squares.

You are not for sale.

She frowned, stepping back out into the hallway. *Not for sale?* They were all for sale. *Begging* the rest of the world to invest in them. Fighting desperately against each other to be crowned the hottest commodity out of all the other commodities-in-training.

Spade joined her in the hallway, closing the door to his room. He leaned against it for a moment, taking stock of whatever he could read in her face. He seemed to be having a conversation with her, *without* her direct involvement, and she tried to school her expression. His eyes switched between hers, settling on the multicoloured eye that wasn't covered by her contact before dropping to her mouth and then her chin.

"You're nice," he said lowly, almost a whisper. Lines suddenly furrowed into his brow. "Sweet."

"Okay." She didn't feel sweet. Or nice. Her mother had been nice and sweet. A perfect Sigma. Isobel felt … different.

His lips twitched. It was weird, to see him almost smile. It didn't look like it came naturally to him.

"Careful." His hand rose, long, graceful fingers hovering over her chest. And then he pressed his pointer finger forward, resting it against her shirt, over her heart. "Don't let them break this."

"I don't think that's how it works." She scoffed a little, hoping he couldn't feel her heart skipping beneath the pad of his finger. He probably could. "If we really had control over who had the power to hurt us, we would all be immaculate."

He tutted like she wasn't understanding him. "If you *let* them, they *will*. They'll fucking *consume* you."

"Who is *them*?"

His frown deepened, that finger tracing up to the neckline of her shirt, where it skirted along the seam. "Us," he revised.

"You?" she asked, confused. She wasn't used to having Spade's full attention. She wasn't sure he was used to giving it either. She felt like a little speck beneath a microscope. Something he was trying to classify. To categorise.

Beautiful, or ugly?

Useful, or a waste?

Valuable, or discardable?

Important, or unworthy?

Instead of answering her, he seemed to focus everything on his finger. "Try it now," he suggested, the very tip of his nail slipping over the edge of her shirt to brush her skin. "Don't let me."

This was a test. A special Spade test. She *knew* it. Knew it by the sudden, calculated look in his eye. She just didn't understand what the test was, exactly.

"Don't let me," he repeated, and then his whole hand was against her skin, flattening to the very top of her chest, brushing up over her neck. He pushed her back into the wall beside his door, leaning his weight into her.

His hair, now dry, smelled like linen somehow. It brushed against her forehead as he drew her up by his hold against her neck. His eyes were detached. Not warm and not cold.

"No offense," she rasped, standing on her toes, analysing him right back. "But you're not that scary. You don't look like you want it, you know?"

His lips twisted, his teeth flashing slightly. "I know. I don't want it. I don't *want,* period. Either I have something, or I don't." He released her suddenly, something gleaming in his eyes that wasn't at all calculated or detached. It was a spark of a promise, a whisper of something that didn't want to step into the light. "When I have something, I possess it entirely." He began to turn away, but not before muttering something beneath his breath that she almost didn't catch. Something that sounded like *just me.* He paused at the steps, looking back at her. "Are you coming?"

"Ah. Yes. I guess." She glanced back down the other end of the hallway. *Still no Theodore.* And it wasn't like she had anything better to do. So she hurried over to where he waited, that little spark still in his eyes.

"Like a puppy," he said, biting back a smile as he watched her. "Cute."

She frowned, partly insulted by the comparison and partly charmed by that unfamiliar spark of something he was letting her see. A little hint of a personality; a secret he usually kept under heavy deadbolt.

THEODORE WAS THE LAST ALPHA TO FIND THEM ON THE rooftop. First, it was Ashford and Niko, who both came up freshly showered, Niko avoiding her eyes and Ashford reaching for the bottle of whiskey Sato had procured. Moses immediately snatched it back.

"Play the game or get your own," he demanded, to which Ashford only rolled his eyes and pulled up a seat.

Niko also sat, but he did it silently, staring out over the edge of the rooftop. Isobel didn't know how badly the rooftop had been damaged, but the officials had wasted no time righting it again. If it wasn't for all the new appliances and furniture, she might not have believed the storm had even happened.

Reed was next, and then Kilian, each of them deciding to join in their game of truth or dare. It seemed to be the theme of her night, though the questions and dares were mostly surface level and silly, just a way for them to pass time.

Until Theodore appeared.

"Where the hell have you been?" Ashford demanded. "I've been texting you."

Theodore ran his gaze over her, like he was checking to make sure she was okay before he turned to Ashford. "Had something to take care of."

"I saw violence," Ashford growled. "You had me worried."

Theodore shot him a wide, disarming smile. "But there *was* violence. Glorious violence."

Moses laughed, evidently enjoying his brother's more devilish side.

"Theo." Reed sighed, sharing a look with Spade.

"What?" Theodore shoved a laughing Moses from the seat beside Isobel, claiming it himself. "And what the hell are you all doing? Isobel was supposed to create drama. Not ... whatever this is. Community engagement? Fun times?"

"I dare you to ignore him for the rest of the game." Ashford slapped a shot onto the low, circular table before Isobel. "He's such an attention whore."

"*Getting* all the attention and *wanting* all the attention are two different things," Theodore grumbled, before glaring at Isobel. "Drink that."

She nibbled on her lip, looking from him to the shot. She had just been doing whatever mindless dare they gave her. Drinking seemed more dangerous, considering what happened the last time she tried having a drink at Dorm A.

"Double dare," Sato grunted, slapping a second shot beside the first.

"Triple." Moses added his, narrowly missing the punch Theodore aimed at his shoulder.

Well, damn.

"Drink it," Theodore repeated, his voice like silk, his eyes tunnelling into hers.

She edged over on her seat, picking up the first shot. She sniffed it and then pressed the edge of the glass to her lips.

"Don't sip it, puppy."

Everyone turned to stare at Spade, faces registering astonishment and disbelief. Reed turned the slowest, his expression remaining blank, but he *did* turn to stare.

Spade was just watching her calmly, that detached look back on his face. "Swallow it all at once."

She did, throwing it back while all their attention was on him. She held his stare as she picked up the second shot and swallowed that one, too, her eyes starting to water, her throat burning.

"Puppy?" Reed finally questioned, when it seemed like nobody else was going to.

Spade met his inquisitive look, and they did that weird "talking without talking" thing where they both just read each other's expressions and turned away, conversation over. Nobody else pressed him. She swallowed the third shot and then fiddled with her phone, drawing it out and turning the camera on Theodore.

"Dare you to ... uh ..." She fumbled for a dare. "Scent everyone in the room and rank them best to worst."

He stood immediately and then started stretching like he needed to warm up. He grinned, moving to Moses and sniffing dramatically around him. "Sixth place." He moved on to Reed. "Fourth place."

"He's thought about this before." Reed looked amused. "He's way too confident."

"Normally, seventh place." Theodore announced when he got to Niko. "But second if I'm having a bad day."

Several of the others laughed. Isobel didn't get the joke.

"Let me guess." Sato held up a hand before Theodore could sniff him. "Last place?"

"You got it." Theodore moved on, waving his hands like he was trying to waft Kilian's scent toward his nose. "Third place!" He moved on to Spade. "Fifth place." And then to Ashford. "Second place—and a little jealous."

"As you should be," Ashford responded with a straight face.

And then it was her turn, and she realised she

should have thought this through a little better. She held up the phone higher, trying to use it as a barrier between them, but Theodore snatched it off her, pressing it down into her lap, the camera covered.

And then his nose was brushing up the side of her neck, and the others were tensing, eyes narrowing on her like she was a bomb about to go off. She felt the warm brush of his breath against her skin, and her hands started to shake, making her grateful that she wasn't trying to hold up the phone anymore. Heat skittered across her skin and saliva pooled in her mouth as his scent wrapped around her, hints of wood and musk and subtle sweetness.

"First place," he announced, drawing back, his pupils blown wide like he really *did* like her scent. "Congratulations, cherry girl."

He dropped back into his seat, pouring out a shot and slamming it down before Spade as Isobel scrambled to stop her phone recording.

"Truth." His voice was deeper than usual. "What is puppy supposed to mean?"

Spade leaned back and shared another look with Reed. They both smiled tightly, and then Spade snatched up the shot and tossed it back. He took the cloth that he had apparently brought to the table with him and wiped the table before setting the glass back down. They were deliberately stirring up Theodore. They seemed to enjoy doing that. Spade filled up another glass and set it before Ashford. "Truth. What happened with the Sigma on your birthday?"

This game is quickly getting out of hand.

"Oscar happened." Ashford's tone was short, his eyes hard on the unlit fire pit in the middle of the table. He didn't seem to be willing to explain further, and Isobel's hand itched to snatch up a glass.

"Figured it out yet?" Sato chuckled darkly, his heavy gaze flickering to all the faces at the table. Several of them exchanged worried glances.

"Most of it, anyway," Reed answered.

Ashford lifted his aquamarine eyes to her, some of the hardness cracking, revealing the curiosity swimming beneath.

She wasn't going to be able to escape that conversation for much longer.

Ashford passed his shot to Sato. "Pick a random number in your recent calls and tell them you 'know it was them.'"

Sato frowned. "I wanted to drink."

"But you want to do this more," Ashford returned.

Sato grunted out his agreement and pulled out his phone, scrolling with a few flicks of his thumb before tapping his screen. The call sound rang around them after he hit speaker, and then a boy answered, his voice husky with sleep.

"Sato?"

"I know it was you," Sato told him calmly, his voice naturally low and rough, naturally terrifying.

It was quiet on the other end before the boy swore, accompanied by the sounds of panicked rustling and items toppling over.

"Listen, man, I swear to fucking god, whatever you think I did—"

Sato hung up. The boy called back immediately, but Sato rejected it, dropping his phone into his lap, and then his eyes were on Isobel, settling on her face with a weight that had her stomach turning. He nudged the shot glass her way.

Everyone tensed up again, but just as he opened his mouth, his phone rang a second time. *Mikel Easton* flashed across the screen. His eyes returned to her after he accepted the call, and he watched her as he listened quietly to whatever Easton was saying.

"I'll be right there." He stood, reclaiming the shot and finishing it before wiping the back of his mouth with his hand. "I'm out."

He strode off without another word, and Isobel felt some of the tension leaving the stiff set of her shoulders. It didn't seem like the game was going to go back to harmless dares and questions, so she stood, glancing over at Theodore.

"We're out too," Theodore said, catching her look. "Later, guys."

"Where are you going?" Moses asked, the storm inside his eyes brewing as he switched his attention between them.

"Nowhere. Staying here." Theodore walked to the stairs, and she hurried to follow, surprised when Kilian also stood to trail them.

"She can't go back—" he started, but Theodore cut him off.

"She's not going back to her dorm. She's sleeping here."

"Where?" Kilian asked as they stopped in front of Theodore's room.

Theodore pushed open the door and then turned, cocking a brow at Kilian. "In my room. Why?"

Kilian's lips twitched in a smile that seemed a little forced. He tapped her shoulder lightly. "Come and jump in with me if you need to."

Theodore dragged her into his room. "She won't. But thanks for the offer." He shut the door firmly in Kilian's face and then sighed dramatically, giving her a bored look. "They think I'm desperately in love with you. It's infuriating."

"Why aren't you? I find *that* infuriating." She bit back a laugh and sat on the end of his bed as he disappeared into his closet.

He returned with a T-shirt and a pair of boxers, holding them out to her.

"No, you don't," he said as she reached for the clothing. "You can wear this tonight. I'll sleep in the lounge. I already got you a spare toothbrush. It's in the bathroom." He lingered, refusing to let go of the shirt as the boxers slid onto her lap.

"Something else?" she asked, emboldened by the whiskey. She didn't feel drunk. She was too aggravated to be drunk. Too disturbed by the appearance of her father. Too haunted by the idea of a mate out there in the world, waiting to take ownership of her.

But the alcohol had calmed her a little. Made things a little quieter in her head.

"Yeah ..." Theodore released the shirt, and his hands were suddenly either side of her thighs, sinking into the edge of his bed. His face hovered over hers, his heat and scent wrapping all the way around her. "It doesn't matter what they think. It only matters what you think. You believe I could never be a threat to you, right? You look so worried all the time. I don't want you to have to worry about me too."

"I don't think anyone worries about you," she admitted quietly. "You're Theodore Kane."

He rolled his eyes, inching closer. His head suddenly ducked to her neck, his forehead resting down, his breath scattering over her collarbone.

"Give me a hug goodnight, Illy-stone."

She lifted her arms hesitantly, wrapping them around his shoulders. He didn't touch her back, but his head turned to the side, his nose brushing along the soft skin of her neck. It was weird the way he made her hug him without really hugging her back. Distracted, she began to run her nails along his sides through his shirt. He shuddered, pulling back like his body suddenly weighed twice as much. His eyes were darker, but not like when he was fighting off ferality. This seemed like a warm darkness. A *hot* darkness. He blinked it away, dazzling her with one of his smiles before he turned and strode from the room.

"Night," he muttered, before closing the door.

She frowned, drifting over to it. She could still *feel* him, which was weird. Maybe it was the alcohol. But he was there, somewhere against her chest, like a soft brush instead of the usual pounding when she felt other people's negative emotions. She frowned, touching the door.

"Caught yourself a Sigma?" Reed's voice sounded

faintly through the door, and she quickly pressed her ear to it.

"Yeah, throw me a pillow, would you?" Theodore's reply was closer than Reed's, but still faint.

He was right on the other side of the thick door. Sitting down, it sounded like.

"I can just put a sensor on the door," Reed offered after a few moments. "You don't have to guard her." Something soft hit the door. A pillow, presumably.

"They put a *bomb* in her room, Elijah. I'm not fucking moving, and nobody is getting into this room. Next person to come near her is joining Crowe in the hospital."

"Crowe?" That had sounded like Spade.

"Never mind. Throw me a blanket?"

Her phone lit up on the bed, and she drifted over, opening the message.

Kilian: You okay in there?

She took it into the bathroom with her to reply as she got changed into the clothes Theodore had picked out for her.

Isobel: I'm okay, but I'll need to go back to my room eventually.

Kilian: I'm with Theo on this one. Why is Gabriel calling you a puppy?

Isobel: He told me to come and I came.

Kilian: ...
Isobel: What?
Kilian: ...
Isobel: Seriously? What?
Kilian: If I told you to come, would you?
Isobel: I mean, I guess?
Kilian: Go to bed.

She set the phone aside and noticed the little basket on the bathroom bench for the first time. Blinking in surprise, she sorted through it, realising it must have been for her. There was a spare toothbrush, toothpaste, a hairbrush, a silk hair tie, face wash, and moisturiser. It looked like one of the luxury baskets students bought from one of the boutiques on Market Street, all the items packed with pale violet tissue paper and pressed, pastel flowers. But Market Street was off-limits to first and second-year students. Still, it wasn't the first time one of the Alphas had boasted connections with officials or older students.

Guilt flooded her as she stared down at the basket, wondering if Theodore had paid money for it. The third, fourth and fifth-year students used popularity points to make purchases on Market Street, but Theodore was still a second-year, which meant he wasn't accumulating popularity points yet. And he was from the settlements. He couldn't afford expensive gift baskets. Unfortunately, he was also incredibly stubborn and would be upset if she didn't use the things he had procured, so she showered using the products, dressed in his clothes, and crawled into his massive bed, burrowing into the sweet scent of him that clung to the pillows.

She hadn't actually intended to fall asleep. She had been busy staring at her phone, wondering how she could convince Theodore to move to a couch, or take his own bed and let her move to a couch, but she must have drifted off while deliberating because she jerked awake when the screen lit up and it vibrated in her hands.

Unknown: Come outside.

She sat up, suddenly full of anxious energy. Her fingers tingled when she replied.

Isobel: Who is this?

Unknown: Niko.

She stared at the screen in shock. *Niko?* The Niko who never spoke to her or looked her directly in the eyes for long? The Niko who seemed to avoid her like she was some sort of weird, Sigma plague?

Niko: It's time for your initiation.

And suddenly it made sense.

But not in a good way.

She kicked her way out of the bed, pacing the floor

nervously until she caught sight of something outside the window. No, not something.

Niko Hart was standing right the hell there. Three inches from the glass. All six-foot something of him. His light, green-brown eyes searched the darkness of the room before finding her, and then he cocked his head to the side, tucking a lock of hair behind his ear. His infectious smile was missing. It usually was around her.

She gulped, kneeling on the window seat and cracking the window open a little. Like most of the other Alphas, Niko intimidated the hell out of her. He was perfect heart-throb material with his tall, muscled body and easy athleticism, his smooth, light-ochre skin, lips the colour of cherries, and bleached-blond hair. He looked like he lived inside posters on the walls of teenagers all around the world. Sweat-soaked and holding a football, a carefree grin on his face, he was the type girls and boys dreamed about, conjuring him outside their bedroom windows with a cocky smirk and eyes that dared them to brave the night as he swung the keys to an expensive, sporty car around his finger.

But that wasn't the Niko she was faced with. This one was stony-faced and impatient, meeting her silent stare with his head still cocked. They were waiting each other out, seeing who would break the tense silence first. His eyes kept bouncing between hers, reminding her that she had taken out her contact, and he finally pressed his lips tightly together, glancing over the oversized shirt she wore.

"Are you going to come outside?" he asked.

"Not until you tell me where we're going." She inched back from the window.

"To the fitness centre." He stuffed his hands into his pockets, and she realised he was still dressed the same as he had been on the rooftop. He hadn't gone to bed yet.

"I have a private lesson with Professor West tomorrow." She returned to the window, opening it a little wider. "I can't be out all night."

He smirked. "Probably best you work out any lingering aggression, then. You don't want to be bringing any of that shit into a lesson with Kalen."

"Lingering aggression?"

He rolled his eyes, pushing the window wide. He leaned into her face, lowering his voice to a whisper. "I know it's in there somewhere."

"Only because *you're* causing it," she muttered, scrambling off the seat so fast she kicked her foot against something, but he wasn't trying to climb through; he was just leaning against the seat, waiting.

He checked his phone and she saw the time flash on the screen. *2:33.*

She had to be up in a few hours, but it didn't look like Niko was leaving anytime soon, so she ducked back into the bathroom and swapped Theodore's boxers for her tights and shimmied her sports bra on underneath the big T-shirt. She added a contact and then slipped out of the window, Niko barely taking a full step back to make room for her.

"Come on," he said impatiently, already striding off.

"This is really how you want to spend your Tuesday night?" she asked, hurrying behind him.

"What do you think?" he grumbled, leading the way around the lake.

Holy damn, the guy walked fast. And somehow made it look like he wasn't even trying. She was almost running to keep pace.

"I don't know," she answered distractedly, keeping her eyes on the ground so she wouldn't fall flat on her face in the dark.

"Let me tell you something the others won't— especially if you're really trying to get a room in Dorm A."

She stared at his broad back for a moment, lost in confusion before almost tripping on the first step leading down Alpha Hill, and then she returned her concentration to the ground. "O-Okay?"

"Too many Alphas living together in one place will eventually start to force a hierarchy. I'm somewhere in the middle, and Oscar is third from the top. So when Oscar says that we all have to force you through an initiation, the only people who really get to ignore him are the Alphas at the top of the chain. Not that they would have participated in the hazing anyway, since they're professors."

Isobel followed him the rest of the way in silence, mulling over that information, but most thoughts of Alphas left her mind as they entered a room. The only thought that remained was how much bigger Alphas were. And how much stronger.

And every other reason she shouldn't get into a *wrestling ring* with one.

"I don't think this is a good idea," she said flatly, staring at the roped boundaries.

"No shit." He kicked off his shoes and ducked between the ropes. "You know what else they won't tell you? They might not hang around the dorm gossiping all day, but there is someone they spill all their secrets to. They speak to me, Carter." He notched his elbows on the ropes, leaning over to settle his stare on her. "I know someone managed to throw you naked into the lake. I know your room was trashed. I know what was written on your wall. I know about the bomb and the blood shower. I know why Elijah is monitoring your room and I know why Theo has you holed up in his room while he guards his door." He paused, then, looking amused. "Pity he only thought about people trying to get in, and not you trying to get out. But most of all ..." The amusement drained immediately out of his features, leaving them blank again. "I know it isn't their job to look after you. But Elijah can't help himself. Bullying is a sore point for him. And Theo thinks he owes you his life. So that's where I come in." He held up the rope, motioning her into the ring. "Your initiation is complete when you can break out of my hold in less than three seconds."

She considered him for a moment before blowing out a sigh. "This almost looks like you're trying to help me," she said, toeing off her sneakers and joining him in the ring.

"I wouldn't thank me yet," he said dully. "Now tell me what happened the first time that Beta cornered you."

She froze, fear skittering down her spine. He really did know everything. "He took me behind Dorm B and tried to kiss me."

Niko nodded, assessing her with narrowed eyes.

His irises were the colour of light moss crawling over rich-brown bark, and standing as close as he was, she thought she could still smell whiskey on him, but he didn't look drunk. He looked ... impatient.

Suddenly, he was advancing on her.

"Whoa!" She skittered backward, but he kept coming, and then her arms were locked behind her back and her jaw was in his grip.

The whiskey scent was stronger. Dizzying almost.

"Seriously?" he groused, releasing her. "That was too easy. Fight back, Sigma."

"That sentence is an oxymoron," she complained, trying to hide the way she had begun to shake. "Sigmas don't fight."

"Bullshit." He crossed his arms. "Imagine I'm the Beta."

"You're too muscly. He's more ... rounded and bulky."

"I said *imagine*."

Two seconds later, he had her cornered against one of the posts, her shoulders pushed back by his hands, his angry breaths huffing against the top of her head. "Stop making it so easy."

"He wasn't as fast as you!" She tried to push him off her, but he didn't even twitch, and his muscles felt like stone beneath unyielding flesh.

He eased back on her second push, and then stepped away from her entirely, moving off the platform and returning with a black strap.

"Maybe this will help," he muttered, directing her by the shoulders to stand in the middle of the platform. He flicked the strap up over her eyes before she knew what was happening and had it tied behind her head before she could duck away.

"What is your ability?" she asked as he drew away, leaving her skin feeling oddly cold. "You're so freaking fast, even for an Alpha."

"I'm strong for an Alpha too." He swept her feet out from under her, and she collapsed like a fragile tower of cards. "But my ability is more ... mental. Like yours."

She pushed herself back up, standing on wobbly legs and pulling her arms up before her face, forming loose fists. "Surprised you'd admit to it," she huffed, awareness prickling all over her skin. It was impossible to tell where he was standing. "Most Alphas would get violent if someone compared them to a Sigma."

He tugged on her ponytail, and she spun around, throwing out her fists, but he had already disappeared again.

"Calling yourself weak is the only true weakness

you'll ever have," he declared, catching her around the neck and spinning her, slamming her backwards against his body. "If you're *sure* you can't do something, it just means you're trying the wrong way. There's more than one way to cross a river, but you just stand in the middle and wonder why you're drowning." He spoke so calmly as she struggled in his hold, her breathing ragged as she battered at his iron grip with her fists and wriggled like a desperate animal caught in a snare. He didn't even seem to be breaking a sweat. "There's more than one way to get out of a bad situation."

He spun her again and forced a terrified squeak out of her throat as he grabbed her legs suddenly and hoisted her. She felt one of the ropes beneath her ass and one of his hands tugging on her hair, dragging her face against his. She could feel the graceful planes of his face, the sloping cheekbones and diamond-shaped jaw.

"There's more than one way to beat someone."

He hadn't pulled her in to kiss her, only to whisper into her ear, but suddenly she wasn't there with Niko. She was back in the chapel, shoved up against the dais, Crowe's heavy body pushing her down, his hands pinning her arms.

Everything went dark for a moment, and it wasn't

the dark of the blindfold. It was all-consuming, flashing right through her brain, the sound of her own rasping breath drowning out all sense. She wasn't herself in that moment, but a memory come alive, a reaction that had taken human form to live like a shadow against her skin, ready to take over at any moment.

Niko must have felt the change because he suddenly whipped off the blindfold and set her on her feet. He took several steps backward, watching her wearily, but she took no notice of him ... because she couldn't even breathe.

She clawed at her chest, searching around with wide eyes before collapsing to the floor, hunched over as she desperately tried to draw in air.

"Ah, shit." Niko kneeled before her, hovering but not touching, his expression taut. "Carter? Here." He lifted her hands, holding them within her blurry eyesight. "Squeeze my hands. Focus on that. Good ... *good girl*. Squeeze harder. There you go." His voice had dropped an octave, husky and deep, soothing and ... practised.

She squeezed his hands until her own hurt and the panic receded, filtering away to wherever it lived inside her body. Not gone, but subdued. She slackened her grip on his hands, and he lowered them to her lap but didn't release her, his thumbs rubbing slow, comforting circles against her skin.

"How did you ...?" She trailed off, unsure how to phrase the question.

"Someone I know." He slipped his hands away, grazing his jaw. It was the first time she had seen his confidence waver. He even glanced quickly at the cameras. *This was a topic he didn't want to discuss.* Well, that was fine with her.

"I told you this wasn't a good idea." She stared down at her lap, twisting her trembling fingers together.

"This is exactly why it's a good idea," he snapped. "But we're done for tonight. When I call on you next time, you need to drop everything. If you try to ignore me or get out of this, I'll turn up wherever you are, pick you up, and carry you here myself. I know you're trying to get views, but I'm pretty sure it's not of your ass slung over my shoulder, right?"

"You're a dick, you know that?" She slipped out of the ring and hastily pulled her shoes back on.

He snorted, following her out of the door and shutting off the lights. "I'm a dick who could have picked something sadistic that didn't help you out at all. Which is what Oscar will do, by the way. So try not to complain about all the people in between me and him who actually *don't* want to torture you."

"Oh yeah? What about Moses?"

"Okay, you got me there." He held up his hands in mock surrender.

"And Theo?" she pressed, annoyed.

Niko laughed outright, casting his eyes over her like he was assessing her in a whole new light. "Maybe you understand him better than I thought, but Theo would never break you. Test you, maybe. Break you? Never."

She swallowed, understanding the implication of what he was saying.

Oscar and Moses might very well try to break her.

And they might even succeed.

6

WE COULD BE FRIENDS

"Iz!" Eve caught her elbow as she hurried toward Fortune Telling and the Mystic Arts. "I thought we were meeting for breakfast?"

"Ah, I'm sorry." Isobel slowed, hitting her forehead. "I ran overtime while I was practising this morning. And I had a mountain of laundry to do."

"I bet." Eve scowled, but refrained from going off on another angry rant over the blood incident. The sudden influx of messages the day before while Isobel had been cleaning had been enough. "I noticed you skipped dinner as well. And your room was empty early this morning."

"My father got here last night. He's staying in the family centre. He convinced the officials I needed extra support because of my situation. And last night I slept in Theo's room."

"Hold up." Eve's nails dug in as she came to a complete stop, her heels suddenly cemented to the floor. "Say what now?"

"Ah ... well my father—"

"Not about *that*! Although it is majorly cool that Braun Carter is here. You slept *where?*"

She shook Isobel for good measure, so that Isobel's teeth clattered together when she tried to respond. "T-Theo was worried about p-people breaking into my room."

"Did he sleep in there with you?" Eve's baby-blue eyes had grown wide as saucers, and she was whispering like the subject of Theodore's bedroom was a national secret.

"No." Isobel laughed nervously. "Of course not."

"Why do you sound like you're lying?" Eve drew back.

"Well, I didn't really end up sleeping much. Niko made me sneak out."

"WHAT?" Eve looked like she wanted to shake her again. "*Niko?* I didn't even know you were friends with him."

"I'm definitely not. It wasn't like that. Sato is making them all put me through an initiation. He said even if the officials give me a room in Dorm A, I still have to pass all their tests as well."

"Sounds like Sato," Eve huffed out, but she still spoke Sato's name really quietly, like someone might report back to him that she was talking about him. "I told you to stay away from him."

"What'd he even do, anyway? Why is everyone so scared of him?"

Eve frowned. "I don't know. That just makes him even more terrifying, though. Like whatever he does, he gets away with it, you know?"

They parted ways when they reached Isobel's first class, and as soon as she stepped inside, the noise level dropped. People openly stared at her. It seemed that she was able to keep her head down and keep to herself in the corridors, but everyone in her first class had actually been waiting for her.

"Hey, Carter!" An Omega boy tried to wave her over to a small group of his friends, but she caught sight of Ashford sitting at their usual spot, smirking at her, and she turned away from the Omega to sit in the chair opposite Ashford.

His brows inched up in lazy acknowledgment, and she folded her arms, letting her gaze drift off to the side, until it twitched, annoyed, back to him. He stretched his legs out, jostling the legs of her chair.

"Morning, Sigma," he drawled. "Don't you look fresh."

She bit back her retort as Professor Vega entered the classroom, clapping her hands to get everyone's attention.

"Ah, Carter!" she exclaimed, her gaze zeroing in on Isobel a little too fast. "Welcome back! Now that you're here, I think we'll break up the pairs for the day and do something a little different."

Isobel glanced back to Ashford just in time to catch him smoothing out the annoyed look on his face, and she missed whatever else Vega said as he caught her eye and mouthed, "You won't escape me that easily."

She scrunched up her nose, whispering back, "I'm not trying to."

He leaned toward her, his boots jostling her chair again. He was wearing black Timberlands this time, and they were heavy enough to really jolt her.

"Lunch time," he said, the words coming out somewhere between a promise and a threat. "I left you alone while you were in hospital, and I gave you time to come to me, but now your grace period is up."

She nodded stiffly, turning back to Vega just as all the other students stood and gathered around a crystal ball that she was setting up in the middle of the room.

Isobel's brow pinched as she noticed the extra crew members gathering in the corner of the room, their cameras surveying the scene, not wanting to miss a single moment of ... whatever the hell was happening.

"Now!" Vega proclaimed with excitement. "Who wants to try first?"

"Try what?" Isobel whispered, turning back to Ashford ... except he was no longer sitting there. He had gathered up his bag and was already halfway across the room. He slipped out while everyone was distracted by Vega and the crystal ball. Not even the extra camera crew noticed.

"Carter." Vega pushed between two of the students, hurrying over to Isobel. "Why don't you come stand in the centre, since it's your mate we'll be trying to conjure ..." She stilled, frowning at Ashford's empty chair. "Where is Ashford?" she asked, her voice turning suddenly sharp.

One of the crew members swore, breaking away to leave the classroom, his steps hurried.

"I don't know," Isobel admitted, as Vega seemed to compose herself, plastering the smile back on her face and taking hold of Isobel's arm.

She pulled Isobel over to the centre of the circle, standing her beside the crystal ball. "Maybe you can try first, hmm?" She placed Isobel's hands around the cold sphere. "Just close your eyes and ask the question in your head: Who is my mate?"

Vega seemed distracted, not really paying much attention to Isobel as she checked the door to the classroom. This whole thing had been set up for Ashford, and Ashford alone. The Mystic Arts class was a joke, and everyone knew it. But Ashford's ability was real, and he had fled before they could use him to get a hint about Isobel's mate.

The crew didn't seem to be able to track him down before the end of the class, and Isobel felt more than a little aggravated by the time she arrived at the gym for her small group session. Having twenty students pretend to describe twenty different versions of her imagined mate in the most dramatic ways possible had worn on her patience.

She knocked on the door and Easton opened it a few seconds later, casting his eyes over her outfit before giving her a nod and standing aside for her to enter. She had managed to keep most of her tights and leotards, since she had plenty of black pairs, and had salvaged enough of her normal clothes to last her until summer break. She had also miraculously saved all of Kilian's shirts, since they had been in her laundry bag when the blood balloons exploded.

"Start on the treadmill," Easton instructed, and she headed over gratefully as he stopped to talk to Moses.

A quick survey of the room showed her that the rest of the Alphas were already there. They were hanging about, mostly, like they had been discussing something, but now they were starting to break apart and get into their individual activities. Isobel didn't want to engage with anyone, so she kept her focus on the treadmill, pressing the speed higher and higher until it felt like her muscles were rubber bands pulled taut, ready to snap.

It was Theodore who leaned over her from the treadmill beside hers, punching the numbers down. He didn't scowl or try to reprimand her, though. He just went back to running, his stare blank as it met hers in the mirror.

And then he smiled.

The smile she ... really liked.

The one that made him look like a superstar. The one that pulled his skin tight around all the angular planes of his face, creating a shifting picture she could probably watch for hours without getting bored. The one that took her breath away. Some of the desperation edged out of her, and she relaxed enough to give him a shaky smile in return.

The rest of the group session passed like a well-choreographed dance. The Alphas skirted around her, and she skirted around them, neither of them offering more than a muttered word or a quick, furtive glance —with the exception of Easton.

By the time the lesson was finished, she felt like she was actually getting *worse* at singing, but her skill was the least of her worries, because as intimidating as being in a shared class with all the Alpha students was, it wasn't anywhere near as terrifying as the idea of a private lesson with just *one* of the Alpha professors.

She was too nervous to eat much during the morning break, and she blundered her way through her first dance class for the day, barely even noticing that Reed sat in the back of the room after he turned up out of nowhere, telling the professor that he had just transferred into the class and wanted to observe the first lesson.

He slipped out before the class actually finished, and she checked the location of the practice room for the tutoring session with West at least six times on her way to the music department. She raised her hand to knock on the door when she found it, but it swung open before she could touch the wood.

"Right on time," West noted, his deep voice rolling

over her. He stood aside, catching her bag by the top handle as she stepped into the room. She jumped as he slid it smoothly down her arms and lifted it away from her, but he ignored the nervous reaction, hanging her bag up by the door and wordlessly motioning to the piano.

The practice room was actually quite large, with soundproof walls and racks of instruments. The grand piano was toward the back, centred on a small stage. The room seemed too bright, but maybe it was West's presence making her sensitive. For a guy his size, he moved completely without sound, with barely even a brush of his black shoes against the carpet. It made her breathing seem absurdly loud, like a nervous rattle on the exhale to bounce against the walls and a dry rasp of an inhale that made her sound like she was hyperventilating.

"Which do you prefer: Carter or Isobel?" West was standing behind her, his presence swelling even larger now that he was out of sight.

She parted her lips, but only a squeak came out, her mind stalling around his scent. It was a smoky and woody vanilla, with hints of bourbon and oak. It was so rich, so strong, it immediately sent her thoughts scattering, her own name rattling around her brain like an empty echo.

"Isobel," she eventually forced out, wishing she could shake her head to dislodge her reaction.

The only Alpha who was able to bowl her over simply with his presence was her father, and that wasn't a good comparison. Maybe it came with age. Maybe all Alphas grew stronger, their power more potent over time.

"Play whatever you like." If West was moving— shifting, pacing, anything—then he was doing it in complete silence. "I'd like to watch and listen for today."

That sounded like a worst-case scenario for her first lesson.

She lifted her hands to the keys, her face heating in a fierce blush when she realised just how badly her fingers were shaking. And just like when he asked about her name, she came up against another wall, her body refusing to cooperate. Her fingers curled in on themselves.

"What is it?" he asked.

"I don't ... I ..." She trailed off, staring at the keys.

"Did I ask you to stop?"

She shook off the memory, the disjointed voice, but it swayed back, reforming like smoke despite her desperate swatting.

"You don't stop until I say so," her father growled, his

hands wrapping around her neck as he bent her head down, inches away from the keys, the dark emotion pouring through him and into her, making a whimper catch in the back of her throat.

"Oh, honey." That had been her mother. Who was now standing beside the piano, staring down at her with sorrowful eyes. *"You remember that?"*

Jesus fucking Christ. She tried to force it all away. The memory *and* her mother.

West was waiting, not saying a word, not making a sound, but she could feel the weight of his eyes on the back of her head, and somehow, she could even smell the change in his scent. It turned sweeter, smokier, like burning sugar. She wasn't sure how she knew, but it wasn't a good sign.

She swallowed and tried again, her eyes starting to burn from her holding her attention too hard on the keys.

"I haven't played in a while." She finally got the words out and felt a small swell of victory that was dashed as quickly as it appeared.

"Why not?"

The memory resurfaced with a vengeance, pushing back so forcefully against her feeble attempts to subdue it. She heard the same disjointed cords that liked to haunt her when she let her guard down. She felt the keys like rough bricks, her sensitive fingers grasping desperately ... and she felt the grip around her neck tighten.

"Braun ... no ..." Her mother had woken up and was crawling toward them, clawing at her husband's pants, his shoes, patting weakly for his attention.

She would have opened herself to him.

She would have taken it all away.

But she had already been used. Filled with darkness and emptied of power. She was useless.

"You'll kill her. You promised. Braun, you promised. You promised."

It was a broken song to accompany the trailing cords Isobel's fingers stumbled over, the sounds turning loud and frightened, clanging calls for help as the storm inside her grew heavier, forming serrated edges to carve out more room as her father squeezed and squeezed and ...

"Isobel." It was a snap, a command.

Her eyes flickered open, her breath rasping as she turned her head toward West, who had moved to her side, his eyes digging into her face. Yellow-amber, sharp and translucent, the pupil contracted to a pinpoint.

"Breathe in," he commanded. His voice wasn't gentle, but deep, with a cold undertone, but her body obeyed him anyway, sucking in a lungful of air like she was starved for it.

"Hold," he clipped, waiting and watching. "Release it. Again." He watched as she breathed, observing the colour that leaked back into her ashen cheeks. She was sure she was bright with shame.

"I'm adding another session," he eventually said, studying her carefully. "Same time, but on Tuesdays. Elijah Reed will take over this session. Is that okay?"

"Um." She cleared her croaky throat, fighting back questions like … are you even allowed to do that? And more importantly, why? "I guess."

"Professor," he supplied, his voice deepening.

"Yes, Professor," she quickly corrected.

"Good." He stepped away, walking to the door. "We're done for today."

Her heart sank low into her gut as she dragged herself toward the library. She had been given an opportunity most students would kill for, and she felt like she had already blown it just because of her stupid piano-related panic. She huffed out a frustrated sound and walked a little faster, but instead of her sneakers hitting the brick pathway, they landed hard against a stone floor, the world around her rearranging in a split second, light flashing across her eyelids like she had accidentally looked up into a sunbeam.

She was standing on the rooftop of Dorm A.

Her hands started to shake, and she shot a hand out to the kitchen counter, leaning against it as she tried to calm her racing heartbeat.

Why are you scared? her mother's voice asked, concern lining her words.

Isobel lost the battle with her racing heart, raising her eyes to the apparition attached to the voice. Her mother stood beside the kitchen, midday sunlight slanting over her blonde locks. She was dressed in that familiar silken pyjama set, with the sky-blue robe knotted at her waist, her feet bare.

Now that Isobel thought about it, it was how she had been dressed back in the family centre as well.

"Mama," she croaked. "What's happening?"

"Oh, sweetheart." The older woman looked heartbroken. "Tell me why you're so scared."

"I just *appeared* here! And so did *you*!" Isobel tried to wrangle control of her voice, but it was too late. Someone had heard her. She could hear footsteps on the stairs leading up to the kitchen.

She spun to face whichever Alpha was about to accost her for breaking into the dorm in the middle of the day. Her chest was rising and falling too fast, but at least she managed to stop her breath from rasping, and she was pretty sure she didn't have a wide-eyed look of shock plastered all over her face anymore.

It was Reed who appeared, pausing at the top of the staircase and blinking twice. It was probably the most shock Reed ever displayed. She got the feeling he wasn't often surprised by things, just like Spade.

"What are you doing here?" he asked. He didn't glance at her mother.

She checked over her shoulder. The apparition was still there.

"I don't know," she admitted. "I just appeared here. Um ... what are you doing here?"

He looked mildly amused at her question before he shook his head. Reed and Spade didn't always attend their classes. Like Sato and Moses ... who she desperately hoped weren't also downstairs.

"It's a side effect of an incomplete mate-bond," he said, stepping fully into the kitchen. He seemed to be about to say something else, but that light slanted over her vision again, temporarily blinding her as the ground seemed to simultaneously drop out from beneath her feet and rise up to meet her at the same time. She tumbled over this time, sprawling out against the brick path outside the music department.

Her mother didn't appear again, but her phone

began vibrating, and she quickly found her feet, glancing at the unsaved number before answering.

"Carter," a brisk, female voice greeted. "This is Bower from the on-site surveillance centre." *An official.* "Where did you just disappear to?"

Her mind began to race, her palm growing clammy around the phone. The cameras on the rooftop didn't cover the kitchen. There was no way they would have seen her appear in Dorm A.

"To the place of my accident," she answered, trying not to lie.

Bower sighed. "We were afraid of that."

"A-Afraid of what, ma'am?" she dared to ask.

Most officials would have hung up on her, but Bower seemed distracted, mumbling to someone nearby before coming back to answer Isobel, her tone still preoccupied.

"That your side-effects wouldn't point to anybody in particular." And then she hung up.

Isobel shoved her phone back into the pocket of her tights and stood there in shock, debating where to go before deciding to just wait in the dining hall for Ashford. It was unnerving that the officials were keeping *such* a close eye on her, but it wasn't entirely surprising. She had to be careful. Especially if she was going to keep teleporting back to the spot where she died like the mate-bond was trying to make sense of this as much as she was. The cameras weren't going to miss a thing when it came to her, and with her father close enough to get his hands on her ... well, it was enough to keep her up at night.

In her *own* room.

Since she arrived before the lunch crowd, she was able to steal one of the booths. At first, she didn't have much of an appetite, but then a wave of hunger suddenly tunnelled through her stomach like it was completely hollow. She started mindlessly piling up her tray, texting Ashford with one hand on the way back to the booth.

She deposited the tray and then ducked back out again. He must have skipped class, because he found her as she was making them coffee.

"For me?" he asked, tapping against the table, his finger lifting to point at the cup she had added several shots to.

She didn't bother asking how he knew. Alpha nose.

"Yep." She made sure the lids were on securely before she swiped hers up, leading the way to the booth she had left her food in.

He didn't get any food himself, and he seemed to pause over her overfull tray when he slid into the booth seat opposite her.

"Hungry?" he asked, leaning back and settling curious eyes on her.

"Starving," she moaned, offloading the dishes from her tray and arranging them on the table. She didn't remember picking up the small bowl of pickles. She hated pickles.

CIAN HAD WAITED FOR HER TO COME TO HIM, TO EXPLAIN herself. He tried to be patient, to not push her, to not overcomplicate a very complicated situation ... but he couldn't let it go.

"What you said on the roof of the library ..." He started to dive right into it, but the Sigma was frowning at a bowl of pickles like she wasn't even listening.

She picked one of them up and nibbled on the edge of it.

He cleared his throat, sitting up and leaning over the table. Her eyes snapped straight to his, the pickle dropping from her fingers and bouncing against the table. Those eyes were a straight kick to his gut—both the honey-coloured one that matched his own hidden iris, and also the multicoloured one. He could see specks of sapphire, like fine glittering dust sprinkled throughout the other colours.

"What?" she asked, shaking her head. "I'm sorry, I'm ... not right today."

"What happened?" he asked, careful not to sound too curious.

She was frowning, munching on a new pickle distractedly. "I teleported."

"You ... what?" It was getting harder to keep his tone neutral.

She suddenly made a face, throwing down the pickle and making a retching sound. She wiped her hands on a napkin and put the bowl as far away as she could. When she refocussed on the dishes in front of her, he pushed it further, to the edge of the table.

"Teleported," she reiterated almost calmly, starting to rearrange the dishes in front of her.

She was separating them with a frown, mumbling beneath her breath. He thought he heard the word "vegetarian," and when he focussed, he could see that she was eliminating everything with meat in it.

He reached across the table, catching her hands. Her eyes flicked to his again, punched into him again, and he forced her palms to the table, weighing them down with his own. Her hands were so pale, her fingers small and delicate. His own larger hands seemed like a stark contrast.

"Where did you teleport to?" he asked evenly.

"To—" She cut herself off immediately, before trying again. "To where I almost died. Pretty much the exact same spot."

Her hands were shaking. He traced along the length of her thumb with his ... and the shaking grew worse.

"Was anyone there, Isobel?"

Her eyes had started to wander to the food again, that confused glint sparking, but they shot back to him at the sound of her name on his lips.

She shook her head, slipped her hands out from beneath his, and leaned back in her seat, crossing her arms.

"Please come here." She spoke on an expelled breath. Nervously. She looked toward the seat beside her. "I don't want to be overheard."

He obligingly slid out of the booth and switched to the other side, stretching his legs out beneath the table. His new vantage point showed him the rest of the hall, and he could see students beginning to filter in for lunch. He turned slightly, setting his arm against the table. She was making herself small, hunching in her shoulders. She smelled ... harassed. Like crushed cherries and branches shoved through a wood chipper. He breathed deeply, curling himself around her, keeping his fucking hands to himself.

"Tell me," he cajoled, because even though he was keeping his hands to himself, his voice hadn't received the memo, and it was trying to persuade her to come closer, where he could scent her better.

Isobel wrapped her arms around her middle, her attention skittering up the expanse of chest that was closer than she had intended. Still, it was better that the cameras didn't overhear this conversation.

She leaned in, refusing to look Ashford in the eyes, and spoke against his shirt, her voice a whisper. "I heard a voice in my head."

"Mhmm." His chest rumbled with the sound, but he didn't say anything else, waiting for her to continue.

As close as she was, she could smell a curious mix of scents on Ashford. If sunlight had a scent, it was exactly the perfume that clung to his dusky skin. He was heat and warmth and the rush of salty seawater. She closed her eyes, distracted for a moment by the heavenly mix.

"What is that smell?" she found herself asking, drawing back so that her eyes could crawl up to his face.

"You're so distracted," he noted with a frown, his

hand lifting like he was about to touch her face, before quickly dropping down again.

But he did touch her. His palm settled across her thigh beneath the table, searing hot, his fingers flexing. "What smell?"

"Like the ocean—"

His touch turned pinching, his eyes narrowing. "Me." The word was quiet and clipped, but he didn't seem angry. He looked surprised. Confused. "Focus, Sigma. What did the voice say on the rooftop of the library?"

"That she was sorry."

His touch slackened, his aquamarine eyes widening. "She? Did you know the voice?"

"Never heard it before." Isobel shrugged a little.

Ashford ducked closer, refusing to let her turn away. "Is it the only one you hear?" he whispered harshly.

Isobel's lips flattened, but she was saved from a reply when the half-closed screen was suddenly pushed back, Niko appearing in the opening.

"There you are," he said to Ashford, ignoring Isobel completely. "We were waiting for you back at the dorm. I'm fucking starving. Are you going to eat all of this?" He reached for one of the pickles, biting off half of it at once.

"It's not mine," Ashford said, easing back from her. He returned to his previous seat, looking completely unaffected by their tense conversation.

"Help yourself," Isobel mumbled.

Niko sat beside Ashford, digging in without being told twice. It was like she had collected all of his favourite foods and arranged them there to wait for him, if the speed of his eating and the sounds he made at each new dish were anything to go by.

Ashford sat calmly in the corner, one arm resting on the table, the other stretched along the top of the back seat. He was smirking at Niko. She started to edge out of the booth, but Reed suddenly appeared, blocking her in. He jerked his chin for her to make room for him, and the look on his face was impatient, so she sighed, shuffling back until she was in the other corner opposite Ashford.

"Keep going," Reed said. "There are more coming."

"I'll just—" She made like she was about to try and climb out of the booth again, but suddenly Ashford was behind her, his hands at her waist, dragging her across the back seat until she was beside him again.

Reed edged around the table to sit on her other side, boxing her in. Spade sat beside him, and then Theodore appeared with a tray. His nose wrinkled, and his eyes flew straight to her and then to the Alphas trapping her in.

They were facing off with each other like a challenge had been issued, and it wasn't until Theodore flashed her his beautiful smile and sat beside Niko that everyone relaxed.

Ashford reached over the table and snatched the sandwich that she had chosen amongst all the dishes she had collected in a haze. It was the only thing she *actually* felt like eating after the strange, ravenous hunger had disappeared. She tried to mumble her thanks, but then Moses appeared with a dark frown directed her way, and the word died in the back of her throat. She busied herself eating the sandwich, taking tiny little bites so that she could drag it out until they all left the booth.

When Kilian appeared, he looked displeased to see her imprisoned between Reed and Ashford, and he exchanged an unreadable look with Theodore before slotting in on his other side.

It wasn't until everyone was deep into a heated conversation about what they were going to do for Ashford's birthday party that she felt another touch against her leg, except this time it wasn't Ashford's searing touch. It was a light tap, just above her knee. Reed was watching her. He bent beside her ear once he had her attention, whispering low, "Is that the first time it's happened?"

She nodded.

He made a slight humming sound. "Do you know why? Why there?"

She shrugged, her shoulders shifting against his and Ashford's arms. "Because it's where I almost died?"

"You did die," Reed corrected automatically. "A bond cannot begin without the heart stopping. Or without the soul disconnecting with the body—depending on whether you buy into the Gifted religion or not."

"Do you?" She set down her sandwich, unable to ignore the uneasy feeling inside her stomach. She almost wished the urge to consume meat and pickles was back.

Reed tapped her plate like he had tapped her leg.

"Finish it." The command was quiet, but he didn't use his Alpha voice. "You need your strength."

"You need to mind your own business," she shot back, a little too loud.

The Alphas weren't talking anymore. They were watching her and Reed. Well, except for Niko. He was still eating, shovelling food in like he wasn't going to get a chance to eat ... ever again.

"You're pale and shaky," Reed noted dispassionately. "You've been skipping meals and throwing out half-finished protein bars after your practice sessions."

"I almost died." She spoke to the table, her tone droll. "I'm stressed." *My father is here.* "And how have you noticed all that anyway? We're not even friends."

"We could be."

Theodore spat water all over the table. "No." He set his bottle down with a little too much force. "She already has me."

"And me." Kilian rolled his eyes at Theodore.

"Yeah," Theodore gritted out. "Like I said."

Reed ignored them both, watching her evenly. Like he had been all week, apparently.

"You don't want to be friends with me." She pushed her plate further away. Reed didn't try to correct her. She was right. "Let me out." She stood, wishing she could use Alpha voice, but apparently she didn't need it, because Theodore stood and bodily dragged everyone out of her way.

"Thanks," she muttered to him, biting back a small smile as she stepped from the booth, hanging her bag over her shoulder.

Nobody tried to fight off Theodore. They liked him too much. They just tagged his shoulders lightly with their fists and then reclaimed their seats after Isobel was free. Theodore remained standing, looking down at her like he already knew what she was about to say.

"See you tom—" she started.

He was already shaking his head. "They put a bomb in your room, Illy."

"There's a camera." She flicked a look to Reed, who only arched an impassive brow in response. "Watch me sleep if you have to." And then she turned on her heel and tried to stalk off, but Reed's voice caught her before she was out of earshot.

His *Alpha* voice.

"Grab a protein bar on your way out."

She frowned as she passed the snack station by the coffee cart, snatching up one of the bars. He hadn't ordered her to eat it, but she did find that asserting a small amount of power and stubbornness over the Alphas had given her back a hint of her appetite. So she ate half of it and threw out the other half on her way to class, just to spite Reed.

7

REBEL LIKE THAT

Isobel checked her emails for the code to the elevator as she stepped into the family centre, punching it into the panel and hitting the button for the eighth floor. She had showered and changed into one of the dresses her father approved of for dinnertime, and selfishly wished her mother's apparition would appear to walk with her as she knocked on his apartment door. But her mother had acted as a barrier for most of her adult life. It was cruel to continue to wish it even after her death.

"Isobel." Her father opened the door, motioning her in, all business. "We're already set up and ready to go. You'll find your outfit changes behind the screen over there. I'll let your new publicist take it from here."

And then he was walking away. He didn't even notice the dress.

"Miss Carter!" The man who appeared before her was slim, with a black goatee and neatly combed hair trimmed short and immaculate. He had reading glasses tucked into his pressed white shirt and an iPad wedged beneath his arm. He stuck the other one out for her to shake.

His grip was firm, like he was trying to impress her.

"Beautiful," he muttered, like she was a doll on display. "The screen barely does you justice. But we'll fix that. I'm Cesar Cooper, your publicist for the time being."

She extracted her hand from his. "Nice to meet you."

"Of course." His hand was at her back now, steering her through the packed apartment as stylists and photographers bustled about, rearranging the furniture and testing out their lights. He hovered a little too close, like he had also taken it upon himself to be her bodyguard. "Now, it was decided that we would do a Sigma theme for your photoshoot this afternoon ..." The rest of his sentence was lost on her as she caught sight of the rack of clothing one of the stylists was flipping through.

"Sigma theme?" she questioned once he finished talking, a ball of lead dropping through her stomach.

"Yes, yes, you know." He deposited her behind the dressing screen, holding the outfit she had caught sight of around the edge as he looked away. He waved it about. "This one first. Hurry now, we're on a tight schedule. You have practice in two hours and Carter is *adamant* that we don't interfere with your training time."

It was a maid costume.

She took it with bile building in the back of her throat, holding it up to look it over. It was ... small. She was used to wearing barely anything while she practised and trained, but this seemed different somehow. The fishnet stockings. The frilly skirt that bounced right out almost like a ballerina skirt. The entire length of her legs would be on show, not to mention the deep, plunging neckline and scant material.

"C-Can I speak to my father, please?"

Cooper popped around to her side of the screen, making her jump a few inches back. He arranged a look of commiseration onto his face.

"Something wrong?" He pulled out his phone, waiting for her to reply like a fix was only a call away, and she was suddenly filled with familiar memories of past tutors threatening to tell her father if she didn't cooperate.

"Has my father approved the photoshoot?" She tried for a different tact. "I just want to make sure."

"Your father approved everything." He was frowning now, his fingers twitching around the phone, but then he slid it away, drawing closer to her, lowering his voice in a conspiratorial whisper. "Are you sure you want me to bring him back in? You know what he's like." His hand slid down her arm as though he was trying to comfort her.

"No need." She gritted her teeth. "I'll get changed."

"Excellent." He squeezed her arm and ducked back around the other side of the screen.

She turned around and stared at her very clear reflection in the glass window behind the screen. Nobody else seemed to be watching, but it was just another low blow that her "privacy screen" wasn't private at all. She quickly stripped off her dress and stuffed herself into the costume. She left the fishnets behind, even though they probably would have helped to cover her legs a little more. The apron layered over the front of the dress turned out to have adjustable straps, so she was able to pull it up over half of her chest. The result almost looked like a ballerina costume. A weird one … but the tight bodice, high neckline, and short, flared skirt was familiar enough.

KILIAN DIDN'T LIKE THE PUBLICIST IMMEDIATELY, BUT WHEN he handed Isobel that costume, Kilian wanted to rip off his hands and bitch slap him with his own broken stubs. Unfortunately, Kilian didn't agree with violence as a first solution, and he wasn't even supposed to *be* there, so instead, he tipped the iPad out of Cooper's pocket when the asshole turned around to watch Isobel's reflection in the glass wall just as she started unzipping her dress. Cooper swore, bending to check that the screen wasn't broken, and Kilian flattened himself to the wall, wondering what the fuck he was going to do. Trip the fire alarm? *Start an actual fire?* Whatever was going on here, it was none of his business. This was some weird Icon family shit.

"Oh, *love* it!" One of the stylists grabbed Isobel as she emerged, saving her from Cooper's permeating frown.

Kilian trailed her as she was whisked through hair and make-up and positioned before the cameras, all the staff acting like they were being timed.

"Here." A feather duster was shoved into Isobel's

hand, and Kilian gritted his teeth so hard they were in danger of cracking.

Not a single person in the room had a ranking ring around their pupil, which meant they were all human, and if the world had taught humans anything, it was that the Gifted were either Icons, or they were *nothing*. None of these humans seemed to care about Isobel, because she wasn't an Icon. They did care about Braun Carter, but the burly man had disappeared almost as soon as his daughter arrived.

Kilian stepped over a bundle of cords, moving to the other wall where he could have a clear view of Isobel. They were instructing her to pose like a ballerina as she pretended to dust the curtains. It was supposed to be alluring. She was supposed to be the perfect Stepford Sigma, but she just looked like a trapped, broken ballerina. She ruined the whole shoot, and Kilian was overjoyed by the frowns of the photographers.

When they made her smile, she somehow looked sadder.

"Okay, we can work with this," the publicist was muttering, pacing behind the cameras and looking like someone had pissed in his coffee. Except Kilian doubted it was coffee in the flask he took a quick swig out of. "We change the tone of the campaign.

Make it look like she's waiting for someone to rescue her."

"So that she can do their chores?" one of the stylists muttered, shaking her head. She looked amused but also a little disgusted, and more than a little defeated.

This likely wasn't the industry for her.

"Next outfit!" Cooper shouted, clapping his hands. "Hustle, people!"

Isobel ducked back behind the screen, and Kilian quickly wrapped one of the cords into a circle on the floor, waiting until Cooper stepped into it on his way over to spy on Isobel again. And then he pulled. And the asshole faceplanted, almost impaling himself on a camera stand. It was beautiful but not nearly gruesome enough.

When she emerged again, she was wearing a wedding dress, and Kilian slackened back against the wall, rubbing a hand over his mouth. Layered in thin, delicate ivory silk, she looked like she was floating on a cloud, intricate beading and embroidery climbing across the bodice and drawing all of his attention to the pale swell of her cleavage, her chest flushed with agitation. Her hair tumbled freely, a simple wreath of delicate flowers tucked onto her head. Her cheeks were rosy, her makeup silver and glittery, her eyes watering.

This was so fucked up. He pulled out his phone and took a picture, sending it to the group chat. The responses were immediate.

Theodore: What the fuck?

Cian: Where the fuck?

Gabriel: Family centre, somewhere around the top floor if the view is anything to go by.

Gabriel: The why is less obvious.

Elijah: Seriously? It's clearly a photoshoot. Her father is an Icon with a penchant for aggressive media campaigns. He will see her partly bonded status as an opportunity.

Gabriel: I said it was less obvious, not that it wasn't still obvious.

Moses: Stop comparing brain size.

Kilian: Yeah, stop waving your big ... brains around.

Theodore: An opportunity to what? To marry her off?

Gabriel: An opportunity for attention. He might be thinking she could win the game, especially if he can drag this out.

Niko: You mean if we can drag this out.

Oscar: Hey Kil. Come and get me.

(Admin) Mikel: Don't get involved, Oscar.

Oscar: You know you want to, Kili.

(Admin) Kalen: Do not get involved, Oscar.

Elijah: Oscar. Don't.

Oscar: Be there in ten, Kiljoy.

Kilian glanced back up at the miserable look on Isobel's face and realised it really wasn't that hard of a decision. He began edging toward the doorway.

Isobel dragged herself behind the dressing screen again, glaring at the third outfit Cooper passed behind the screen.

"We should shoot her sitting on the windowsill or something, looking out, with that sad look on her face ..." He strode off, talking to one of the photographers, some of his words drifting back to her. "Daydreaming about her mate ..."

She quickly slipped on the silk nightie and dressing gown, shoving her feet into the silken slippers while angrily knotting the sash around her waist. She was too busy trying to get dressed as quickly as possible to realise exactly what she was putting on, and it wasn't until they were directing her onto the balcony that she realised what they had inadvertently done.

They had dressed her as her mother.

Had her father picked this? Because he thought all Sigmas were the same?

She stared down, suddenly deaf to the people around her, her fingers rubbing against the lustrous material. She would always find her mother like this in the middle of the night. Out on the balcony. Contemplating the fall. Contemplating her choices. Weighing up whether she could bear to leave Isobel or not, most likely.

It was hard to admit that. Hard to face that. When it was all she knew, it was almost normal, but she had been away from that penthouse long enough now that none of it looked normal anymore.

"I'm done," she croaked, stepping off the balcony.

Cooper was getting in her face, but she tuned him out, glancing away from his twitching goatee. She snatched a coat from the rack of clothing and ducked behind the useless screen to hastily swap out the dressing gown for the coat, clutching it closed at her throat as she shoved her feet into her shoes and tried to leave the room.

She might have made it, too, if her father hadn't returned at that moment.

"Everyone out!" he bellowed, gripping her arm and preventing her from going any further.

He didn't use Alpha voice. They were humans, after all. He might have been a fully-fledged citizen, but he had his own set of rules, and using his abilities on humans could land him in jail, Icon or not. Still, they scattered like they believed he would do something terrible to them. Like they had been the ones to let him down. Like they would be punished, after he finished dealing with her.

Once the room was clear, he gripped her other arm, drawing her up as he bore down on her. "Have you forgotten your place, daughter?"

His fury battered against her chest with heavy fists, forcing her to crack in increments, until his poison could begin to leak in. He was the only one who could overpower her in this way, but he hadn't had much reason to do it with her mother alive.

She started to grow weak as his heavy emotion flooded into her. He always had so much rage. So much bitterness. So much hollow darkness just searching for a bad emotion to latch onto. He shook her a few times, her teeth snapping together, like he was settling it all into her system. Jostling it into place. Making room for more. He waited until he heard her hiss of pain, and then he set her down, leaving her to rub the bruises already forming on her arms.

And then something changed.

It was almost imperceptible, but she felt it. It was a strange shift in the tension, like something had been added. A breeze from a window that had been sealed shut. He frowned, realising his phone had been vibrating, and she edged away as he answered the call, her eyes flicking between the door and the carpet. She wanted to flee, but that would only make things worse.

And what's this? an unfamiliar voice asked.

She jumped at the sound that sprouted inside her head, spinning to find a man standing a few feet away.

He had endless black eyes and was heavyset, with a fierce, broad brow and tightly curled hair, and he was staring straight at her, a gold Alpha ring wrapped around onyx pupils.

"Crap," she muttered, when her mother appeared right beside him, flicking her curious attention between them.

"Who's this?" her mother asked.

"Double crap." Isobel turned away from them, though it made the hair on the back of her neck stand on end to put the man out of her sights.

Her father was cursing into his phone, his face reddening, his pacing taking on a violent edge. He had been mad before, but this was something else. This was the sort of thing she really *should* run from. She needed to wait for whatever bad news he had just gotten to pass before she tried to face him again, or she would end up with more than just bruises.

"Ah ..." The deep, crooning voice behind her drifted along the back of her neck. "He's invisible."

"Who are you talking about?" her mother questioned.

"My little wolf," the man replied, striding past Isobel like he didn't give a shit about her, even though she was pretty sure *he* was a figment of *her* imagination. Not even her own psychotic creations respected her. He moved to the wall, right beside the door, and slammed his fist against it, growling when he couldn't seem to get a grip of anything.

"Think you're untouchable now, do you, little fuck?" he seethed.

"What the hell is he doing?" Isobel hissed out of the side of her mouth as her mother moved to stand beside her.

"He's trying to grab that boy by the throat."

"What bo—" Isobel froze, her eyes slamming into her mother. "A boy like me or a boy like you?"

Her mother smiled sadly. "You mean is he alive? He is. He's just invisible."

Great. Now the ghosts she kept accidentally materialising were trying to attack her only other Alpha friend. She ran to the door as her father spun around to pace back to the wall of windows. After flinging the door open, she glanced at the spot on the wall the man was now starting to pound against with fists that couldn't seem to catch anything, spittle flying from the edges of his mouth as the curses died away to grunts and growls.

"Get out," she whispered, hoping Kilian heard her.

She ran to the elevator, slamming her finger into the button as the man with dark eyes chased her, both he and her mother disappearing as the elevator jolted into action. She rested her head against the wall, trying to calm her racing pulse.

"Kilian?" she whispered.

"Not just him," a gritty voice whispered back, close to her ear.

She spun around, clutching the handrail in the elevator, her wide eyes travelling between a suddenly visible Kilian and Sato.

"Does your father always touch you like that?" Sato asked in that quiet, dangerous tone.

"Is it any of your business?" She shook out her hands, which were tingling too much, the shock trying to take hold of her body.

Kilian was considering her carefully, a disturbed look on his face.

"Yes," Sato answered plainly.

She waited for him to elaborate. He didn't.

"*How*?" She drew out the word, her exasperation clear. "How is *any* of this your business? *Why* were you both following me? I've been out of the hospital for days. If I was going to tell anyone the truth about where my accident happened, I would have."

"How did you know we were there?" Kilian asked, drawing her attention from Sato's impassive expression. "You looked right at us."

Ah, she was back to playing the "answer all questions with more questions" game with the Alphas.

"Are you little wolf?" She lifted a brow at Kilian, who only looked confused.

The elevator doors opened, and she and Kilian stepped out, but Sato remained. Kilian quickly shot out his hand, holding the doors open, his eyes flicking between Sato and Isobel ... because Sato looked like someone had just shot him in the chest at close range. Which for anyone else, looked more like "a little put off."

"What did you say?" he whispered, his voice cracking.

"So it was you." She watched as he slowly started to walk toward her. She edged backwards, and Kilian monitored them warily, hovering close by like he thought he would be required to intervene at any moment.

She held up her hands when Sato got too close, but

he only pushed into her, her hands slipping against his chest, her butt hitting a chair behind her.

"Where did you hear that name?" he asked quietly, his chest rising and falling evenly against her palms. He seemed so contained, full of self-control, but there was something off about the façade. Like it was a trap.

"Someone told me," she hedged. If it had just been Kilian, she might have confided in him, but admitting to Sato that she heard voices and saw apparitions of people who were dead or made up or *something* was not on the cards.

"Who?" He was so close, his hands gripping the top of the chair he had backed her into, caging her in. He was leaning down, trapping her in the glittering, angry darkness of his eyes.

"That's enough." Kilian pulled him back, and they faced off as a snarl ripped out of Sato's throat,

"Get out of here." Kilian delivered the order in Alpha voice, and she didn't have to wait for very long to guess who he had issued it to. Her feet were already moving her to the door.

She fled the family centre, strangely glad to be back under the watchful eye of the cameras again, until she realised that she was still only wearing the stupid, silk slip beneath her coat, and she was late for the practise time she had booked.

For all the bravado she had shown at lunch time, she was hesitant when she finished catching up on the *Ironside Show* with Eve that night and shuffled back to her room. She checked that her door was locked properly several times and even shifted a pile of books in front of it for good measure. It wouldn't keep anyone out if they busted the lock, but it would make a sound when it toppled over.

She sat on her makeshift bed, hugging her knees to her chest and staring at the blank wall she had gone to all the trouble of trying to decorate when she had arrived at Ironside. Since her room had been trashed the first time, she had started treating it less like *her* room and more like the storage closet it was initially intended as. It was just a transient place. Somewhere for her to store her stuff until she managed to force her way into Dorm A.

She slept with the light on that night. Fully dressed. Unable to succumb to the vulnerabilities of darkness or soft, comfortable clothes. If it hadn't been for the camera watching over her, she might not have dared to sleep at all.

"Nice to see you again, Carter." Annalise Teak stood aside, motioning her into the small meeting room within the family centre. "This is my partner, Charlie."

Isobel offered both women a small smile, moving to the bright yellow armchair that sat facing them across a small coffee table.

Charlie didn't get up to greet her but offered a warm smile from where she was still seated, her shoes kicked off and her legs crossed in the chair. The silver Beta ring around her iris was stark against dark eyes, matching her silver nose ring and eyebrow ring. She had short dark hair that swept over her face and more dangling silver piercings stepping up along her earlobes. But other than the piercings and the way she was seated, she seemed to be dressed just as professionally as Teak.

"We grabbed you a coffee," Teak said, picking up a takeaway cup from the sideboard by the door and offering it to Isobel.

"Thanks." Isobel took a sip, not at all surprised that they knew how she liked her coffee. They might have the Gifted rank rings around their irises, but Teak was as good as an official.

"So, you've been going to all your classes." Teak folded into her own chair, sounding impressed. "You only took a day off to clean your room—I'm sorry about that, by the way."

"Why? Did you do it?" Isobel snapped her lips shut, wanting to palm her face immediately. Just because Teak and Charlie *looked* approachable—just because Teak also had a Sigma ring—didn't mean anything.

Teak likely held Isobel's future in her hands.

These sessions weren't just for Isobel. They were a way to monitor her, to assess her, to *experiment* with her experience. She wouldn't have expected anything less from the officials. She had actually expected more.

Charlie smirked. "Don't look so scared. This is a safe space."

"So you won't be reporting back everything I say?" Isobel challenged.

Teak clicked her tongue in a disapproving sound. "I'm a bond specialist, Isobel—do you mind if I call you Isobel?" She waited for Isobel to shake her head before she continued. "I serve dual roles. To support any student who has initiated a mate-bond, and to keep the officials informed of every minute step of the process. I won't be reporting on what you say unless it directly affects your bonding process."

"You're her first, though," Charlie added, winking. "So she already has a soft spot for you."

"And possibly my last." Teak smiled slightly. "Since it's so rare." She opened up the cover on her iPad, checking something on the screen before looking up at Isobel again. "You teleported yesterday and appeared at the scene of your death?"

"Yes. It wasn't for long."

"And you were alone? There was nobody there?"

Did her mother count? She hesitated. "No."

They shared a look before Teak put aside her iPad. She seemed to carefully consider her words before she spoke again.

"What you're going through must be terrifying. You don't seem very eager to find your mate. Why don't you tell me about that?"

Isobel tipped her head back against the chair, setting her coffee aside as her stomach clenched painfully. She wrapped her arms around her middle and thought about her father. Was he in the building? Would he punish her for what had happened the day before? Had he calmed down?

Suddenly, tears filled her eyes, and she hastily swiped them away, clearing her throat. "Since I came to Ironside, I've been able to decide things for myself. What I eat, when I sleep, whether I watch the show or not."

For a moment, neither of them seemed to know

what to say, but then Charlie tilted her head, speaking in a curious tone, "Most people find Ironside to be quite restrictive. There might be more luxury here, but there are less rules in the settlements. Less eyes on you. What else can you do here that you couldn't do before?"

"Sleep through the night," Isobel admitted quietly. "Even with people trashing my room and rigging booby traps for me, it's easier here."

"And what makes you think that a mate will take those things away from you?" Teak asked carefully, like she knew she was tiptoeing around a subject that could shut Isobel off at any second.

"I'll belong to whoever it is." Isobel glanced between the women apologetically, not wanting to offend them. "I won't be in charge of myself anymore."

"Why do you think that?" Teak asked, sharing another look with Charlie. "You don't have to worry about upsetting us."

Isobel shrugged. "You have some sort of file on me, right?"

Teak straightened up again, patience written into the soft expression on her face. "Of course."

"I bet it's extensive."

Charlie snorted. Teak shot her a quick look of chastisement that still somehow managed to look soft and loving. Teak was the perfect Sigma. It made Isobel sick to her stomach.

"Yes." Teak refocussed on Isobel. "It's extensive."

"What happened to my mother?"

Teak froze, searching her face. "You were informed by your father in early February—"

"No." Isobel interrupted. "I know she's dead. I want to know what happened exactly. I've searched online. It wasn't reported on or announced to the public at all."

Teak's eyes turned briefly sharp, like something was clicking together in her mind as she watched Isobel fidget in her seat. "I was told your father is staying here in the family centre to better support you. And that you would be meeting with him every afternoon for the foreseeable future. Are you not comfortable speaking to him about it?" she asked plainly.

"I don't know what comfortable feels like." Isobel issued the information almost like a challenge to the woman across from her. "Not around my father."

To her credit, Teak didn't even bat an eyelash. "Understood. I'll find out what I can, how does that sound?"

"There isn't any information about it in my file?"

"No." Teak still had that sharp, considering look in

her eyes. "Your parents lived the lives of an Icon and his mate. The OGGB didn't attend your mother's death —the human police force did."

"But the OGGB knows everything," Isobel persisted.

It made her nervous that they were using the formal acronym for the Official Gifted Governing Body instead of just saying "the officials." It was like she was already chained to a desk in an interrogation room, a group of humans in suits on the other side of one-way glass, wondering why she was questioning things she had no right questioning.

"The way things worked" was not a topic up for discussion. That was what anti-loyalists did. They questioned things.

"Have you had any other side-effects?" Teak suddenly steered the conversation away from her mother. "Anything strange, different, out of the ordinary?"

"Just weird cravings." *And seeing dead people.*

"Any cold and flu symptoms? Sudden depression or feelings of hopelessness?" Teak was tapping away on her iPad.

"Some headaches, chest pains, and ... mood changes, I guess."

It took the rest of the hour to answer all of Teak's

JANE WASHINGTON

questions, but Isobel was surprised when Teak suddenly changed the subject again, right as Isobel was getting up to leave.

"I'll dig into what happened to your mother." She was avoiding eye contact as she packed up her things. "And Charlie is going to give you her number, in case of emergencies."

"I am?" Charlie asked, at the same time as Isobel said, "She is?"

"Yes of course." Teak brushed them both off, still busying herself with stuffing her iPad into her bag. "It wouldn't be appropriate for me to give mine out—I'm here for the sessions the officials have appointed and nothing more."

Charlie suddenly got up, holding out her hand for Isobel's phone. "I'm a rebel like that." She rolled her dark eyes. "Always doing things behind my mate's back."

Teak snorted softly but still refused to turn around. Isobel hesitantly handed her phone over and then took it back once Charlie was finished with it. She thanked them both, slipping out of the room, and hurried to lunch before she could run into her father.

8

TOSSING AND SPINNING

Isobel slumped back into her chair, dropping the polished cutlery as the credits for the latest Ironside episode aired. She was seated at an eight-person dining table in the penthouse apartment with her father, his assistant, his agent, his marketing manager, and Cooper. They all muttered quietly and took notes as the episode played, while her father just sat there staring stoically at the projected screen.

After skipping her scheduled meeting with him the day before, he had finally summoned her on Friday morning with a curt email.

Isobel,

As you know, you earn a monthly stipend during your time at Ironside. My financial advisor has been putting these amounts aside for you into a fund to be accessed when you graduate. Every time you disobey me or fail to attend our scheduled meetings, I will deduct money from that account.

Your absence last night cost you three months of your salary.

Do not let it happen again.

I will see you at 6:00 p.m. tonight. We will watch the show together.

Regards,

Your father.

So there she was, wishing she could disappear into the floor after watching the one scene she had been dreading. The officials had finally decided to air the footage of her emerging naked from the lake, and time had slowed down—both on-screen and off-screen—as she was sandwiched between Reed and Spade.

Her nudity was blurred out except for that moment, not that it was needed.

She hadn't actually realised how tightly she was pressed between them at the time, and she could have done without the knowledge. She also could have done without the entire world having the knowledge, or the visual to go along with it.

Her father, however, didn't seem bothered.

After asking her the date of the incident, he launched into a discussion with Cooper about all the reasons the officials might have delayed showing it until now.

When he finally turned back to her, she caught a flash of the temper she had been bracing for. "They should be overloaded with content," he snapped. "They shouldn't be sitting on clips for this long because they don't trust that you'll provide them with regular content to air."

He didn't wait for an answer. He just swivelled back to his team, and they continued to discuss her right over the top of her own head. He wrapped up the meeting by standing and gathering everything into his briefcase. The others all immediately scrambled to get their things together and leave the dining room.

"I'll be returning home for the weekends," he told her. "So I'll see you again on Monday. You have two days to make something happen for the cameras."

She fixed her gaze down. "Torturing someone only works when they aren't asking for it. How do I make something happen?"

She could feel her father's embarrassment of her pouring out of him. "Acting dumb doesn't suit you anymore, Isobel." He held the door open but mostly blocked the opening. "We all know what you're doing with the Alpha boys—" He held up his hand, cutting off the confused question forming on her lips. "I'm not disappointed. I'm actually impressed. I didn't think you had it in you. And you're playing them perfectly, staying just far enough away to draw them in, to make them fight over you. As I watched you on-screen this year, I finally thought ... that's *my* daughter. But you aren't a master at the game yet. You need to listen to me. You need to heed my warning. *Do more*. People get bored in the blink of an eye around here." He stepped aside, waving her through. "Make something happen."

CIAN DRUMMED HIS FINGERS ON HIS LAP, STARING AT THE flickering flames of the fire pit they had set up on the bank of Alpha Lake. He forced a smile as someone shouted over the back of Kilian's chair at him. He just assumed it was some sort of drunken birthday greeting, but his mind was elsewhere. If elsewhere was about as tall as his bicep with strawberry blonde hair and an ass that was made for leggings—which was fortunate for her, since she seemed to live in workout clothes.

The Sigma was hearing voices.

And she was avoiding him and the others ... but not for much longer.

Even if the cards hadn't suggested that tonight

would be eventful, he would have known it by the fact that even Oscar and Moses had come down from their perch, relocating to one of the picnic tables that had been set up around the lake. They sat on the table, their legs planted on the seat, drinks in their hands as they glared a forcefield into existence, causing students to stumble away from the non-existent barrier. It had already gotten to the point of causing a few injuries. People were actually walking *into* the lake just to skirt around the table with a maximum amount of buffering distance between them and the perceived danger.

Cian knew that Carter would be involved in whatever happened tonight, because he had pulled her card again. *The Moon*. It never appeared to him in any other capacity anymore, only to signify something to do with her. It was *her* card now, and it wasn't a good one. The card usually referenced danger, darkness, or deception. He wanted to think that it was warning *him* about *her*, but ... well, he knew better.

There was a reason it kept popping up, over and over, like it was obsessed with her.

It was trying to warn her. Trying to get to her.

He did another sweep of the gathered students before glancing back to Oscar and Moses. Kilian was also watching them, a small smile on his lips.

Theodore, Elijah, and Gabriel were taking up the other chairs around the fire pit, collectively suffering through the ministrations of their pretend girlfriends. Or at least Theodore was. Elijah and Gabriel just flat-out ignored theirs. At least Elijah was letting Ellis sit on the arm of his chair. James had tried to sit the same way on Gabriel's chair, but he had abruptly slammed his cup down on it to stop her. Now she was perched beside Ellis, their heads bent together as Elijah scowled at their backs and Gabriel scowled at their fronts.

Elijah and Gabriel practically existed as a single atom. Coming between them was a bad idea, physically or otherwise. Cian gave it ten minutes before one of them lost their patience. Probably Gabriel.

Niko stumbled out of the dorm with a girl tucked beneath his arm. One of the popular fifth-year Betas. A contender for the Icon crown. Cian watched them with an eyebrow quirked.

"She is definitely not Asian," Kilian commented, having traced his stare.

Cian smirked. "Maybe he's working his way up to it."

"Up to what?" Theodore asked, latching onto their conversation with a desperate look on his face. Wallis was starting to get a little handsy, and he didn't have Gabriel's innate ability to be rude as fuck.

"Who do you think?" Elijah muttered, staring up at the sky with a bored look.

"Now it's a who?" Theodore strained away from Wallis and craned his neck to try and find who they were talking about. "Niko?" He frowned, standing and accidentally toppling Wallis onto her ass. "Who's that? Who's he working up to ...?" He squinted, no doubt cataloguing the small blonde girl Niko had chosen. "That's not fucking funny." He levelled a glare at Cian before helping Wallis up, but he didn't reclaim his seat. He scrubbed the back of his neck, glancing around for an escape.

"Let's go find better drinks," Elijah muttered, coming to his rescue.

Gabriel stood, and the three of them escaped into the dorm. Oscar and Moses tracked them with bored eyes, assessing whether they were giving up on the party or not.

Cian pulled out his phone, losing patience, but as he hovered over her name, he realised he had nothing to say.

It's my birthday. Get your ass over here.

They weren't even friends.

He didn't even want her company.

He stood with a disgusted sound, shoving his phone away again. "Bathroom," he muttered to Kilian, stalking off toward the dorm.

ISOBEL CHECKED HERSELF IN THE MIRROR AGAIN, RUNNING her hands over the pale blue bodice of the dress Kilian had gifted her. Eve had helped her stitch it up, and she had miraculously cleaned away the bloodstains from Crowe's assault in the chapel.

"I'm so glad this was in my sewing box this week instead of with your other clothes," Eve commented, playing with the hem of the short skirt. "Kilian bought this, which means Kilian touched this, which means it must be protected and preserved at all costs."

Isobel laughed, but the trepidation still settled in her stomach. It was Sunday. Her last chance to "make something happen," and her only chance to fulfil the favour Sato had demanded of her.

"Come on." Eve tugged her hand, trying to drag her out of the bathroom—not for the first time that night. "We're going to miss the party at this point."

"Please just go ahead of me," Isobel begged. "I haven't finished my hair."

"Are you sure?" Eve pouted, glancing at the door. Isobel had already delayed her.

"Yes! Go!" Isobel flashed her a smile, pushing her to the doorway before turning back to the mirror.

She reached for the curling iron just so that she would have something to do, but her vision grew blurry before she could touch it, and a sudden flash of light burned into her retinas.

"Crap," she muttered, a second before the bathroom blinked out of existence and she found herself sandwiched between two hard surfaces.

The kitchen island on the rooftop of Dorm A was pressing into her ribcage, while something else wedged into her spine. Theodore, Reed, and Spade were on the other side of the island, staring at her like they thought they were hallucinating. Theodore glanced into his cup and then back up at her, his mouth opening and closing.

She heard a rumbling sound behind her, and two jean-clad thighs suddenly pressed into her sides, trapping her. Someone was sitting on a kitchen stool right behind her, and judging by the dusky golden skin peeking out through a tear in his jeans, it was Ashford.

"Sorry!" she squeaked, eyes wide on Theodore. She worked to lower her voice, wary of the camera facing the rest of the rooftop despite the party noise below. "I keep teleporting here because it's where I died."

She felt Ashford's touch against her shoulder

blades, shifting her hair over to one side of her neck. He leaned forward, squeezing her harder with his thighs, the heat of his chest suddenly scorching along her spine.

"This is one way to wish me happy birthday." He was using that teasing voice he sometimes goaded her with. The tone that implied she was too innocent to understand that he was flirting with her.

"Your birthday was almost two weeks ago," she shot back, pretending to be immune to him even though she had gone cold and stiff with shock, and he could definitely feel it. "And I already gave you a present."

"You gave me a heart attack," he countered. "Do you often expose people to their phobias and call it a gift? Who the hell taught you how to be a Sigma? You're doing it *so* wrong."

He was obviously still teasing her, but that hit a little too close to home, and she flinched.

Theodore rounded the counter and inserted his hands under her arms. He lifted her clear of Ashford, setting her gently on her feet.

"Can you loop the cameras?" he asked over her shoulder, as his hand slid down to hers, his fingers pushing between hers before clasping her tightly and using the hold to pull her against his side.

"Already did," Reed answered. "You've got about a minute."

"Good." Theodore pulled her toward the stairs. "We just need to get you out the front of the dorm, and you can tell the officials you teleported to the trail again. It's lucky you died in one of the blind spots. Makes this easy."

"Yeah," she drawled. "Super lucky."

He turned as he reached the front door, pushing it open as he smirked at her. "You're not going to come and hang out with me, are you?"

"I might," she hedged, slipping past him to get outside. His eyes seemed to darken as she brushed against his chest, but the front of the dorm wasn't well lit, so it was hard to tell. "See you later."

He only hummed in response, the deep sound chasing her as she hurried toward the lake. She had probably beaten Eve to the party, so she pushed through the students that were laughing, jumping, and dancing as she tried to find Wallis. Someone had set up speakers around the corners of the lake, the music bouncing across the water, amplified so loudly it actually hurt her ears. There were also a few tables with ice-filled wooden buckets lining the surface, bottles nestled inside, with mountains of paper cups a jostle away from toppling onto the ground. The tables were tucked up against the outside of Dorm A, right by the window looking into the living room—though heavy, dark curtains had been pulled across the glass. It was just out of sight of the cameras, so there would be no footage of what people poured into their cups.

When she tumbled out of the fray of people that she belatedly realised were all crowded into a designated dance area ringed by sparkling red lanterns, she found that there was a piece of paper in her hand. Frowning, she glanced back to the tightly pressed mesh of people, but nobody was staring back at her. She unfolded the note, brow furrowing.

You have the blood. You have the guts. But do you have any skin in the game? Need some help with that?

"Hey!" she shouted over the music, causing a few people to glance over. She waved the note above her head. "Who slipped me this?"

They might as well have looked straight through her, and nobody answered. She folded the note up with a scowl, slipping it into the pocket of her dress as she moved toward a section of the lake that didn't seem as busy ... though it quickly became apparent why.

"You really thought that was going to get their attention?" Moses scoffed, shaking his head at her. He and Sato were both seated on a picnic table facing out over Alpha Hill—though they had been turned toward the dance area. Behind them, she could see Kilian heading their way. There were a gaggle of first years following him with their phones clutched to their chests like they wanted to take pictures with him. Theodore met Kilian halfway, and they stopped to talk to each other, both of them glancing over at Moses and Sato with frowns on their faces, before including her in their assessment. Kilian jerked his head, probably telling her to get away from the table.

She glanced away, back to the broody Alphas before her.

"What does it say, little rabbit?" Sato tilted his chin toward her pocket. The question was almost friendly.

"Some nonsense." She folded her arms. "Anyway, I'm here. How do you want me to get Wallis' phone?"

Sato smirked. "You're here." He shared a look with Moses, who rolled his eyes.

"She's here," Moses agreed.

"Do you want a reward?" Sato purred. "I've got one in my pants for you."

"Okay, *that's* disgusting." Moses suddenly turned on Sato. "The fuck is wrong with you? She's basically my sister-in-law at this point."

Sato tossed his head back and laughed, drawing far more looks than Isobel's shout had. He looked kind of ... beautiful. Like a demon led into the light and offered wings for a single flight. Until he stopped, and the fantasy crashed down to the ground. He pulled a carrot out of his pocket, waving it at her.

"If you want your reward, you have to do the task," he said silkily.

Why the heck did he have a carrot in his pocket?

She turned her back on them, her eyes darting around for somewhere to escape to before landing on the drinks table. She hurried over to it, pouring some juice into a cup just for something to do. Theodore and Kilian seemed to relax now that she wasn't talking to Moses and Sato. They were slowly wandering over to a circle of wooden beach chairs set up around the fire pit. Wallis, Ellis, and James were there, talking to the same group of first years that had been trailing Kilian. They were taking photos with the Beta girls, but Ellis scattered them before Kilian and Theodore stepped back into the circle.

Isobel tightened her grip on the plastic cup, her attention wandering back to Sato. He was regarding her coolly, giving her his full attention like the only reason he decided to come down to the party and pretend to be normal was to watch her squirm through the task he had demanded of her. Moses was watching, too, but he didn't look half as pleased. He looked ... exhausted, actually. She frowned, shoving away the sense of empathy that crept up on her. He stared back, bored, an eyebrow cocked.

She couldn't believe he was her first kiss.

What the actual hell.

A small, hard smile twitched over Sato's lips, like he could read her mind, and she quickly spun around, groping blindly for one of the bottles of alcohol. Whatever it was, she doused her juice in it before steeling her spine and heading over toward Wallis.

"Puppy." Spade appeared at her side, Reed hemming her in on the other side.

She didn't pause, and they kept pace with her.

"Yes?" she finally sighed out when he didn't say anything else.

"What is Oscar making you do?"

"What's it to you?" she grumbled, annoyed they were so perceptive.

"Either it's good enough to drag them down here into the middle of a party, or *you're* good enough. We'd like to know which."

"It's me." She gritted her teeth, flashing him a tight smile. "Do you believe me?"

He looked amused.

"I guess you don't need our help, then," Reed said casually.

She slowed her pace, and they slowed with her.

"You'd help?" she asked, her tone thick with suspicion.

He shrugged, his oversized shirt shifting. Even now, they were still dressed like they were on their way to dance practice. "Never know until you ask."

"I have to get Wallis' phone." She stopped walking completely, still far enough away that the group of people around the fire pit wouldn't be able to hear her.

"And what will you be doing with it?" Spade asked.

"Giving it to Sato."

"For what purpose?" Reed this time.

"I don't know. I'm sure if you stand somewhere in his vicinity, you'll figure out just by looking at his face or whatever it is you two do to know everything all the time."

"It's called perception," Spade said dismissively. "So that's it?"

"No. After Sato is done with it, I have to return it."

"And what are you willing to do in return for our help, hmm?" Reed stepped in front of her, blocking her view of the fire pit, his cold eyes switching between hers in an examination of some kind. "Will you trade a favour to Sato for a favour to us?"

A special Reed test, this time. She should *obviously* switch out Sato for them. People weren't mortally terrified of them. People didn't warn her about them. Their own *friends* didn't warn her about them. The only problem was ... *what if that wasn't the right answer?*

"No thanks."

ELIJAH STEPPED OUT OF HER WAY, NOTCHING HIS SHOULDER against Gabriel's as the Sigma walked away from them, a little flounce in her step.

"Good puppy," Gabriel muttered, his eyes boring into the back of her head.

Elijah smirked. "For now. We have time to corrupt her."

"Not that we're interested in that," Gabriel said tonelessly, still watching her.

"Not at all," Elijah agreed.

They both moved to catch up, reclaiming their previous seats. Ellis must have fished a set of balls out of the lake because she somehow thought it would be a brilliant idea to perch on his lap. She took one of the cups of beer he had set down by the leg of his chair, knocking it against his.

"Cheers, babe!" She flicked her eyes over his shoulder like she was reminding him that other students were close enough to hear them.

"That's not for you." He reclaimed the beer before

she could put her lips on it, returning it to the base of his chair.

But he didn't kick her off his lap. There were too many people for that. He heard a quiet sound beside him and turned in time to see James perch on Gabriel's knee. The two Beta girls must have come up with their plan together.

Gabriel's jaw flexed, his eyes narrowing as he lifted his arms away from the chair. As a dancer, he had trained himself to withstand physical touch, but only when he expected it. When it came as a surprise, it was a major trigger for him. Elijah calculated that he had probably fifteen seconds to remedy the situation before Gabriel had a meltdown on camera.

"Spin the bottle," he announced, standing and righting Ellis before she fell flat on her face. He grabbed James' arm, hauling her upright and pulling her a few feet away from Gabriel. "Everyone find your own ... seats." He shook his head as the circle filled up with girls faster than he could even finish the sentence.

"It has to be boy-girl," one of them complained,   . edging back to make the circle larger.

Gabriel stood, pushing his chair back. He brushed off his clothes like he was trying to shake invisible dust away and then shoved his hands into his pockets.

Probably surreptitiously tapping against his leg in a comforting pattern through his pocket. Elijah also moved his chair back, notching it up against Spade's before tipping his beer to his lips, draining it quickly. He picked up an empty soda bottle and tossed it to Kilian, who positioned it on the side of the fire pit, and then he hunted down the Sigma. She was trying to escape the circle while stealing glances at Wallis. He took her by the shoulders, steering her to his chair.

She went willingly enough, casting him only a little bit of side-eye. Gabriel was right about the puppy thing. He turned her, and she let him. His hands crept around her hips. She let him do that, too, though her mouth pinched into a firm line. He hoisted her up, sitting her on the arms of his and Gabriel's chairs before falling back into his seat. Gabriel did the same, folding his arms tightly across his chest and edging toward Carter like she could shield him from the touch of everyone else.

He definitely didn't realise he was doing it, or he would have probably stormed off to join Oscar and Moses ... except that was no longer an option, as Moses was dragging a fold-up chair over to their circle. Students edged away, some of their laughter dying off. The circle was almost completely silent by the time Oscar joined.

"What are we playing?" Oscar drawled, and several people flinched at his gravelly voice.

And then Niko and Ashford appeared, carrying fold-up chairs of their own. More students scattered, making room for them, though several girls immediately crowded back in as soon as they were seated.

"Anyone else want a seat?" Theodore spoke up, looking considerably more upbeat now that he wasn't forced to house Wallis on his lap.

Only the Alphas had actual chairs. Everyone else was sitting on the ground, except Carter. She was perched between him and Gabriel like she was their little Sigma princess. The notion was almost absurd enough to make him laugh out loud.

"No?" Theodore glanced around, pretending to be oblivious to the way all the girls were going absolutely mental over his sweet, thoughtful expression.

What a tosser.

Theodore caught Elijah's eye, saw the annoyance there, and winked, before stepping forward to spin the bottle.

9

HYPOCRITE

ISOBEL FELT WEIRD.

Not weird from the alcohol or from the game that was about to unfold in front of her. Not weird because all the Alphas were glaring at Sato like he was about to do something evil. Not weird because she had just spotted Bellamy sitting beside Wallis, laughing casually with the girl on his other side.

She felt *really* weird.

The hair on the back of her neck stood on end, and her fingers tingled. Her skin was extra sensitive. Even the slight breeze that managed to permeate the tight throng of students was like sandpaper against her skin.

Theodore touched the bottle, winking at Reed as he spun it, and she jumped up to stop him because she *knew*. She *knew* it was going to land on her. Ashford stood with her, snatching up the bottle before it could stop spinning.

"It should be ladies first," he scolded, tossing the bottle in his hands a few times. "So, who wants it?"

James jumped up, rushing over to seize the opportunity.

Isobel sat back down shakily, her eyes hypnotised by the spinning bottle. And then the feeling came again, stronger this time, except she had no idea what it was supposed to mean.

Sato started laughing before the bottle stopped, like he, too, was being swamped with sudden feelings of dreadful premonition ... but he was delighted by them.

The bottle landed on Theodore.

Moses chuckled.

The rest of the students all gasped, holding their breath for a reaction from Theodore ... who was glaring at Sato.

Because *that* made sense.

James looked a little too pleased as she approached Theodore, considering she was supposed to be pretending to be Spade's girlfriend. She planted her hands on the arms of his chair, bending down like she was posing for a photo as she tried to plant her lips on his. He turned his head at the last second, letting her kiss his cheek before he grabbed her arms and gently set her backwards. He waved off the disappointed sounds of the onlookers as he spun the bottle again.

"That's my friend's girlfriend, people." He laughed, standing by and waiting for the bottle to stop.

Isobel's hands were twisted so hard in her lap her nails were starting to dig in. She had that *feeling* again, but this time she ignored it. She wasn't like Ashford. She was just letting her anxiety get the better of her. She worked on extracting her nails from her skin and was so focussed on persuading herself to ignore the feeling that she almost missed it when the bottle stopped.

On her.

Just like she thought it would—no, *knew* it would.

Theodore turned to her, dramatically surprised, sharing looks with all the gasping students who were whipping out their phones. He was playing to the crowd. Being the perfect Icon-in-training.

"Now *that* one has a mate." He tutted, wagging his finger at some of the girls giggling behind their phones. "So *obviously* ... I can't let you all watch this."

Cue the shocked laughter. The cheers. The mad rush of whispering. Theodore disappeared from the circle and came back with a beach umbrella that must have been stuck into one of the picnic tables. The laughter and cheering increased in volume, and everyone was in such a frenzy that they didn't even notice several of the Alphas jumping to their feet, like they were about to interfere—all while still shooting glares at Sato, which still made about as much sense as it had a minute ago.

Theodore stopped before her, reaching around her to set the stem of the umbrella against the armrests behind her, and then he slowly pulled the canopy down, enclosing them while the students howled and jostled, trying to get close enough to see something.

And then suddenly it was just him.

Theodore Kane.

Perfect and stormy-eyed. Frowning and breathing heavily, like the umbrella had weighed a tonne. His smell enveloped her, his heat creeping over her skin, his hair brushing her forehead. She couldn't draw in air. Couldn't breathe. Couldn't admit in a million years that she would have traded a million moments for just this one. She just *couldn't*. She had a mate.

A mate who she belonged to.

Like a fucking goat.

She swayed forward, kissing him suddenly, her lips touching lightly to his. She only intended it to be a quick brush, a secret little *fuck you* to what had become of her future, but as soon as she began to retreat, he chased her. He kissed her hard enough to halt her movement, both of them freezing for a second, his breath a hard rasp against her lips as he released her. He seemed to be in shock, his expression shattered, his eyes burning. His amenable social mask had completely collapsed, his gaze shuttering as defeat painted his features and he took her lips again. The guilt passing insistently from his chest to hers barely even permeated her mind, which seemed to be completely drugged by the vicious kiss. It wasn't soft and sweet, or gentle and slow. He kissed her fast and hard ... like a part of his brain was screaming at him to stop and his body was doubling down on the decision to fuck his brain. It was like he was trying to stamp himself against her mouth so that she would taste him for the rest of the night. So that she would still feel his lips when she closed her eyes to go to sleep. So that she might never forget as long as she fucking lived.

A touch landed over her thigh, firm and insistent, but it didn't belong to Theodore, who still held the umbrella stand behind her back. It was enough to ease her back, eyes wide.

Theodore sucked in air on a surprised breath, gaining some space himself, his eyes heavy as he stared at her mouth. He ran his tongue between his lips, nostrils flaring, eyes glittering so dark they were almost black, his pupils blown out.

The pale gold hand on her leg was familiar. Long, graceful fingers that she had seen on the piano keys.

Reed.

He squeezed her gently, and she eased back another inch. Theodore looked … relieved. And pissed. But she wasn't sure who he was so angry at. He lifted up suddenly, opening the umbrella, and the touch disappeared from her leg in the blink of an eye.

Theodore slid back into easy showmanship like nothing at all had happened, taking the umbrella back to his seat "just in case" and wiggling his brows at James, like he was inviting her to give him another shot.

Slowly, the eyes turned back to Isobel, waiting.

She swallowed, slipping off her perch and approaching the bottle, trying to hide the tremble in her legs and hands. *It was so quiet.* Nobody really believed that Theodore had kissed her or *would* kiss her. You didn't mess with mates. Some of the students were looking warily at the bottle, like they couldn't decide if they wanted it to land on them or not. On one hand, it would be a guaranteed highlight if she actually kissed someone. On the other hand, if her mate turned up any time soon, whoever had decided to disrespect her bond would probably be completely trashed online—Isobel right alongside them.

She sucked in a breath, positioning the bottle in the hopes that it landed somewhere near Wallis, even though a darkly amused Sato was on one side and a smirking Bellamy was on the other. But the position felt off. She adjusted it again, and then again, until the ache in her chest eased.

"Just spin it, Sigma!" someone shouted. "Stop teasing!"

She flicked it into a spin, stepping back, and then back further. The ache didn't spring back up inside her chest, but another feeling took its place, sinking into the pit of her stomach. It was almost like someone had cast a curse over them all, aiming for maximum impact whenever anyone stepped forward to spin the bottle.

The tip wavered, resting just before Wallis.

Stopping at Sato.

His dark eyes narrowed, all traces of amusement suddenly wiped from his expression. She waited, hoping he would just storm off and then she could kiss Wallis instead, while surreptitiously stealing her phone.

But Sato only shifted his hips forward, getting more comfortable in his chair. "Come on then, rabbit."

That word. *Rabbit*. It echoed around them, passed from mouth to mouth like a rebounding whisper against narrow walls, tinged by confusion and astonishment. It was like he had known all along this would happen, like he had singlehandedly orchestrated this exact situation when he told her to steal Wallis' phone ... but that was completely impossible.

Unless he was working with Ashford.

She glanced at the dusky-skinned Alpha, only to find him agitatedly twisting his tangled hair into a bun, his mouth etched into a deeply disturbed frown.

Okay, no help from him, then.

She walked over to Sato with that sinking feeling in her stomach getting even heavier. His legs were spread enough for her to step between them, but she didn't. She stopped at his knees. Gulping.

His fingers lifted from where they had been resting against his thigh, tangling with the hem of her dress. He didn't exactly tug, just rubbed the material between his thumb and forefinger, his influence steadily wrapping around her. It was some combination of the heavy, dark look in his eye and the cloying, dangerous scent that clogged her throat. It didn't scream of danger; it screamed at her to step closer. It wasn't until she shifted between his knees that the saccharine thickness in her throat began to burn, but it didn't seem to be enough for him. He tugged lightly on her dress until her legs hit the edge of his seat, and then he released her, his hand falling back to his thigh. He still hadn't made any movement to lean forward or sit up properly, and it didn't look like he was going to. She pulled in a deep breath, closing her eyes for a moment to steel herself.

"I'd be terrified too," someone whispered, close enough for Isobel to hear them.

She opened her eyes again. He was too freaking far away, relaxing back into the chair. She would have to copy the pose James had used on Theodore. That thought made her sick, and she didn't particularly want to examine why. But the other option was to sit on Sato's lap, and that made her sick with fear.

Just get it over with, a voice inside her screamed.

So she turned and perched on his thigh.

"No way did she just do that," someone exclaimed, not even trying to be quiet.

"Is she insane?"

"Is she actually going to kiss him?"

"Is he actually going to *let* her?"

"It's not like anyone is going to punish him for it. It's *Sato*."

That half-smile twitched across Sato's lips before disappearing again, and he cocked a brow at her.

"That's right," he spoke in his normal, gravelly tone, apparently uncaring of who overheard him. "Don't try faking me out, Sigma. I'm the last person to care about your mate."

Wallis was just out of reach, but thankfully, she had pulled her phone up and was already snapping pictures, so it was easy for Isobel to reach over and pinch it between her fingers.

"That's too close," Isobel said. "Are you trying to get a photo or get inside our mouths?"

Wallis only rolled her eyes, looking a little annoyed as she folded her arms across her chest. Thankfully, she didn't demand her phone back just yet.

"You wish," Wallis muttered beneath her breath.

Isobel shifted closer to Sato, ignoring the look in his eyes and the firmness of his body, because as relaxed as he *looked*, he was actually coiled like a snake, every muscle tensed, making his whole body as hard as a rock. She planted her hand on his shoulder and suddenly shifted her weight, drawing her knees to the chair either side of his thighs.

His other brow jumped up, his cocky expression giving way to veiled surprise.

"Rock-paper-scissors?" she suggested, casually

dropping the phone onto his lap. "If I win, you back out of the game. If you win, I'll back out of the game."

His arm wound around her back, lifting her and dragging her closer, his other hand transferring the phone from his lap to his pocket, using her body as a shield to hide what he was doing. The dress Kilian had bought her was already short, the material thin, ruffled like silk, so when he dragged her forward, the skirt rode up her thighs.

And then Niko surprised her, his voice ringing clearly across the circle. "It's just a game, Carter. Back out anytime you want."

"Have you been paying attention?" Sato asked, his eyes drilling into hers. "The Sigma doesn't back out."

"Maybe she should," Niko returned calmly. "Maybe nobody taught her how to."

Isobel blinked like she had been dragged out of a sudden haze; the adrenaline of the competition Sato had created between them dissolving as Niko successfully encouraged a very different memory to the front of her brain.

Crowe.

She flinched, her body tightening, but Sato acted before she could withdraw. He stood, planting her on her feet, and then grabbed her wrist.

"It's going to storm," he announced, not even

glancing up at the sky. "Better head home, kiddos." He squeezed her wrist once and then released it, his eyes settling on her briefly. "Go thank your knight in shining armour, Carter."

He stalked off, and she turned her eyes to the sky, frowning. *How did he know?* She didn't get a chance to thank Niko, because he was already striding after Sato. Ashford followed, looking pissed as all hell. Reed and Spade were having a silent conversation as they also followed, their bodies tense. Theodore was rubbing his hands over his face, muttering something about the storm to the people trying to get his attention. Kilian was sitting in his seat, frowning after Sato, but he didn't get up.

Isobel spotted Eve trying to make her way through the crowd and started toward her, but someone stepped into her path.

"Honestly." Bellamy looked impressed. "How do you do it?"

"Honestly?" She tried to side-step him. "Don't talk to me."

He reached for her arm, and she violently pulled it away, taking several steps back.

He sighed, shaking his head. "Look, whatever you think I did, I *didn't* do it."

"I think you drugged me."

"I didn't," he said immediately.

"I think you left me for ... what?" She narrowed her eyes on his face and then looked down at his chest, cracking open her wall just enough to taste any bad emotions that might have been waiting on the other side. What she felt surprised her. It wasn't guilt, or regret, or even nothing at all—to indicate he was pleased with what he had done. It was fear. *Fear that he would be caught*?

"I was drugged," she insisted.

"Not by *drugs*," he whispered back, before sucking in a breath and backing away from her like he had just said something he regretted. "Look, never mind. But I had nothing to do with it, okay?"

Eve popped up just as he pushed away, disappearing into a group of second-year Betas.

"Are we really breaking up the party just because Sato—" she started, before blinking up at the sky. Raindrops were falling, sudden and heavy.

"I guess so," Isobel answered the unfinished question. "But I have to ... finish something. See you back at the dorm!"

"Okay, find me later, though!" Eve hurried off as the wind picked up, scattering the students like leaves.

They must have all been a little on edge after the last storm ripped through the mountain behind Dorm

A. Wallis was making her way over, probably to ask for her phone back. Isobel quickly took off after Sato, hesitating outside the dorm before glancing over her shoulder and pushing inside.

Of course there was a professor standing on the other side.

"I meant to knock," she lied, stopping short before she collided with Easton.

He was frowning down at her, his scars made deeper by the shadows cloaking the room. *Why wouldn't they turn any lights on?* Probably so that partygoers wouldn't get the insane idea that they were welcome inside.

"You should go home," he suggested. "This storm is going to get worse."

She nodded, shifting nervously from foot to foot. If she claimed that she was running after Sato, he wouldn't believe her. People didn't run *toward* Sato. Easton's frown furrowed deeper, his annoyance battering against her chest. He stuck his hands into his pockets, his head tilting to the side.

"It isn't a good time." He sighed, like he didn't really want to deal with her. "The guys are ... going to be busy for a while."

"I'm free as a bird." Kilian's silky voice declared, his hands landing over her shoulders.

She glanced back to see that he, Theodore, and Wallis had just entered the dorm.

Kilian spun her around, and she knew they were about to ask for Wallis' phone so that they could send the other girl home, so she blurted the first thing that popped into her head.

"Let's keep the party going." *What the fuck was she doing?* "You want to keep the party going, right?" She turned to Wallis.

Theodore's eyes narrowed, a tinge of his frustration knocking against her chest. The poor guy had probably been manhandled all night and wanted to escape.

"Ah, sure." Wallis squinted at Isobel like she didn't understand what her game was. "I'll stop the other girls from leaving."

She slipped back out into the rain, and Isobel found herself stuck between Kilian, Easton, and Theodore. None of them looked particularly happy.

"I had no choice," she groaned.

Kilian's grip on her shoulders softened, and he eased his expression into a gentle smile. "Oscar isn't done playing yet?" he guessed.

She shook her head miserably.

Theodore's frown darkened, and his eyes flicked

up over her head, probably focussing on Easton. "Where is he?"

"Rooftop," Easton grunted. "Sort this shit out, before the storm gets worse. I mean it." He stalked off, disappearing into the room closest to the entryway a few seconds before Wallis, Ellis, and James poured back into the dorm, lowering their arms from the hair and make-up they had tried to save from the rain.

"Can we ..." Isobel started to hurriedly whisper to Kilian, who grabbed her hand and pulled her toward the staircase before she could even finish the question.

"We'll be on the rooftop!" he shot over his shoulder.

The others followed almost immediately, but Kilian pulled her fast enough that they still reached the rooftop with a few moments to spare.

Sato was sitting at the kitchen island going through Wallis' phone while the rest of the Alphas crowded around him, speaking lowly and furiously. The rain was pounding down hard, so she didn't catch anything they were saying. Before she could even warn Sato, the phone did a disappearing act, and the others reached the top of the stairs.

"We're continuing the party," Theodore announced. He didn't exactly sound thrilled. "Help me bring the drinks in."

He didn't issue the order to anyone in particular, but Niko and Ashford followed him back down the stairs while James and Ellis hovered around Wallis. They didn't look like they wanted to be there anymore, and they kept shooting their attention between each of the tense Alphas and the staircase. Isobel was at a complete loss. She wanted to make them feel more comfortable, but this wasn't her dorm. Thankfully, Reed got off his stool, wordlessly offering it up. Sato and Moses also got up, preferring to huddle in the corner of the kitchen, hoisting themselves to sit up on the counters. Sato stretched out a long leg, planting his boot on the edge of the kitchen island before digging into his pocket and fiddling with a phone in his lap. Due to his positioning, it was impossible to tell whose phone it was. Moses leaned over, pointing out a few things on the screen and muttering low in Sato's ear.

"What kind of game do you want to play?" Kilian asked, notching his chin onto the top of her head, his arms wrapping around the front of her chest, pulling her back against his hard body.

Wallis took Reed's vacated stool, eyeing Isobel and Kilian like a puzzle she didn't particularly understand, while Ellis and James just looked like they had a front-row seat to heaven, as though witnessing Kilian give *anyone* affection caused them ecstasy, but they only had a front-row seat; they weren't actually *in* heaven, and the frustration and bitterness behind the fascination was clear to see.

Isobel couldn't even blame them.

Kilian's bergamot and bark scent wrapped all the way around her, his thumbs brushing against her shoulders, his warm body lulling her somehow. She sank against him, and his hug tightened. She tried to distract herself by thinking of all the party games she had seen play out on the *Ironside Show* over the years.

"Clothesline," she blurted, naming the last game she remembered seeing, because it got a lot of attention on the website.

"Clothesline?" Ellis asked, looking confused.

"The game where you divide into two teams and stand in a line." Wallis craned her neck, looking around the kitchen for a suitable space as she explained. "Then the person at the front of the line takes off an item of clothing, puts it on the ground, and goes to the back of the line. You keep going until someone forfeits, and then the other team wins."

Isobel had gone stiff with regret, and Kilian was laughing softly against the top of her head, but she forced the regret down. Her father wanted her to make shit happen, and nothing would guarantee her a highlight like a bunch of Alphas removing their clothes.

Theodore passed her and Kilian with one of the wooden buckets of drinks from outside. "Well, we can't do girls versus boys," he noted, obviously having heard Wallis' explanation. "That would be a quick victory."

Niko and Ashford carried the other buckets, dumping them onto the table before they started pouring out drinks into the paper cups.

"Not much room up here, though." Isobel spoke to the ground. She was terrible at being devious. "We should go downstairs." *Where there are cameras.*

"Oh, should we?" Kilian chuckled.

Wallis, Ellis, and James all looked up with bright, excited eyes. Despite being labelled as the official girlfriends of three of the Alphas, they still hadn't been given much screen time. Maybe the officials knew more than they let on. That was a terrifying thought.

"Let's go, then." Theodore had two cups, and he lifted one of them to Isobel as he passed, as though to let her know it was hers.

Kilian released her to pour himself a drink, and she hung back as everyone else walked downstairs, blowing out a tense breath when it was just her, Sato, and Moses left in the kitchen.

They didn't even look up.

She walked over to them, moving between the counter and the island until she stood on the outside of Sato's lifted leg. "What are you doing with the phone?"

Moses jumped off the counter, staring her down. "Only what she deserves," he stated coldly.

"Just for breaking into Sato's room?" she asked, her brows flinching into a confused frown.

"Just?" Moses laughed darkly, and Sato dropped his leg—the only barrier between her and Moses.

Moses stalked forward, stopping an inch from her, his eyes darkening with anger. "What if the roles were reversed, Sigma? What if a guy had broken into *her* room? What if she had woken up with him on top of her? Groping her? Grinding on her? Trying to force her to fuck him?"

"You should report her." Isobel shrank back, regretting the questions already. She couldn't even look at Sato. "Or ..." She took another shaky step back. "I don't know ..." She suddenly wanted to throw up. Just because Sato was a strong, terrifying Alpha, it didn't make everyone's actions against him harmless. She *knew* that, but her fear of Sato had temporarily overridden her sense.

"Or what?" Moses stepped to the side, blocking her

view of Sato even though she hadn't been trying to look at him. "Have you tried reporting injustices here at Ironside, Sigma? Do you think they only ignore you? Could you possibly be that self-centred?"

"Fuck off," she shot back, earning a dark chuckle from behind Moses' back.

"What would you do?" Moses pressed, closing the distance between them again. "If it was Theodore she had assaulted. Tell me." *Alpha voice.*

She answered without thinking. "Ruin her." Theodore was precious.

Moses narrowed his eyes, the storm in them churning. "Prove it. Consider this my initiation."

Sato slid off the counter, appearing beside Moses. He held out Wallis' phone, his dark eyes unreadable.

"What did you do?" Isobel asked, staring at the phone instead of taking it.

Sato gripped the strap of the tiny handbag she had been wearing across her body, dragging her against him as he unzipped the bag and wedged the phone inside.

"I took control of her life." He spoke in a low, warning tone. "I could destroy her now ... but I think I'll let you do it instead. In your own way, of course."

"I'm not that kind of person." She folded her arms tightly.

"Bullshit," Sato growled.

"I'm a *Sigma*!" she shot back. "You're asking me to go against my genetic fucking make-up."

Moses smirked at her. "Yeah, you're a Sigma. You always do what you're told, don't you?"

She didn't answer.

"You never fight back?" Moses continued. "You're completely and utterly subservient? Why don't you kneel right now? Why aren't you curled up at our feet like a good little Sigma pet?"

Crack.

She wasn't sure what happened. Just that her hand stung, her mind was full of noise that sounded like rage, and Moses' lip was split, blood staining the teeth he flashed in a sudden, surprised smile.

Sato was laughing, a glittering light sparking to life in his eyes. Moses licked at the blood on his lip before crowding her against the counter.

"You're a fucking hypocrite, Carter," he seethed, low and raspy, but there was a change in his expression. It was the clearest she had ever seen the storm in his eyes. They flicked between her own eyes and then down to her mouth as he licked his lip again. It was like he was searching for more of whatever she had just done to him. Another taste of her violence. "*You* are the one who acts like Sigmas are weak and pathetic, not us. *We* think Sigmas are the strongest of us all and *we* know what's inside you." His hand was suddenly right in the middle of her chest, pressing up against her ribcage with his palm as he forced her to bend slightly over the island behind her. "Such pretty darkness and nowhere to wear it, right?"

"Your choice," Sato suggested mildly, leaving the rooftop. His voice lingered behind like a haunting echo.

"This is it," Moses added quietly, still pressing her in place. "Tonight is all you have. Embrace your darkness, or you're out before you even get in."

10
HARDLY PROFESSIONAL

SHE BARELY HAD A CHANCE TO ABSORB WHAT HAD HAPPENED before her phone started vibrating. She pulled it out to check the messages.

Unknown: I know you lied, Sigma.

Unknown: And I know what you lied about.

The next message was a screenshot of a picture, taken from the top of Alpha Hill, showing the time stamp of when the picture was taken. It was her and Ashford walking into the dorm after their confrontation on the library rooftop. She frowned, her fingers itching to respond, to demand who was messaging her, but then a video came through, and she clicked on it.

Whoever was taking the video was pressed up against the outside of Dorm A, the camera angled to the clear sky, capturing faint shouts from the rooftop above. The sounds of commotion continued, glass shattering and heavy things being tossed around. And still ... clear skies. The person behind the camera suddenly moved away from the dorm, the ground jolting back and forth as they ran away, but then they stopped and pulled the view back up, focussing on the dorm again. On the window into the lounge, specifically, where they must have spotted movement.

Kilian was there, a limp body in his arms. Petite, pale limbs. Tousled blonde hair. It was her. He cradled her close to his chest, her face resting in the crook of his neck, and then he lowered her to the couch set against the window. The other Alphas were there too. Moses, Ashford, Sato, Reed, Spade ... even West. They were all gathering in the room. The camera switched up to the rooftop, too far away to hear the commotion any longer, but long enough to show the clear sky.

Isobel's breath caught in her throat as she leaned against the counter, gripping her phone even harder. The video dragged on with no real focus except for the faint breathing of whoever was filming, until Easton suddenly appeared at the window. He was too far away to see for certain, but it looked like he was covered in smudges of blood. He raised his hand to the glass and seemed to have his head tilted up to the sky.

The camera also tilted back up to the sky, watching as dark clouds gathered, before falling back to Easton. The sudden sound of thunder rumbled through the phone speakers, and then the video ended.

Her heart was beating fast enough to make her dizzy, but another screenshot was already coming through. It was a picture of her leaving Dorm A in pristine, freshly washed clothes before she climbed the fire trail to where she had pretended to die. Because it was a screenshot, she could see the time and date stamp at the top.

Unknown: One of the Alphas has an illegal ability, and you lied to protect them. But how far are you willing to go?

Unknown: Tell them anything about these messages and I'll release everything. This is between you and me. Our own private game.

The sender was right. She *had* lied to protect an Alpha with an illegal ability, but they were wrong about which one. It turned out Moses and Theodore weren't the only ones. A sudden crack of lightning fissured across the rooftop, making her jump and scurry toward the stairs, her heartbeat pounding somewhere in the back of her throat.

Had Easton created this storm too? And why?

It was Sato who had ended their game, claiming there would be a storm. And then he had stalked inside … where Easton was standing right in the entryway.

And *then* the rain started.

She made her way to the common room on shaky legs, her phone burning a hole in her pocket.

"Finally," James grumbled, giving her a bit of side-eye. "They look like they want to kick us out."

"You're on my team, baby." Kilian waved her over, and even with the panic and trepidation tripping through her system, she still wanted to laugh at the two teams that had formed.

Sato, Moses, Ashford, Spade, Reed, and Niko were gathered on one side of the room, drinking and looking generally disinterested while Theodore, Kilian, and the three girls were on the other side, looking like their patience was wearing down to nothing. Theodore wedged a cup into her hand as she joined them.

"We can't lose," he told her. "It's up to you, me, and him." He jerked his chin at Kilian.

"What about us?" Wallis asked, sounding a bit miffed, though she still kept her tone within the appropriate, Alpha-worship range.

"You're barely wearing anything," Theodore commented, tipping his beer to his lips as his eyes scanned the other side of the room.

"I'm wearing less," Isobel pointed out, playing with the hem of her dress. The other girls had on skirts and tops.

"You have something else," Kilian whispered in her ear, when Theodore pretended he hadn't heard her.

She turned slightly, giving him an inquisitive look over her shoulder.

"Trust me." His lips quirked. "They'll stop the game before you do."

"You first," Theodore grumbled at Moses, who headed the other line forming before he cut a quick look to her and Kilian. "Since you have the advantage."

The "advantage" was probably the extra layers of clothing the guys seemed to be wearing.

Moses smirked, kicking off a shoe and picking it up to take with him to the back of the line, where he placed it on the ground. Theodore did the same thing, and the rest of them followed. One shoe, and then the other, the "clothesline" growing longer and longer. When the guys moved onto their socks, Isobel found herself at a disadvantage. She was the only one who was wearing sandals. She slipped the hair tie from her hair, trying not to look like she was a thousand miles away. If she wasted this highlight opportunity, her father would kill her. She decided to tease out her hair on her way to the back of the line, blowing a kiss to a glowering Moses.

The Alphas were *insanely* competitive.

She wanted to ignore the messages she had received, but she couldn't, so she tried to quietly weigh her options as they played, the boys growing more boisterous with every passing minute, throwing taunts and jibes at each other. Sato pulled out the carrot at one point, biting off the end before tossing it to the ground. And then clothes really began to come off, and she started to feel the buzz of the alcohol. Theodore was first, flashing his broad, strong back as he pulled his shirt over his head.

"Don't be intimidated," he taunted Moses. "There always has to be a bigger twin."

Moses looked like he couldn't roll his eyes any harder if he tried. He tore his shirt off, revealing a torso as perfectly muscled as Theodore's but littered with scars. Isobel took one of her earrings off, earning a laugh from Kilian and a few narrow-eyed looks from the other line. Reed removed the reading glasses that had been tucked into his pocket, Kilian removed his shirt, and Wallis skipped the headband, necklace, or earrings she could have taken off, whipping away her shirt instead. She walked confidently to the back of the line, brushing her hand against Theodore's chest as she passed, her purple satin bra glinting obnoxiously.

Isobel fought the rush of acid that spilled onto her tongue, swallowing it down with another large gulp of whatever drink Theodore had made for her. It tasted like whiskey, so maybe she shouldn't have been drinking it so fast. She admired girls who were as confident as Wallis, but something about Wallis touching Theodore didn't sit right. Not when Moses had forced Isobel to think about the other girl breaking into Theodore's room and molesting him. Not when she thought about the fact that Wallis *had* done exactly that to Sato.

Spade's shirt came off next, and he folded it neatly on his way to the back of the line, looking like the whole game was a huge inconvenience to him for the simple fact that he had to place his clothes on the floor. Isobel decided to help him out—probably because she was tipsy—as he stared distastefully at the next spot in the line of items. She picked up Theodore's shirt, dropping it into the other line. Spade immediately placed his shirt on top of Theodore's but then stopped before her, holding his hand out.

"First rule of playing with Alphas," he said softly. "Kindness will get you killed. No cheating, puppy."

She frowned at his hand. "What do you want?"

Instead of answering, he tugged at the strap of her handbag, pulling it over her head. He placed it in the line where Theodore's shirt had been and took his place behind Reed, who was staring at Spade's hand like he expected it to burst into fire from touching her.

She blew out an annoyed breath, glaring at Spade as the line moved on. James and Ellis both decided to follow Wallis' lead, taking their shirts off, and Isobel found herself looking to the guys for a reaction. Theodore, Moses, and Kilian didn't seem to be watching, almost like they were being gentlemanly—though it was hard to think of Moses as gentlemanly. Reed and Spade were just straight up disinterested. Ashford and Niko didn't turn away, but there wasn't any interest in their eyes. Sato stared at the fallen clothing like the whole game disgusted him, and it made her curious as to why he was even there.

She found herself forgetting the phone that had been burning a hole in her pocket the whole time as she realised she was standing between Kilian and Theodore, both shirtless, both edging a little closer to her to move away from the girls either side of them. The heat of their bodies, the soft roll of their power, the combination of their scents mixing together, the whiskey on her tongue ... it was a sensual ocean she could drown in if she didn't actively keep her head above it all. Theodore's sweet amber was the perfect earthy companion to Kilian's citrus and floral bergamot, both scents lighter than usual, more cloying, a perfume that thickened with every brush of their bare skin against her arms, chest, or back as she huddled between them.

When Sato practically tore his shirt off, a scowl firmly fixed to his lips, she found herself backing into Kilian, seeking comfort from the black gaze that tunnelled into her. Kilian's hands landed on her hips, and Sato's eyes flicked down, narrowing slightly before he dropped his shirt into the line.

"I'm here, baby." Kilian's voice was soft against her temple, his grip tightening somewhat as a shiver travelled through her body. He was trying to comfort her, but it was having the opposite effect, winding her up even tighter.

She was struggling to breathe evenly when Theodore's hands moved somewhere near his groin and the sound of a zipper speared the room. He chuckled, his arm jerked, and then he turned around, flashing a torn-off button as he held his pants together with his other hand. He was smirking in a victorious way, but when her eyes flicked down his corded forearm to where he was holding the top of his pants in his fist before darting back up again, the amusement seemed to have fled. His eyes flashed and his chest expanded on a deep breath before he forced the smile back into place.

"Would your team stop fucking cheating?" Moses growled, glaring at Theodore's back as he slipped off a dark metal ring and stalked toward the back of the Line.

Isobel stepped forward, glancing toward Reed, who had taken Moses' place. He was assessing her quietly, reading her face like he already knew that she had nothing but her dress left to take off. She played with the hem, chewing on her lip. She could feel so many eyes, and a quick sweep of the line showed that they were all watching and waiting, their attention heavy, like this was another test. But they weren't just watching her; they were watching Reed, like they expected him to forfeit then and there. Theodore and Kilian were actually glaring at him. Niko didn't look happy either.

Her attention returned to Reed, whose lips twitched in amusement. He cocked a brow, almost like an actual question.

Do I look like I'm about to forfeit?

"All at once, puppy." Spade's words drew her attention and made Reed's smile almost twitch into full effect.

She stopped playing with the hem of her dress and pushed her fingers beneath it, finding the waistband of her panties. She rolled them down her legs and balled them into a fist. She walked to Spade, giving him plenty of time to stop her as she reached for his pocket.

"First rule of playing with Sigmas," she muttered, pushing her panties into his pocket. "Never underestimate your opponent." She was being petty. She knew how particular he was. How much he was triggered by hygiene. He was probably having an actual aneurysm knowing what was in his pocket as she withdrew her hand.

James choked on an astounded laugh. Ellis looked mildly impressed. Wallis was staring at Isobel like she had grown a whole other head. And the others ...

Something had shifted. An insidious energy was leaking into the room like a slow fog, raising the hairs on her arms. Their faces were so blank—even Spade's. It was impossible to tell where it was coming from, but it froze her to the spot. The other girls picked up on it a little late, but they still realised at some point.

"Ah, do you have my phone?" Wallis stage whispered. "I think we should go."

Isobel pointed to her handbag on the floor. "In there."

Wallis edged toward it, but she wasn't moving fast enough, because Sato barked: "Leave. Now."

"Wow." Isobel forced a laugh from her throat as the other girls scrambled to escape the dorm after Wallis retrieved her phone. "You guys really hate losing, huh?"

She bent to retrieve her items from the floor, but Kilian caught her shoulder, shaking his head at her. He didn't say anything else, and she straightened, her frown bouncing between them.

"You've been drinking," Theodore explained, his voice rough. He shifted his attention to the glass wall, probably watching through the intermittent flashes of lightning as the other girls ran away. "You'll have to stay here tonight."

"I'm not *driving* back to the dorm," she groaned. "I can walk just fine." *And she still had to find a way to ruin Wallis' life while dealing with the messages on her phone.* "And I've got stuff to do."

"You've had one win tonight. Don't get greedy," Reed advised, his jaw tense.

"Stop patronising me," she growled, whirling on him.

"Then ..." He stepped up to her, glaring down at her. "Think it through, Sigma. This bond is something new, something we haven't seen before, right? So how do you know that completing it will work the same way?"

She frowned, trying to sort through her muddled mind to figure out what he was trying to say and why he was suddenly saying it now. The Anchor permanently marked the Tether to complete a mate-bond. But her mate still hadn't appeared, so that meant ... *she could also complete it without them?*

"For fuck's sake." She threw up her hands. "I'm a *little* drunk. I'm not going to get into an accident and scar myself permanently by *walking home*."

"A little drunk?" Kilian asked, quickly picking her up before she backed into a coffee table.

Light flashed through the room, and she met his eyes, her own widening.

"Uh-oh," she said, as the room started to slip away.

The cat-like yellow-green of Kilian's alarmed stare transformed into deep blue with uneven black splotches. A face full of scars. A hard mouth parting in shock. She was sprawled ungracefully onto Easton's lap, a call tone chirping from the laptop on his desk and a slew of curses tripping from his lips. He rolled his chair back and shoved her down, pushing forward just as the call tone stopped and a woman's voice filled the office.

"I thought you were going to call at nine?" She had a husky voice. Textured, pretty. Angry. "Why are you still in your office?"

"The boys are having a party." Easton's words were clipped.

Isobel was trapped beneath the desk, her whole body struck with shock and a heavy wave of dizziness. Maybe she *was* drunk. The alcohol seemed to have knocked her off course from her usual teleporting spot.

"The party broke up?" the woman asked. She sounded politely interested now, but there was an edge to her voice.

"Some of them came inside," Easton replied, sucking in a breath as Isobel tried to shift beneath the desk.

He rolled forward further, his hand landing on her head, his fingers tunnelled roughly into her hair, holding her in place against his thigh, the tension in his grip unmistakable.

Don't move.

She clutched his leg in shock, biting back a whimper. His leg was like stone, carved in hard lines of tight tension.

"Yes, that's what I'm referring to." The woman was a little impatient, now. "The girls left. Except Kane's little girlfriend. Sounds like she teleported to the fire trail again."

The woman was an official.

"Ah." That was Easton's only response.

"Will you visit tonight?" The official's voice turned silky, lowering to a purr. "Or do you want to play a game?"

Easton's fingers flexed, sending a jolt of sensation through Isobel's skull and down her spine. It tingled through the length of her folded legs, resembling anxiety or fear ... but it wasn't a great resemblance. More like a tacky imitation. His grip on her hair was unyielding, his body coiled with tension, but it wasn't anger battering against her chest in waves. The emotions rolled over each other too quickly to properly identify, but it was clear he was uncomfortable, ticking down the seconds until he could release her. He wasn't mad at her but alarmed at the situation, reacting on instinct.

"I'll visit," he said.

"Are you sure?" The official's husky chuckle seemed to impossibly ratchet up the tension in Easton's body, but he was saved from an answer by a loud knock on his office door.

He swore, his breath sawing out before he raised his voice. "What?"

"We've got a problem," Theodore announced, opening the door. "Isobel—"

"Teleported to the fire trail again," Easton swiftly interrupted. "I know. I should go and deal with this, Tilda. I'll see you later."

"Why do you need to deal with it?" Tilda returned, the sensual edge to her tone ripped away.

Isobel could move her head just enough to see through the gap in the backboard of the desk to where Theodore was backing out of the office and closing the door again.

"Because Theo is about to march out into a fucking storm to go looking for her." Easton worked to get his tone under control, letting the roughness bleed out of it. "I have to keep my Alphas under control. I'll see you later."

He slammed the laptop shut with his left hand, his right hand releasing her instantly. He jerked his chair back, staring down at her in shock.

"Are you okay?" He was rubbing the thigh she had been leaning against agitatedly. "Did I hurt you?"

"No," she lied, too shocked to move.

He held out a hand, and she just stared at it.

"Please don't stay down there." His jaw was tight, his tone shaky, his discomfort still rolling over her.

She placed her hand in his, and he pulled her up, standing from his seat.

"Are you sure I didn't hurt you?" he asked as she wobbled on the spot, his gaze tracing over her hair. "It would have been bad if she had seen you."

"I know," Isobel blurted. "About the storm." She pointed to the window.

Easton frowned, falling back into his seat. His eyes narrowed, examining her face, before he motioned to one of the chairs on the other side of his desk. "Do you want to sit down?"

She perched her butt on the edge of his desk, remembering a little too late that she wasn't wearing any underwear. Easton levelled her with a cold expression.

"On a *chair*, Carter."

"Right." She popped off the desk and fell into one of the chairs, having enough foresight to close her legs.

He rolled forward, folding his arms across the desk. "What do you mean you *know* about the storm?"

"I know it's you," she said plainly. "I know you have an illegal ability. It's not just Theodore and Moses. I don't even think it's just the three of you. I think Sato has one too."

Her statement was met with silence, and then he stood, rounding the desk. He leaned against the other side, towering over her with his arms crossed, his eyes guarded as he considered her.

"Is that so?" he asked quietly.

She wanted to bang her head on the desk. *Why did she say any of that?*

"I'm not an anti-loyalist," she hurried out, glancing to the door. "But ... I won't tell anyone."

He scoffed. "No shit, Carter. If we thought you were going to tell anyone ..." He let the rest hang in the air between them. Not quite a threat, but the suggestion of one, if she chose to take it that way.

"Then why have they been following me?" she demanded, pointing at the door.

"Accidents happen." Easton unfolded, standing tall again. "Like right now. Students get drunk and run their fucking mouths."

"I'm not like that."

"Then why aren't you wearing underwear?"

The question was so sudden, so unexpected, she was left sitting there with her mouth open. She glanced down at herself, frowning. "How can you tell?"

"You sat on my desk." He closed his eyes, pinching the bridge of his nose. "I'm an Alpha. I have an Alpha nose. Get up."

She stood before she even realised she was obeying

and twisted her face into something like a wince. "Sorry, Professor."

He closed his eyes tighter. Pinched the bridge of his nose harder. And then he was walking to the window, yanking it open.

"Go around the dorm and come in through the front again. It will look like you walked down from the trail."

She glanced at the storm outside. "You couldn't make it a little less ... torrential, could you?"

He gave her a flat look. "You teleported into my lap while I was video calling my girlfriend and then put your scent on my desk," he said tonelessly. "Trust me when I say the storm is the safer option for you right now."

"Should I ..." She chewed her lip, knowing somewhere in the back of her mind that this was going to be a painfully awkward memory in the morning when she was more sober. "Like ... clean your desk or something?"

He stepped forward, and she backed hastily toward the window. Without saying anything more, he kept advancing and she kept retreating until she was hanging half out of the window. He set his hands against the sill either side of her, leaning forward until she was an inch from tumbling out.

"Fuck's sake," he grumbled, looping an arm around her waist. He lifted her, his other arm slipping beneath her legs.

He held her gently, despite his rough voice, and leaned out of the window, dropping the arm from beneath her legs. Her bare feet hit the muddy ground, and he carefully withdrew his other arm, waiting until he was sure that she wouldn't fall over.

"Hurry up," he snapped. "Before you catch a cold."

"It's not even that col—" He had already shut the window.

She glanced up at the sky with a frown on her face, blinking against the heavy droplets of water. The storm seemed agitated. Just like Easton. She hurried around to the front of the dorm and knocked on the door.

Theodore opened it a few seconds later, the look of concern on his face switching to something like exasperation as he eyed her.

"I thought you used the opportunity to run home," he said. "I was just about to check Dorm O."

Dammit, why didn't she think of that?

The other Alphas spilled into the hallway, but it was Kilian who stepped around Theodore and picked her up.

"Let's get you cleaned up without muddying the

carpets, hey?" He had his arms looped around her, lifting her feet several inches from the ground, and while she was grateful that he hadn't picked her up any other way that might have flashed the other Alphas, she was still feeling how much the movement had lifted her dress to the tops of her thighs.

"Want some clothes to change into?" he asked, as he walked past the others, completely ignoring them.

"Kil." Theodore's voice was a harsh bark. It was enough to have Kilian stopping in his tracks and looking back.

"What?"

"Let her shower on her own, at least?"

Kilian chuckled, his eyes drifting down to meet hers. "Why?" he asked, mischief sparking in the yellow-green depths. "Nothing we haven't done before."

He pushed into his room and had the decency to wait until the door was closed before he started laughing. He carried her into the bathroom and set her down on the tiles, backing out immediately despite his teasing in the hallway.

"Help yourself to any clothes," he suggested. "I'll just be outside." He opened the door to his room, revealing Niko, his fist already raised to knock.

"Oh." Niko looked from Kilian to her. "You were kidding."

"Are you sure?" Kilian sounded like he was trying to hold back another laugh.

Even Isobel tried to bite back a smile. Kilian's mischievousness was just too infectious.

Niko didn't seem to think so. He ignored Kilian's response, turning his attention to her. "Let's go."

It took her a few long seconds of blinking back at him to realise what he was talking about, and then it dawned on her.

When I call on you next time, you need to drop everything. If you try to ignore me or get out of this, I'll turn up wherever you are, pick you up, and carry you here myself.

Well, fuck.

II

AND THE ASSHOLE IS BACK

Niko watched as it took the Sigma a little too long to figure out what he was talking about. He completely ignored the way Kilian was blinking at him in confusion.

"I can't," Carter said, holding herself in the bathroom doorway. "I'm ... a little inebriated."

He dragged his eyes down to her muddy calves. "Clean your feet and come."

"I'm getting really sick of you Alphas ordering me around," she grumbled, stepping away from the doorway. The shower turned on, and Kilian waved a hand in front of Niko's face.

"Um, what?" Kilian asked.

"Initiation." Niko gave him a tight smile.

They all knew about the initiation tasks Oscar had

demanded they give her. Realisation lit in Kilian's eyes, along with a spark of curiosity.

"Can I watch?" he whispered as the water turned off.

Niko laughed. "I don't think so. She can barely get it right without an audience."

"Because you're twice my size." Isobel sniffed in disdain, coming out of the bathroom. She was a little bit adorable when she was drunk, with just enough fire to raise the hackles of every Alpha in her vicinity.

Niko pulled out the sandals he had stuffed into his back pocket, tossing them to the floor at her feet. "Let's go."

She mimicked him beneath her breath, and he chewed on his lip to keep the amused smile at bay.

"Just as bad as Easton," she continued, grumbling like she was too drunk to realise they could hear her.

"What did Mikki do?" Kilian caught the back of her dress before she left the room.

"Pulled my hair." She pouted. "Pushed me under his desk. Dropped me out of a window."

"*That's* going to need unpacking," Niko noted. "But later. Let's go, before everyone gets out of Mikki's office."

Carter nodded, following behind him as he took off down the hallway. Kilian was headed straight to

Mikel's office, probably hoping to catch an explanation for whatever Carter was talking about.

They headed into the rain, and he shrugged off his jacket, holding it out for her.

"Can't we wait until I'm sober or it isn't raining?" she complained, pulling the jacket on and tugging the hood up. She completely disappeared inside it.

"If you're going to drink and let down your guard around dangerous people, then no," he returned.

He couldn't stand the thought of how vulnerable she was all the time. Half of it was because she was his mate—and unlike the other Alphas, he actually *did* believe that mates were destined. It didn't mean that he was ever going to accept her, that anything would ever happen between them. If it was completely within his control, she would spend the rest of her life never learning of the connection between them.

It was just how it had to be.

He was the first of his parents' children, and they had made their expectations of him known since he was old enough to understand what they were talking about. He was an Alpha with an ability he could easily hide. That made him popular and non-threatening. He was a definite shoe-in for Ironside. Which meant, at the very least, he could send back money every month, and at the very most, he would become an Icon. He had a chance to raise his culture, his family, his heritage out from the ditch it had been shoved into. There was a reason Gifted from other countries fled to America, begging for refuge in the settlements. Japan didn't have an Ironside. All they had were *akuma*. Malevolent fire spirits, who they believed were infecting humans and turning them into ... well, *him*.

He wasn't naive enough to think that becoming an Icon would change his country's perspective on the Gifted. Instead, he was banking on their greed. It was America's greed that saw to the safety and limited rights of the Gifted, and where America led, the rest of the world at least considered following. Even if only for a moment.

"You're a talkative one, aren't you?" Carter spoke up behind him, following his hurried footsteps through the rain.

She almost had to run to keep up with him, but he considered that her warm-up, so he didn't slow down.

"What would you like me to talk about?" he asked, trying not to sound like a total dick. Like he didn't want to talk to her at all.

He *wasn't* a total dick, but he also didn't really want to chit-chat with the Sigma. She was trouble. She never did what anyone expected.

"Why are you actually forcing me to do training

right now? Kilian wasn't serious, you know. Well not about showering with me *that* time, anyway."

He almost stumbled. "You're a very talkative drunk."

"I seem to be getting drunker. I think it's the mate-bond. It's making everything wonky, you know? It teleported me all wrong, and now it's making me sloshed."

Unfortunately, he did know. She had ten mates, and at least eight of them had been drinking. He pulled his phone out as they pushed into the fitness centre, opening the group chat.

Niko: Stop drinking. You're affecting her somehow.

Theodore: I already stopped.

Kilian: Stopped a while ago.

Elijah: Barely even started.

Cian: Where are you? I'm not drinking.

Niko: Training. Is anyone drinking?

Moses: Guilty.

Oscar: Guilty. And not stopping.

Niko: I need her conscious, asshat.

Theodore: The fuck for?

Oscar: Come here and call me an asshat again. Bring the Sigma. Two birds, one stone.

Mikel (admin): She is not your toy, Oscar.

Oscar: Are you sure? Because she looks exactly like this toy I had as a kid.

He sent through a picture of a stuffed rabbit.

Niko rolled his eyes, tucking his phone away and ignoring all the incoming message vibrations. Oh well, he tried.

Isobel narrowed her eyes at the bunching muscles beneath Niko's soaked T-shirt as he pushed into the same training room as before.

"Seriously," she said, as he shook wet strands of hair out of his eyes. "Why tonight?"

"Didn't you need a break?" He avoided looking at her. "An escape?"

"That doesn't mean I wanted to be beaten up." She huffed.

"I'll walk you back to your dorm after we're done." He dangled the offer before her tantalisingly. "And deal with Theo and Kilian so you don't have to."

"Why?" She squinted at him, shrugging out of his oversized jacket. "Do you have a hero complex or something?"

"I have manners." He frowned back at her. "If you don't want to be there, you shouldn't have to be there."

"It's not that I don't want to be there," she hedged, kicking off her sandals. "I am trying to move there, after all."

"Liar." He said it so casually, reminding her of the first highlight Ironside had featured of him. They had called him a human lie detector, saying that his Alpha abilities were the sharpest they had ever seen. Niko himself had told her that he was stronger, faster than most Alphas.

"How's your sense of smell?" she asked, her face scrunching up in worry.

"Fine." He quirked a brow, waiting for her to elaborate.

It was on the tip of her tongue to warn him that she still wasn't wearing underwear—her mistake with Easton still fresh and traumatising—but the alcohol clouding her judgement was making it hard to decide if it was more or less embarrassing to talk about it, so she eventually just shrugged and slipped past the ropes, waiting for him in the middle of the mats.

Niko walked back to the door, his pace calm and measured. He flicked the lights, dousing the room in darkness.

"I don't want to blindfold you again," he explained, somehow finding his way over to the ropes.

He ducked beneath them, his outline barely visible, and stopped before her.

She waited until her eyes adjusted to the dark. "I can still see you," she pointed out. *Barely*. "You still don't look anything like the guy who attacked me."

"You still haven't learned to use your imagination." His hands landed on her shoulders.

She pushed them off.

He let out a sound of mild amusement, his hands flashing back into place faster than she could react. One second, he was holding her by the shoulders, the next, she was on her back, the breath knocked out of her. He held her down lazily, easily, counting to three, and then he released her, pulling her back up to her feet.

"Are you trying?" he asked, curling behind her. He knocked her legs out from beneath her, and she tried to grab onto him, to pull him down with her, but he had already slipped away.

"Yes," she groaned, when he didn't even bother to pin her down again. "I've just had a *really* tough day, and I feel like my limbs aren't cooperating with my brain anymore."

"Focus more on the tough day, less on the limb-to-brain cooperation."

She tried to do as he said, dredging up thoughts of

the text messages she had yet to deal with, and the "initiation" task Moses had demanded of her. He was asking her to choose between herself and another person. To be the selfless Sigma she thought she was supposed to be, or ... something else. The kind of person who could dish out her own justice and claim what she wanted, uncaring of who she hurt in the process.

Niko sent her sprawling again, and she managed to catch a hold of his shirt this time, so she only landed on her knees before pulling herself up again.

"What happened?" he asked, sending her down again twice as hard.

She wheezed, holding her stomach. "Just wondering if I have a dark side or not," she panted out, as he held her down with a foot against her arm.

He picked her up again. "Must be a small dark side. Like the size of a freckle or something."

"Nuh." She bent over, still clutching her stomach, and he gave her a minute to regroup. "I slapped Moses today. Made him bleed. Was badass." She wheezed out a pained breath between each statement.

"Okay," he allowed. "The size of a cookie, then."

"Stop making my dark side sound cute." She suddenly straightened and tried to throw a clumsy jab at him. Even in the darkness, he seemed to see it coming from a mile away, and he easily caught her hand and then her other hand, twisting them behind her back.

"Ow ow ow!" She tried to stomp on his foot and somehow managed to knee him in the groin instead, jolting him off balance.

They went tumbling down, and she scrambled to take the upper hand, trying to pin his arms to the ground while she straddled his waist. He froze, his chest swelling beneath her, a faint vibration travelling from his chest right through to her core.

Oh fuck oh fuck oh fuck.

"Carter." He growled her name. "Does Gabriel still have your underwear?"

"It's not a power move if I ask for them back." She was close enough to see his eyes close, like he was praying for patience.

"One," she whispered. "Two ..."

He flipped her.

She had expected his competitive streak to kick in, but not quite in that way. Now he was weighing her into the mat, her hands captured the same way she had been holding his, his hips a heavy weight against hers. She tried to hook one of his legs by wrapping both of hers around it, but then she didn't know what to do. She only succeeded in pressing herself right against his thigh.

He growled out a sound that was both displeasure and reprimand. "That was a mistake." He swore roughly. "I have to walk back into the dorm after this."

She didn't get a chance to reply, because her mind suddenly wavered, like how the world around her shifted before she teleported, except this time, she didn't go anywhere. At least not physically.

But she was suddenly inside someone else's head, standing inside their body.

"Holy shit," she whispered, as the eyes that didn't belong to her looked over a woman suspended from the ceiling. The woman was petite, with a lithe and athletic body and darkly tanned skin. Her muscles strained as a strong male hand—belonging to the body she had just hijacked—reached out, spinning her in a slow circle. She wasn't entirely naked, but she might as well have been, with the delicate wisps of cream silk that bunched beneath the ropes crossing over her body in beautiful, terrifying patterns.

"What?" Niko's voice sounded far away. "Carter? Isobel? What the hell?"

"C-Can't move," Isobel whispered back, like the person whose body she was inhabiting might be able to hear her.

"Why? What happened?" Niko's hands were flying all over her body, but they only held a whisper of the pressure they would have in reality.

There were other sensations more pressing to her in that moment. Like the cock rising hard against the front of the pants the stranger was wearing, straining to escape, and the way his large hand cradled it as he looked over the woman, whose face she couldn't see. Only her long, auburn hair twisted into a plait.

He squeezed himself, and a bolt of pleasure rippled through Isobel.

"I'm inside his head," she whispered shakily. "My mate."

It seemed like Nico had stopped touching her, but she wasn't sure. The stranger's hand released his cock and drifted over the gentle curve in the woman's spine before retreating. He dug into his pocket and pulled out his phone, reading the notification that popped up on the screen without opening it.

Hidden member (open group chat to view more): Blackout.

The stranger stared at his phone a second longer before sliding it away. He stepped away from the woman, tugged the zipper on his pants up, and left the room, locking it behind him. The woman called out to him, but he was already far enough away that the sound was muffled. He kept his eyes firmly on the floor, not giving away any details until he was behind another door. He switched off the light, and that was that.

She couldn't see anything.

She could only hear his breath and feel the maelstrom of emotion that whipped around his chest. Trepidation. Frustration. Guilt.

"Carter?" Niko's voice permeated through the darkness, calling her back. "What can you see?"

She drifted back to herself, blinking up at Niko, who was bent over her, fingers on the pulse at her neck. Some of the tension seemed to leak out of his posture when their eyes connected in the dark.

"He went into a room and turned the light off," she said, scrambling upright and leaning closer to Niko so that she could whisper, "*Right in the middle of fucking someone.*"

"What?" Niko reared back, searching her face before leaning forward again.

"Well, he hadn't really started yet. I think. He had her tied up and hanging from the roof ... *ohmygodwhatifshewasunconscious.*" The words all ran out of her at once, and she tried to jump to her feet, but Niko caught her arm, dragging her back down to the mat.

"I'm sure she was conscious," he said dryly. "But he obviously knew you were in his head."

"No, it was because of a weird text he got." She frowned. "I don't know what I just saw. None of it makes sense. It was like a weird fever dream. Are weird fever dreams side-effects?"

"I'll ask." He tapped at his phone for a bit, the screen lighting up his face and showing how he chewed on his lip. "Elijah said yes." He turned the screen off again. "And not even I'm comfortable leaving you alone anymore, so I'm taking you back to Dorm A."

She didn't even bother arguing. She mentally couldn't handle anything else for the night, so she just followed him meekly from the fitness centre, burrowing into his jacket again until they arrived at the dorm. The overwhelming heady feeling no longer permeated her brain, washed away by the rain, or whatever that weird vision had been. Niko led her into the dorm and then promptly disappeared. Probably switching out his pants as quickly as possible.

She surveyed the empty common room before padding over to Theodore's door and knocking softly. He opened it, stepping aside for her to enter, watching her warily.

"What happened?" he asked. Maybe Niko had

forewarned him, or maybe it was written all over her face.

"Where do I start?"

He closed the door, leaning back against it. He considered her quietly before opening his arms. "Start wherever and whenever you like. Come here."

She stepped into his warmth, twisting her arms around his muscled torso, brushing her nose against his clean shirt, inhaling his warm scent. One of his hands fell to her left shoulder, the other lightly cupping the back of her head. He wasn't really hugging her back, more like giving his hands somewhere to rest.

She could feel the questions burning from his chest to hers. His impatience battering against her despite the way he held his body deliberately relaxed against hers, allowing her to sink into his strong muscles.

"Sorry for kissing you in the game." She spoke against his shirt, hoping he wouldn't even hear her.

Both of his hands twitched. "It was just a game."

"Why do you never hug me back?"

He huffed out an amused sound. "I'm hugging you back right now."

"No, you're not." She wiggled against him, drawing a quiet rumble from his chest.

His arms suddenly banded across her back, pulling her off her feet and flush against him. He stepped toward the bathroom, planting her outside the shower.

"I'm not Kilian," he rumbled. "You're going to need to wash yourself. But first ... are you okay?"

She sucked in a breath, then quickly told Theodore the events of her night, skipping over the disturbing text messages she had received. She started with teleporting to Easton's lap and ended with seeing her mate and his ... *girlfriend*?

It didn't hit her until she was saying it out loud.

Her mate had a girlfriend. Or at least he was sexually active. Or ... just *really* into people swinging from the ceiling? She didn't understand what the weird text was about. Maybe it was a settlement thing. Maybe the ceiling-swinging was a settlement thing too.

Theodore's emotions seemed to run the entire gambit from amused to disturbed. His hands had landed on her shoulders at some point, his thumbs rubbing a comforting pattern over her collarbone. It was past midnight, and she had a full day of classes in the morning, but her night wasn't done yet.

"I'm sorry you're going through this." Theodore's thumbs stopped stroking as he considered her with a heavy expression. "But you aren't going through it alone. What can I do to make it easier?"

She smiled and slipped her arms around his waist, hugging him tightly even though he kept his hands on her shoulders, fingers pinching in. He hummed, the sound emanating deeply from his chest before he gently peeled her off, softening the action with one of his wide, sunny smiles.

"You could sleep in your own bed," she said. "That would make me feel better."

"I can't." He chewed on his lower lip, the movement making her focus on his mouth a little too hard.

"I meant by yourself," she quickly corrected. "I'll go sleep in the common room."

He considered it, albeit unhappily. It came as a surprise to her that she had *any* kind of power over Theodore.

"Please?" she hedged, ducking to catch his eye.

"Go to Kilian," he expelled on a hard breath. "But ..." He disappeared from the bathroom, returning with a long-sleeved T-shirt, a hoodie, a pair of boxers, and a pair of drawstring sweats. He dropped the bundle onto the counter. "Wear these. Just in case. Wait." He ducked out again and then dumped a pair of socks onto the pile.

"Theo. I'll overheat."

He cut her a look, his brows lowering. "I don't need to sleep in my bed, but I need to feel like there's someone nearby to protect you."

What did that have to do with her overheating?

"Okay." She forced out a smile, watching him relax slightly. "Thanks."

He left the bathroom again, shutting the door behind him this time, and she turned on the shower, pulling out her phone to consult the messages she had gotten earlier. It seemed the sender had grown frustrated at her lack of a response.

Unknown: You can't ignore me, Sigma.

Unknown: I have nothing left to lose.

Unknown: Don't test me. I will turn it all in to the officials.

Unknown: One of those Alphas went psychotic on the rooftop, didn't they? Which means Professor Easton isn't the only one with an illegal ability. But Easton tried to cover it all up.

Unknown: And then there's you. Lying about how you entered the Death Phase.

Unknown: Were you and one of the Alphas trying to force a bond? Was it Theodore?

Unknown: It didn't really work out, did it?

She shook her head, scrolling through the

messages with dread sinking lower and lower through her stomach.

Isobel: Who is this?

She quickly put herself through a scalding shower, tapping her phone screen as she hastily dried herself off.

Unknown: Your new master.

She battled the urge to throw her phone against the wall.

Isobel: Cut to the chase. Tell me what you want.

Unknown: There's a secret club for students to be mentored on the Icon track. Almost every winning Icon was a member, but they don't snitch. I want to know everything. What it's called. Where they hold their meetings. How to get invited.

She wanted to scoff and ask why they hadn't chosen *any* other student to blackmail for the information, but the answer was surprisingly obvious. Her father was a winning Icon.

Isobel: How long do I have?

Unknown: They won't make it easy, so I'll give you until the start of summer break, and then your secrets are public. Don't test me, Carter. I really don't have anything to lose. And remember: one word to the Alphas and this game is over, and all your lives are ruined. Play nice now.

And this could officially go down as one of the

weirdest days she had been through since starting at
Ironside.

She slipped back through Theodore's room to the
hallway, earning herself a smirk from the Alpha
reclining against the headboard of his bed as she
almost tripped over the miles of soft cotton he had
insisted she disappear into.

When she reached the hallway, she ignored
Kilian's door, tapping lightly against Moses' instead.
Almost too lightly, but he must have heard, because it
opened a few moments later.

"Carter." He leaned against the doorjamb, crossing
his arms. "Sleeping over again, are we?"

"Haven't done much sleeping." She hugged her
torso, looking up and down the corridor before
settling her gaze at his feet. "I need more time."

"No."

"I don't know how to ruin someone's life in a
single night."

He stepped back, kicking the door wide, and she
hesitated before stepping lightly into the room. He
nudged the door shut and then flicked on a lamp
before sitting on the edge of his rumpled sheets.

"Were you asleep?" She leaned against the back of
the door.

He ran a hand through his tangled dark hair, eyes

dragging over her clothes like he was trying to find her inside them. "Was trying to be asleep. Why the fuck are you wearing practically everything Theo owns?"

"Honestly?" She held up one of her palms, the sleeve hanging down over her fingers. "I have no idea. We made a deal. He would sleep in his own bed if I went in with Kilian—who is probably already asleep so I'm probably going to feel like an asshole either way."

Moses rolled his eyes. "Something tells me he'll survive." He looked down at his hand, smoothing it distractedly over his thigh. "I'm sorry for being a dick earlier."

"Which earlier?" She squinted at him, catching the small twitch of a smile that he beat back.

"Just the last time. On the rooftop. The thing with Wallis? It's a sore point. For all of us."

"It's ... assault," she dared, softening a little when it seemed like Moses wasn't about to come for her throat again. "Attempted rape. You don't need to make excuses or explain. You should be angry."

"Hmm." His eyes flashed, that dark storm shifting into something heavier as he chewed on his lip, considering her. "It might seem like I'm torturing you, but I've accepted that you'll be moving here. We all have."

"Sato?" she asked, feeling her own lips pull up as he flashed her a wry grin.

"It's our own fault, Oscar included. We can't exactly blame you."

"How?" She reared back, confused and a little astounded. That didn't sound like a sentence that would *ever* come out of Moses Kane's mouth.

"We've been fucking with the cameras since we got here. Covering up for me, for Theo, for ... all sorts of things."

Like Easton.

"What's that got to do with me?" she asked softly, scared that too much input from her would remind this version of Moses that the *other* version of Moses wasn't anywhere near this forthcoming ... and also hated her.

"The officials think we're wigging out the electronics." He looked torn between annoyance and amusement. "Too many Alphas in one place. They think our energy is too strong. And they think, like most of the rest of the world, that the demure, blank-slate power of a Sigma might just be the fix to their Alpha problems. They want to put you in here to even us all out. I'm sure if you weren't enrolled, they would have pulled a Sigma from one of the settlements to pose as a cleaner and ... you know." He watched her carefully before he continued. "Be our house slave and regulate our emotions."

She slackened against the door, letting loose a weak laugh. "I've been trying so hard for nothing."

"Not for nothing." He shrugged. "The officials like their puppets to dance. If you slacken off now, they'll just find another way to pull your strings. You and us? That's what the people want to see. They like the scrappy little Sigma who thinks she can get in with the Alphas, and they like wondering if we're going to let you in, or if we're just fucking with you."

"I would also like to know that," she deadpanned.

"Who hasn't been clear?" he challenged, raising an eyebrow. "I want you gone. Sato wants you gone. Niko wants you gone. Elijah and Gabriel like puzzles, but they get bored quickly. For every person Cian interacts with regularly, that's another person added to his psychic register, and he already has nine housemates. He doesn't have the mental capacity for you. And Kilian and Theo? If it were up to them, you would already be living here, earning a punishment from the officials for not playing their little game."

Well ... when he put it that way.

"I guess that's pretty clear." She tried not to sound disappointed, but it was harder to hear from Moses that he wanted her gone when he *wasn't* scowling at her or threatening her.

"Anyway." Moses rubbed his shoulder. "I didn't give you that task just to be an ass. You've already proved you can keep a secret, but you'll need more than that for us to trust you. Can you stand up for yourself? Will you stand up for your friends? Can you be ruthless? Can you fight? Will you pull your weight?"

She frowned at him. "By dishing out *your* version of justice?"

He licked his lips, like he could taste her trembling moral high ground. Like he could devour her *and* the shaky ground she stood on with a whispered bribe. Like he thought she was just as corrupt as he was.

"There's no justice for Gifted." He leaned back on his hands, his legs parting wider, his head cocking to the side, his posture slouching. He was tired. "There's especially no justice for Sigmas. You want to run with us? Learn to make karma happen your own way. Dorm A is where good girls go to die."

And the asshole is back.

"Fine." She sighed, thinking about the messages on her phone. Maybe Moses was right. She was being too weak. Her blackmailer hadn't bothered with any of the Alphas, even though the video incriminated

Easton the most. They had gone straight to her. "But I need more time."

"I'll give you until the end of the year." He flopped onto his mattress, stretching one leg out and bending the other. His hand rested over his stomach, where his shirt had risen a few inches with his movement, showing a hint of the tanned muscles she had witnessed earlier. "That's one more term," he said, as she opened the door.

Like she didn't already know.

12
WHERE GOOD GIRLS GO TO DIE

KILIAN WAS AN ANGEL MOST OF THE TIME, WITH GENTLE touches, hair as soft as down, and a protective streak that was somehow less like the overbearing aggression she was used to associating with the word *Alpha* and more like ... a warm hug.

But that was when he was awake.

After awkwardly tapping on his shoulder while she stood by his bed like a creeper, he rolled toward her, shoving his face into her stomach—*low*, on her stomach. He pushed at her clothes, like he was trying to find an inch of skin, and she didn't even know if he succeeded or not, because when he released a deep, rattling groan, the sound shooting through the room, her brain turned to mush.

He had her underneath him in a second.

"Off," he grumbled, trying to get all the material out of his way.

Shit. She was swimming in Theodore's clothes. Maybe he thought she *was* Theodore.

"Kil-Kilian!" She gripped his shoulders, her nails digging into the warm, exposed silk of his skin. He wasn't even wearing a shirt.

His head lifted from the crook of her neck, his eyes narrowing sleepily on her face. "Off," he repeated. "You'll overheat and die."

"Oh ... I thought you were—"

He tore off her pants, socks, and then wrangled her out of the hoodie, stripping her with hasty, deft hands until all she had left was the long-sleeved shirt and Theodore's boxers. He pulled the blankets up to her chin and dragged her into his arms, holding her head against his chest.

"Sleep," he muttered.

It seemed like an impossible command, except that with the bare covering of clothes between them, his smell was permeating the cocoon he had made with the blankets. He smelled like a garden. Sweet, fresh, warm. It was like curling up beneath a bergamot tree, safely tucked away from the buzzing heat, tantalising fruit swaying comfortingly above as the gentlest breeze stroked against her skin. It was like drinking too much wine and collapsing onto a cloud, and he knew it. He made a soft, buzzing sound in his throat, like a hum that travelled to his chest, and she was done for.

Asleep in three seconds flat.

When she finally woke up, it was with a hammer of panic in her chest that quickly faded into confusion. Her limbs were languid, the sheets tangled about her legs, sunshine slanting across her skin from the window.

Wait ... sunshine?

She was always up before the sun.

Seconds away from panicking again, she was sidetracked by a tray of food set up beside the bed. Coffee, just the way she liked it. Juice. Bagels. Fruit. Pastries. She sat up, staring around the empty room. Kilian was gone, but his scent remained, a faint echo of what it had been the night before.

When she reached for the coffee, she found a note beneath the mug.

Eat something more than a protein bar.

She was pretty sure Kilian had also turned off her alarm, and she fell back against the pillows, picking her phone up off the tray. She hadn't missed any classes, but she had missed all her scheduled time in the practise rooms. Unfortunately, she had also just had *the* best sleep of her entire, miserable life, so it was hard to be mad about it.

She wanted to bask in the fully rested feeling for a moment longer, so she crossed her legs, reached for a bagel, and pulled the latest episode of the *Ironside Show* up on her phone, propping it against the tray as she ate her breakfast.

It was hard to return to her own dorm after practice that night. It seemed so cold and inhospitable, like an abandoned viper's den. Empty and undisturbed ... but with a lingering threat that harm could slither beneath the door at any moment.

She avoided it as long as possible, locking herself away in Eve's room as Eve picked through her hoard of snacks, chatting all the way through Monday's episode. Eve only grew quiet or pensive when Isobel or one of the Alphas featured on-screen. It was rarely ever Isobel alone, and they had stopped trying to speculate as to her relationships with the Alphas. It was now public knowledge that she was trying to get into Dorm A. The speculation was more to do with whether she would succeed or not, and which paring would prove the most entertaining if she did succeed.

"Will it be Carter and Sato?" Ed Jones' voice teased her through the speakers. *"So much tension."*

"Everyone's terrified of Sato." Jack didn't sound convinced. *"We could get that content if we put anyone in a room with him."*

"But it's the focus.*"* Ed cackled. It was practically gleeful. *"The way he watches her. I think he's planning something."*

"Should we warn her?" Jack joked.

"Oh, I think our adorable Sigma has well and truly clued on," Ed said. Their adorable Sigma? What the fuck? *"How about Theodore, then? The fan favourite?"*

"I don't think I can bear to watch that Shakespearean tragedy," Jack groaned out. *"The fans will overthrow the government if we break Theodore Kane's heart."*

"That poll was rigged—"

"What poll?" Isobel asked beneath her breath, interrupting the show.

"Can Carter and Kane be 'just friends?'" Eve answered with an eye roll. "It was a landslide *no*, by the way."

"What about the other dark horses?" Jack was propositioning. *"We barely got anything interesting out of them until Carter came into the picture and started stirring up trouble in Dorm A. Now we're seeing a whole new side of Sato, Reed, Spade,* and *the other Kane twin."*

"Moses hasn't given any indication of interest since the Valentine's Day party, but Reed or Spade could be interesting ..." Ed continued to discuss which Alpha-Sigma pairing would be the most entertaining, even when the images on-screen switched to the fifth-year antics on Ironside Row.

"I vote Kilian." Eve spoke around the stem of a Twizzler.

"Oh my god, same." Isobel fell back against the bed, staring at the ceiling. "I think I'm addicted to his scent. I smell it everywhere I go."

Eve stopped chewing, her eyes widening. "What?"

Isobel glanced over, confused at the blank look of shock on Eve's face. "What did I say?"

"You mean like his deodorant, right?" Her eyes grew wider, almost like a warning.

"Uh, yes." Isobel sat up straight. "Obviously."

Eve let out a nervous laugh, looking even more confused. "Okay, good. I've eaten too much candy. Let's go brush our teeth."

Isobel expected it, but she was still shocked when

Eve dragged her into one of the shower rooms and started up a shower to drown out their conversation.

"Now tell me what you actually meant," she demanded, gripping Isobel's arms.

"Exactly what I said." Isobel frowned. "I know his scent. Not his deodorant but *him*. I know it's not really a Sigma thing—"

"It's *exclusively* an Alpha thing." Eve reared back, looking like she was on the verge of passing out, her next words almost a whisper. "Or a mate-bond thing."

"Hold up." Isobel laughed nervously, shaking her hands between them. "That's not ... his eyes ... and it's not just him. I know lots of people's scents."

"What's mine?" Eve shoved out her arm, pushing her wrist beneath Isobel's nose.

Isobel sniffed, suddenly unsure. "Moisturiser? Candy?" She spent a lot of time with Eve, and the other girl actually didn't have a distinctive scent.

"Jesus Fucking Christ." Eve started pacing. "That's just my moisturiser and the candy I ate. Who else's scents do you know—that you're sure of?"

"Uh ... well ..." She stalled, her frown deepening, her heartbeat kicking into overdrive. "I guess all of the Alphas."

"*All* of them?" Eve stalled, her mouth falling open. "Are you *sure*?"

"Yeah? I mean, the smells are kind of weird, like they wouldn't be deodorant or soap or anything. Except maybe Theo's or Spade's." Now *Isobel* was starting to panic, because it was far too easy to distinguish each individual scent in her memory, even the ones she had only managed to decipher once or twice.

"Easton smells like a storm—"

"*Professor* Easton?" Eve choked, her face pale. "Did this all start before your Death Phase, or after?"

"Before, but it got stronger. Why is it important?"

"Because it's one of the extra Alpha senses that some Gifted mates get. Like how Alphas all have extra strength and speed, and some Anchors will magically show supernatural strength or speed if they need to protect their Tether. Only Alphas can scent people, but some bonded can do it—probably because it helps them know what their mate is thinking or feeling, through the variations of their scent."

"Right." Isobel scratched the back of her neck, hoping she wasn't about to make a mistake. "I should tell you something."

What colour had remained now sapped from Eve's face with every word, as Isobel went through the actual events leading up to her Death Phase. The only things she left out were Theodore, Moses, and Easton's illegal abilities.

"Do you think the mate-bond is reaching out to the Alphas who were with you when you died, because your mate is too far away?" Eve whispered, her voice dry and cracked. "Have you told your bond specialist any of this?"

"Not yet." Isobel chewed on the inside of her cheek. "I don't know who to trust."

"I mean, it's good to be careful," Eve hedged. She didn't look convinced, so Isobel began to take out her other contact while Eve continued. "But it's not like you did anything super wrong. You could just tell them you were worried they would think one of the Alphas was your mate—*what is that?*" She was pointing at Isobel's other eye.

"It's the reason I'm being careful." Isobel replaced the lens while Eve stared at her, a vacant look creeping behind her eyes.

"Both your eyes changed," Eve said tonelessly.

"And if the officials find out, everything changes." Isobel stared hard at Eve, trying to convey the seriousness of the situation. "As soon as I turn twenty-one, I'm no longer the daughter of an Icon. They can do whatever they want with me, but there's no way I get out of this without becoming a research project.

It's bad enough that my mate wasn't there with me in the Death Phase, but I get the sense something *like* that has happened before, at least. That's why they were waiting for me to die in the hospital. They thought my mate was already dead."

"Maybe they wouldn't turn you into a science experiment?" Eve sounded hesitant, her eyes darting to the door of the shower room like an official would bust inside and arrest her for doubting them. "I mean you're already different, but they're leaving you alone, right?"

"No. They're just waiting, and watching, very closely. They seem to think this will all magically resolve through the side-effects of prolonging a bond. And maybe they're right. I'm pretty sure I was inside his head last night."

After she caught Eve up on everything else that had happened last night and finally told her the bad news about Isobel's father stealing her away for spring break, they escaped the bathroom.

"I was planning something epic for spring break to get your popularity up." Eve was pouting, dragging her feet on the way back to their rooms. She paused before her door, fiddling with the handle. "The whole Mate Finder campaign is ... pretty brilliant." She watched Isobel carefully. "It just ... doesn't seem like your style."

"Wait until you see the photos," Isobel grumbled.

ISOBEL CHECKED HER EMAILS AGAIN AS SHE MADE HER WAY TO the fitness centre. She had received yet another temporary timetable while she ate breakfast with Eve that morning, telling her the location of the additional tutoring session West had added onto her calendar.

The fitness centre was so massive that there were still areas of it she hadn't explored, and it was toward one of those sections that she walked now. An indoor climbing range, with two sections walled off from the rest of the range. One of the doors had a sign on it.

Private Session in Progress.

She knocked on the door and West opened it a moment later, stepping aside to let her in.

"Good," he said, by way of greeting. "You're dressed properly."

She glanced down at the tights and loose shirt that she had already put through one dance class and two practise sessions for the day.

"Is this still, um ..." She was unable to hold West's gaze, her eyes darting off to the side to avoid the weight of command he seemed to emanate without any real effort. "A piano lesson, Professor?"

"I offered to mentor you onto the Icon track. I thought I would start with piano, since you listed it as your backup speciality, but it has become apparent that you have a bigger problem that needs fixing first." He picked up a harness, tossing it over to her.

She caught it with shaking fingers, holding it uncertainly as he moved to stand before her.

"Trust," he said.

"I don't want to trust anyone," she blurted, adding quickly, "Professor."

"Harness," he responded, a subtle demand riding his rough timbre. It was almost a compulsion, without a hint of Alpha voice. A very interesting, and terrifying, talent.

She untangled the harness, her face flaming as she tried to figure out how to put it on.

"Step through here." He pointed without touching her or the harness. "Yes, right leg. Good. Now your other leg through here. Yes. Tighten these straps. Clip this around your waist. Perfect. Good girl. Tighten that strap. How does it feel?"

She took a deep breath. "Fine." *Suffocating*.

He was wearing workout gear. She didn't notice until he was securing his own harness. He looked ... different. In his suit, he could be a bodyguard, or a suave agent from the old spy movies her mother used to watch. He would have to be the big Russian one, who liked to punch people and mostly communicated in grunts and diminishing glares. They would have to call him the Red Bear or something.

In workout gear, he suddenly transformed into the handsome, all-American agent, trading his glower for an omniscient spark and dry charisma. It made her mind twitch with the need to see him in a full set of occupational costumes, like a boxed set of Alpha Ken dolls.

"Are you listening, Carter?" West's voice cut through her thoughts with a sharp, barked edge, though his face was still lined in deliberate patience.

"Sorry, Professor." She shuffled to the wall where he was standing.

He clicked a carabiner onto her harness, giving it a light tug that had her jerking forward another step nonetheless.

"Have you climbed before?" He took a hold of the other end of the rope, standing back and finally giving her the mercy of turning his attention somewhere else.

"My father sent me to a few indoor obstacle courses to prepare for Ironside Row," she answered. "They weren't strictly climbing."

He nodded, his eyes turning back to her as he dug

something out of his back pocket. A small handful of black cloth.

"I spoke to your dance teachers." He closed his hand around the cloth, drawing her attention back to his face. "They said you never partner up."

"Nobody ever wants to partner with me."

"Not that you ask them." His lids grew lazy, his expression pointed. "I've seen you dance. You're dynamic, highly energetic, incredibly athletic, and strong. You're an acrobatic dancer, but you're small and graceful. You're a quintessential flyer, but you shy away from acrobatic partners. You're cutting your talent off at the knees and you know it. If you can't learn to trust, you won't make it onto the Icon track, let alone anywhere near the finish line."

"I'm not trying to get onto the Icon—"

"Don't." He sighed, shaking his head. "Don't be an insipid cliché of an Icon's daughter, Carter. At what point do you think your objection to fame becomes ostentatious?"

Her lips slammed shut, her eyes narrowing. "It's not an act. Are the cameras on? I thought this lesson was private."

"They are off." He flashed her the screen of his phone, showing 51:03:23 ... and counting. The minutes remaining for their lesson. "And I didn't say it was an act. I'm asking you to gain some *awareness*. Every student here has traded their lives for a shot at what you were given from birth. You're undermining every settlement kid whose most far-reaching dream is to send a monthly Ironside stipend back to the settlement to put food and medicine in the hands of their family. They don't even dare to dream of the Icon track, but if they were offered half the opportunities you had been ...?" He let that hang in the air between them like an accusation as he shook out the length of black material from his fist. "Turn around, *princess*."

The last word was whispered, his tone jaded, almost as if she wasn't supposed to hear it. He sounded as though he suspected he was wasting his time, and that hit harder than his words.

She turned slowly, swallowing back tears from the lecture as the material suddenly flashed over her eyes, effectively blinding her. He securely tied it off behind her head, and she *felt* him hesitating behind her.

"I'm sure there's more to the story," he murmured in a light rumble. "I'm sure you've been a victim your whole life—truly a victim, not just acting like one—but you need to shake it off. Step out of that skin. An Icon is a role model. You could actually *help* people. People who were victims just like you."

Dorm A is where good girls go to die.

Everyone wanted her to change.

And if she were honest with herself, she really wanted that as well. She just didn't know how to.

"We'll start here," West told her calmly, turning her in the right direction, lifting one of her hands to rest against the wall, his smoky vanilla scent digging right into her pores. "From here on, you don't move an inch unless I tell you. Are you ready to trust, Carter?"

Fuck no. "Do I have a choice?"

"Professor."

"Do I have a choice, Professor?"

"That should have answered your question. Right hand up, two handspans above your shoulder." *Alpha voice.*

Her arm jerked, puppet-like, racing to obey faster than it did even with her father's Alpha voice. She winced, gripping the handhold and resting her face against the wall as her heartbeat tried to break through her ribs and unhook her from the rope.

"Left hand, just above your head."

Free from Alpha voice this time, she took her sweet time reaching for the second handhold, and then the first foothold, and the second. Her arms were stiff, her muscles trembling in fear. Every time he asked her to release one of the grips or move, she had another mini panic attack all over again. She had no sense of time or distance, and her jaw was aching from how hard her teeth had been pressed together. West directed her calmly and patiently. After forcing her to take the first step, he kept his Alpha voice at bay, but an even worse punishment came when she realised she had reached whatever height he had intended for her and she now had to make her way back down again.

As soon as her feet hit the cushioned floor, she collapsed, her head between her legs as she tore off the blindfold. West's voice was fucking *echoing* inside her head, her ears·straining for a word of warning even now.

He crouched before her, his powerful thighs bunching. "It's up to you, now."

She lifted her pale, sweaty face, meeting his hard eyes with confusion in her own. "What is?"

"Whether we continue this or not."

"Why me?" Her voice was hushed, and she forced the rest out before he could give her another lecture. "Ranks stick together. So you either don't believe anything will come of me, in which case you're wasting your time, or you think I could be an Icon, in which case, you're betraying your rank. You should be promoting your Alphas over me."

His hard lips shifted, but then he swiftly rearranged his face, hiding whatever emotion had just been about to show. "I knew there was some pride in there somewhere," he grunted, standing and offering her his hand. "But you left out a third option."

She watched his hand like she was waiting for it to suddenly transform into a claw and take a swipe at her before she hesitantly placed her fingers in his. His power rolled over her *hard*, making her stumble as soon as he pulled her to her feet, her head reeling. He dropped her hand, turning toward the door.

"I believe you have it in you." He opened the door and pulled down the Private Session in Progress sign. "What better way to monitor your progress than to ensure I'm the one guiding it?"

She spoke to the closed door, her voice low, "But you *are* enabling it, which means you don't really think I'm a threat at all." The truth was pretty clear. He *was* monitoring her, but not because he thought she could win. It was because she was getting close to his Alphas. He thought she was a threat, but not to the game. She was a threat to his boys.

Still, news of her getting special treatment from the Alphas must have started to spread, because people now gave her a wide berth like she was Moses or Sato—but less scary. The other students didn't quite know how to treat her anymore. Even her dorm room remained suspiciously untouched. Even Eve was getting some funny looks as she accompanied Isobel to her piano lesson.

"So, Reed is taking over from Professor West for this one?" Eve asked, nodding toward the door that already had a Private sign stuck to the outside.

"I think so." Isobel paused outside the door. "But these lessons always seem to be the complete opposite of what I expect, so who knows."

Eve chuckled, giving the door a wary look. "Good luck."

Steeling herself, Isobel knocked and opened the door, sticking her head inside. Reed was already sitting there, playing the beautiful grand piano that she hadn't had a chance to explore the week before.

"Come in," he muttered, his eyes never leaving the keys.

She stepped inside and was about to shut the door when a cameraman suddenly appeared out of nowhere, his assistant pushing the door wide.

Isobel pretended to ignore them, scattering away from the door and approaching the piano. Reed stiffened, his fingers falling from the keys, a short sigh slipping out of his mouth. He didn't need to look to know their lesson was no longer private.

"Sit," he commanded, edging off the stool and

hovering beside it. "I don't care what you play, just play something."

Reed's presence wasn't quite as stifling as West's, but with the additional crew members, she was still no less relaxed. Her fingers were stiff, her tongue thick enough to choke on as she pulled her heavy hands up to the keys. Reed curved himself around her back, his hands notched against the piano, caging her in. A haze of cloves and woodsmoke settled around her, her skin tingling. She never would have guessed that she would take comfort from Reed, but the baffling effect was undeniable. Some of the tension lifted from her limbs, her back straightening until she could feel the brush of his arms around her. A weight she hadn't even realised she had been carrying around unlocked with a heavy groan from around her heart, and she drew her first full breath since waking up in Kilian's bed the other morning.

None of it made sense. *Especially* the fact that Reed seemed to know he would have that effect on her.

"Play, Carter." He pulled back, and she did. Her fingers drifted to the starting notes, pressing down without the panic.

It wasn't smooth. Not at first.

She had to work to block out the disjointed sounds of her memory. The vision of the keys shifting in and out of focus as her father's fingers constricted against her throat. She had to swallow past the rasp of ghostly pain.

She played Yiruma and reminded herself that she could breathe. She drifted into Yann Tiersen and convinced herself she was safe. She jumped from Chopin to Avicii, then Satie and Beethoven. She had no idea how long she played for, because once she started, it was hard to stop. She closed her eyes as her muscles took over, accompanied only by that smoky, smouldering fragrance. It was so unlike Reed, yet it suited him perfectly. She could imagine him standing by a fireplace, lighting a candle before settling into a chair to read a book, his reading glasses propped onto the edge of his nose.

She could imagine herself there too. Curled up on a fluffy rug, her head on a pillow, her eyes fixed to the flames, lulled by cinnamon and cloves as warm hands bundled her up, lifting her from the floor and resettling her in his lap, his book falling open on her thigh, his voice softly rumbling as he began to read out loud—

She stopped playing, the song ending on a soft sound to accompany the sigh that slipped from her lips, even as a small part of her brain rioted.

That vision had felt a little *too* real.

She scrambled off the piano bench, shooting Reed a suspicious look. He was staring back at her, his eyebrows dipped, little furrows appearing between them.

"You need to work on your pacing." His voice was pitched low, husky. He cleared his throat. "And one more thing." He pulled out his phone, his fingers flying across the screen.

Her own device vibrated with a message, and she yanked it out, opening the chat.

Unknown: It's so glaringly obvious, it's painful. Consider this my initiation task. Figure out what we're hiding. I'm ready to graduate from these childish games.

She saved his number, watching as he left the room without another word. The camera crept toward her phone, and she quickly turned off the screen, forcing a secret smile.

"Just texted me to tell me I'll never be as good as him," she lied, pretending she was talking to herself as she rolled her eyes and followed him out of the room.

As soon as she was clear of the building, she replied to his message.

Isobel: Is it something you're hiding from me, or from …?

Reed: From you. From them. From ourselves. That's your first and only hint. We carry a lot of secrets, and if you're going to be one of us, you need to be clever enough to keep them all in line. So prove your cleverness, Carter.

"Prove this. Prove that," she grumbled, shoving the phone back into her pocket, even though a little thrill raced through her. Unlike Moses and Niko's tasks, this one was a riddle. An invitation to dive into the secrets of the Alphas the way she was already craving to do and figure out what nobody else had been able to.

13

FAKE BASTARDS

When Isobel pushed into the family centre the next day, she was surprised to find Ashford sitting at one of the empty tables. His long legs were stretched out beneath the table, his head jerking up like he had been napping as the door fell closed behind her.

"Carter," he drawled, standing and unfurling his tall form. "Ready for your appointment?"

"Um." She stared at him. "How do you know—"

"Really?" He smirked, interrupting. "I'm psychic, doll."

"Right." She cast him a confused look and then moved to the elevator. He followed. "What are you doing?" she asked.

"Coming with you." He pressed the button to call the elevator.

"Nooo." She drew the word out slowly. "You're not."

The doors opened, and he ushered her in, advancing on her with his arms wide, confident that she would scramble out of his reach and right into the elevator, which she did. He pressed the correct floor and leaned against the wall, crossing his arms.

"Ashford." She folded her arms. "What the fuck are you doing?"

He rolled his lower lip between his teeth, looking like he was smiling at her harsh tone. "Moral support," he claimed easily, even though it was a bold-faced lie.

"I don't need moral supp—*Ashford!*"

He was striding from the elevator, knocking on the door to the office she met with Teak and Charlie in.

Teak opened the door, her brows inching up at the vision of Ashford—who had reached for Isobel at the last second and was now dragging her against his side.

"Cian Ashford." He stuck his free hand out to Teak, the other still anchored heavily to Isobel's hip. "One of Carter's friends. She was nice enough to let me hijack her session for a few minutes."

"Okay." Teak recovered smoothly, arranging a polite smile to her face as she stood aside, waving for Isobel and Ashford to enter.

· · ·

303

Cian dragged the Sigma into the room, and because there was only one chair, he dropped her into it, enjoying the little surprised puff of air that escaped her. He perched on the arm, his hand landing over the top of her head. He stroked her hair as he focussed on the third woman in the room. Indian American, if he had to guess. She had a silver Beta ring, stark against inky eyes. She cocked a pierced brow at him.

"Charlie," she introduced herself. "We weren't expecting you, Mr Ashford."

"Please." He showed her all his teeth. "My dad is Mr Ashford."

She looked like she wanted to smirk at him, but instead, she arranged a professional expression onto her face, turning to share a look with Annalise Teak, the reason he was here.

"To what do we owe the pleasure, Ashford?" Teak skipped right to the point, not buying his supportive friend act for a second.

Still, he kept petting the Sigma's hair. It was soft and silky, and the touch seemed to quiet her until she was content enough to sit back and wait to see what he had planned. Her scent matured from the crushed cherry he knew well, to something softer, subtler. Her head tilted back a little, just the smallest fraction, like she was unconsciously preening under his touch.

Of course she was.

They were intrinsically tied together by the soul. She was *alive* because of him. Well, him and the others. They were the only people who could give her comfort now.

"Now that you mention it, I do have a question." He twisted a lock of strawberry blonde hair between his thumb and forefinger, his attention fixed on Teak. "Have you ever heard of a Sigma speaking to the dead?"

Carter grew eerily still, a small hand whipping up to smooth her hair out of his grip. He leaned over her, planting his elbow against the back of her chair and using his fist to prop up his head. Teak and Charlie went just as still, sharing another quick look.

"Interesting." He straightened, looking between them. "You have."

"Why do you ask?" Teak sat down, crossing her legs, levelling him with a cool stare.

"You're an official and a Gifted *and* a Sigma." Cian shrugged lightly. "There's no better person in the world to ask, in my opinion."

"I didn't ask why me." Teak narrowed her eyes. "I asked why you would ask such a question."

"Because I don't do well with mysteries." He suddenly grew serious. "I want answers, and I realised

I won't get them from the Sigma until she has them herself."

Carter suddenly shot to her feet, spinning in a cloud of sunbeam hair and starlight-and-gold eyes, glittering with fury.

"Get out." She pointed with a shaky finger to the door.

So. Cute. She looked like she was ready to strangle him, even though she probably couldn't strangle a raggedy toy. It almost made him want to invite her to try.

"Sit down," he countered, biting back his Alpha voice. "I wouldn't put you at risk, Isobel."

That made her pause, a brief flash of confusion butting up against her anger. She must have felt his frustration, because her hand was rubbing absently over her chest. She fell back into the chair, sullenly, and tilted her head up to cast a barely tolerant expression over him.

"The cards were clear," he told her, trying to make his voice sound more kind, more … empathetic. "These two are your allies. They won't betray you to anyone." *Not even the officials.* He left that part unspoken.

Teak made a sound of indignation, while Charlie hid another smile.

"Liaising between Isobel and the OGGB is my *job*,"

Teak announced, a hint of gravel in her words. "They have her best interests at heart; it would be impossible to *betray* her to them."

He rolled his eyes. "Bullshit." The cards didn't say they were *his* allies, but they were definitely Isobel's. Even if they didn't realise it yet. "You have a choice right now. Isobel can speak to the dead. Now tell me ... will you be *liaising* that information?"

Teak stiffened, turning wide eyes to Carter. Her lips were stiff. She didn't want to ask. She didn't want to be put in the position of having to choose between the little Sigma who probably reminded her far too much of herself, or the officials, who quite literally held her life in their hands.

But she would choose Carter.

The cards were clear on that.

And Carter really needed someone on her side.

ISOBEL STAYED SILENT, THE SESSION WELL AND TRULY TORN out of her control by this point. The longer Teak looked at her, the more the understanding seemed to settle over the other woman's face. Teak consulted her notes, cleared her throat, and then peered at Charlie from beneath her lashes, before finally turning back to Isobel and Ashford.

"No," she whispered, a pallor falling over her skin. "I won't be passing this information on."

"But you've heard of it happening before?" Ashford pressed.

Isobel wanted to kick him. Or hug him. Or sit back and let him ask all the questions she never would have had the guts to ask in a million years.

"They questioned me quite extensively about it when I applied to be their bond specialist," Teak answered stiffly. "I don't have any personal experience with it, but it's clearly happened before. When they put Charlie through her clearance course, they asked her if she suspected I might have developed that particular ... anomaly. It must only pertain to Sigmas."

"But you have theories?" Ashford pressed, petting Isobel's head again.

She let him, even though Charlie was watching them closely. Ashford was a touchy person. It probably said as much in his file.

Teak sighed, tossing aside her notes and leaning forward. "Isobel, just tell it to me straight. Are you ... hearing voices? Seeing things?"

Isobel nodded stiffly, too scared to utter the words aloud.

"How often?" Teak fell back against the chair like she couldn't really believe it.

"I think ... when I'm really scared?" Isobel whispered. "At first it was just my mother's voice. Then I started seeing her. Then ..." She glanced up at Ashford.

"Then she heard my mother," Ashford supplied calmly. "Saying something only my mother would say. Something only my mother would say *after* her death, if that makes sense."

"It doesn't," Charlie provided. "And the least you could do is spill your secrets after forcing Isobel to spill hers."

Isobel decided then and there that she *really* liked Charlie.

"My mother stole one of the guard's cars and tried to drive it off a cliff with me in the passenger seat." Ashford was rigid, his agony pressing against Isobel's chest, making it hard for her to breathe comfortably. "She had a change of heart and tried to hit the brakes, but it was too late. We hung off the edge for fifteen minutes while she begged me to climb out the window. I was eight. As soon as I was out, she started to say something, but the car tipped, and she disappeared. I think she was trying to apologise."

Isobel's head hung low, remembering the pain in the voice that had spoken to her while Ashford and her were on the rooftop.

"I'm sorry," Isobel repeated the words on a whisper. "She ... she said she was sorry."

"I know." He resumed stroking her hair, his hands steady, but Teak was like Isobel.

She could sense the agony emanating from him in waves.

"I'm sorry." Teak frowned, a spark of genuine sorrow in her eyes.

"I also saw Sato's dad, I think." Isobel forced the words out.

"Oscar's dad?" Ashford's voice turned sharp. "While Oscar was there?"

Isobel nodded. "He was ... something else."

"Hmm." Ashford stopped touching her, his posture suddenly guarded. "So, what do you think?" he asked Teak.

"I think it's highly irregular that you're so invested," Teak answered. "You and the other Alphas. I think it's suspicious that West and Easton both agreed to tutor her, and I don't think it makes any sense for all of you to show so much interest in her. *But* ..." She flicked her attention to Isobel. "You're like a vault. It's incredibly difficult to get information out of you, so maybe that's it. Discretion is an invaluable attribute around here."

"She has other attributes." Ashford sounded like

he was holding back a laugh.

Charlie rolled her eyes. "I met an Alpha or two during my time at Ironside," she said calmly. "I was even friends with one of them, for a time. She explained how Alphas get territorial, how they form pack-like structures when too many of them are together in one place. And she told me how competitive it gets—she emphasised that, most of all. I would caution you against turning Carter into a game just because Theodore Kane is interested in her. She has a mate. That is not something to be messed with."

"Are we messing with it?" Ashford didn't even skip a beat. "Or are we helping ease the ache of a *mate* who can't even be bothered to show their face? I think she gains a great deal of comfort from us. We're the only ones who bother to give her any, after all."

"I think this is getting off topic," Isobel said pointedly.

"It's finally getting *on* topic." Charlie rolled her eyes, but she softened it with an understanding smile. "If the Alphas are helping, then I'll stop butting in. I just ... I know how they are."

Isobel felt her lips pulling up at the corners. Finally, someone who didn't fall at the feet of the great and mighty Alphas.

"I think we can help." Ashford's voice turned to steel. "Not by violating her bond, but by respecting there *is* one. One which is being ignored."

"We have used surrogates before," Teak mused, considering him slowly. "Where bond-mates have died or been away for extended periods of time. It does ease the side-effects."

"Great." Ashford didn't sound thrilled, but he kept pushing ahead. "So what can I do?"

Hold up ... what?!

"Why you?" Isobel interrupted.

"Because I'm the one who gate-crashed your session." He cut her a tight smile. "In return, I'm offering to help." He didn't particularly look like he wanted to help, but she couldn't think of anyone invested enough in her life to force him to help. Except perhaps her father ... but Ashford was also an Alpha, and he didn't seem like the sort to be easily pushed around.

"Touching helps." Teak was already writing a list. "Physical comfort. Sleeping beside a warm body. Anticipating her needs, like a real mate. Presents, pampering ... In the half-bonded states, most Anchors will spoil their Tethers, easing the trauma of their recent death and making them feel welcome in this world. It can be a difficult thing for the mind to accept

—coming back from the dead. Tactile things that help to ground her soul to the real world, like feeding her or making her living space more inviting."

Isobel scoffed quietly.

"I don't see Isobel easily accepting any of that," Teak continued, a small smile twitching over her lips as she continued to write. "So I suppose your biggest challenge would be finding ways to ease her half-bonded state that she will actually allow." She tore the page out of her notebook, handing it to Ashford. "I'll inform the officials that you've offered to be a surrogate."

Ashford made a humming sound, tucking the note away. "As your mate has already pointed out, we Alphas can get a little competitive—"

"I'll inform the officials that several of you may be surrogating," Teak corrected, looking like she was suppressing a small chuckle. "Will I get a straight answer if I ask why?"

"Theo," Isobel answered, her cheeks flooding with colour. "They think we're too close. The others like to ... um, monitor us."

"Ahh." Understanding sparked in both Teak and Charlie's eyes, along with a heavy dose of amusement.

"Poor Theodore," Charlie muttered.

"Yes, yes, poor Theodore," Ashford agreed,

standing and moving to the door. "Thanks for the session, ladies. Was a pleasure. Come on, doll. I'll hold your hand all the way to your next obligation like a good fake mate."

Isobel stood, but ignored his hand, quietly thanking Teak and Charlie before shouldering past him. He must have hung back to say something because she managed to get the elevator to herself, but he caught up to her soon after she hit the pathway leading from the family centre. He captured her hand, his fingers pushing between hers. Tingles immediately shot up her arm and she tried to jerk it free. He held tighter, twisting their hands across her front as he dropped his arm over her shoulders, anchoring her into his side.

"If Theo liked me so much—"

He laughed, cutting her off. "*If*. Right."

"He would have kissed me first," she finished.

Ashford stalled, his eyes fixing to a point on the path ahead. "Say what now?"

"The game? Spin the bottle?" She peeked up at him, trying to ignore that *incredible* sunshine and seawater scent that clung to his skin and hair. He smelled like a god of the seas just as much as he looked like one.

Isobel wasn't one of those people who thought the

Gifted were descendants of old gods, but it was almost easy to entertain the thought when she recalled Ashford rising from the water of Alpha Lake, slicking his golden hair back from his face as water ran in rivulets from his perfectly carved body.

They were walking again, Ashford keeping silent. "Maybe I'm wrong," he eventually said, a slow smile creeping over his face. "It happens. What are your plans for spring break?"

"Mate Finder tour," she sighed out. "I'll be visiting all the settlements on a PR tour with my father and his team."

"Ah." He scoffed. "The wedding dress."

Had he seen the posters already? She winced, opting not to answer. He was steering her toward the fitness centre as though he had a copy of her schedule.

"What's the plan?" he pushed. "The city settlements first and then the outreach ones?"

"No, there's too many to do it that way. It has to be based off their location. We're starting with the Hudson Settlement and ending at the Mojave Settlement."

"Interesting. So you're visiting all fifteen, then?"

She nodded, trying to ignore the ball of lead in her stomach.

"How macabre," he surmised.

She snorted. "Nobody else seems to think so. The PR team thinks it's brilliantly romantic. A real Cinderella story. I'm Prince Charming, of course."

"Of course."

"Ashford?"

"Call me Cian."

"Why would I do that?"

"Why should you call me by my name?" He opened the door to the practice room she had booked without her making any sort of indication that it was the right one.

She slid past him, frowning when he invited himself inside and closed the door, leaning back against it with his arms crossed.

"Why are we talking like we're friends?" she asked.

A laugh rumbled out of him, and his arms relaxed, falling to his sides. "I like physical contact, too, you know."

She smirked. "I know."

"Well, it's hard to get close to people in this godforsaken environment. People either want to use me for screen time or in the hopes they can hitch their ride to an Icon. And you've met my friends. They're not very cuddly."

"Kilian—"

"*Kilian* is part of the problem," he spat, squinting

at her. "I'm so fucking jealous that he gets to be all over you with no strings attached. I just ... swindled a similar deal."

"Careful," she whispered, when all other words failed. "They'll make you get a fake girlfriend."

He only smirked, raising his voice. "Stop trying to reject your surrogate mate. I'm here as long as you need me. As long as you only need me for the next ..." He pulled out his phone. "Well, tonight, I guess. The busses come to take everyone back to the settlements for break early in the morning."

"You're going home?" she asked, feeling a strange pang of anxiety.

"Yes." He smiled, but it was tight. "Are you going to dance?"

"Are you going to watch?"

"Tempting, but no. The guys have been texting me. Gabriel gets antsy when I leave it up to the last minute to pack." He opened his arms for a hug. "Will this tide you over?"

She stared at the open, inviting space, holding her breath so that she wouldn't breathe him in. "Do I look like I'm struggling?" She tried to sound droll, but her voice was a squeak.

"Pretty much always," he answered, wiggling his fingers at her.

"I feel fine," she promised.

"Oh, for fuck's sake." He surged forward, wrapping one arm around her back and the other around her thighs, and then he hoisted her up, her whole body slapping along the front of his, the breath leaving her chest in a whoosh. "You're impossible," he grumbled. "Just relax and accept the hug."

Easier said than done.

Ashford—*Cian*—didn't have a very *relaxing* presence. His scent clogged up her brain, filling her with images of slow-rolling waves crashing against his bare, muscled back. She could almost taste it. Salt and skin. Heat.

His face nudged into her neck, his chest filling with a deep, searching breath. It vibrated out on a groan. "Okay, *wow*. Syrup on skin, that's quite a smell, Carter."

"Isobel," she grumbled. "If we're going to be friends."

His arms tightened, his chest still vibrating. "I'm thinking very unfriendly thoughts."

"Oh my god, put me down!" She hit his shoulder, and he obliged, laughing. He pushed a few messy locks of golden hair out of his face. "See you round, cherries."

She quickly locked the door behind him, her face

flaming bright red. She really didn't want to admit it, but her body felt lighter after the hug, her limbs more languid, though her chest tightened the minute she was alone. It was difficult to tell which emotions were from the strain of her half-formed bond and what was simple anxiety for the upcoming settlement tour, so she bundled it all to the back of her mind as she began to dance.

Several hours of practise later, she managed to grab some alone time with Eve before a group of Omegas descended to drag her friend off to dinner.

"See you at GMS!" Eve called, grinning as she skipped out of the room. The Green Mountain Settlement, Vermont. Eve had come from one of the outreach settlements. It was the ninth stop on Isobel's tour. Also Kilian's stop.

She skulked back to her room, packed her bags, and then sat on her makeshift bed, staring at the wall. That panicky feeling was rising again, and the harder she tried to ignore it, the more insistent it became. She didn't want to leave. Ten days seemed, unreasonably, like a lifetime. She wasn't sure how long she could go without ...

Without who?

She frowned, scrubbing her hands over her face. It seemed impossible, but ... Reed had said it was obvious. *So glaringly obvious, it's painful.* And if she could use contacts to cover up her eyes, then ...

"No." She laughed to herself, falling back and staring up at the ceiling. Except ...

"No!" she said again, a little more forcefully this time as her heart beat faster and faster. She *did* keep teleporting to Dorm A. And even now, she was itching to walk over there. It was an effort to stay where she was, to not reach for her phone to text one of them. She wasn't sure who, exactly, just that her mind kept drifting back to Dorm A.

Fuck.

She was mated to one of those asshole Alphas, and they were collectively hiding it from her.

Even Theodore.

Even Kilian.

And *Cian*, that fake bastard.

With a small growl, she jumped up, stalking all the way outside. She needed a plan, but her mind was wiped clean of everything except anger. Her phone vibrated in her hand, and she furiously swiped at the screen.

Theodore: You better not leave without saying goodbye.

She pulled up short, mulling over the message, and hands suddenly landed over her shoulders, darkness shrouding her vision, the thick black cloud cutting out the surrounding lights.

Not this again.

"Couldn't let you leave without a little send-off celebration," a voice purred into her ear as several sets of hands restrained her. Something was pressed into her mouth, choking off her scream. "We heard about your little Cinderella campaign. But how will you land a pretty prince if your face is all fucked up?"

That didn't sound good.

She struck out with her arms and legs, trying to twist out of their hold and land hits wherever she could. A few people grunted, the grip on her arm slipping, but there were too many of them, and they managed to drag her into a nearby building, shoving her up against a stone wall. One of them immediately punched her hard in the stomach, making her double over and clutch herself. They kicked at her until she fell to the ground. A boot made contact with her nose, and wet warmth gushed over her face. She stopped trying to fight, curling into a ball and wrapping her arms around her head. She choked back all sound, taking the beating as silently as she could, so the alarm that suddenly rang around them was piercingly loud in comparison.

"Saved by the bell, bitch." One last kick, and

footsteps pounded away from her, a door falling shut.

The dark cloud lifted, and a small form crouched beside Isobel, hands reaching around to the back of her head to untie the gag shoved into her mouth.

"Thanks." Isobel spit out blood, pulling up to a sitting position and falling back against the wall as the alarm continued to shriek through the stairwell. "Eve?"

"I heard them talking about it on the way to dinner," Eve said, her mouth a firm, angry line. "I tripped the alarm. Are you okay?"

"Who was it?" Isobel asked, ignoring the other question. She wasn't sure if she could stand.

"A group of Omegas and Betas. I'll help you file a report. I know all their names. Come on, let's get you to the medical centre."

It was slow going, and Isobel was pretty sure one of her ribs was cracked, but Eve took her weight and patiently helped her every step of the way, falling quiet after Isobel's almost violent reaction to the question of whether Eve should call Theodore to help.

It wasn't until several hours later, when she was lying in a hospital bed, staring out at the night sky through the tall window, that she really allowed herself to go through her memories of the day she woke up in Dorm A and made her way to a room just like this one. She had waited, back then. With Eve her only visitor.

She had waited to find out if she would die without a mate.

When all the while, her mate had been *lying* to her.

Hiding from her.

She had always known the Alphas were playing their own game at Ironside, but the lengths they had gone to in order to frame the entire narrative was shocking. They weren't just controlling what the officials saw. They were controlling what *she* saw, and this was *her* fucking life.

She wanted to be angry—she *was* angry—but there was a tiny seed of doubt in the back of her mind whispering that Kilian and Theodore wouldn't lie to her without a good reason. That seed sprouted, growing thin, unsteady branches. Reed had *told* her they were hiding something and had even challenged her to figure it out. He had said they were hiding it from themselves as much as they were hiding it from her.

She supposed all the answers rested with the *who*, and not the why.

Which one of them was her mate? What was so special about him that the others would all protect him from *her?*

14
OSKIE

"THERE WE GO. ALL BETTER!" THE MAKE-UP ARTIST, Serena, stepped out of the way of the mirror, tapping her brush to expel any excess powder.

Isobel turned her face from side to side. It was clear that she was swollen, but the glittering dark eyeshadow and pristine contouring helped to hide her bruises. Nothing could hide her limp, but they had to choose their battles.

"Champagne?" Serena offered—*again*—as the air hostess passed through the centre of the plane with another tray.

Isobel shook her head, watching as her father held up his finger for another glass. The private plane had several rows of comfortable seating, but it was growing excruciating all the same. Every time she tried to switch positions, a sharp bolt of pain travelled simultaneously down her tailbone and through her ribs.

She checked the time on her phone, counting down the minutes until she could take another dose of painkillers as Cesar Cooper broke away from the bubble of conversation surrounding her father, moving to the empty chair opposite Isobel.

"You look lovely," he told her, patting her knee encouragingly. She pulled her leg back, but he didn't seem to notice. "We'll be landing in the private airfield in New York soon, and then it's a short drive to the settlement. We've got a limo for you, of course. The rest of us will come separately, since the Ironside crew want to shadow you. Did you look over the schedule?"

She had spent a sleepless night in the hospital glaring daggers through the emailed schedule, fuming over what the Alphas had done to her and planning her revenge. The beating she had received was nothing compared to knowing her mate had been beside her all this time. Lying to her. She still had no idea who it was, but she would be visiting each of their settlements, and after a conversation with her father over breakfast in her hospital room, she had found out exactly which settlement each of them were from. He cared far more about her apparent scheming than the fact that she had been dragged into a stairwell and assaulted. He had given her that "you're finally starting to act like my daughter" look again, after patting her shoulder and telling her that jealousy was a given at Ironside. It was actually a *good* sign.

She had turned the conversation quickly back to the schedule to avoid snapping at him or bursting into tears.

Theodore and Moses were in Hudson. Her first stop. Sato was in the Ozark Mountains. The third stop. Then the Green Mountains for Kilian, and the Protected Redwood Settlement Region for Niko— stops nine and ten. Reed and Spade were at number twelve. Piney Woods. Then to Rock River Valley for Cian, and Easton's home settlement, the San Bernardino Mountains. Finally, her last stop was the Mojave Desert, where West was from.

Since they only had ten days to visit fifteen settlements, she had requested to prioritise the first eight of the Alpha stops, and her father was happy to oblige, thinking she was planning some way to use the Alphas to create drama on her tour.

"Well, let's just go over it again, then." Cooper

drew out his tablet when it seemed like Isobel wasn't going to answer him. "They've prepared a spot for you to receive visitors in each of the settlements. So as soon as you arrive, we'll invite the lucky applicants in to meet with you. Your father has requested that the following Alphas be rounded up and added to the line-up, as you requested: the Kane twins, Elijah Reed, Gabriel Spade, Kilian Grey, Niko Hart, Cian Ashford, and Oscar Sato. We'll make sure they're first in line, so you can spend as much time on them as you would like."

Isobel nodded, fiddling nervously with her phone. Theodore and Kilian had both tried messaging and calling her before she left. Thankfully, they didn't think to check the hospital.

"We asked the bond specialist to prepare some interview questions for you, but she suggested you just look at their eye colour," Cooper was saying.

"What if they're wearing contacts?" she asked quietly. "Those 'Gifted Eyes' places are really popular online. It's easy to recreate even the most unique eye-colours with rank rings."

"We're going to the settlements." Cooper rolled his eyes. "The Gifted can't afford such things."

"Right." Isobel flushed, looking down into her lap

before forcing her head back up again. "Let's just say they could, though. What then?"

"I'm not a bond specialist, darling." He reached out, grabbing her hands. His were clammy, a little sweaty. She resisted the urge to jerk hers away as his thumbs swiped against her skin. "You could always touch them?"

He released her hands when she tugged them, and she resisted wiping them against the seat until he was returning to his own spot for landing. She separated from the rest of her father's posse when they touched down, sliding into a limo with the film crew from Ironside, who all spoke to each other as though she was invisible.

To pass the time, she pulled out her phone and scrolled through Twitter, reading the comments on the official Mate Finder tour announcement made by Ironside.

@the_witching_hour: There are posters of Carter all over my settlement. Look what happens when I trace the golden ratio over her face! Is she perfect? #perfectbeauty #goldenratio #matefinder #findingcarter

@foodiefinds: Loving all the drama and suspense. The Kane twins came home just for the #matefindertour! First stop is Hudson! Might as well just end it here. Heh. #looknofurther #findingcarter #teamtheodore

@artistic_visions: Is it just me or does Carter have some sort of connection to every Alpha at Ironside? Gonna be a long tour. $100 says they don't let her talk to anyone else. #matefindertour #justicefortheprofessors #findingcarter

@screenqueens: @IsobelCarter turned 18 this year, so she shouldn't be getting all these special privileges anymore. Braun Carter needs to stay in his lane and stick to the rules. @OGGBOfficial what's the deal? #policethegifted #OGGB #giftedbehavingbadly #settlementsgonewild #findingcarter

@geniustwins_speedy: **RE: @screenqueens:** *The age of independence is 21, idiot.*

@fandomfanatic: Carter wants attention, not a mate. Check out this before and after picture. Proof of plastic surgery! Maybe plastic interferes with the magic? #matefindertour #findingcarter

@MRS.kane98: Theodore looks at Carter the same way my Labrador looks at cheese and I'm so here for it. #matefindertour #findingcarter #justicefortheo

@travellingavery: **RE: @MRS.kane98:** *I'm willing to bet my house on Sato. Haven't heard a thing he's said all season because his abs are so distracting. (If they aren't showing on screen, I stare at a screenshot of them on my phone instead).*

@olivia_filmsthings: **RE: @MRS.kane98:** *Reed is the*

kind of daddy that would treat you right and I'm here for it. #justiceforreed

*@emma.garcia12: **RE: @MRS.kane98:** What about Spade? He could ignore me all day and the second he says my name imma still be like "Yes, spaddy?"*

*@CAOfficial: **RE: @MRS.kane98:** As the official owner of Ashford's online fan page, I'm shocked and appalled. There's only one true daddy.*

*@screen.savvy: **RE: @CAOfficial:** Ashford is the man, the myth, the f**kboy legend. Carter should watch out for that one.*

Isobel barely refrained from rubbing her eyes and smudging all the make-up, opting to put the phone away instead and stare out of the window until they rolled to a stop at the gatehouse to the Hudson Settlement. There were huge Mate Finder banners at the front of the gatehouse, with streamers strung between them.

One of the cameramen leaned his head into the window, letting out a low whistle. "The officials are excited about this. I heard they're throwing a party for each of the settlements, hoping to get everyone involved. They even brought in alcohol. Don't know what the buggers did to deserve it, though."

"Shut up, Ryan, you racist prick." Another of the cameramen gave Isobel an apologetic look. She ignored it, and they were soon rolling past the guardhouse. The Hudson Settlement was one of the four main city posts, and one of the biggest. There were crowds already forming, held back by spaced-apart bodyguards in black fatigues.

"I had no idea I was this popular," Isobel said softly, following the black rope that was keeping the crowd contained.

"You kidding?" It was the same cameraman who had snapped at Ryan. "You could win this thing. And win a life out in the real world for one of these people too."

Out in the real world.

If one of the Alphas actually turned out to be her mate, then ... well ... for the first time in her life she had to admit, the chances were *good* that she would be living the life of an Icon.

The crew exited first, fanning out to capture every moment as she stepped out of the limo. The stylists who dressed her in the plane had explained that each of her outfits had been inspired by the cities she was visiting. For the first stop, she was dressed in a cropped Beastie Boys T-shirt with a slit right down the front, bridged by gold pins, the subtle muscles of her torso brushed in faint gold dust above the hem of loose, high-waisted jeans with large slits down the side seams, showing off the stylish black boots that hugged her calves. Everything was expensive, sponsored by actual designers in exchange for her mentioning their names on camera. Since it was the first question asked by the crew once she was out of the car, she didn't have to worry about remembering to do it.

The crowd started screaming as she walked past them, and she tried to smile through the noise, too terrified to make eye contact with anyone. They were holding their hands out over the barrier, but when she moved toward one of them, one of the Ironside crew darted forward.

"Touching is only for the meeting room," he advised quickly. "This way, Miss Carter."

She let them usher her toward the closest building, which had even more people packed behind ropes, filling the sides of the room. She thought she even recognised a few faces from Ironside. There was a table at the other end of the room, two chairs on either side. The crew directed her to the larger, high-backed chair facing the rest of the people, and a hush fell over the crowd as someone called for the first "volunteer" to come forth.

Despite how angry she was at him, her body relaxed as soon as Theodore's tall form stepped into the doorway, the sunlight turning him into a brief silhouette before he was striding for her table.

"Volunteer, eh?" He sank into the opposite seat, crossing his ankle over his knee and cocking his head at her, brushing a few locks of hair from his face. "You doing okay, Illy?"

"Why?" she asked, pretending to sound bored. She even pulled her hand up to examine her newly painted nails.

A little flop of confusion struck against her chest from his direction. She glanced over his shoulder, spotting a line forming behind him, headed by Moses. Her father and Cooper stepped into the back of the room. She steadied her breath, pulling her chin up as she turned her attention back to Theodore. The weird ball of tension that had taken up residence in the back of her throat was slowly snaking out of her ... but was it because Theodore was her mate, or because this was simply how she reacted to him?

"This is quite the Ironside Special." Theodore abruptly changed tack, motioning around the room. "How exactly do you plan on finding your mate through all the streamers?"

Isobel *hated* that he was turning on his charm. "I brought one of those special little torches," she answered. "Borrowed it off my bond specialist. Shows when someone is wearing contacts."

He narrowed his eyes on her, and the confusion flopped against her chest a little heavier. "Liar," he whispered.

"Hmm." She forced her eyes to drift over him. "But I've got nothing on you."

There.

There it is.

Panic.

Despite his calm, unaffected face, the heavy weight of panic was pressing in against her.

She was fucking *right*.

"If you had to guess." She notched her elbows onto the table and propped her chin on her hands, leaning toward him. "Which settlement would you say my mate was in?"

"I'd say one wouldn't be enough." He stood, winking at her, every chink of his armoured charm still in place. "You're going to need a small army of them to get through the lines forming." He chuckled as several people within earshot broke into whispers, a few giggles bursting through the crowd.

"Kiss her!" someone shouted.

Theodore laughed harder, holding up his hands as he slowly backed away, leaving Isobel with a horrible, empty feeling inside her chest. Theodore was a phenomenal actor. It was impossible to tell what was real and what wasn't.

Moses dropped into the vacated seat; his expression far more curious than it had been while he was standing in line.

"Lovers spat?" he asked, reading Theodore better than she ever would have.

"Something like that." Isobel crossed her arms, dropping her blasé act. "How about you, then? Which settlement do you think my mate is hiding in?"

"What makes you think he's hiding?"

"So it's a he?"

"Do I look like an official, Carter?"

She leaned over the table, grabbing his collar and putting her lips by his ear. "*Worse*," she whispered, her voice barely audible.

A low, dangerous sound rose up from his chest, and she uncurled her fingers, dropping back into her chair. "They told me to touch the volunteers." She kept the fear from her tone, reminding herself that she had the upper hand. "And I know he's hiding. I was inside his head."

There. Again. The briefest flash of panic.

"Again?" Moses asked carefully.

"So what do you think?" Isobel ignored his question. "Which settlement is he hiding in?"

OSCAR DROPPED A HEAVY BOX AGAINST THE COUNTER, pulling out his phone as it vibrated with a text message. He swiped the screen as a droplet of sweat fell against the glass.

Theodore: She knows.

It was to the group chat.

"Motherfucker," Sato swore.

Lily gasped behind him, carrying her own, much smaller box. "Oskie!"

"Pretend I didn't say that." He confiscated the box off her, adding it to a pile in the corner. "I told you to stop carrying stuff. Go play on your iPad."

"How much did it cost?" she asked, shuffling onto the patched-up couch and pulling the iPad back into her lap. He had already preloaded it with endless games.

"It was free." He stole it from Ironside. "I won it at Ironside." He bopped her on the nose before opening one of the boxes and beginning to throw utensils into one of the two kitchen drawers.

The house was tiny. More like a hut, with one bedroom and a living area big enough for the couch and a tiny trestle table. But the roof wasn't collapsing, like the last one. Lily didn't tell him about it, and he had to rein in his rage that she had been living with rain dripping all over the place for months.

His phone vibrated with another message, and his neck pricked as he waited to see how long he could ignore it. Three spoons and a potato peeler later, he cracked, reaching for the device.

Moses: She definitely knows, and she's pissed.

Kilian: How pissed?

Moses: She's out for blood.

Oscar: Oh well, it was going to happen eventually.

Theodore: Easy for you to say. She already hates you.

Oscar: There's a fine line. And I'm the only one who didn't pretend to be her friend, so I guess I've just taken your place as favourite, pretty boy.

Theodore has left the chat.

Moses: Seriously, O? I'm the one who has to deal with him now.

Elijah: How can you be sure? Add Theo back.

Theodore has joined the chat.

Theodore has left the chat.

Elijah: I swear to fucking god. Add him again, and tell him Oscar is muted.

Theodore has joined the chat.

Oscar has been muted.

Elijah: How can you be sure?

Theodore: She's my mate. I'm fucking sure.

Moses: I'm also 100% sure.

Oscar signed out and opened the handy security app Elijah and Gabriel had been working on, cracking Kalen's password in half a minute.

Oscar has been added as an admin.

Oscar has been unmuted.

Oscar (admin): Nobody puts baby in the corner.

Gabriel: Wow. You're actually enjoying this.

Cian: He was designed for chaos. He feels right at home.

Oscar has been removed as an admin.

Kalen (admin): Everybody calm down. We've had time to plan for this.

Kilian: We didn't think it would happen so soon.

Niko: I'm not ready.

Cian: I knew today was going to be a shitshow.

Gabriel: Thanks for the heads-up.

Easton (admin): We were never going to be ready. But she's proved she can keep a secret and I think it's pretty obvious she doesn't want a mate. Maybe we can work something out?

Moses: She's not in a negotiating mood.

A picture popped up on Oscar's phone, sent by Moses. He picked it up, biting back a chuckle at the image on-screen. Carter was levelling a simmering stare at Moses from across the room, ignoring the poor girl sitting across the table from her, obviously trying to get her attention. Carter looked like she was seconds away from drawing her finger in a line across her throat, threatening Moses for all the cameras to see.

Kilian: Oh my god, she's so cute when she's mad.
Theodore: She's mad at you too.
"Oskie."

The little voice had his head jerking up. Lily's face was green. He quickly hunted down a bucket, pushing it into her hands just as she started to retch, the sandwich he had made her an hour ago resurfacing. He sat beside her, holding her dark curls out of her face until she was finished.

"Oskie?" she tried again, her face now pale and sweaty. "Will I lose all my hair again?"

"No, sprout. This won't be like last time."

Last time, he almost lost her.

And then West turned up, out of nowhere, offering him a way out. Join Ironside. *Win*. Lily would never have to go through that again. At first, it was just a way to give her a better life after she won her battle against Leukaemia, but then the cancer came back.

They spent every cent beating it the first time around ... the second time? They had nothing left.

She managed a tremulous smile, her black-ringed eyes crinkling at the corners. The Sigma ring was almost invisible with how dark her eyes already were.

"Will the Sigma come to visit us?"

The question had him clamming up, but Lily was too busy reaching for her iPad again. She clicked into YouTube and started scrolling through the trending videos, some of which were clips from the Ironside episodes. She skipped to the reels, tapping to pull up a short video of Carter sitting at the same table Moses had sent a picture of. She was smiling politely at a boy across from her.

"She's coming here in two days," Lily said, as Oscar decided to busy himself cleaning out her bucket and fetching her a cup of water to wash her mouth out with.

He wrung out a cold cloth, managing to talk her into lying down so he could cover her sweaty forehead. She was still clicking through videos, but she tugged on his pocket before he could return to unpacking the boxes.

"Will she?" Lily asked, wide black eyes imploring him.

She had developed an unhealthy obsession with

Carter in the time that had passed since his last visit. She watched Ironside religiously in the town hall every night and followed all the fan pages on her beat-up old brick of a phone. As the only Sigma in the Ozark Settlement for a good few generations, she idolised Carter for being like her ... and for dragging Oscar into the screen time drama. She somehow thought he and Carter were friends.

"She might," Oscar hedged. He *had* to go and see Carter. The gaggle of Ironside assistants and managers that had already turned up to prepare for Carter's arrival had made it clear that he would be the first in line to greet her, just like Theodore and Moses had been. But if she really had figured out what they were hiding from her, then it wasn't a meeting he wanted to involve his sister in.

"I'm not old enough to go to the hall and meet her." Lily pouted, picking at the iPad case. "Do you think she'd have time to come here?"

"I'll ... ask," he said.

She huffed, like she knew he was lying. "Jackson said I was going to go bald again and I'll be ugly."

"What?"

"Jackson. He said Sigmas are useless but *ugly* Sigmas are a waste of air."

What the actual fuck?

"Where does Jackson live?"

"Row J, House 3. He lives with his grandma. She hates when people lean up against her house. Said she was going to put out pigeon spikes. What are pigeon spikes?"

"I thought you were starting third grade, squirt. And you've got an iPad now too. I'm going to step out for a bit. You better know what pigeon spikes are by the time I get back. And how to remove them."

"Okay, Oskie."

He rearranged the cloth, flipping it over to the colder side, and then he stepped outside, his eyes narrowing.

Row J, House 3.

Could he make the little boy disappear without anyone noticing?

THEODORE SLID INTO A SEAT AT THE RICKETY TABLE, the weight of his body threatening to collapse it. He had already broken one of them, and he had only been home for one day. His father was boiling water for shitty tinned coffee, giving him some major side-eye. Usually, Moses was the moody one.

"So, um. It didn't go great, then?" his father ventured, lining up cups and plates of cookies.

He always pulled out extras, hoping some of their friends came over when they visited ... but they didn't have any friends. Not at home. It was too risky—*especially* in the Hudson Settlement. Not even their father knew about their ferality. Their mother had taken it upon herself to guard that secret since the day Theodore was born. Luckily, the midwife was late to the birth, or she might have noticed that Theodore was born with spidery black veins that only disappeared when his Sigma mother sucked the darkness into herself.

She opted to birth Moses on her own, just in case.

And then she decided she couldn't risk another child.

"It ... was fine." Theodore fiddled with the cup when his father pushed it into his hand. "She's having a bad day."

"Oh." Benjamin Kane frowned, darting his eyes to the door, waiting for Moses, or the friends that would never come, or *heck*, maybe even Isobel Carter herself. "I thought I might get to meet her."

"Someday maybe. Sorry, Dad."

"Your mom would have liked her." Benjamin flashed a grin full of teeth, some of that Kane charisma flashing across his face. It was a broad and handsome face, his smile just a little crooked, smile lines around his grey eyes, white peppered through the dark strands of hair that were still full and thick despite his age. He wore his beard trimmed short, and he stroked his hand across it now, still staring at the door.

Moses stepped through as Theodore drained half of the coffee, drowning out the taste by shoving one of the sugary cookies into his mouth. They sent money home, just like everyone else, but this year the officials had jacked up the prices at all the commissaries. Most households were now lucky to afford half their usual grocery shop.

"She's coming," Moses grunted, tucking his phone into his pocket and plucking one of the extra cups from the counter. He snapped it down onto the middle of the table. "Looks like we'll finally get to use one of these extra cups, eh, Dad?"

Benjamin jumped up, rushing to the door. "What? Oh, she really is coming. Oh god. Is the place clean enough?" He quickly began wiping spilled coffee grinds from the counter. "I should have baked something. She's probably starving."

"She flew here on a private jet," Moses muttered, rolling his eyes. "She probably had caviar for breakfast."

Their father paled even further, staring at the cracked coffee cups.

"Dad." Theodore patted the seat beside him. "Sit. Relax. She doesn't care."

"Well, she cares about *something*." Moses shared a look with Theodore, brows pushed high. It said: *Are we really doing this?*

It likely wasn't even Isobel's idea. The officials were driving this trip, and any of them would be stupid to assume otherwise. As soon as his father sat down, Theodore sprang up, beginning to pace beside the table.

"Did you do something?" Benjamin asked, frowning at him. "Did he mess up?" He directed that to Moses, who smirked.

"You could say that."

"And you?" Benjamin pressed, now just about as white as a sheet.

"You could say that," Moses repeated, sounding chipper.

Benjamin let out a sound like a strangled cat. "For crying out loud, the timing. Can't you just apologise?"

"Might not cut it—" Theodore snapped his lips shut as a knock sounded against the door Moses had closed.

Moses remained in his chair, his arms crossed. Benjamin was shell-shocked, staring at the door, listening to the very obvious sounds of a camera crew on the other side.

Theodore slipped around the table and pulled the door open, forgetting about the crew instantly. He wanted to say it was because he was used to it—the attention, the cameras—but he would be lying. It was the way Isobel was hunched in the opening, twisting her fingers together like she did when she was scared or nervous. She had put on such a brave face before, but in between then and now, someone had obviously forced her to prolong the encounter, and she had run out of bluster.

"So you're going to say goodbye before you leave, this time?"

Why did he fucking say that?

Her eyes flashed up, mismatched and angry. As always, he focussed on the galaxy colour she left uncovered. The warm, speckled, honey-gold colour made his insides twist up nervously, because it was the colour he saw in the mirror whenever he switched out his contacts.

"If you'd prefer I didn't—" She began to turn away, but he quickly reached out and grabbed her wrist, dragging her into the house.

He stepped up behind her, his hands lightly

clasping her shoulders, his body tight against her back. *You're not going anywhere.*

"Dad, this is my friend Isobel. Isobel, this is our dad, Benjamin."

"Nice to meet you, Mr Kane."

Fuck, her voice was so sweet when she was cowering back against him. His father was a Beta, and Theodore was fairly sure that her issues were mostly with Alphas—or Ironside students in general—but she still seemed nervous as all hell.

"And I'm Braun Carter," a voice boomed, a tall shadow falling across the entryway.

Isobel flinched, sinking even further into Theodore. *Ah, that explained it.* He gave her a little squeeze, steering her to the other side of the table. Moses stood, angling his body just slightly in front of her as they faced off against Braun.

Benjamin had finally found his legs and was enthusiastically pumping Braun's hand. "My wife and I watched you grow up on Ironside," he gushed. "Well … I suppose we grew up with you, but you weren't watching us."

"It's a pleasure." Braun glanced around their small house. "Isobel has told me so much about your sons. They seem to be really hitting it off."

Isobel coughed, and he shot her a quick, hard look, making her tense up further.

She hadn't told him shit about them.

Benjamin flicked his silver-ringed eyes between father and daughter before stepping back and offering Braun the seat furthest away from where Theodore and Moses weren't even pretending to be doing anything other than guarding Isobel. Benjamin wasn't stupid. He raised two Alpha sons, even if he didn't know about their ferality. He knew that they could get possessive.

"Coffee?" Benjamin asked, just as Braun's eyes began to drift over to Isobel again. "I remember you used to drink quite a bit of it. Actually, I think I might ..." He started rustling through the cupboard above the stove, pulling down the brand of coffee he liked best. Braun Carter's face was on the packaging. "I'll make you the special stuff!"

He dumped out the old pot and looked over his shoulder. "Theo! Come and help your old man out." There was half a bark to the words, and Theodore set his mouth into a grim line before taking a step back from Isobel and moving to his father's side.

Benjamin handed him the coffee packet before moving on to his next target. "Moses, why don't you show Braun and Isobel the rest of the house?"

"There's only two other rooms," Moses muttered, though he stepped to the side. Isobel followed him, and he looked down at her, his brows pushing together before he took her hand and pulled her down the short hallway.

Braun held back, waiting for one of the cameramen to dart after them before he followed.

"Were those bruises under her make-up?" Benjamin hissed lowly, leaning into Theodore so that the rest of the crew wouldn't be able to overhear.

Theodore gritted his teeth, nodding. It was the last topic of conversation he wanted to broach. He had noticed the second he sat down across the table from her, and it had taken everything in him not to lose his shit. He was still trying to tamp down on his instincts.

"From *him?*" Benjamin whispered, giving up all pretence of coffee-making.

Theodore took over so that the crew wouldn't take any interest in their conversation. They were all crowding after Isobel and Moses, completely obsessed with the fact that Moses was holding her hand.

"Him, or the other students. Hard to tell with her."

"She's limping." Benjamin's expression was torn.

"Hmm," Theodore agreed. *Don't think about it.* The last time she was hurt, he turned feral, and she *died*. He needed to keep a tight wrap on his emotions.

"I didn't think Moses liked her."

"He likes her well enough. He just doesn't like her liking me."

Benjamin scoffed, the heaviness immediately lifting from his eyes. "You two never did share well."

They were quiet after that. Benjamin didn't understand why his wife suddenly applied for them to relocate to the Hudson Settlement, and he understood even less when she began to introduce her sons as twins instead of brothers ... but he had learned to let a few things slip. Years of taking on the ferality her sons battled to keep at bay had created a madness inside her, and he loved her too much to ask her to change, especially when she asked for so little.

His father didn't question when eight rare Alphas suddenly all came of age to enter Ironside at the exact same time, even though he knew at least one of them was a lie. The outreach settlement they had come from didn't keep birth records, so the only danger now was if he let something slip in front of the cameras. So they didn't speak again until Isobel, Moses, and Braun returned.

Isobel sat between Theodore and Moses, her eyes directed to her lap as Benjamin naturally picked up on the safest topic of conversation: Braun Carter.

Theodore tuned them out more or less immediately, bending his head toward Isobel's.

"You don't want a mate," he said lowly.

She grew eerily still, and Moses pitched closer until their heads were all bent together like they were sharing a secret.

"No," she affirmed quietly.

"Then maybe you can understand." Theodore sat back as Braun shot them a look. He didn't give a fuck about the older Alpha, but he didn't want Isobel punished for being rude, and Kilian and Oscar had made it clear that not all of Isobel's injuries over the past couple of weeks had been caused by Ironside students.

She didn't reply, and it was a physical effort not to pull her back when Braun stood, announcing that they had to stay on schedule.

"See you soon," Theodore muttered, watching her trail her father out of the house.

She glanced over her shoulder, looking like she would rather stay with them and their chipped mugs and stale dirt coffee ... even though she was probably still fuming at them.

He took a step toward her, but Moses gripped his arm, halting him before any of the crew noticed.

"Bye," Isobel whispered, turning to follow her father.

A growl built up in the back of his throat, but he bit it down, forcing an easy smile as the cameras turned back to watch them standing in the doorway. He leaned against the door jamb, waving lazily, before stepping back and slamming the door.

"Let's go for a run," Moses snapped, more of an order than a suggestion.

Theodore nodded, storming into their shared bedroom to change his clothes.

He needed to work out some aggression, and he needed to do it fast.

15

WELCOME TO THE GAME, I GUESS

Isobel closed the door to her room, leaning up against it as exhaustion tunnelled through her. They had spent most of the day at the Hudson Settlement, staying for the beginning of the celebration that night before flying to Maine. Someone had organised rooms for them at a lodge near the North Woods Settlement, and she had exactly six hours before she had to be up again for the whole hair and make-up routine.

She locked the door first and then put herself through a scorching shower, but she couldn't seem to do anything about the bone-deep chill that had settled in her veins. It had been like that on the plane on her way to New York and again on the way to Maine, but now it seemed to be worse than ever. She was shivering by the time she stepped out of the shower, pulling on her pyjamas and diving into the bed, where she curled into a ball, fighting back a full-body shudder.

She managed to drift off to sleep, but when she woke up, her throat was raw, her eyes itching. She told Serena that she was sick when the styling team poured into her room, but the other woman just waved her off with a smile.

"At least the swelling is going down," Serena stated cheerfully, already setting up her make-up station. "So, for the North Woods theme, we have some *delicious* Balenziaga boots and a Burberry flannel dress with a matching trench. You'll be nice and cosy, and you can hide tissues in the pockets."

Isobel didn't bother answering, because they weren't going to listen to her anyway. She wasn't their client. Her father was.

She sank back into the chair, becoming a doll for them to play with as her eyes sought out the window, wondering what the next stop had in store for her.

Oscar glanced down at Lily for the fifth time, checking that her cheeks were still flushed with anticipation and not pallid with nausea. She had fallen asleep just before they announced Carter's arrival, messing up the braided hairstyle she had forced him to copy from a TikTok video, but she didn't care.

She was trying so hard to stand up on her tiptoes that he eventually gave in and swung her onto his shoulders, pushing his way to the front of the line. People turned to snap at him as he carelessly brushed up against them, but as soon as they saw his face, they scattered.

That was how he ended up standing by himself right at the roped boundary the officials had set up. Carter stepped out of a shiny black Jeep, a film crew pouring out of a companion car to capture her walk past the gathered crowd. Lily gripped his hair. *Hard*.

"Oh my god," Lily breathed, just as Isobel's eyes swept their way.

The Sigma paused, attention flicking back to Oscar. She was dressed in a forest-green slip dress, the material practically transparent, with gold foil and beads stitched magically into all the right places. The dress probably cost enough to buy Lily another five huts, all with impeccable roofs. But Carter looked like she was freezing. She hugged her arms around her body, allowing the officials to sweep her past the people as she shot them shy, soft smiles. She paused when she got to Oscar, but the officials moved her along again, muttering something about saving everything for the table.

She glanced at him over her shoulder, gold dust glinting along her cheeks. They had rolled her in glitter and gold, and it still wasn't enough to cover up her pain. Luckily for her, the "damsel in distress" posters had already perpetuated the marketable image of a Sigma in need of saving, so she was playing right into their strategy, looking all small and cold.

"She looked at me," Lily gasped, finally releasing her death grip on his hair. "She's so pretty."

"I've gotta go to the meeting hall." He swung her down, walking her to the edge of the crowd. "Go straight back home, okay? I'll meet you there."

He waited until she was skipping back toward their row before he turned on his heel and stalked into the meeting hall, striding toward the table Carter was seated at. They were standing over her, waiting for her to finish an energy drink. Maybe she wasn't being peppy enough for them.

"The first volunteer for the Ozark Settlement," some guy announced. "Oscar Sato."

He pulled out the seat across the table from her, and they stared at each other for a few moments, neither of them speaking.

"Was that your sister?" she eventually asked.

He dipped his head in a short nod, before narrowing his eyes as she sniffled, a shudder passing through her small body. He made a disgusted sound, shrugging out of his jacket and tossing it across the table. "They could have at least put you in something warm."

"It's freaking hot," she complained, ignoring his jacket.

She had a fever.

"Put on the jacket." He didn't even bother biting back his Alpha voice, and she frowned as her limbs moved to obey. Even though a thin bead of sweat had formed on her forehead, she still hugged the jacket close, her nose dipping to the collar. Something raw and urgent rose in his gut as she tried to scent him, and he took a deep breath to steady himself, his lungs filling with the smell of burning cherry trees. It was a new fragrance on her, something he had never smelled before.

It was alarming.

"When did you eat last?" he asked, his voice rumbling with more gravel than he had intended.

She lifted a slender shoulder. "They served breakfast on the plane."

"Which you ... ate?" He stared her down.

She pursed her lips, choosing not to answer.

"Fuck's sake," he growled. "Didn't Cian apply to be your surrogate mate? You're getting sick. You won't survive the tour at this rate."

The camera crew crept closer, reminding him that their conversation wasn't private. Good. Ironside would probably have to act on that.

"I've survived long enough at Ironside with no mate in sight." Her tone was sharp suddenly, her mismatched eyes narrowing in a flash of fury. Oh, she *definitely* knew. But did she know about all of them, or just one of them? "Why do you think I won't last ten more days?"

"Because you have a fever." He kept his voice low and even, the opposite of hers. "Maybe the stress of the tour is pushing you over the edge. You need a surrogate."

"You need to stop pretending you care." She stood, still hugging his jacket, still shaking. "I need a break."

She slipped behind the group of people crowded behind her table, ducking away from the camera crew. The group consisted of her father, his team, and a bunch of officials. Oscar made to follow her, but one of the cameramen intercepted him.

"Don't bother," the guy said with a shake of his head. "We'll be heading to your house as soon as she's done with the volunteers." They called for the next volunteer, ushering Oscar away, and he gripped the swiftly rising need inside his chest, crushing it in an invisible fist. He wouldn't let his chaos out to play within a hundred miles of his sister, and he wouldn't resort to manual chaos by punching the cameraman either.

He hoisted himself up onto the scaffolding out the front of the hall, pushing aside the curtain of streamers they had hung up to hide the plastic sheeting where a window should have been. He tugged the sheeting down, leaning into the opening where he had a clear view of Carter, and then he pulled out his phone.

CIAN LET HIS HEAD FALL BACK AGAINST THE WINDOWSILL, the sounds of Emily and Harper's moans washing over him with all the soothing texture of a fucking gravel road. He should take up smoking. Or drugs. Or basically anything to plug the hollow need bottoming out inside him. His dick got hard just like always, but the pleasure was empty and hollow.

Boring.

That's why the girls were on round three without him. He didn't even want to watch. He just wanted them to finish and fuck off, even though this was their house.

He heard them both flop to the mattress, giggling, and he let his eyes drift up to what he could see of the sky above through the window.

"Ashford," Harper called out. "Your phone."

He dragged himself upright, falling onto the end of the mattress as Harper looped her arms around his neck, dropping the phone into his lap.

"Who's that?" she asked, as he swiped to open the picture Oscar had sent. "She's *gorge*—holy shit, it's Isobel Carter."

Cian stood, Harper falling back to the bed. "Pleasure as always, ladies."

"Wait, you're leaving already?" Emily was reaching for his belt. He took another step back, catching her wrists with a smile.

If anyone could have persuaded him to let go for a little while and forget his problems, it was the Turners. They were a no-strings couple who loved inviting the occasional guy into their bedroom, and he happened to enjoy—on occasion—the carefree, joyful way they treated him like one of the battery-operated toys in their bedside table.

"I'll be back tonight," he promised, dropping a kiss onto Emily's forehead and Harper's cheek. There had been a moment where Harper tossed her head back, her blonde hair cascading to the bed as Emily went down on her. He thought he felt a little twinge of something then, and he was just fucked up enough to know that in the dark and with a lot of alcohol, he might be able to imagine strawberry blonde streaks in that hair.

"Actually, never mind. I might just go celibate for a while."

The girls chuckled, like they thought he was joking.

He was halfway home, still staring at the picture Oscar had sent, when his phone rang.

"Cian Ashford?" an impatient voice asked as soon as he accepted the call.

"Yes?"

"We are in need of Carter's surrogate mate. Are you available?"

He froze, his brows jumping up. "I am?" It came out more like a question than a statement. His parents weren't going to be happy, but if Carter wasn't in too bad a shape, then they would be back in Chicago in a week or so anyway. "Is she okay?"

"We'll send a car. Please be ready to leave in half an hour. You'll be meeting her in Colorado."

They hung up, and Cian jogged the rest of the way

home, whistling for his brother as he passed the crowded centre square, where Logan was hanging with his friends.

"Where's the fire?" Logan asked, catching up with him. "Thought you were going out with the Turners tonight."

"I'll explain when we get home. Just keep up." Cian slapped him lightly across the back of the head, kicking up the pace as they neared Archer Avenue. All the narrow lanes in the RRV Settlement were named after actual Chicago streets, but none of them were big enough to comfortably drive a car through. They burst through the door of number eleven, finding their father and stepmother in the tiny living room. They were better off than most families, even though the commissary prices were jacked up enough that they could barely afford food anymore. Both of his parents had actual jobs within the settlement, and they even had a tiny house with two bedrooms the size of closets and no shared walls with other houses.

Cian was pretty sure the money he was sending home was actually going to the neighbours. His Omega parents were like that. Kind and generous to a fault.

"Dad, Emma." He rushed past them, opening the door to the room he shared with Logan. "They're sending a car to pick me up!" he shouted back through the door as he shoved his things into a bag. "I'll be back when the Mate Finder tour comes through here in a week or so."

All three of them appeared in the doorway in a flash.

"What? You're leaving?" his father asked, sounding appalled. "You only just got here. You're supposed to be here for the whole break. Your party is tonight!"

"Shh, Arthur, did you even listen to him? He's being added to the Mate Finder tour!" Emma exclaimed, before she turned her excited gaze on Cian. "Do they think you might be Carter's mate, sweetheart?"

Logan scoffed, flopping down onto the bottom bunk. "He wishes."

"They're calling me in as a surrogate. She must not be doing too well."

"Oh." Emma looked crestfallen. "That's not good. But why you?"

"I offered. Just before the break. Thought something like this might happen."

"Thought, or...?" His father trailed off, looking at the tarot cards Cian dropped into his bag before zipping it up.

"It wasn't like that." Cian hooked the bag over his shoulder. "Sorry about the party."

"Don't worry about it." His father clapped him on the back. "We'll just postpone it. Keep us updated, okay? Don't let them force you into anything you aren't willing to do."

Cian flinched, shrugging off the reminder. There were plenty of people who would pay for an hour alone with a young Alpha, it turned out. His parents had intervened on more than one occasion.

"Love you," he shot over his shoulder, hurrying out of the house.

Isobel was struggling.

She managed to make it through all the volunteers in the line with a polite smile on her face, but it dropped too quickly when she rose to shaky feet, following the direction of one of the crew as they assisted her to the exit.

"We'll stop in at Sato's house and be wheels up in a couple of hours." Cooper appeared beside her. "There's a doctor waiting on the plane already."

"Thank you," she said, focussing on where she was walking. They had given her the thinnest heel to walk in, and the Ozark Settlement only had dirt roads.

Cooper dropped his arm around her shoulders, and she immediately ducked out from beneath the weight.

"Uh, it's not my jacket," she explained lamely. "Sato is an Alpha. He's sensitive to smells."

"I might not be Gifted, but I'm not an idiot." Cooper was trying to sound good-natured, but it was clear he was annoyed. "It's a two-hour flight, and then you have the night off. Spend it wisely, because we need you ready to go in the morning. We're doing another two stops."

She nodded silently, following the crew to a narrow lane packed with houses no bigger than huts. Sato's door was already hanging open, his broad back visible as he stirred something in a pot over the stove.

"Sigma! Carter!" a little girl screamed, racing to the open door. She leaned against it, her chest heaving, her eyes wide.

She had a Sigma ring.

Sato tensed but didn't turn around.

"Well, hello there." Isobel knelt down, putting herself on eye level with the girl. "What's your name?"

"My name is Lily, but Oskie calls me squirt. You can call me squirt too if you wanna." She sucked in a breath like the sentence had worn her out, and Isobel noticed the fine sheen of sweat dotting her forehead.

"Lily." Sato glanced over his shoulder, his brows pulling together. "Please sit down."

Lily ignored him, swaying on her feet as she blinked at Isobel. "Did you find your mate?"

"Not just yet," Isobel muttered. "I'm *so* tired after trying to find him all day. Is there somewhere we can sit down?"

"Yes!" Lily grabbed her hand, leading her over to the couch that was wedged wall-to-wall in what looked to be the only living space.

Isobel sat down. She could have stretched out her legs to touch Sato in the kitchenette. Lily jumped up onto the couch beside Isobel, her hand clutched around a wet cloth, still staring at Isobel with that dazed, wide-eyed look. There was a bucket pushed just slightly beneath the couch, and a small basket of medications on the trestle table.

"I like your home," Isobel told the little girl. "Do you live here by yourself?"

"Noo." Lily drew out the word, flashing an adorable missing tooth. "I share it with Oskie. What's wrong, Oskie?"

Isobel blinked over at the tensed Alpha at the stove. His emotion was radiating out, nudging against her chest with a dark feeling. *Lily could feel it too.*

"Nothing, squirt." He slapped down several bowls

and then heaped them with what looked like cheesy pasta dotted with peas.

He stuck forks into each bowl and brought them over to the couch, dropping one into Lily's lap and one into Isobel's lap before sitting up against the wall, his long legs stretching out. One of them wound behind Isobel's leg, the heat of him brushing across her ankle.

"Eat," he grunted, forgetting his bowl as he fixed Isobel with a hard look. "It's Lily's favourite."

"Monsta pasta!" Lily stabbed her fork into the bowl, but she made a face when it came time to force the food past her lips.

"Just a little," Sato said to her, softening his voice to a gentle, soothing rumble.

Lily popped a piece of pasta in her mouth, turning to grin at Isobel. "He made monsta pasta for you. He usually makes me toast when I'm sick."

There were too many medications in that little basket. Isobel wanted to ask, but that dark emotion was still battering against her, and the camera crew were *way* too quiet, all packed against the other side of the room, some of them still outside. As curious as she was, it would have been wrong to air their private business to the whole world.

So she shut up, and she ate. The pasta was

surprisingly good, the cheese perfectly melted with a hint of pepper.

"How old are you?" she asked Lily, who was kicking her legs, tapping against Sato's arm with every swing.

"I'm eight years old," Lily replied. "Is Oskie your mate? You can have my room. I sleep on the couch most nights anyway."

The hut was only big enough for one other room, the walls so thin that she could hear the people moving around in the neighbouring hut. Did that mean Lily was completely alone?

Sato's father certainly seemed to be dead ...

Isobel stilled, the fork clattering from her fingers. The horrible "ghost" who called Sato "Little Wolf" ... he had been this adorable little girl's father?

"Ah ..." She wracked her brain for a response to Lily's question while Oscar just leaned back against the wall, watching with heavy eyes and offering no help at all. "My mate will have an eye like this." She pointed out her multihued iris. "Two people forming a bond will always have an eye that matches colour."

"Who has an eye *that* colour?" Lily asked, squinting.

"When you find them, you let me know."

"Okay." The girl giggled. "And if you find them, you'll let me know?"

"Hmm." Isobel lifted her gaze to Sato again. "Do you think it's possible?"

"No," he responded flatly. "Your mate clearly wants to stay hidden. Learn to live with it."

She set her bowl aside. "I'm fine with that. He better hope I don't find out who he is."

"Why?" Lily asked, licking cheesy sauce off her fork instead of actually eating.

Isobel sighed, glancing over to the doorway. She could see her father's shadow outside, Cooper beside him, their eyes burning into her. She wanted to deliver a message. To Sato. To the other Alphas. To everybody who watched her tremble today. But she had to be careful, or she would end up in a worse state tonight.

"Because I'm a Carter," she settled on, holding her father's gaze. "My mate is playing games with me … but *real* Icons aren't made to lose. They're going to regret playing games with me."

One of the cameramen stepped forward immediately, his voice loud. "Are you officially announcing your intentions for the Icon track, Miss Carter?"

Her father was smiling wolfishly, a steely look in

his eyes. Sato looked like he wanted to drag her outside and ... punish her somehow.

"I am." She stood. "And I've overstayed my welcome."

She shrugged off Sato's jacket, draping it over Lily's shoulders, before she bent to give the girl a hug. "It was so nice meeting you, Squirt."

Lily choked on a small squeal, returning the hug tightly. Sato stood as the crew all backed out of the house, lowering their cameras. He reached over her shoulder just before she followed, slamming the door and separating her from everyone who had followed her there.

"Lily. The jacket." He kept his eyes on Isobel, crowding her up against the door.

Her back hit the solid surface, Sato's muscled body pushing up against her front. Lily must have handed over the jacket, because Isobel was suddenly wrapped into it again, Sato's hands rubbing over the material.

"This should help," he muttered lowly, his cheek brushing against the top of her head.

"How?" Isobel whispered back, her heartbeat thundering.

"Because I'm an Alpha." He smirked, easing back. "Same reason they agreed to let Cian be your surrogate. We're fucking potent. We're the perfect balm for a soul reaching out for something to ground it." The corner of his lips twitched, dark eyes drifting over Isobel's face. "You haven't figured out who it is." It was a statement, not a question.

"And you've known all along," Isobel returned, her words barely more than air.

He hummed, the sound vibrating through his chest and into hers. "Welcome to the game, I guess."

16

THOROUGHLY FUCKED UP

THEY CHECKED INTO ANOTHER LODGE IN COLORADO, COOPER
pulling her aside as they filled the reception area.
"Here's the card for your room." He held it out for her.
"We have a surprise for you in there."

"Oh. Thank you." She took the key card, wincing
when his fingers brushed against hers. The surprise
was probably another dress, just as uncomfortable as
the one she was wearing.

It smelled bad, now. Like sweat and sickness.
Not even Sato's drugging oleander scent could
drown it out. Isobel was concerned, because the
outfits were only on loan from the designers who
created them, but there wasn't much she could do
about it. She was getting sick. Sato's jacket seemed
to help, but her body was failing her. Her spine

ached, her ribs were on fire, her throat was raw, and her nose was so blocked she could barely breathe.

She said goodnight to her father and headed toward her room with a pounding head, all of her thoughts focussed on the shower that waited for her. Or a bath, if she was lucky. She entered the room, dropped her bags by the door, flicked the lock over, and leaned her forehead against the wood.

She felt fucking *lonely*.

Surrounded by her father and his team, it was like being home again, except this time, her mother was missing. She almost wished she was back at Ironside having the shit kicked out of her.

"Tough day, Carter?"

She spun so fast, she needed a minute to fight off a wave of dizziness and nausea, but she was pretty sure she wasn't hallucinating the tall boy by the window. Ashford—*Cian*—resumed drawing the curtains before opening his arms for her.

His golden skin looked a little drawn, tension lining his face, though he was wearing a soft smile that looked forced, just for her. His hair was pulled into a messy bun, gilded strands teasing his neck. She stepped up to him and slapped him clear across the face. His head turned to the side. It was a little underwhelming. She had imagined him stumbling back against the wall.

"I deserve that," he said tightly.

He held out his arms again, and this time she stepped up against his chest, allowing him to wrap them around her while she kept hers swaying by her sides. It felt *amazing*. His scent was like a salty wave that washed right over her, cleansing her of all the people she had touched, of all the stilted smiles she had laboured over.

She turned her head, nudging closer, her cheek pressing to his chest. He wasn't soft anywhere, but her eyelids started to droop, her hands twitching to wind around his torso and hang on. Instead, she tucked them into fists and fit them beneath her chin. One of his hands was at her mid back, just holding her tightly against him while he brushed strong, sure fingers through her hair.

"You've had a girlfriend before," she mumbled, swallowing when she realised her mouth was pooling with saliva. "You're way too good at that."

"I've had a few. And some of them have also had girlfriends at the same time, so maybe they count as double."

She snorted. "I'm so fucking angry at you."

"I know, sweetheart."

"Am I?" she asked.

"Are you what?"

She pulled back a little, squinting at him. "Your sweetheart?"

"I don't do girlfriends anymore," he said, pretending he didn't know what she was really asking. He picked her up suddenly, both arms bound around the small of her back as he hoisted her against him. He kicked into the bathroom, sitting her on the counter. As soon as he stepped away to run the bath, the cold settled back into her bones, making her shiver. She sneezed, and when she spoke, her voice was a rasp.

"Who's my mate, Cian?" It was her first real moment to talk to one of them without any people or cameras nearby.

Instead of answering, he retrieved a bag of supplies from the other room and began sorting through them. Isobel leaned over, spotting the hot water bottle and medicine inside. "What's that for?"

"Teak told them to pick it up. Along with me." He dumped half a packet of Epson salts into the water. "Apparently Oscar freaked them out by declaring to all the cameras that you weren't going to survive the tour without a surrogate. Teak told them that extra stress would exacerbate your symptoms."

"Why won't you tell me who my mate is? You can trust me."

"It's not about trusting you." He sighed, sitting on the side of the tub as the water ran behind him. "Not anymore, at least." He rubbed his hands over his face. "Have you considered that your mate might not be ready to reveal themselves?"

"Have you considered that I didn't get that choice?"

"Would you have acted any different if you *had* the choice? You keep a lot of secrets."

She grew quiet, fiddling with her fingers.

"That's what I thought," Cian muttered, standing and pulling his shirt over his head.

"W-What are you doing?" She stared at his sternum, gawking just a little bit. She had seen Cian shirtless more than once, but it was different when there weren't any cameras, and they were only a few feet away in a steam-cloaked hotel bathroom. He had two new tattoos, long-stemmed roses that angled up and over his shoulders. She was also pretty sure his nipple hadn't been pierced the last time she had seen him half-naked. She swallowed, unable to tear her eyes away from him.

He tossed his shirt onto the counter beside her, kicking his boots off one at a time. "Teak said skin-on-skin contact was what you needed. She said to stick to you like glue until you stopped shivering."

Isobel quickly sat on her hands to hide the tremble in them. "I'm not shivering anymore."

"Relax. Making a move on you is the last thing I want to do, no offense."

"None taken?"

He laughed, catching the way she scrunched up her nose. "I'm sure you already know you're beautiful." He grabbed her hips, sliding her off the counter and setting her on her feet. He lifted away Sato's jacket and then her dress was whipped over her head without much warning. "They're saying you have a *scientifically* perfect face."

"But my mouth is too narrow," Isobel added, crossing her arms over the skin-toned bodysuit that had come with the dress. "Yeah. I've heard. I've also heard about all my plastic surgery and how it's interfering with the bond magic so maybe don't believe everything you read on the internet."

Cian chuckled, bending to slip off her shoes. He turned off the water, shucked his pants, and stepped in wearing only a pair of short cotton boxers, his hand held out to her. "Come on, then."

She gave him a dubious look, wondering if it would be weird if she picked up Sato's jacket again.

Probably.

"Just pretend I'm Theo." Cian gave her a taunting look, wriggling his fingers.

She scoffed, slapping her hand into his. "Why can't I just be mad at you?"

He gently manoeuvred her over the rim of the tub and then pulled her down into the water, putting her back to his chest. There wasn't enough room to squeeze between his thighs so she ended up on his lap, the tub deep enough for the water to still reach the top of her ribs.

"Probably because that wounded little soul of yours is desperate for comfort." He gathered her hair into his hand, using it to tug her head back against his shoulder. "You still aren't relaxing."

"Yeah, no shit," she hissed out. "I've never done anything like this before."

"Will it help if I tell you to relax again?" There was a hint of laughter in his voice. "This isn't exactly comfortable for me, either, you know."

She tried to force her muscles to loosen as his big arms stretched along the sides of the bath. Her phone began vibrating on the counter, and she used it as an excuse to pop out of the bath. Almost immediately, she was freezing again, and she frowned, shivering as she glanced back to Cian.

He cocked an eyebrow at her. "Cold?"

"Yeah." She stepped back into the bath, the water uncomfortably hot until he dragged her back into his lap, his arms wrapping around her middle.

She held her phone out of the water, basically melting into his addictive scent. "Why am I cold when I'm not touching someone?"

"Your unfinished bond is straining. They call you the Tether, right? Because you're the one that died?"

"Um. Yeah." She was busy trying to ignore the erection pressing up against her thigh.

"Without an Anchor, you're just a string between death and life with nothing holding onto the life side. If you're not careful, you could slip away. Unfinished bonds are especially painful for the Tether, and if the Anchor is missing, just about any physical contact will do, though the more powerful Gifted are obviously preferred."

"How do you know all of that?"

"Elijah and Gabriel." He loosened his hold on her when it seemed like she wasn't going to try popping out of the bath again, and he returned his arms to the edges of the tub, shifting slightly beneath her. His grunt was one of discomfort, his scent swelling until it was heavier than before. "They did a lot of research after what happened to you."

"To me, *and* to ...?" She remembered the phone in her hand and glanced at the notification.

Theodore has invited you to download a secure messaging app.

"The hell?" Cian breathed, apparently also seeing it.

She clicked on the link, and her phone began installing something automatically. "Ah, shit!" She tried clicking out of it, but Cian captured her wrist, his voice muttering silkily by her ear.

"It's Elijah and Gabriel's app."

"Oh. Why am I downloading it?"

"I would also like to find out."

The app prompted her to enter her phone number, and then she received another notification.

Theodore Kane has invited you to a group chat.

Cian stiffened behind her, and the bath suddenly felt very awkward, which was strange, because it definitely should have started to feel awkward earlier. She accepted the invitation and then opened the group chat, staring at the single message on-screen.

Theodore: We have a proposition for you.

She frowned, trying to see who the group members were, but she only encountered an error message.

This feature is currently hidden.

Cian leaned over the bath, dragging his pants

toward him and digging into the pocket. His screen was full of notifications. She returned to her own phone, tapping out a message.

Isobel: What is it?

She felt it a few seconds before it happened, but only had time to thrash toward the edge of the bath before the world was shifting and re-shaping around her. Her vision went blurry and then resettled ... with her still in the bath. She was panting, curling into a ball with her arms hugging her knees.

"What is it?" Cian rumbled, lightly tugging her wet hair from her face.

"Almost ... teleported, I think. I don't know."

His phone started vibrating like crazy, and he reached over the side of the bath for it, cursing.

"We should get out," he said carefully. "Try not to look down at yourself."

Try not to look ... Oh. Oh, come on, what the hell?!

"He's inside my head?" She stared at the wall, her brain threatening to explode, her voice pitching. "My mate is inside my head?"

"Almost-mates," Cian corrected distractedly.

"Like there's more than one?" She laughed nervously, even though she knew he meant that her mate and her were "almost mates."

Except he was quiet.

And when she glanced up at him, he looked like he was biting his lip hard enough to draw blood.

"There's *more than one?*" Isobel screeched, scrambling to find her feet.

Cian handed her a towel, and she reached for it, her fingers trembling against the cold that sank immediately back into her bones. But she never grasped the towel, because the bathroom was gone in a flash of light, the tiled walls replaced with faded wallpaper and an old, bronze hanging lamp. Big, rough hands steadied her, fierce gold eyes staring down at her ... except West's eyes weren't the same shade. One of them was yellow-amber, like the eerie glare of a nocturnal creature, and the other was yellow-gold, with familiar honeyed flecks.

She started hyperventilating, and he immediately picked her up, sitting her on a stiff couch and pushing her head between her legs, his hand passing like a shadow over her spine, stroking so lightly she could barely feel it. But she *did* feel it, and it was comforting as *hell*. Warmth spread from his touch, igniting her blood, his vanilla scent tasting richer, headier than the last time she had scented him.

"Breathe," he reminded her, and she gulped that scent until her lungs were full, her head spinning in a bourbon-tasting haze.

"Y-You," she choked out, disbelief and fear making her voice small.

Of all the possibilities, West was the worst. He was … well, he was a lot like her father, to be honest. They didn't look alike, but West was the only Alpha who was potent enough to rival Braun Carter.

"Yes," he said, after a moment. "And all the others."

She whipped her head up fast enough to make the room spin. After blinking several times to clear her vision, she found herself only a few inches from West, who was crouched before her, his face lined in concern.

"*All* the others?" she croaked faintly.

"Ten of us, to be exact."

He pushed her head back between her knees as the whole hyperventilating thing started up again, but it didn't seem to be enough this time. Even his Alpha voice telling her to breathe couldn't make a dent, and she found herself tipping toward the floor, darkness spreading across her vision.

KALEN (ADMIN): SHE'S HERE. IN THE MOJAVE Settlement.

He stared at the Sigma laid out on his bed,

debating for a moment before forcing his phone up to snap a quick picture. They were going to want to see with their own eyes that she was okay.

Theodore: What the fuck happened?

Well. Mostly okay.

Kalen (admin): She fainted. All good, Cian?

Cian: Other than a terrified erection, yeah.

Kilian: Bro. Wtf.

Cian: We were in the bath, asshole.

Oscar: You're her assigned surrogate, fuckface, not her hired escort.

Cian: They quite literally told me to get in the bath with her. Even changed her room to one with a bath. Fuckface.

Kilian: It's weird, her father pimping her out. But why the terrified erection?

Cian: I let slip that she has more than one mate. Cue terror. Dick still hasn't received the message. Would very much like the Sigma back.

West (admin): Doesn't look like she's coming back.

Elijah: You're near enough to Ironside. It's, what, an hour's drive?

Kalen (admin): I have permission to come and go between here and Ironside. I'll drive her back there

once she's awake and I'll send her down the fire trail.
This is a fucking disaster.

Gabriel: *Why did she faint?*

Kalen (admin): *I was about to put in my contact,*
but I hadn't reached my room yet.*

Elijah: *Fuck.*

Theodore: *Fuck.*

Cian: *Fuck!*

Kalen (admin): *I told her she has ten mates. She*
knows.*

He set his phone aside while the expletives rolled in, pinching her delicate wrist between his fingers as he checked her pulse again. She was ice cold. He picked up the phone again and swiped out of the group chat, tapping on Elijah's contact. He put the phone on speaker, setting it onto the bed as he stalked to the wardrobe, pulling out all the extra blankets he had.

"We're both here," Elijah answered. "What is it?"

"She's freezing," Kalen snapped, trying to tuck the blankets around her. "And shivering. Her lips are blue."

"It shouldn't be that bad, especially if she was just with Cian." Gabriel was the one to speak. "Maybe the side-effects are twice as severe because there's so many of us. She's not having withdrawals from one of us being across the country; she's reacting to all the individual mates scattered to all corners."

"Just tell me what to do," Kalen growled, biting back the urge to say: "As long as it doesn't involve getting in the bath with her."

"She needs skin-to-skin contact," Elijah said. "Strip off to your underwear. We know she's basically already naked, even though you tried to cut off that part in your picture. We were in her head earlier."

Kalen pushed his reservations aside, tearing off every layer except his boxers. He slid into the bed beside her, hauling her against his side as he wrapped his arms tightly around her.

"Now what?" he asked.

"Pile on blankets so that your scent bakes into her," Elijah instructed.

Kalen kept her stuck to him with one arm as he reached for the blankets, hauling the layers over them. He tucked them carefully around her body, feeling her skin start to warm. "Anything else?"

"Yeah," Elijah drawled. "Try not to make her pass out again the second she wakes up."

"Massage her," Gabriel said, before Kalen could bark at Elijah. "Drown her in your scent as much as possible, especially where her veins are closest to the skin. Her wrists, forearms, temple, and neck."

"Fucking fantastic," Kalen ground out. "This is *exactly* what I had planned for my Saturday evening. Scent-marking a goddamn unconscious person."

"Person." Gabriel snorted. "We already know who's in your bed, Kalen. Maybe we should leave you to it—"

"If you hang up right now, I'm going to put my fist so far through your face that I'll be able to tie your fucking shoelaces."

"This got violent quickly," Elijah muttered, before hanging up the call.

Kalen resisted the urge to smash something, the restraint making his hands shake as he began to rub Carter's cold fingers. The furrowed lines on her brow eased, and he looked at her face for cues as he moved onto her forearms. The furrows returned. He brushed his thumbs across her temple, and her expression softened again, her breath less choppy. He used his body to roll her over, settling himself on top of her, though he was careful to prop himself up enough so as not to crush her with his weight. This freed one of his hands to stroke her temples, feathering touches across her forehead. She looked more like she was sleeping peacefully. The first woman to sleep in this bed, let alone step into his room.

And that was when he remembered ...

The door downstairs clicked, announcing the arrival of his girlfriend.

Fuckkkkkkkkkkkkk.

He slipped out of the blankets, tucking them carefully around Carter, who immediately looked like she was in pain again. He swore, swiping up his phone and tapping out a quick message as he grabbed the box of contacts from his sock drawer and practically poked his eye out trying to shove one of them in. He flew down the stairs, meeting Josette in the hall, where she was hanging up her coat.

"Sorry I'm late." She gave him a kiss, holding up a bag. "I ordered Italian from Gianna. I swear that lady is going to be the richest person in this damn settlement now that she can charge through the roof because of the commissary prices."

"You're an angel." He took the bag from her, leading her into the kitchen. "What did you need to talk about?"

"Well …" She sat at the small circular table as he began opening lunchboxes of pasta, smoothing her hands over his grandmother's favourite tablecloth with a small frown on her red lips. "I figured this was the only way to get you to invite me into your house. This place is harder to get into than the settlement is to get out of." She laughed at her own joke, but the sound tapered off when she saw the look on his face.

He was annoyed.

She immediately got up, moving behind him and winding her arms around his waist. His naked waist. Shit. She sniffed him. "You were about to have a shower?" she asked suddenly. "You smell kinda sweaty."

Because he was just trying to smother himself in blankets.

"Josette." He spun, pulling her hands away from his skin and holding them in his. "It's got nothing to do with you. I just don't—"

"Don't like people in your private space." She rolled her eyes. "I know. But like ... why do you even need a private space?"

"Because I'm surrounded by cameras all day long." He sharpened his voice. "But you don't need to make up an emergency if you really want to come over. You can just ask me."

"What if you say no." She pouted, blinking up at him.

"I might. Sometimes. Can you be okay with that?"

She sighed, shrugging. He had been dating her for a year, and he was well-acquainted with that look. Josette was the type of woman who believed, unfailingly, that she would always get her way eventually. It was why she was okay with dating someone who lived at Ironside and was away most of the year. It was why she let him sneak away from Ironside just to fuck her and leave again as soon as it was done.

She was playing the long game. Well, that and she also liked to be fucked.

His phone started ringing, and he pulled it to his ear. "Yes?"

"This is your fake emergency call." Elijah sounded bored. "Blah blah emergency blah."

"Is everything okay?" Kalen bit out.

"Clearly not."

"I'll be there in an hour."

"You're a terrible actor. You only have one tone: angry."

Kalen hung up, wincing at Josette's crestfallen face. "I'm sorry. They need me back at Ironside. I have to leave right away."

"But it's late," she protested. It was feeble. Josette was a hardcore loyalist. She got a real kick out of saying that she was dating an Ironside professor. She even had a framed picture of President Grant and the Gifted Ambassador Brooks shaking hands and smiling victoriously hung up in her kitchen.

It was precisely the reason he had chosen her to date.

"I'm sorry." He kissed her deeply enough to leave her breathless and giggling before he packed up the lunchboxes, ushered her to the door, and helped her back into her coat. "I'll call you tomorrow," he said, closing the door after her.

He locked it this time and then immediately pulled out the contact, because his fucking eye was still stinging.

Taking the stairs two at a time, he found Carter shivering. He pulled back the covers and carefully positioned his body over hers again, trying to soothe back those lines of distress on her face. She softened, melting beneath him, and he felt a flush of heat spear through him that *definitely* wasn't appropriate. He dipped his nose to her temple, pulling in a breath. His scent was all over her. Rich, boozy, cherry-vanilla hitting him hard. He felt a groan building up in his chest and quickly tamped down on his reaction, easing to her side so that his hips weren't resting over her soft thighs anymore.

He absently traced his fingers over her neck, leaning forward to sniff her again every now and then. It was like micro-dosing on the most dangerous drug. He didn't even realise how high he was getting until his stroking of her neck had turned into a tight grip, moving her face to the side so he could brush his nose up along the pale, addictive line of her throat.

He pulled back, closing his eyes and laying one arm heavily across her as he stared at the ceiling. *Should he break up with Josette?* He had absolutely no intention of acting on the half-formed bond. But ... it seemed wrong. His reaction to the Sigma was painfully strong.

It was also completely illegal.

And thoroughly fucked up.

17
LOW BLOWS AND SHARP SHOTS

THE FIRST THING ISOBEL BECAME AWARE OF WAS BLAZING, tingling heat. It soaked her head to toe in sweet vanilla liquor, making her blood sizzle and her head swim. The room was pitch black, and there was a body beside her. She brushed her nose across warm skin, her head struggling to clear as she climbed closer to the source of the delicious aroma. The body was warm and *big*, and everywhere she touched, the skin beneath her fingertips lit up, the very tops of her fingers doused in a golden glow. She traced patterns of light, her breath catching as tingles exploded throughout her body.

The chest beneath her was vibrating, scattering the light into puffs of sparkles beneath his skin that twinkled into nothing. She pressed down harder, bringing the light back, and traced up to his neck, skirting rough black stubble decorating a fierce jaw and tunnelling her hands into silky, short black hair.

The chest vibrated harder, and the thick thigh she had been straddling shifted up, big hands grasping her hips. He began to lift her away, but she clamped her thighs, holding onto his leg as she sank her teeth into his neck in punishment. The sparkles lit up her mouth, and those big hands pressed her down again, grinding her onto his hard thigh. She whimpered, withdrawing her teeth, and kissed across his hard jaw until she was staring into mismatched eyes circled by a swollen Alpha ring, pupils blown out.

West.

As in *Kalen* West.

As in *Professor* Kalen West.

Her memories rushed back in a vicious assault, the sparkles beneath her touch dying instantly.

"Oh my god," she breathed, swaying.

"Do *not* faint again," he growled in Alpha voice. "*Especially* if you're going to wake up in that state again."

"Oh my *god*," she wailed, scrambling to get off him. She tripped over a small mountain of blankets that decided to come off the bed with her, almost face-planting into a wardrobe. "I'm *so* sorry, P-Professor."

He winced. With moonlight slanting in a perfect spotlight over his expression, she could see the utter misery written all over his face. "Just ... call me Kalen in private. It'll make things easier."

Because he was her mate. "Look, I don't think ..." She backed up until she hit the wardrobe again, holding her hands out in front of her. The tremble was gone, a contented warmth snuggled deep down inside her. *Weird*. "I don't think I could ever—"

"Carter. Calm down."

"Isobel."

"Isobel." He scrubbed a hand down his face. And that was when she realised he was almost naked ... or *was* naked. It was hard to tell, with the blanket twisted over his lap. "I won't be completing the bond. Ever. None of us will."

"Oh." Her brows pinched in. She wasn't sure how to feel about that. Relieved? Rejected? Suspicious? Definitely suspicious.

"Theodore was just about to propose a deal before you teleported." He flicked the blanket back, flashing a pair of boxers as he grabbed for his clothes on the floor and started pulling them on. He was powerfully built, the breadth of his chest impressive, each sinewy muscle shaped to perfection. Even the chiselled ridges of his upper abs and obliques were cut sharply, but maybe that wasn't an appropriate thing for her to notice.

"He was going to tell you who your mates were if you promised never to reveal us to the officials," West continued, oblivious to her ogling. "Can we make that deal now?"

She frowned. "I ... I don't like the alternative. Either this has never happened before and we become the control group of a new OGGB experiment ... or it *has* happened before, and I don't want to know why all of those people have disappeared."

"Precisely." He purred out the word like he was complimenting her, and for some reason, it made her want to climb all over him again.

She frowned harder, crossing her arms over her chest. "Do you have ... um ... a shirt or—"

He was already reaching past her, dragging a coat from his closet. He held it out for her, and she shyly slipped her arms into the sleeves, holding her breath as he secured the buttons with fast, blunt touches. He pulled out a pair of black socks that were long enough on her that they disappeared beneath the hem of the coat, and then he grabbed a box of contacts from the same sock drawer, covering up his honey-gold eye.

"So we have a deal, then?" he asked, stepping back

from her. "Nobody ever finds out about this, and we never act on it?"

She chewed her lip. "Nobody should ever find out about it."

"And you won't act on it?"

She closed her eyes, shaking her head. "For now."

He rumbled with a growl. "Isobel ..."

"No." She held up her hand. "You can't force me to do anything. I have no idea what I'm going to feel like in the future."

"You can't, don't you understand?" He gripped her chin lightly, turning her eyes up to his. After whatever weird bond-mate skin-on-skin thing he had done to get rid of her sickness, he seemed to be considerably more at ease with touching her. "You have ten *Alpha* mates. Choose one of them only if you want to watch the boy you love being torn apart by the rest of them. Us. It has to be this way." He pulled up the hood of the coat he had dressed her in, tucking all of her hair away. "We have to drive back to Ironside. It's about an hour from here. We'll hike to the fire trail from the outside and you can say you teleported back there. Okay?"

She nodded, following him through the lovely old house that was a lot bigger than the Kane's home or Sato's hut. It just didn't really look like Kalen's style. The wallpaper was old, lace doilies covering faded, hand-carved furniture, and a big piano sitting on the second landing.

"Do you live here by yourself?" she asked as they walked down the stairs.

"It was my grandmother's house." He spun, facing her in the entryway and glancing toward the kitchen. "Have you eaten today? Oscar said they aren't taking care of you on that fucking tour."

"Um. No ... I haven't been feeling well—"

He had already turned his back, striding into the kitchen. She drifted to the doorway, watching as he poured out some juice. He pushed the cool glass into her hand. "Drink."

She sipped it as he pulled out ingredients to make sandwiches. Salad. Cheese. Meat. She made a soft sound, and he looked down at the sliced ham he had just pulled from the fridge.

"No meat?"

She shook her head.

He tossed it back and then got to work on the sandwiches, his deep voice rolling through the kitchen. "My grandmother was Silla Carpenter."

"The Alpha Icon who gave up everything to live in the settlements?" Isobel drifted another few steps into the kitchen, her eyes wide as she continued sipping the juice. It was sweet and cool, and exactly what she needed.

Kalen nodded. "She taught me everything I know. She was a musical prodigy. She had perfect pitch and an eidetic memory."

"Wow. Are you a prodigy too?"

He laughed, shaking his head. "I have all of her knowledge and none of her natural talent. Not like Theo."

"Is he a musical genius?"

Kalen wrapped the sandwich, fitting it into her coat pocket as he waited for her to finish the juice. "He has more talent in his little finger than most people have in their wildest dreams, but no. The real genius is Elijah. He's the only one I didn't train. I didn't need to. He can play anything he hears, no matter the instrument."

"You taught them *all*?"

He took her empty glass, setting it in his sink before leading her back to the entryway. Either he was avoiding her question, or he was in a hurry to get out of there, because he didn't respond. "Wait a few minutes and then walk out of the house. Follow the road straight ahead all the way to the end. Don't stop and talk to anyone. Slip through the boom gate while I'm talking to the guards and go to the fence on your left. It's dark enough that they won't see you in this coat. Walk down the road until you can't see the lights of the guardhouse anymore. I'll pick you up there."

"Okay." She swallowed, wishing she had her phone.

"You'll be okay," he promised, tugging the hood further around her face before flicking off all the lights and opening his door. "See you soon."

She waited and then stepped outside, closing the door behind her. Kalen lived at the far end of what looked to be the main road through the settlement. She was elevated on a small hill, just high enough to get an idea of the layout before she began hurrying down the road. She crossed her arms, hugging herself as she kept her head down, focussed mostly on the socks that only looked like shoes from a distance. Still, it was probably better than borrowing shoes from Kalen. She would look like a clown.

At the other end of the road, a pair of headlights suddenly switched on, flooding over the guardhouse, drawing three men from within. They approached the vehicle and began chatting with the driver, their body language non-hostile. Isobel slipped beneath the boom gate and skirted off to the side, not daring to take a full breath until she was fully encased in shadow and nobody was shouting after her. She didn't pause but kept going, kicking into a jog when she heard the sound of a car door slamming in the distance. She didn't stop until only the headlights of the car following her were visible, and then she turned to wait, stepping forward when it pulled over a few feet ahead of her. West leaned over the passenger side, opening the door and flinging it open.

"Hop in."

She slid into the seat, quickly buckling up, her breath rattling in her chest. Her ribs ached worse than ever.

"Eat your sandwich," he said, flicking her a look. "And unbutton that coat. You're sweating."

"You're so bossy." She shrugged open the coat and pulled out the sandwich.

He waited until she had finished all of it before he dropped his phone into her lap. "Please text the others to let them know you're fine. They won't fucking leave me alone. Use the group Theo invited you to."

"Okay." She clicked on the familiar app, staring at the list of messages. "Which group is that?"

"It's called Carter."

She clicked on the correct group, trying not to read the other messages.

Kalen: Um, hello. It's Isobel.

Elijah: Good. You're alive.

Gabriel: How was the cuddle?

Theodore: What cuddle?

She clicked on Kalen's profile, changing his screen name to her own.

Isobel: How do you know about that?

Gabriel: Who do you think told him how to do it?

Theodore: WHAT. CUDDLE?

Cian: Calm down, psycho. She was almost hyperthermic. It's a bond thing.

Kilian: Great. Cian and Kalen do "bond things" now.

"What are they saying?" Kalen asked, wincing at the barrage of text message notifications.

"Kilian is sarcastically saying that it's great you and Cian do bond things now."

"I do not," he growled, before softening his voice. As much as he could. "Relay that. Please."

Isobel: Kalen said he does not do bond things.

Niko: Hey, Isobel. I'm glad you're okay.

Isobel: Hey, Niko.

Kilian: ...

Elijah: ...

Theodore: Wow. Two stones walk into a bar.

Isobel: Shut up.

Theodore: You're an adorable stone.

Oscar: Let's revisit the cuddling discussion.

Kilian: Give us details, baby.

Isobel: Why? She frowned down at the screen.

Oscar: Not every day I get leverage over Kalen.

Kilian: I just like details. I'm a detail-oriented guy.

Isobel: This is ... weird.

Easton: Thank you for letting us know you're okay, Isobel. Have you had a discussion with Kalen?

Isobel: Yes.

Kilian: While you were cuddling?

Isobel: No.

Elijah: ...

Gabriel: ...

Theodore: Is there anything you want to ask us, sweetheart?

Isobel: Um.

Isobel: No.

Cian: ...

Kilian: Aw. Baby stone.

Easton: I know it's awkward, but are we in agreement on this remaining a secret?

Isobel: I won't tell anyone. We can pretend it didn't happen.

Cian: Easy enough with us all living close to each other ... but the longer we prolong it, the worse the side-effects will get. Specifically, for you. And we won't be able to go home for the holidays unless one of us is with you. That's pretty obvious now.

Isobel: Okay. She sucked in a breath, gathering up all of her courage.

Isobel: Will you still be a surrogate, Cian?

Oscar: Fucking hell.

Moses: See? It's already starting.

Cian: Of course, doll. But it can't always be me. You might form an attachment to me.

Isobel: No danger of that.

Cian: Wow.

Moses: Hahahahaha.

Isobel: Sorry, I didn't mean it like that. I just don't want to belong to anybody. Especially not an Alpha. I ... have things I don't think I could ever get over.

Easton: Understood. Say no more. Is anyone else available to help ease the side-effects, if needed? It's better for Isobel to know who she can turn to without making people uncomfortable.

Kilian: I'm available.

Theodore: I'll be mad if you don't.

Gabriel: You can come to me if the others aren't available.

Elijah: I'm out for now, but available to talk anyone through it, or in an emergency.

Niko: Sorry, Isobel, but count me out.

Isobel: Please don't be sorry.

Moses: Try not to take this personally. But hard pass.

Isobel: You, on the other hand, should be a little bit sorry.

Oscar: Come to me, if you dare.

Elijah: ...

Gabriel: That's disturbing.

Theodore: Highly disturbing.

Isobel: Thank you for offering, Kilian, Theo, and Gabriel.

Oscar: How pointed.

Elijah: Technically, I also offered.

Isobel: Technically, thank you too.

Oscar: Ignore me one more time, Carter.

Isobel: THANK YOU SATO FOR YOUR SCARY INVITATION.

Kilian: So ... about the cuddling.

Easton: Make another group. Some of us don't need to read this.

A few seconds later, a new notification popped up.

Kilian has invited you to a group: Everyone except Mikki.

She snorted, clicking on it.

Kilian: Tell us.

Moses: Did he pop a stiffy?

Cian: Let's not bring stiffies into the conversation.

Moses: Did YOU pop a stiffy?

Isobel: Cian did. And Kalen, I don't remember.

Elijah: ISOBEL. You weren't actually supposed to answer that question.

Kilian: But I am SO glad you did. I'm dead.

Moses: I was going to remove myself from the group. Now I think I'll stay.

Isobel: Shit. I'm sorry.

Kilian: Don't be. Cian always has a stiffy.

Theodore: Weird thing to claim about someone.

Kilian: Have you met him?

Cian: You're mistaking size for rigidity.

Kilian: Settle a debate for us, Isobel.

Isobel has left the group.

She quickly reverted Kalen's name to what it was before and handed his phone back. He turned it off before slipping it into his pocket. "They're a lot, aren't they?" His eyes briefly drifted over her before facing the front again.

"I can't tell if they love each other or hate each other. They fight like ..."

"Brothers," he supplied. "They're very close. Especially Niko, Elijah, and Gabriel. They grew up together before Eli and Gabe transferred settlements. And Theo and Moses actually are brothers. Their teasing is just teasing. All of them would kill for each other."

"Hmm." She played with the sandwich wrapper as

Kalen fiddled with the radio dial. "Whose head did I go into, back at Ironside? The guy who got the blackout text?"

He froze and then swore, swerving the car to avoid a pothole in the road he had been too distracted to see. "Maybe it's best if we don't talk about that."

Oh. *Oh*. It was him.

Yikes.

"Yeah okay." She turned to the window, her face flaming red, and they drove the rest of the way in silence.

It was strangely comfortable, even though there was this gigantic, awkward thing hanging between them. Easton and West had both helped her to lay down some pretty solid boundaries, and despite the bizarreness of the situation, she was feeling more at peace than she had since waking up and finding out that she was half bonded.

Nobody was trying to claim her or own her.

They were acting like they could hide this, potentially forever.

When they arrived at Ironside, Kalen turned off his headlights and manoeuvred off the main road, taking the direction of the service road up the side of the mountain. They reached a gate with plenty of warning signs on it, but Kalen got out and unlocked it, pushing it wide.

"Special Ironside friends," he explained, getting back in the car.

"Must be nice to be an Alpha," she muttered as they crawled the rest of the way up the rough road.

"You'll have us all beat for fame and influence after this whole Mate Finder thing," he returned. "Your father is ... smart."

Maybe it was Kalen's naturally gravelly voice, but it almost sounded like he was about to insult her father. He pulled the car over, lifting from his seat with far too much grace for a man his size, and then he was holding open her own door. "You'll need to leave the coat."

She shrugged it the rest of the way off and also removed his socks before slipping out of the seat. He kept his eyes well above her bodysuit as he walked her over to where she could just make out the end of the fire trail through the desert shrubs.

"I wish I could give you some shoes." He glared down at the uneven path, his voice rough. "Will you be okay?"

"I'll be fine," she promised.

She was lying, but luckily, he didn't know that, and he left her with one last heavy look.

The journey down was painful and punishing, and she was pretty sure one of her ankles was bleeding from her accidentally kicking a cactus. She was limping when she finally got to the medical centre, and they ushered her into a room to treat her feet as the triage nurse called her father.

She was nodding off in her chair when the small gaggle of people walked into the room several hours later.

"You poor thing!" Cooper reached her first, yanking open the blanket the nurses had given her like he needed to check her over for injuries or something.

She quickly snapped the blanket closed again, standing with a slight wince to face her father.

"We can't adjust the schedule for any illness or injury," he told her calmly. "So make use of Ashford in the time you have left."

She nodded, and they left the family centre, returning to the same van that had taken them to the private airfield last time. It was a short flight, but she was still completely exhausted by the time she shuffled into her room.

Cian was sitting on the bed, fiddling with his phone, his expression drawn. It eased when he looked her over, but only slightly, and his eyes narrowed when they landed on her bandaged feet.

She shuffled to her bag, her limbs heavy. She hunted for her toiletries and pyjamas until Cian huffed out a frustrated sound, taking over. He piled everything onto the bathroom counter, started the shower for her, and then paused in the doorway, giving her a sceptical look. "Do you need help?"

"I'll be fine." She gave him a tight smile, closing the door before stripping off the hospital gown and her bodysuit.

Cian had already turned out the lights when she emerged again, but his strangled sound hit her when she opened the door, flooding light into the room.

"What are you wearing, Isobel?"

She quickly switched off the bathroom light, stumbling her way over to the bed that they were apparently sharing. "Pyjamas," she mumbled, falling onto the unoccupied side of the bed and letting out a deep sigh. "Fuck, I hurt."

His face appeared above hers, shadows digging into his frown lines. "Where?"

"Ribs. Back. Feet. Everywhere. I'm so fucking tired."

"Wow. Two fucks. You must be *super* tired."

She groaned, closing her eyes. His touch fluttered over her ribs, and her eyes flew open again, readjusting to stare at him.

"I've never seen pyjamas like these in real life," he muttered, his touch still ghosting her ribs. The heat of the almost-contact spread lower until she could feel it almost like an actual caress against the inch of skin between her tiny shorts and fitted, lace-edged tank.

"My father packed more of my clothes from home before the trip."

"So these are rich girl pyjamas?"

"I guess."

He rumbled out a sound, falling to his back, his chest swelling with a deep breath. "You felt my boner."

"Abrupt change of topic." She stared at the ceiling, suddenly wide awake.

"Not really." He chuckled. "But if I'm going to be doing this ... skin-on-skin thing with you ... there's a conversation we need to have first."

"Do you want me to ignore it, if it happens again?"

"Carter. You're killing me."

"Sorry. What's the conversation?"

"You seem pretty innocent. Painfully blunt, but innocent."

"That's probably accurate."

He let out a laughing breath. "Yeah. I don't want to give you any mixed signals."

"Tell me what a boner is supposed to mean, and I

won't get any mixed signals. I didn't realise it was so nuanced."

"It depends on the situation." He was outright laughing at her now. She could tell by the tone of his voice, even though he was managing to hold back the actual laughter. "But in any situation with you, it means nothing, okay?"

"Okay." She shrugged, even though he probably couldn't see it. "Can we sleep now?"

"Yeah, we can sleep. Come here. Get your skin."

He didn't wait for her to move but tugged her half over his bare, muscled chest before dragging the blanket up to her arms, his hand landing over her head. She inched closer, already soothed by his heat, her eyes growing heavy. His free hand rubbed lightly along the middle of her back, brushing the small indentations of her spine through her thin shirt with his knuckles.

His brushing touches dragged her under, and she woke up to the sound of someone banging on the door what felt like ten minutes later. She groaned, throwing her arm over her eyes to block out the sudden light. Cian rolled away from her, pulling a pair of jeans up over his boxers before walking halfway to the door. He paused, glancing back at her. The banging continued.

"Here." He ducked back to his bag, pulling out one of his shirts and tugging it over her head.

She grumbled out an incoherent sound, still half asleep as he pushed off the bed again and unlocked the door, letting in the stream of people that made up her styling team.

They dressed her and did her make-up while chatting with each other. Cian cocked a brow from the armchair he had parked himself in, sharing a look with her as they discussed—with each other, not with her—the fading bruises on her face, and the new injuries they would have to cover up on her feet.

"You know they're talking about adding another surrogate mate?" one of the make-up artists whispered.

"What?" Isobel asked, glancing between her and Serena, who the other woman had been talking to.

"Just because of your little teleporting thing," Serena said, patting Isobel's hand. "It's going to really disrupt the schedule if that keeps happening."

They dressed her in another nature-inspired dress, with another pair of annoying heels, and then they were packing her into another Jeep to travel to the San Juan Settlement, Cian pressed in beside her.

"Instructions are to stand behind her, not beside her," one of the cameramen told Cian. "We want people to know you're acting as her surrogate mate, but we don't want you to intimidate them. They need to see her as available."

"She does a great job of that," Cian returned, his lips twitching. "Comes across as super available."

Isobel snorted.

The cameraman gave him a funny look. "Yeah. Right."

They arrived at the settlement, and the crew piled out first, leaving Isobel a single moment of calm and quiet before she stepped out to the sound of cheering. They began ushering her in the direction they wanted her while she smiled and waved at the crowd that had gathered to meet her. She was passing down the cordoned-off main street when the shots rang through the air. There was a short delay, and then people started screaming.

Cian was there in a second, grabbing her wrist and tugging her in the opposite direction to the commotion. She could hear the officials and the crew shouting both of their names, but Cian just looked over his shoulder at her, eyes hard.

"Just run," he barked in Alpha voice.

"We should hide!" she shouted back, her throat catching on a sob, her body trying to fight against his order.

She lost the fight, sprinting to keep up with him as he dragged her through the fleeing crowd and behind the very last building at the other end of the main road. They were tucked between the back of the building and the settlement boundary wall.

People were still screaming, the shots still ringing out. She could hear sirens in the distance already. She held her hands over her ears, the tears falling freely. It didn't matter that Cian was watching her cry, as long as he was the only one. He tugged her to his chest, his arm wrapping around her shoulder. She wasn't sure how long he held her before he tugged one of her hands down.

"It's safe," he said gently.

"Is this a settlement thing?" she asked, her throat raw from crying.

"No." He sucked in a breath. "This is new."

18
SURROGATE NUMBER TWO

Isobel and Cian were escorted back down the main street, past blood-stained drag-marks through the dirt and ambulances helping out the officials who had been injured and the humans in fatigues who had been doing crowd control. They weren't touching the Gifted. The Gifted were being carried off on stretchers, an assembly line forming, leading to a building with a small crowd outside. Most of them seemed to be grieving instead of panicking.

She felt numb as they corralled her into a waiting car, catching only a brief glimpse of her father, Cooper, and the rest of their team before one of the officials was urging her inside. She made it onto the plane, where her father gave her a grim nod before disappearing behind a curtain to talk to his crew. She and Cian sat in silence until her father came back out, sitting opposite them.

"I've been told that Oscar Sato inspires fear in people," he said, quickly adding, "Even though he's not allowed to actually fight, of course."

"He scares the shit out of people," Cian confirmed. He didn't sound anywhere near as confused as Isobel felt.

"Who was the shoot—"

Her father spoke over her.

"And you?" he barked, looking at her. "Does the Sato kid scare the shit out of you? Could you put up with him being your second surrogate?"

She would have preferred Theodore or Kilian, but she was starting to see where her father was going.

"I'm ... fine with Sato, but if I have a choice—"

He cut her off again. "We'll arrange for him to meet us in Nevada. The shooter left some kind of manifesto. Something about Icons being used to perpetuate a system of oppression. He was anti-loyalist scum. And now he's dead." Braun stood, straightening his jacket. There was a blood splatter on his collar. "The officials are going to tamp down on the celebrations in Nevada, Montana, and possibly Washington until they've upped the security. Sato's appearance should scare off any attempts aimed directly at you."

"Sato has a sister," Isobel rushed out, before he could walk away. "She's sick. She needs ..."

He was walking off.

"Fucking asshole." Cian watched him go with narrowed aquamarine eyes.

Isobel swore, pulling out her phone and shakily navigating to the group chat, because she was too much of a chicken to message Sato privately.

Isobel: I'm really sorry. I tried to stop him.

Cian glanced down at his phone and visibly cringed. "They're going to think something happened to you," he said, his fingers flying across the screen.

Cian: They're pulling you in as her second surrogate, Oscar.

Oscar: Fucking why?

Cian: There was a shooting in Colorado. At the settlement. I'm fine. Isobel is fine. So is her fuckwit of a father.

Elijah: You know she's in this group, right?

Isobel: He kind of is a fuckwit.

Oscar: Not kind of.

Kilian: Yeah, they're not exaggerating.

Gabriel: People are starting to post about the shooting. I can see why they would want Oscar.

Isobel put her phone aside and pushed into the bathroom. She immediately fell to the toilet, throwing up violently. She could still hear the sounds of people screaming and the *pop pop pop* that seemed to bounce down the street after her.

She struggled to her feet, washing her mouth out and then scrubbing away the smudged make-up on her face. Cian was leaning against the wall opposite the bathroom when she got out. He offered her a bottle of cold water, and she immediately pressed it to her forehead.

"Thanks," she croaked.

He nodded. "Do you want to talk about it?"

Heck no.

"I ..." She dropped her arm, the bottle hanging by her hip. She shook her head. "Do you?"

He was staring at the floor, the hint of green in his eyes more prominent than usual. His thumb was rubbing across the tattoos on his hands, his expression vacant. "I'm worried about my family. The settlements have a very fragile ecosystem. Sometimes it feels like a stiff breeze can start a domino effect from Mojave all the way to Washington."

His fear was pressing so tightly to her chest that she had actually mistaken it for her own. She cracked herself open, allowing it to slip between her walls, flooding through in a steady stream until his shoulders were easing back and his forehead was crinkling in confusion.

"Did you just …" He stared at her, his hands forming loose fists before relaxing again. "You didn't have to—you *don't* have to. That's not why I'm here."

"I know." She fell back into her seat, turning to the window. He was there because he couldn't legally say no to the officials.

Isobel was in the bathroom when Sato arrived. She could hear him through the door.

"They expect all three of us to share a bed or something?" He didn't sound happy.

Why should he?

She sighed, bracing her hands against the sink as she sucked in a steadying breath. They were cramming Nevada, Montana, and Washington into the next day to make up for the temporary "blip" in the schedule, as Cooper had put it. The man was insane. Several people had been shot right in front of his face, and all he could talk about was how to spin it, how to use it for *traction*.

She spun to the door, pulling it open and staring at

the two boys inside her hotel room. Cian groaned, doing a quick sweep of her appearance before looking up at the ceiling. Sato had gone very still, his dark eyes flashing with a hint of something she couldn't quite make out.

"What are you wearing?" he asked bluntly.

"Hello to you too," she responded haughtily, just as Cian replied, "Rich girl pyjamas."

"I didn't request you," she told Sato. "This was out of my control."

"I know." He narrowed his eyes on the hem of her shorts—which were barely more than underwear, because she hadn't expected to have people *sleeping* with her—before turning away from her with a tense sigh. "It's fucked up, what happened." He dropped his bag onto a low table between two cosy armchairs, tugging it open to grab out a few things. "Mind if I shower?"

"Go ahead." She rubbed the back of her neck nervously, quickly skittering out of his way as he passed her.

Cian had his lips quirked up, watching her in amusement.

"What should we do?" she asked him, perching on one of the armchairs. "I have no idea if I can sleep."

"Me either." He rubbed his eyes, falling into the armchair opposite. "Let's order food."

She popped up, wincing as her ribs screamed from the too-fast movement. He glared at her, also rising to his feet.

"You said you were feeling better," he accused, his eyes tracing over her skin.

"It's not the bond." She forced a quick smile, trying to side-step him to get the room service menu.

He stepped into her path, and she collided with his chest, wincing again.

"Why do you keep doing that?" He gestured to her face. "Flinching like moving is causing you pain?"

"Because it *is*." She rolled her eyes.

"Where? What happened?"

"I got the shit kicked out of me on the last day before break. I was pretty banged up. I've done a lot of running over the last two days, and I think it's made things worse. Happy now?"

He actually looked like he wanted to commit violence, his Alpha ring growing bright and gold, but he wrestled back his reaction until he looked almost impassive.

"I thought the bruises were from your father. Do you know their names?" he asked quietly.

"Yeah. I already reported them."

Cian scoffed, shaking his head. "Do you have a copy of the report?"

"Yes."

"Forward it to me."

"No." She crossed her arms over her chest.

He pulled out his phone, calling someone while he kept his eyes locked on hers.

"Hey, Elijah." His hand landed on her shoulder, holding her in place. "I need you to pull a report—"

Isobel quickly snatched the phone off him, fumbling to end the call before she slapped it into his chest. For some reason, Niko's slightly accusatory words were coming back to her, reminding her that it was her own job to look after herself. Not theirs. Reed was triggered by bullying; Niko had made it sound like he wouldn't be able to tolerate bullying of any kind, even if it had nothing to do with him.

"Why do you think you need to do something about this?" she asked Cian. His hand covered hers, but she wasn't releasing his phone yet.

"Who knows." He shrugged. "Maybe because you called me a surrogate mate. Maybe because I'm a toxic dude who thinks you can't handle things yourself … or maybe because I'm fucking terrified that next time one of us will be too close to you when someone permanently scars you."

She deflated, her hand falling away from his phone. He caught it and then had the audacity to call Reed again. "Yeah, sorry," he said. "I need you to pull the report Isobel made on the last day of term. Thanks."

He hung up, considering her quietly.

"I thought it was specifically your mate who had to scar you?" she asked, swallowing.

"It is. Usually. But nothing about this is normal. We don't know if one person marking you completes the bond with all ten, or if you could mark yourself. We don't know anything. We need you to be careful."

"That explains all the weirdness the night we played clothesline." She scrubbed a hand across her ribcage before slipping past him—successfully, this time—to pick up the room service menu.

"Yeah," he said, tone heavy with sarcasm. "*That's* what all the tension was about. It had absolutely nothing to do with you rolling down your panties and slipping them into Gabriel's pocket."

"I feel bad about that," she admitted, looking up with a guilty expression. "He probably had to burn those pants."

"Only one way to find out." Cian fell back into the armchair, texting on his phone.

She looked through the menu, biting her lip. "What should I order?"

"Whatever you like. Mikki has us on a pretty strict diet, but Mikki isn't here right now."

"What's the diet for?" she asked absently, picking up the room phone.

"The muscles you're always drooling over," he quipped, making her drop the receiver.

She cursed beneath her breath, picking it up again and glaring at Cian, who only cocked a brow back at her in challenge.

Okay. He had a point. "Is that weird? You guys are just ... *very* fit."

He smirked. "Some of the comments online can be a bit ... invasive. And just a heads-up, Elijah, Gabriel, and Niko don't like to be fawned over. But you can pant over my muscles all you want, doll."

"Stop flirting with me. I don't pant."

"How about I keep flirting with you, and we see who's right about the other thing?"

The door to the bathroom opened, saving her from a response. Sato gave Cian an exasperated look, like he had heard some of their conversation.

"Pizza okay?" she asked, glancing between them.

"Who's paying?" Sato asked, looking at the menu in her hand.

"My father."

"Rich girl pyjamas and rich girl pizza." Sato surveyed her for a breath. "Pick whatever you want. I'll eat it."

She hit the button to call for room service, ordering two of their gourmet pizzas.

"Will that be all, Miss Carter?" the lady on the other end asked politely.

"Yes, that's all—" Both boys looked up, shaking their heads. "Uh. Actually. One more please. The pepperoni. Thank you."

She moved over to the corner they had set themselves up in, perching on the wide sill of the window between them, plucking her phone off the table.

"You don't want to check that." Sato looked like he was smirking on the inside. Which wasn't a good sign.

She clicked on the string of notifications taking her to a group chat that didn't seem to include Kalen or Easton. She flicked up to the first message.

Cian: Hey, Gabe, what did you do with Isobel's panties, you dirty dog?

Gabriel: What do you think I did with them?

Theodore: I think you pinned them to a specimen board.

426

Kilian: I think you extracted DNA off them to study in a lab somewhere.

Cian: You're holding them right now, aren't you?

Elijah: He's actually holding a bottle of liquor. He looks like he wants to drown in it.

Kilian: Poor Gabriel. Must be hard. Is it hard?

Moses: Lol. Yeah. Is it?

Niko: Stop talking about boners in the group chat.

Isobel groaned, setting her phone aside and shooting Cian an accusatory glare. He grinned back at her, his lips sinuously curved and sly, his gaze lazy and heavy. She was starting to seriously reconsider not complaining about the surrogates that had been chosen for her. Cian was by far the most sensual *and* the most sexual, and Sato made her blood run as cold as he made her skin run hot, which was a weird and unfamiliar combination.

Neither of them were comforting or easy.

She didn't have that weird sickness anymore, but she actually attributed that to West, not Cian.

Cian was suddenly swearing, his eyes flying from the screen of his phone to her. "You have two broken fucking *ribs*, Isobel?"

The room suddenly dropped into silence, two angry Alphas advancing on her. She had no idea what to do about it, so she reacted on instinct, hesitantly prying open her walls to accept the deluge of their anger.

"Stop." Sato's voice cracked like a whip, the Alpha command forcing her to cut off the stream of their emotion. "Show us."

She scowled, her eyes darting around them, looking for an escape. There was nowhere to go. She tugged on the hem of her lace-lined top, and Cian's hand shot out, covering hers. It seemed like he was about to stop her, but then he released her hand. She tugged the material up, showing the mottled bruising across her ribs and stomach.

"Turn around." Sato's voice was the softest she had ever heard it, and she was pretty sure that was a bad thing.

She turned and felt fingers against her back, brushing over tender spots. She dropped the material, spinning around again. Something was wrong, putting her immediately on edge. Sato was too still. Cian was too blank.

They both pulled in deep, rattling breaths.

"Let me take it—" she started, but Cian's face darkened, and he stepped forward, crowding her personal space.

"You really need to stop doing that. We watched you *die* because of that."

"Cian." Sato's voice was a deep rattle, the single word sounding like a warning. Cian closed his eyes, battling something back before he took a measured step away from her, muttering quietly, "Don't move."

He pulled out his phone, turning it on speaker. The ringing was the only sound in the room as Sato stared at Isobel, danger flicking between them. Fear choked up her throat. She didn't even dare breathe too deeply.

The hell was going on?

"Can you two seriously not last even two hours—" Reed's voice filled the room, drowned out by Sato's savage growl. "What happened?" he asked, sudden and sharp.

"Isobel is hurt." Cian was keeping his voice low. "No skin broken, but Oscar is losing it."

Reed must have pulled the phone away from his face, because the string of furious words he uttered were faded, barely audible, and then he came back, his tone even and soft. "Isobel?"

"Mm?" She was too scared to speak.

"You know what to do, don't you?"

"Submit," her mother's voice urged. "Baby, you've done it a thousand times."

The apparition was there, standing behind Cian and Sato. And then suddenly the dark-eyed man was back, glancing around the room.

"Fancy hotel," Sato's father huffed out. "Only seen places like this on the TV." His eyes connected to the back of Sato's neck, narrowing. "There's my little wolf."

Isobel sucked in a breath, closing her eyes tightly. "Please god, not right now."

Sato rumbled darkly, forcing her eyes back open again.

"Submit." Her mother was ignoring the other man, focusing only on Isobel. "I taught you how to deal with this, baby. This is not a boy. This is a predator."

"Alphas have an animal brain, Isobel." Reed was speaking again, a note of urgency to his voice this time.

Her father had called it a beast, not an animal.

She didn't want to do this anymore.

She didn't want to submit anymore.

"Isobel …" Cian's voice was almost pleading. "Just—"

Sato stepped forward, and Isobel collapsed, tears gathering in her eyes as she curled into a ball, her arms hugged over her head. Her father preferred her to lay her cheek on the ground, baring her neck for submission and her back for punishment, but she couldn't bring herself to do it.

Sato snarled, the sound menacing, making her shiver.

"Isobel. Sweetheart." It sounded like Cian tried to take a step toward her, but Sato shoved him back. "Fuck. Okay. Elijah. Talk her through this. She's misinterpreting, probably because of her fucking dad. She's curled in a ball on the ground."

"Toss her the phone," Reed demanded.

Suddenly, it was sliding beneath her face. She reached down, her shaking fingers fumbling with the device. She picked it up, fumbled to turn off the speaker, and pressed it to her ear. Tears were flowing down her cheeks, even when she closed her eyes tightly.

"H-Hello," she whispered.

"Isobel," Reed breathed out. "Oscar isn't himself right now. There's a part of his brain that thinks you belong to him, and someone else has hurt you. You need to show him that you're okay."

She cracked her eyes open, breathing shakily into the phone. "How?"

"Stand up, sweet girl. Don't cower. He won't hurt you."

Every instinct she had was screaming otherwise, but she clung to the measured, even tone of Reed's voice, slowly rising to her feet. Sato loomed closer, his gaze black. She shuddered, searching for the black veins that didn't appear.

"I'm okay," she said shakily.

He just stared at her like he didn't hear her.

"Tell Cian he needs to leave the room," Reed said quickly. "He's being perceived as a threat. Oscar is guarding you."

"C-Cian?" She flicked her eyes over Sato's shoulder, causing him to let loose another terrifying rumble. "Can you please go for a walk?"

"Like fu—"

"Please," she whispered, keeping her eyes on Sato this time. "Reed will tell you if you need to come back."

"Don't go far," Reed specified.

"Not far," Isobel added, hearing the door open and close.

"That voice on the phone is lying to you, girlie." Sato's father was whispering into her ear. At some point he must have drifted behind her to get a better look at Sato. "My little wolf is very capable of hurting you. It's how I designed him. Other Alphas try to ignore their hindbrains. I taught my little wolf to embrace his."

"Is he gone?" Reed asked.

"Mm," Isobel affirmed quietly.

"I need to go too. He's listening to me now. He needs to feel completely alone with you."

"Wait," Isobel squeaked. "Please don't—"

"He won't hurt you," Reed promised.

"Oh he'll more than hurt you," the apparition whispered in her other ear. "He'll break you."

The call went dead, and Isobel's hand fell to her side, the phone dropping with a thud against the carpet. Sato drew closer, his nose passing over her hairline.

"You're terrified," he rasped out.

"N-No, I'm completely okay." She tried to think of *anything* else to change her scent to something more pleasant, and the first image that popped into her brain was surprising enough that some of the fear actually did drop away, shock taking its place. For some reason, it was West's smoky vanilla scent that filled her brain. She remembered how warm and safe she had felt, waking up with him. And the glow when they touched, the sparkles that danced beneath his skin everywhere her fingers drifted.

Sato's nose brushed her hairline again, his rumbling softening to something less dangerous. His fingers caressed the backs of her hand, and then something cool and metal slipped between their touch, making her jump and look down. Delicate gold chains were snaking around their wrists, binding them together. Sato wasn't paying any attention to them. He gently pushed her back against the windowsill, bending to trace his nose across her jaw. The chains continued up their arms, another chain snaking from her waist to his, pulling his hips into hers. He grunted softly. She lifted her arm, marvelling at the give in the chains. They stretched, allowing her to move, before tightening when she dropped her hand back to his.

As soon as he felt her fingers against his, he turned his palm, pushing his fingers through hers, locking their hands tightly together. The chains glinted happily, lit from within by a familiar golden glow.

Isobel gasped, her fear disappearing entirely. She could feel them everywhere now. Cool and smooth against her skin, a contrast to the burning of Sato's hand when it cupped her jaw, drawing her mouth to his. It was the most natural thing in the world to sigh into his kiss, to embrace this new way of surrendering, to open to him and answer the firm demand of his tongue as the glossy, satin feel of metal smoothing over her skin brought her so tight up against his body that there was no room left for fear or anger.

She twisted her arms around his neck as he released her hand, the chains slipping away and reforming as he cupped both hands to either side of her face, groaning into her mouth. His kiss changed, becoming less exploratory and more dominating. He tasted like the sweetest poison mixed with cherry. A bittersweet brandy, like the fancy desserts the cooks would make for her family on special occasions. She never really craved those desserts, but now she wondered how she had ever gone a day without them. She sucked on Sato's tongue, trying to savour their combined taste, and he rewarded her with a growl that vibrated all the way through her body, making her desperate to rub up against him.

The chains dripped between her fingers like water as she gripped his hair, his hands falling from her face. He caught her thighs, pulling them up around his waist, the chains securing her against his body so that she wouldn't fall. Finally, she had something to rub against, and she fit her aching core against the stiff, throbbing cock that was stuck up against his stomach.

He tore his mouth away, his hands flexing against her thighs. "Carter ..." His voice was rough with restraint.

She ignored him, wriggling for more friction. His chest swelled, a heavy growl radiating up from his chest, one of his hands releasing her thigh to flash up to her neck. He squeezed, his tongue thrusting viciously into her mouth, cutting off her air supply completely as his kiss turned rough, but then he seemed to wrangle his restraint back into place.

"Carter," he tried again, his tone edged in sharpness. "You can stop."

She blinked, her eyelids heavy, reality threatening at the edges of her mind. She didn't want to stop. There was a slow fire building through her body, and the chains were beautiful.

Delicate. Exquisite.

She wanted more. More heat. More glowing metal. More friction.

Sato sat on the edge of the bed, looking down between their bodies as he gently began to lift her. The chains easily slackened as he carefully repositioned her, drawing her legs to one side. This wasn't what she wanted. She pouted as his eyes drifted back to hers, dark with fire, burning a path of tingles over her lips before they connected with her own eyes.

Guilt.

It niggled at her walls, trying to worm its way into her pretty golden moment.

It was the hint of his emotion that finally swept away the drugging haze that had descended over her mind.

She had just kissed Sato.

Sato had just kissed her.

Grinding had been involved.

She could still feel how hard he was, throbbing beneath her thighs almost in time with the throbbing between her own legs.

What the fuck.

What the fuck.

She screamed.

The door flew open almost immediately. Cian paused, staring at them in confusion before kicking the door closed and stalking over. He was holding a few pizza boxes, and he set them onto the table. Isobel started hyperventilating, the chains no longer beautiful and pleasurable.

They slackened, the magic falling away from them, but that meant they no longer moved with her, and when she tried to scramble away from Sato, they pulled tight, biting into her skin.

"What the actual fuck?" Cian stared at the chains.

"Bond magic," Sato gritted. "Practically drugged her."

"I'm right *here*," she seethed, trying to escape again.

The chains almost cut into her skin, and both boys suddenly screamed, "Stop!"

She froze, breathing hard, her hair falling messily about her face.

"Careful," Sato growled, hauling her right up against his chest until the chains all slackened again.

"You be careful," she ground back. "Or I'll tell the group that you just had your tongue—"

Sato's hand wrapped around the lower half of her face, cutting the words off. "Unless you want to send another Alpha off the rails, I wouldn't finish that sentence *or* carry out that threat."

She tore her face away, scowling.

Cian was watching them with narrowed eyes. "I'm going to untie you now, okay? Try not to move."

He bent down before them, searching for where the chains ended or began, his touches feather-light, like he could tell how over-sensitised Isobel was. He stood, his brow crinkling. "I think if you both stand, I can just lift Isobel out."

Sato stood, still holding her against his chest. Cian rearranged some of the chains, holding them out to make room for Sato to drop her legs. As soon as her feet hit the ground and both of them straightened, the chains started to slip down their bodies. Cian picked her up, and Sato helped to pluck her legs safely out of the tangle. The second she was free, she jolted away from them both, her chest heaving with panicked breath, her face flaming with embarrassed colour. She had been rubbing herself all over Sato like ... like some kind of *animal in heat*, no thoughts in her brain except the beauty of the chain and a desperation to ease the ache in her core. And what made it worse was that Sato had said *she* was acting drugged.

Not *we*.

He had been thinking clearly and rationally—or at least as rationally as he ever thought.

That made it so much worse.

Had she *assaulted* him? No ... that wasn't right. He had kissed her first. He had kissed her back.

She hunted through the pizza boxes, trying her best to ignore the way the two Alphas watched her, waiting for some sort of a reaction. She found the vegetarian option and stole a slice out of it, perching back on her windowsill to chew and flick her attention between them cautiously.

"Should we talk about this?" Cian asked.

She picked up the TV remote and turned it on, stubbornly facing the screen. He took a step toward her, like he was about to insist, and she narrowed her eyes at him, pointedly turning up the volume until he shook his head, holding his hands up in surrender.

19
GLITTERY, GLOWING THINGS

Isobel had the bathroom door cracked after she finished brushing her teeth, peeking at Cian and Sato on the Alpha-sized bed. It was the biggest size you could get, but they still made it look small, the free space between them practically diminutive.

Sato had his eyes closed, his head tipped back, his hands in his lap. He had been video-chatting with Lily while Isobel was in the bathroom, but now his phone was silent. Cian was spread out on his back, his arm bent over his eyes. Both had decided to sleep in their boxers, following the infernal instructions given to them by Teak.

If she thought seeing Cian strip in a steam-clogged bathroom was confrontational, it was nothing to seeing them both stretched out over the bed. Sato's hand drifted down his abs, scratching a spot just above the hem of his boxers.

Isobel swallowed.

"You're panting again," Cian called, sounding amused. The asshole must have been able to see under that arm.

She scowled, stepping out of the bathroom. "I've had plenty of skin-on-skin contact," she said, hugging herself. "You can put some clothes on."

"Isobel." Cian lifted his arm from his eyes, fixing her with a look. "Get over here. You need sleep."

"I'm scared," she admitted.

Sato's eyes blinked open. They both considered her.

"Of what?" Cian finally asked, though there was a note of trepidation in his voice. A hint of defensiveness too. On behalf of Sato, who—true to Reed's word—hadn't actually hurt her.

She gulped, a realisation crashing into her.

They made out in front of Sato's father. His dead *father.*

She hadn't even noticed the ghosts disappearing.

"Of gold things and glittery, glowing things," she admitted, casting her eyes over the pile of delicate chains poking out of her bag.

"You shouldn't ever trust me," Sato mumbled.

"Not on anything except this. In that aspect, at least, you're safe with me."

"In that aspect, you're safe with all of us." Cian patted the bed. "Consent is black and white, sweetheart. A simple no will do when you're uncomfortable."

She nodded. She didn't need to doubt it. Not with the way Moses had reacted to Sato being assaulted. Not with how Niko had talked her through her panic attack like he had done it a hundred times before.

Not after seeing the message on the back of Spade's door.

I am not for sale.

She climbed toward the centre of the bed, and they both inched to the very edges, giving her as much space as possible as she burrowed beneath the blankets. Cian flicked off the lights, shifting a little closer. She turned into him instinctively, seeing that he had opened one of his arms for her. When she wiggled closer, he spun her around and tucked her against his chest, just like the night before.

She found herself face-to-face with Sato, whose head had tipped to the side, his dark eyes glittering as they stared into hers.

"Goodnight," she whispered.

"Night, little rabbit."

As soon as she closed her eyes, the *pop pop popping* flashed back into her mind, and she furrowed her brow, trying to push away the memory of screaming, of her heart beating through her chest as she covered her ears and sobbed.

Maybe the memory was just as bad for Cian, or maybe he could smell her distress, because he rearranged his arm beneath her head, putting his scent right near her nose. She instinctively rubbed her nose against the golden skin, sighing as salty seawater and warm sunlight washed her mind clean.

SHE WOKE UP TO BASHING AGAINST THE DOOR AGAIN, HER head groggy as she struggled to a sitting position. Sato was already up, tugging his clothes back on. He stalked toward the door as Cian rolled from the other side of the bed, also reaching for his clothes.

"Wait," Cian muttered, causing Sato to pause. "Rich girl pyjamas."

Sato glanced back to Isobel. "Do you have anything to wear over that?"

Isobel rubbed her eyes. "They're literally about to dress me."

Sato scowled. "Humour us."

She didn't get a chance to, because Cian was already tugging a shirt over her head.

Sato let in the team, and they got to work on her, keeping their chatter to a bare minimum. There were bags under their eyes, and they moved slower than usual, several of them jumping for no reason.

And Sato wasn't helping the situation.

"When is she going to eat?" he demanded, pulling one of the assistants up short by the arm.

"I d-don't know," the smaller man stuttered. "I c-can get something."

"Make sure you're the only one who touches it." Sato's voice was gruff, but the assistant jumped like he had just been screamed at, rushing out of the room.

He returned with croissants and coffees for all three of them. Isobel tried to hide her baffled smile in her coffee as the assistant bumbled through an offer to help Sato with anything else he needed. Cian rolled his eyes, kicking his booted feet onto the table as he texted on his phone. He was acting like he had already forgotten about the day before, but it was more likely that he was obsessively checking in with his family.

After Serena took her into the bathroom to change into the short black dress and thigh-high leather boots they had chosen for her first stop of the day, she slumped back into the make-up chair, pulling out her phone.

The group chat was full of notifications again, but she clicked on the messages from Reed first. The first was from last night.

Elijah: I guess silence is a good sign.

The next message had only come in an hour ago.

Elijah: What happened?

She squinted at her phone, wondering what the hell to say.

Isobel: He didn't hurt me, like you promised.

Elijah: I was bluffing.

Isobel: Awesome. I hate you.

Elijah: What happened?

Elijah: I would like to know what worked, in case it happens again.

Isobel: If it happens again, I'm never talking to any of you again.

Elijah: Easy solution. Stop getting hurt.

Isobel: It's my life. I'll get hurt if I want to get hurt.

Elijah: You want to get hurt?

Isobel: Of course not.

Elijah: Fine, we'll talk about this later.

Isobel: When you can read my face and know my thoughts with your weird "perception" thing? I think not. We're never having this conversation again.

Elijah: So something definitely happened.

Isobel: What the heck? You can do it over text?

Elijah: Tread carefully there, sweet girl. You're walking through a minefield.

Isobel: Sato, Cian, or Alphas in general?

Elijah: If we're all landmines, then Oscar is a nuclear bomb.

Isobel: How so?

Elijah: Just heed the warning, Isobel.

She traded her phone for the coffee and kept quiet as they finished her hair and make-up. She went down with Cian and Sato, and they all packed into the limousine that had been conjured at some point. The crew were still refraining from their usual loud gossiping, choosing to flick wary, hesitant stares Sato's way for the entire car trip.

The poor people of the Great Basin Settlement weren't much better off. Or the Glacier Settlement. Or the Olympic Settlement. Three plane trips, three outfit changes, and three settlements later, she barely had enough energy to stand upright for a shower before she was collapsing into bed. She wasn't sure when the boys joined her, but she woke up to Sato absently fiddling with her hair at some point in the night. She sleepily pulled out of Cian's arms, edging toward him without really realising what she was doing. It was instinctual. She knew that her warmth and scent would comfort him as much as Cian's comforted her. It was Cian's drugging, heavenly aroma that had perfumed her into peaceful dreams for several nights now when she should have been tossing and turning with nightmares.

She curled herself along the side of Sato's body, her hand slipping over his stomach, and went back to sleep almost immediately.

In the morning, his arm was wrapped around her, keeping her firmly in place, his fingers still tangled in her hair even though he was deeply asleep.

Until the team started banging on the door to wake them up.

Cian tugged a shirt over her head, and she shuffled to the bathroom, surprised to find a coffee and a wrap waiting for her on the desk when she got out.

The banners, streamers, and general fanfare were back when they arrived at the Black Hills Settlement, but the number of men and women in black fatigues had doubled, and the crew were searched before Isobel was allowed out of the car.

They kept Sato away once Isobel was seated, evidently learning from the disastrous last three stops of the tour. They positioned him at the entrance to the hall ... where he still managed to intimidate the hell out of everyone, but at least it was from the other end of the line this time. After two hours of holding people's hands and listening to all the prophetic dreams they claimed to have had of her, they left Black Hills and boarded the plane for Vermont.

They wrapped her in a dress that looked like syrup dripping down her body for the Green Mountains Settlement, since Vermont was apparently famous for maple syrup. It was incredibly hard to walk in, especially with the heels that wound up her ankles, chains dripping down to dangle over her feet. The dress was strapless with a sculptural silhouette, and she genuinely had no idea what it was made of. It *looked* like shiny gold plastic, or, well ... syrup. The only thing she knew about it was that it was Versace, and they wanted her to come in to do a photoshoot so they could put up Mate Finder billboards in the major cities with their brand stamped across the bottom. Her father said yes. The Ironside officials said no. Her contract with the academy took away bits and pieces of her father's ownership of her, transferring it to them instead. It was the first time she had seen her father's authority being overruled, and it put him in a terrible mood.

Cian and Sato—who had been eerily quiet ever since she emerged from the makeshift dressing area on the plane—were following her closely, practically on her heels. One of the assistants tapped on Cian's shoulder, reminding him that Isobel needed to look approachable and available, but Sato scowled at the poor woman, and she quickly scampered off.

Isobel shook her head before resuming her search of the crowd for Kilian's white-blond hair.

KILIAN WAS GOING TO BE LATE, AND IT WAS ALL BECAUSE Aron was a jealous asshole. Kilian had spent all his time at home since returning for the break. Never far from his phone. Always on the edge of panic.

Things weren't going smoothly.

Isobel spoke to them in the group chat, and she didn't seem angry at them anymore, but he had lied to her, and he was probably the only one she had trusted fully. And now he was late to the hall where he was supposed to be first in line to meet her so that she could scowl at him or slap him or ignore him completely ... but Aron didn't give a damn about any of that.

"Can we do this later?" Kilian tried to side-step him again, but Aron blocked him, gripping his arm.

"You've had a week to talk to me," Aron accused.

"Exactly." Kilian sighed, gently prying his fingers

off. "So you choose today—right *now*—to make a stand?"

"Because I'm jealous, babe." Aron gave him a soft, self-depreciating smile. "I thought I could just sit back and let it all unfold, but it's driving me insane. Even knowing you're just sleeping two lanes down from me, it still burns that they're showing footage of you and her."

"They're probably showing footage of her with a lot of people," Kilian deadpanned, pointing to the nearest Mate Finder banner. "That give you any clues?"

"Kili!" His adoptive mother, Sao-Yeong, was rushing over, carrying a bag with what looked suspiciously like a lunch box inside.

He groaned. "Eomma. Mom. No."

She held out the bag to him. "I made hwayeon and topped it with cherries instead of flowers."

Then she winked.

Sometimes he really regretted that he was so fucking close with his mother.

She had *no* filter.

She turned to Aron, arching a sharp brow. "Are you making my son late? He's the most important applicant!"

Aron huffed out a laugh, raising his hands and backing away. "Sorry, Mrs Gray."

She harrumphed at him, digging out the lunchbox and pushing it into Kilian's hand ... before shoving him down the path toward the hall. "Your father got there early with the camera. He's waiting to take pictures. He bought new film just for this."

She rambled all the way there about what he should say to Isobel and all the food she had cooked just in case Isobel wanted to come and have tea before she left again, and then she kissed his cheek outside the meeting hall, holding a hand over her heart like she was sending him off to his first day of settlement school.

He rolled his eyes, holding back a laugh as he saw his adoptive father in the back of the hall. Frederik Gray was a Beta, just like his wife. He had immigrated from Germany. She had immigrated from Korea. They argued over which of them would buy the end house on Maple Lane, because it had a second floor with views over the wall and space for a tiny shop out the front.

They ended up buying it together.

And then they rented out the top floor to Kilian and his birth mother, not to make money, but because the guards were letting drugs into the settlement and

Kilian's mother was no longer capable of looking after him. She spent her last days in the rocking chair by the window, staring out over the wall and holding her veins like she thought they were going to fall out.

Kilian had been four.

His eyes connected with his adoptive father. Frederik held up his camera, waving excitedly. Kilian waved the lunchbox back, making the older man shrug out an apology, looking only partly chastised.

Isobel was sitting down, and he skipped to the front of the line, catching sight of a frowning Oscar and Cian a few steps behind her. It looked like the crew were attempting to tell Oscar to stand somewhere else.

Oscar was pretending he couldn't hear them.

Kilian smirked, sliding into the chair opposite Isobel. "Interesting companions," he noted, swallowing as his eyes settled on her face.

God, that face. She looked better than the first few days of her tour. The make-up was thinner, playing up her natural beauty instead of trying to hide her away, though a dozen dissection videos online were proving that the heavy make-up had been to hide bruising and swelling.

Her dress was also giving him a minor heart attack, but it explained why Cian and Oscar were hovering so close. People in the crowd kept catcalling, shouting at her to stand up for them again.

"Yeah, it's been interesting." She didn't look angry. She looked ... sorrowful. She nibbled on her lip, somehow managing to not smudge the lipstick they had put on her. "I'm sorry." She flicked her gaze up to his quickly, before looking back down at the table.

She was apologising ... for being his mate?

Of course she was.

"Should we make out?" he joked, wiggling his brows at her and trying to lighten the mood. "How have you been testing all the other applicants?"

She grinned. "Not like that."

"So, then how? Is there a questionnaire? Is there a test?"

Her eyes sparkled and she leaned forward, dropping her voice. "There's just one question."

"Ask the question, baby."

"What did Spade actually do with my panties?"

He snorted, slumping back in his chair, a smile splitting over his face. "You're dying to know, aren't you?"

"Desperate," she agreed.

Behind her, Cian coughed.

Kilian glanced up at him. "Something to say, Surrogate Number One?"

"Isobel gets very anxious when people bring up erect male organs."

One of the cameramen stepped away, tugging up his shirt to drown out a laugh. He looked like he was choking.

"Nobody brought up erect male organs," Isobel groaned, turning to glare at Cian.

"They were bound to come up." Kilian was biting back a laugh. "The longer we talk about your panties, I mean."

Another camerawoman was going down. One of the assistants was red in the face, trying hard not to make a sound.

"Nothing is ..." Isobel struggled. "Going to come up—"

Kilian lost the battle against his laugh.

"You're the worst," she finished lamely, crossing her arms and pouting at him. "What's in the lunch box?"

"My mom made you sweet rice cakes. They have cherries on them. Because she thinks she's hilarious."

"No gifts." One of the officials stepped up to the table, confiscating the lunch box.

"Sorry," Isobel muttered.

"I'm sure there's more at home. Will you come and visit quickly before you leave?"

She smiled and nodded, and he stole one last glance at her before giving up his spot to the next person in line. Eve—Isobel's Omega friend—darted past him, almost diving over the table to give Isobel a hug before the official stepped forward again and barked at her.

They had tightened security even further since the shooting in Colorado. His parents had even paused the illegal export of their paintings through the commissary delivery driver. It was the first time they had stopped in twenty years. He was pretty sure all the guards knew about it; they just didn't care.

Still, it wasn't worth getting in trouble with tensions so high.

Isobel finally stood, her dress making creaking sounds like leather or latex stretching out. It clearly wasn't designed for sitting. Cooper appeared at her side, his hand sliding around her waist.

"We'll do a stop at Grey's house and then make an appearance at the settlement party tonight. It's a six-hour flight to California, so you should try to get some sleep on the plane. We should arrive around 3:00 a.m."

"Okay. Thanks." She pretended to stumble to break

his grip, and Sato shouldered past him, knocking him out of the way and taking his place at her side.

He didn't even try to be subtle about it.

Cian appeared at her other side. Behind them, she could hear Cooper complaining to someone about the two Alphas.

"Isobel!" her father barked.

She sighed, stopping and waiting for him.

"Stop hiding behind your surrogates." He looked pissed off. "I spent a small fortune on this tour so that the settlements could see *you*, not them."

"Yes, Father." She hurried to keep up with him, losing sight of Cian and Sato as he barged ahead of their group. "Would it be okay if I stopped in really quickly to see my friend before we go to Kilian's house?"

"What friend?"

"Eve. Please? Just a really quick visit. She told me her house is on the way to Kilian's."

"Fine. *If* you stop hiding behind the Alphas. I haven't given you this opportunity for nothing. I want you dancing at this party tonight. Signing autographs. Taking pictures. Do *something*."

"Yes, Father."

He gestured to Cooper, breaking away to speak to the other man privately. Isobel walked on her own, following a bustling assistant who led their entire group to Kilian's house. When Isobel spotted Eve waving from the doorway of a different house, she split from the group, holding up her hands to her father to indicate that she would only be ten minutes.

"Come in!" Eve moved to open the door and almost collided with a boy leaving the house. "Oof. Sorry, my friend was just leaving."

The boy grinned at Isobel, holding out his hand. He was tall, with floppy dark hair and laughing eyes. "Hey, I'm Aron." He held out his hand for her to shake, but he didn't try to prolong the encounter, waving back to Eve and strolling away from the house while whistling beneath his breath.

"Come in, come in," Eve tried again, tugging her through the door and kicking it closed. The crew had congregated on the other side of the road, uninterested in the visit.

"My parents are helping set up for the party, so you can meet them tonight." Eve sank into one of the chairs at the kitchen table, her leg bent up, her chin resting on her knee. "You look ... really happy," she noted. "Did you ..." She lowered her voice to a whisper. "Did you find out who your mate is?"

Isobel chewed on her lip, casting a quick look around the house. "Is anyone else here?"

"No." Eve's blue eyes flew wide. "Oh my god. You know who it is. Tell me right now!"

Isobel laughed nervously, the sound only half-hearted. She made the split-second decision to relay what had happened, desperate to confide in someone *other* than the Alphas, hoping it might clear her head of all the muddled feelings fighting for dominance inside her. She could trust Eve; even if there was nobody else in the world, there was Eve. And it would be nice to feel like someone was on her side, keeping her secrets. The Alphas all had each other, but she had no one.

The story came together in a disjointed sort of way. She told Eve about the glowing light beneath West's skin after she teleported to his house, and the golden chains that had wrapped around her and Sato. Eve didn't say a thing throughout her entire explanation and sat in silence for a few minutes after, her face ghostly pale.

"Holy shit," she finally croaked. "I mean ... I really thought you were Kilian's mate, but *all* of them?"

"Why Kilian?" Isobel blinked. That seemed random.

"You know I've heard about the golden light thing." Eve's leg dropped from the chair so she could lean forward in excitement. "I've heard of people who could make it appear just by thinking about their mate. You should try! Think of Kilian. He's my favourite."

Isobel winced. "I'm not sure ..."

"Isobel," her friend groaned. "You have ten mates and I have zero. Let me live vicariously for a moment!"

"Right." Isobel deflated. Eve had always harboured a crush on Kilian. Maybe this was difficult news to hear. "Sure. Sorry."

"Okay, close your eyes!" Eve sat up, clapping her hands beneath her chin animatedly. "Think about Kilian and try to ... funnel those thoughts into the light. It should appear."

Isobel was dubious, but she did as the other girl instructed, closing her eyes and summoning thoughts of Kilian. She thought of his soft, pillowy lips and how euphoric of a feeling it had been to feel them teasing hers in a kiss that had gone from gentle to firm at the flick of a switch. She thought of his bergamot and bark scent and how it had drugged her into having the best sleep of her life ... and then she went back to focusing on his lips.

Apparently, she had a thing for Kilian's lips.

She liked the way they formed a smile that was never far from artful. She liked when they pursed as he frowned. Fuck it, she even liked the way he chewed his food.

"Are you thinking about the light?" Eve asked.

"Yes." Not even a little bit.

She tried to imagine light beneath her skin with the vision of Kilian's teeth digging into his lower lip to distract her, and she was just about to claim that it wasn't going to work and apologise to Eve when something suddenly pulled against her wrist.

She opened her eyes, distracted by the soft lines of light that had sparked to life, glowing from within her veins, spidering from her wrist to her forearm. She gasped, so distracted that she didn't even pay any attention to the way Eve had been tugging against her wrist until someone came up behind her, shoving a ball of material into her mouth.

She tried to scream, but whoever was behind her was holding the gag too tightly, and only a muffled sound came out. She tried to fight them off, but her arms pulled tight, her body jerking, unable to move away from the table. Everything seemed to happen in slow motion after that. Her eyes crawled back, horrified, to fix on her friend. Eve sat calmly across from her, her chin resting on her palm, her elbow notched against the table. Isobel's wrists were zip-tied, another tie disappearing beneath the table, anchoring her arms there.

"He's right behind you." The apparition of her mother appeared behind Eve. "Jerk your head back."

Isobel didn't even think. She just did it, rearing her head back with as much force as she could. She connected with something, and pain radiated through her skull as a male grunt sounded.

"Push the chair back," her mother said.

She shoved the chair back as hard as she could, landing on her knees as her arms were pulled taut.

A body fell behind her, but he was up and rounding the table a second later, swiping his arm beneath a bloody nose. It was the boy from before. Aron. He had a knife, and he was bent over Isobel's captured arm, examining the light in her veins. Eve was smirking, regarding Isobel with a suddenly haughty expression.

"You're so fucking gullible," she told Isobel. "You literally believe everything everyone tells you. It's like you were raised in a cave."

Isobel groaned through the gag, trying to lean away from Aron, the zip ties digging into her skin. The table was too long for her to go around it, but maybe ...

"Just get up onto the table. Kick. Fight."

She tried to obey her mother, but Aron was faster.

He flashed behind her again, that knife digging into her neck. "Move an inch and I'll kill you, Sigma."

Eve stood, perching on the edge of the table as she pulled something out of her back pocket.

A scalpel.

"I know what you're thinking," she said with a sigh, examining the small, precise blade. "You're thinking that I'll never get away with this, right?" She leaned over Isobel's arm, tracing her glowing veins with the tip of the scalpel, not quite breaking the skin. They were even brighter now, like Isobel's panic was fuelling them. "You're thinking that you have all those big, strong Alphas protecting you. But I have a gift, you know?"

She applied some pressure, and blood welled around the blade. "Of course you don't know." Eve laughed softly. "It's illegal. Or at least ... the way I use it is illegal. Want to see?"

She pressed the blade in harder, bringing tears to Isobel's eyes. Light began to spill out with the blood.

She was suddenly dizzy, suddenly weak. She slackened, and Aron pulled his knife away, laughing. She blinked, trying to bring Eve into focus.

She remembered this feeling. It was like being drugged.

"You've tasted my power before." Eve's voice was a

floating discombobulation, a haunting sound to accompany the weak, muffled scream Isobel tried to muster. She was so weak, so dizzy, slumping over the table until her forehead smacked into the wood. But she barely felt it, because the pain in her arm was already filling her body to the brim.

It wasn't the pain of being cut.

It was the pain of having her light pulled from her body.

It was the pain of knowing that irrevocable damage was being done. She was only a tether, and Eve was sawing away her strings, relieving her of the anchor that held her to this world.

Her vision filled with endless darkness, a tight buzzing sound echoing through her mind. She couldn't see, but she felt every strand of light that was pulled from her veins. She mourned the threads that were thin as wisps and the foundational fibres that held so many strands together. She mourned as she floated, disconnected, adrift in a world of pain.

Soon, the rending of her soul was the only thing that existed. Everything else was lost to the anaesthetised haze her mind had succumbed to. She couldn't so much as twitch a finger or discern the voices that she was sure had been speaking over her only moments ago.

And then, miraculously, the haze lifted.

She stared through blurry tears as the room came back into focus, a relentless knocking sound filling the space. The room was empty. The table was covered in blood and thin, flickering threads of gold filled with fading, sorrowful light. They were spilled out like entrails all around her arms.

The door crashed open behind her, and the room filled with people. The noise hurt her head, and she winced with every shouted word. Hands were reaching for her arms, and her broken heart jumped into her throat, the words expelled violently from her chest.

"*Don't touch them!*" She was talking about her strands of light.

She was going to vomit.

She was going to die.

Someone cut the ties from her wrists, and she immediately slumped over the table, shielding her strings with her body. She screamed at anyone who drew too close as she inched back just far enough to gather her flickering lights. She picked up each one, her tears washing away some of the blood, only for it to be replaced by fresh blood from the wounds on her arms.

She gathered up every single one of the threads, and then she collapsed, slipping off the chair.

She needed ... if only she could ...

The light that flickered across her closed lids was weak and feeble, but she felt her body hit the ground, jerking her eyes back open.

"Isobel? *What the fuck?*"

Kalen.

That was exactly who she needed.

His face swam over her, his amber eyes shadowed with horror, his mouth tight with fear.

"Take me back an hour," she rasped, bringing her hands to her chest.

Her grip finally weakened, her threads flickering their feeble light one last time before slipping from her slack fingers.

To be continued ...

BONUS SCENE
HURRY

THEODORE FELT IT FIRST.

The tearing inside his heart.

The breathless terror that swept through him for no reason.

He collapsed, his father rushing to his side, Moses appearing a second later.

"Phone," he groaned, dropping it twice after Moses handed it to him. He groaned, clutching his chest and ignoring Moses and Benjamin's panicked questioning as he hit Oscar's number.

"Something's wrong," he rasped as soon as the call picked up. "Where is she?"

He didn't even care that his father was right there, listening to every word.

Moses dropped next, gasping for breath, his hand ripping at his shirt like his chest was on fire.

There was no reply from Oscar. He must have dropped his phone, because Theodore could hear screaming in the distance, and what sounded like several people's footsteps pounding against the ground beside the phone. The device in his hand began vibrating with text messages and beeping with incoming calls.

The others were feeling it too.

He tasted ash on the back of his tongue, but he worked to swallow it down, hiding his face from his father. "Moses?" he asked, still staring at the ground. "Moses!"

"Here," his brother grunted, voice too tight and too rough. He was fighting it back, but he was failing.

He needed Theodore.

Theodore crawled to where he had collapsed against the wall, refusing to meet his father's eyes as Benjamin knelt before them both, gripping their shoulders.

"Just tell me if I should get the doctor?" their father demanded, his voice surprisingly steady.

"No," Theodore said, gripping Moses's hand. "No, Dad. Everything is fine. Moses, close your eyes and count back from ten."

His brother made a sound that was barely human.

"Out loud," Theodore barked in Alpha voice.

"T-Ten." Moses gripped his hand so tight his nails were drawing blood. "Nine."

Theodore opened his eyes, staring at the phone a few feet away; dread wanted to pull him under, but he had to stay afloat. If he lost control, Moses didn't stand a chance.

"Eight."

And then they would lose their father.

"Seven."

Because Benjamin didn't heal like an Alpha, and he wouldn't survive one going feral.

"Six."

The pain was getting worse. *Why was it getting worse?*

"Five."

He flicked his eyes to the phone again, and his father quickly retrieved it, pushing it into his free hand.

"You're doing great," Benjamin told Moses, his voice shaking, before turning back to Theodore, his eyes wide in alarm. Theodore nodded, and Benjamin moved to Moses' other side, taking his other hand. "You're doing great, my boy." He swallowed, ignoring the trickle of blood now running down his hand from one of Moses' elongated claws.

"Count," Theodore reminded Moses.

"F ... f ... *fuck!*" Moses was on his feet suddenly, the darkness receding from his wild eyes. "Why does it *hurt* so much?" There were tears glittering on his cheeks.

Theodore watched as his father quickly pushed his hand into his pocket, hiding the wounds Moses' claws had caused. The older man got up, turning on the radio and pulling the curtain over the one window in the room.

"I'll find out," Theodore managed to get out, speaking through the pain as he tapped on the screen of the phone, bringing up all the notifications.

Before he could click on any of them, Kalen was video calling him. "Moses," he hissed, drawing his brother to his side as he accepted the call.

"Everyone stay silent unless I ask a question." Even over the phone, Kalen's Alpha demand was crippling, forcing Theodore to bite his tongue. Literally. He winced, breathing hard as he surveyed all the faces on the screen. Kalen had video-called the entire group.

"Oscar," Kalen said, after a moment. "What happened, exactly?"

Moses gripped the phone, dragging it closer to his face before clicking on Kalen's square, changing the view until it filled the phone's screen. Kalen's phone seemed to be on the floor, the camera facing up at him as he bent over it. He wasn't looking at the screen, but at something else. His face was etched in concentration ... and there was something else there. Something buried in the lines around his eyes.

Fear.

"She went into one of the houses to visit her friend." Oscar began speaking, his throat sounding raw. "She was taking too long, so one of the assistants knocked on the door. Nobody answered. We kept knocking. I broke down the door. She was tied to a table, her arms cut open, these ... glowing strings spilling out. It looked like a messy surgery to extract those strings. She wouldn't let anyone touch them. And then she disappeared."

"She's here." Kalen was speaking almost distractedly. "She teleported to me."

"Permission," Theodore forced the word out, fighting against Kalen's influence.

"Speak. Keep it short."

"Did you take her back in time?"

"Not yet."

A chorus of angry, disbelieving sounds rose through the speakers.

"Cian," Kalen snapped. "Explain. I need to concentrate."

"I had a ... feeling ... when Sato was forcing his way into the house." Cian's voice was rough. He didn't sound good at all, and that terrified Theodore more than anything. *What did he know?*

"I was just frozen and cold all over," Cian continued, his voice breaking. "I called Kalen because I could feel that all the pain was reaching for him, like the bond knew he was the only one who could fix her. I thought she might teleport there. I told him they took something from her, and he couldn't take her back in time until he returned what they stole."

"I'm putting the strings back," Kalen gritted out. "Almost done. She's lost a lot of blood."

It's like she's already dead.

Theodore shook the memory off, gripping his sanity with every reserve of strength he possessed.

"Hurry," he forced another word out, his head pounding as he defied Kalen again. "Please hurry."

'I HOPE YOU ENJOYED TOURNER!

If you want to chat about this book or catch all the teasers for my next book, scan the code below to check out my reader's group!

If you enjoyed this book, please consider leaving a review. Indie authors rely on the support of our incredible readers, and without you guys, we wouldn't be able to continue publishing. Thank you for everything you do for the indie community!

Thank you!!
Jane xx

CONNECT WITH JANE WASHINGTON

Scan the code to view Jane's website, social media, release announcements and giveaways.

Made in the USA
Las Vegas, NV
08 September 2024